## THE
## MAN OF BRONZE

*By James Alan Gardner*

EXPENDABLE
COMMITMENT HOUR
VIGILANT
HUNTED
ASCENDING
TRAPPED
RADIANT
LARA CROFT: TOMB RAIDER: THE MAN OF BRONZE

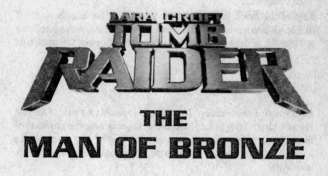

# THE
# MAN OF BRONZE

## JAMES ALAN GARDNER

**BALLANTINE BOOKS • NEW YORK**

A Del Rey® Book
Published by The Random House Publishing Group

Copyright © 2005 by Core Design Limited

All rights reserved under International and Pan-American Copyright Conventions. Published in the United States by Del Rey, an imprint of The Random House Publishing Group, a division of Random House, Inc., New York, and simultaneously in Canada by Random House of Canada Limited, Toronto.

Del Rey is a registered trademark and the Del Rey colophon is a trademark of Random House, Inc.

www.delreybooks.com

ISBN 0-345-46173-8

Manufactured in the United States of America

First Edition: January 2005

OPM 9 8 7 6 5 4 3 2 1

To Eidos and computer game creators everywhere,
without whom I'd have written at least
twenty more books, and maybe won
the Nobel Prize.

# ACKNOWLEDGMENTS

Thanks to Linda Carson, Paul Witcover, Steve Saffel, and the folks at Eidos for editing and advice. Also thanks to Mike Resnick and E. E. Knight for their great work on the previous two Lara Croft books.

At one point in this story, a character says, "The best time to make money is when blood runs in the streets." He is paraphrasing Nathan Rothschild, a banker during the French Revolution and the Napoleonic Wars. (The Rothschild family made a fortune by following Nathan's cheerful little maxim.)

Also, Lara quotes the first two lines of the poem "Fire and Ice" by Robert Frost ("Some say the world will end in fire/Some say in ice") and the last verse of "The Hunting of the Snark" by Lewis Carroll ("In the midst of the word he was trying to say . . .").

Finally, for those unfamiliar with certain British terms, I offer the following definitions:

> petrol = gasoline
> car boot = the trunk
> car bonnet = the hood
> electric torch = flashlight
> Sweeneys = rapid-response police team

# 1

## WARSAW: THE BELL TOWER WAITING ROOM

The Stare Miasto district of Warsaw is an illusion. It appears to be centuries old, with buildings dating back to the 1200s and a city wall erected to fend off the Mongol hordes. But the district's venerable appearance is false. Stare Miasto was leveled during World War II—not a stone left standing—and everything you see is a twentieth-century reproduction made to look aged using rubble that was left after Hitler and Stalin pounded the city into ruin.

In other words, Stare Miasto is a counterfeit antique: well built and lovely, but fake.

I know about counterfeits. I've seen many. My name is Lara Croft, and I collect old things.

It was December—a clear cold night with the snow ankle deep. Warsaw's streets were empty, except for a few late stragglers whose breaths steamed ghostlike into the air. Their heads were probably full of Christmas: presents to buy, food to cook, decorations to string over the hearth. My thoughts, however, were elsewhere. I'd been called to Warsaw by a friend . . . and my friend was in trouble.

His name was Reuben Baptiste: born in Trinidad, educated at Cambridge, and a useful fellow for someone in my line of work. Reuben was a freelance research assistant. He had a knack for finding exactly the right paragraph in exactly the right book—often in dusty libraries where the books were uncatalogued and stacked in random heaps on the shelves. Reuben had a good eye for deciphering faded hieroglyphics and for spotting inscriptions so faint they were almost invisible. Above all, he could *talk* to people. He could talk to scientists of the Royal Society in their clubs off Piccadilly; he could talk to native shamans as they sat around smoky campfires; he could talk to people in rest homes and coax out the story of how they'd once seen something odd fifty years ago while strolling beside the Nile.

Of course, Reuben had his shortcomings—all his knowledge came from books and conversation, not from hands-on work in the field. He'd never entered an ancient tomb or even visited an archaeological dig. Still, he was excellent at what he did. Whenever I was too busy to do such chores myself, I'd hire Reuben to track down information for me. He, in turn, always sent a heads-up my way if he came across something of interest . . . so when he telephoned to say, "Drop everything and meet me in Warsaw," I hopped the first plane from Heathrow.

Before leaving, I *did* take a moment to ask Reuben what he'd found. He said he couldn't tell me till he got permission from his current employer . . . and, no, he couldn't say who that was. But if everything worked out, this unknown employer would be eager to sponsor me on a chance-of-a-lifetime expedition, and I'd be eager to go.

That's all Reuben would say. I didn't press for details. One reason I valued Reuben was that he never divulged the secrets of those he worked for.

When Reuben first called me, we'd arranged to meet at the Bristol, Warsaw's most exclusive hotel, so distinguished it's listed as a Polish national monument. Just after my flight landed, however—while I was queued up at customs, moving at a snail's pace because Okęcie airport was in the middle of a high security alert—I checked my messages and found a voice mail from Reuben, saying, "Forget the Bristol; meet me at Dr. Jacek's."

His voice sounded bad: breathless with pain. I pushed my way through customs with unladylike haste.

\* \* \*

Dr. Jacek's clinic lay on the edge of Stare Miasto, housed inside what was once the Church of St. Anthony the Great. The church was a victim of recent history. Much had changed when Poland won its independence from the Communist bloc, and one of those changes was a gradual outflow of people from Warsaw's inner city into new surrounding suburbs. Fewer residents meant smaller congregations . . . until finally the bishop had to close several lesser-used churches. One church was converted into insurance offices; one became an experimental theater; and the former Church of St. Anthony the Great—unsanctified with all appropriate rituals—was sold to Dr. Stanislaw Jacek for use as a private clinic.

Jacek's wasn't your usual medical center. It was one of those solid-steel-doorway places you can find in any major city if you follow a trade like mine: a clinic where no one asks awkward questions about bullet wounds and where they always carry antidotes for cobra venom or curare. Strange creatures prowl the back streets of Warsaw—everything from bioengineered horrors to biblical monstrosities—and the victims usually end up at Jacek's. Often, patients are sent discreetly from more conventional hospitals: places that prefer not to handle patients whose flesh is mutating into acidic goo.

But when I arrived, the place seemed quiet. I knocked on the steel door—three quick knocks, two slow, two more quick—and was admitted by a motherly receptionist with a heavily armed doorman behind her. He looked ready to shoot me with a Heckler & Koch MP5 A5 submachine gun, until the receptionist gave him a scolding little slap. "Ach, this is *Lara*. She's a friend." Apparently, however, I wasn't enough of a friend to be allowed into the clinic fully armed. The receptionist said, "Sorry, no exceptions," as the doorman plucked my pistols from their holsters and locked them in an imposing metal vault behind his desk. I noticed several other guns in there before he closed the vault door.

"Lots of patients tonight?" I asked as I hung my winter jacket on a coat stand.

"Just your friend Reuben," the receptionist said. "He told us to expect you. Go up to the private waiting room; he'll join you as soon as the doctor finishes bandaging him."

"Bandaging him? What happened?" I moved toward the corridor that I knew led to the treatment rooms, but the doorman blocked my way. He didn't actually point his gun at me, but he tightened his grip on it.

"Please," the receptionist said. "Just wait. It won't be long. Then your friend can tell you whatever he wants you to know."

She pointed toward a door that led to a stone-lined stairwell. Grudgingly, I started up the steps.

The private waiting room was set aside for people who'd accept a little inconvenience in exchange for staying out of sight of other visitors. It lay halfway up the church's bell tower: a shabby room with shabby furniture . . . but then, everything at Jacek's had an air of cheapness. Dr. J. enjoyed being a penny-pinching old curmudgeon.

Despite the ragged decor, I liked the room. This level of the tower had tall glass windows on all four sides, giving splendid views of Stare Miasto under its burden of snow, plus the Vistula River, black and not yet frozen over, rolling frigidly off to the east. When I first arrived, the room was empty; I passed several minutes gazing out onto the city, idly plotting escape routes across the rooftops. Soon, though, I heard footsteps coming slowly, painfully, up the stairs.

I turned. Reuben Baptiste appeared in the doorway. He tossed me a cheerful wave, then nearly fell over from the effort. A moment later, he toppled into a nearby chair and sat there panting.

He looked dreadful. Reuben's skin was normally a rich Caribbean brown, but now it resembled half-melted wax. I could see a greater quantity of skin than usual—Reuben's shirt was in tatters, and the tatters were burned around the edges.

Much of Reuben's face was smeared with clear ointment, no doubt applied by Dr. Jacek. Jacek had also taped thick white dressings on Reuben's left side: one at the front and one at the back. I'd worn similar bandages a few years earlier when a bullet had passed in and out of my body, breaking two ribs on its way through. Fortunately, that shot did no permanent damage to my internal organs. I was afraid Reuben hadn't been so lucky—he breathed with short little gasps as if his lungs couldn't get enough oxygen. Still, if Reuben had been *seriously* injured, he'd be down in Jacek's operating room, not staggering up to meet me. Reuben was still able to walk, and that was a good sign . . . I hoped.

One other detail: Reuben had a stainless steel attaché case handcuffed to his left wrist. The case showed a swath of charred smudges across its metal surface.

"Lara," he wheezed. "Glad you're here."

I went and crouched by his side. "Who did this to you, Reuben?"

"Don't know."

I narrowed my eyes. "Don't know or can't say?"

"Don't know," he repeated.

"Can't even make a guess?"

"Really, truly, Lara, I don't know what's going on." He smiled weakly. "You're the one who people try to kill. Me, I'm harmless."

"Next you're going to say, *Honest to gosh, Lara, it can't possibly be related to this metal thingy locked on my wrist.*"

He shifted his eyes away. "I can't talk about that—it's confidential. I don't give away *your* secrets when I'm working for *you.*"

"At least tell me what happened. How did you get so banged up?"

Reuben let his head slump back against the chair.

"When I phoned you," he said, "I wasn't in Warsaw. I was in Athens."

"What were you doing in Athens?"

"I can't tell you till my employer gives the okay. But it's big, Lara. It's—"

His voice broke off. He winced in pain.

"Broken ribs?" I asked.

"Just one. At least that's what Dr. Jacek says. Feels like I've snapped half a dozen." Reuben took some quick tortured breaths. "Anyway, after I called you, I caught a flight here. Arrived at Okęcie a couple hours ago. Nothing out of the ordinary till I got to the rental car office. I'd made arrangements several days earlier so they'd have a car waiting . . ."

I tsked my tongue. "Reuben, you should know better. Giving several days' notice of where and when you'd be? A person with enemies can't take such risks."

Reuben made a face. "I didn't realize I *had* enemies." He tried to breathe, then flinched at what must have been another jab from his broken rib. After swallowing the pain, he continued.

"The rent-a-car agency had two people in the office: a kid, maybe nineteen, and an older fellow who seemed on edge. In retrospect, I realize the older guy was acting suspicious—he shooed other customers out the door and even snapped, 'No cars! We have no more cars!' I should have noticed he was clearing the office of everybody but me. I was just so tired and jet-lagged . . . Oh, don't scowl, Lara, I know that's no excuse. Anyway, the older man gave me the keys to a car and told me where it was parked; but the kid volunteered to fetch the car for me. I'd, uhh . . . well . . . my current employer has deep pockets and gives me a huge expense account, so I'd splurged on something fast, sleek, and sporty. A Lamborghini Diablo."

My eyebrows went up. "You can *rent* a Lamborghini Diablo?" Dear, oh dear, whatever happened to exclusivity? I resolved to sell my own Diablo before people thought I'd gone bargain hunting at Hertz.

"You can get good cars if you call far enough ahead," Reuben said. "I could see the kid wanted a chance behind the wheel, even if he only drove it in from the car park. The older guy said no, no, no, but I decided to let the kid have a thrill. I handed him the keys and said, 'Be my guest.'" Reuben sighed and lowered his eyes. "I thought I was doing the kid a favor."

It wasn't hard to guess what had happened next. I said, "Go on."

"The kid went to get the car. The older guy had a strange look on his face. After a few seconds, he went into the back room—didn't say a word, just left. I stood at the window of the car company's office—they had this big plate-glass window overlooking the lot—and I watched the kid drive up. Beautiful red sports car . . ." Reuben shook his head sadly. "At the last second, I noticed a rack of free road maps on the side wall of the office. I went to grab a map of Warsaw in case I needed it . . ."

"Which," I said, "is what saved your life."

He nodded. "The car blew up right outside the office. If I'd been standing at the window, flying glass would have cut me to shreds."

Reuben fell silent, brooding. I wanted to reassure him—pat his shoulder or even give him a hug, tell him I understood—but I couldn't force myself past the restraint of my upbringing. *Lara, dear, one mustn't intrude. However much one feels, one really mustn't intrude.* Maybe Reuben preferred it that way: both of us pretending he wasn't on the verge of tears. That "kid" who'd wanted to drive a Lamborghini had died in Reuben's place.

Survivor guilt is cruel. There's no reason to blame yourself for a death that's not your fault . . . yet deep in your soul dwells a sense of obligation when the bullet meant for you hits somebody else. You've incurred a debt you can never repay.

"It's not like the movies," Reuben murmured. "When a car explodes. It's not a dramatic burst of fire with stunt-

men jumping up off trampolines to simulate the force of
the blast."

"I know."

He glanced at me angrily . . . but something in my face
must have told him I *did* know what it was to endure an
explosion. To feel the wall of heat slam into you: burning
your eyes dry, popping your eardrums, pounding your
body like a thousand simultaneous punches, knocking
you off your feet and throwing you backward with a fire-
driven force so far beyond mere human strength that the
humiliation is almost as excruciating as the moment of
impact.

Then for a time, there's nothing. Even if you're conscious, you can't see, hear, or feel. Your senses are numb
for a tiny grace period as your brain seeks to deal with
what's happened. Suddenly everything floods into aware-
ness: light if your eyes haven't been burned out of their
sockets, sound if there's anything left of your eardrums,
and a lot—a *lot*—of pain.

"I blacked out for a while," Reuben said. "I don't know
how long. When I woke, I felt burned head to toe . . . lying
in a heap against the wall, maps littered around me, some
of them smoldering . . . and the older guy from the rent-a-
car agency was bending over me. I thought he was trying
to help—giving me first aid. Then I saw he had a butcher's
knife the size of a machete. He was assessing my wrist,
trying to decide the best way to cut off my hand."

Reuben held up his arm, the one with the attaché case.
It didn't surprise me that the rental car man had intended
to perform an impromptu amputation—I had no doubt the
attaché case was the target of the whole explosive exercise. Such cases were built strong enough to keep their
contents safe from fiery jolts. I assumed the original plan
had been to blow up Reuben in the Diablo, then hack the
case off Reuben's corpse. Why would the rental car man
have been carrying a knife if he hadn't expected to use it?

The only surprise was the man's hesitation before doing
the deed. He must have had hours or days to prepare for

the amputation—plenty of time to get past any squea-mishness. So why the pause? Unless the man had always pictured slicing into skin charred to a crisp and was dis-comfited by the sight of Reuben's relatively unburned flesh.

But I pushed such questions aside. Looking at Reuben's arm, I saw it was very much intact. "I take it you con-vinced the gentleman not to carve you up?"

"Forcefully so." Reuben gave a slight smile. "He thought I was still unconscious. Never saw the punch coming. I got him a good one in the nose, which dizzied him enough for me to knock the knife from his hand. Then I clubbed him a few times with the attaché case. That was that."

"But he wasn't alone?"

Reuben stared at me. "How did you know?"

I pointed to the dressings on his front and back. "Aren't those bullet wounds? So you faced more than a meat cleaver and an exploding car."

"Oh. Right." He looked down at the bandages as if he'd forgotten about them. That was a bad sign—if his burns were so serious, he didn't remember getting shot . . .

After a moment, Reuben said, "The fellow with the knife *did* have a friend. Waiting in a parked car. That must have been the getaway plan: the man in the office would grab my attaché case, then he'd be picked up by the chap in the car. They'd race off before the police arrived. Lucky for me, the driver had parked a long distance away. I sup-pose he wanted to stay out of the blast radius. So he was far enough off that when he shot at me, he missed. Mostly. Dr. Jacek said the bullet went in and out without hitting anything significant."

Reuben pressed his hand against his side. In the quiet of the waiting room, I heard blood squish under the gauze.

"What kind of gun did the man have?" I asked.

"I don't know. A handgun. Average size."

I grimaced. Average size? What did that mean? When this was all over, I'd have to teach Reuben a few things about firearms. "Did the gun have a silencer?" I asked.

Reuben shook his head. "I doubt if the man came expecting to shoot. He thought I'd be killed in the explosion. The gun was just insurance if something went wrong."

I shrugged. Reuben was probably right. "So this second man shot at you?"

"As I was clambering over debris to get out of the office. There wasn't much left of the front of the building. I was lucky the whole place didn't collapse on my head."

"That probably wasn't luck," I said. "If they wanted to kill you but save the attaché case, they'd use as little explosive as possible. They'd also make sure the Diablo only had a few drops of petrol, to reduce the chance of fire. No more damage than necessary."

"Easy for you to say," Reuben muttered. "It looked like chaos to me. Things blasted in all directions . . . then this guy started shooting."

"What did you do?"

"I dropped to the ground, gasping. Nearly skewered myself on broken glass. Isn't that strange? I'd just been shot, but what stands out in my mind is being afraid of a bit of glass."

"Sharp glass can be lethal," I said. "Besides, the brain does odd things when you receive a major injury. Sometimes it fixates on trivialities as a way of blocking out pain."

Reuben gave me a look. "You know all about major injuries, don't you? But I'm learning, too. After a second, I barely felt the bullet. My mind was racing, trying to think how to escape." He shrugged. "Then I caught a break. You know how some rent-a-car offices have a board where they hang the car keys? The explosion knocked things around so much, the key board had landed in the parking lot—only a few steps from me. Even better, some of the keys stayed on their hooks. So I grabbed all the keys I could and started trying to find a car that matched."

"The man with the gun had stopped shooting?"

Reuben nodded. "There were dozens of parked cars between him and me. I kept low, out of the line of fire. After a while, I heard the getaway car's engine rev. I thought, *Maybe the gunman has decided to run.* But no such luck. He started coming my way."

"A determined fellow." Also a fellow who was strangely unafraid of the police. These people had blown up a car near an international airport . . . a misdeed that would draw *massive* attention from concerned officials. Not just the Polish authorities; Interpol would get involved, as would MI6, the CIA, Russia's FCIS, and a dozen other organizations that got nervous whenever "explosion" and "airport" appeared in the same sentence. It explained why Okęcie had been on high alert when I arrived—Warsaw was now a global hot spot. Either the men who attacked Reuben didn't realize they'd kicked over a hornet's nest, or they believed they were safe from international manhunts.

"The keys I'd found," Reuben continued, "had tags giving the license plates of the corresponding cars. The first matching car I came across had been too close to the blast—it'd flipped completely over on its roof. But the second car was still okay. I crawled inside and got it started just as the man who'd shot at me drove up."

"Whereupon he shot at you again?"

Reuben nodded. "He hit the driver-side window, but I'd kept my head down. All I got was nuggets of glass down the back of my neck. Then I floored the accelerator and took off."

"With the villain in hot pursuit."

"My first car chase," Reuben said. "I'd tell you every detail, but I don't remember a thing." He gave a rueful smile. "Okay, I remember being terrified, with occasional moments of blind panic. But how I got away—it's just a blur."

"I understand," I told him. "You drove at high speeds taking ridiculous risks until you found you'd lost your pursuer."

"That sums it up," Reuben said. "For five minutes, I zigged and zagged like a maniac. Then all of a sudden, there was no one behind me. No one on the streets at all.

So I pulled to the curb and passed out." He closed his eyes, as if the memory embarrassed him. "When I woke, I felt so woozy . . . I was supposed to drive to my employer's place, but it's three or four hours out of town. I'd never make it unless I got patched up first."

"So you discarded your vehicle and came here?"

Reuben hesitated.

"Oh no," I said. "Reuben, please tell me you got rid of the car you were driving. The one that was seen by the man who shot you. Please tell me you left it miles away."

"Um. Well . . ."

I glanced out the bell tower window. The streets of Stare Miasto are closed to automobile traffic, but the clinic was on the edge of the district. I could see a car park immediately across the way . . . and at this hour of night, there were only a few vehicles in the lot. It was hard to tell in the dark, but one of the cars might have been missing its driver-side window.

"Reuben," I said, "the people who are after you will surely ask, *Where would a gunshot man go when he needs medical attention?* This clinic will immediately come to mind; they'll surely check it out. If you were so careless as to leave your vehicle across the street, like a beacon saying, *He's here, he's here . . .*"

Reuben flinched and turned toward the door. "We'd better go."

Beneath the bell tower, four identical black Ford Explorers slid to a stop in the slushy street. "Too late," I said. "We now have a situation."

# 2

# WARSAW: THE CLINIC'S UPPER FLOOR

I turned from the window. "Tell me this, Reuben. Whatever you have in that attaché case . . . please say it's not just money. If the people in those cars are thieves wanting cash, let them take it. We can unlock that handcuff—"

Reuben interrupted, "I don't have a key. Either to the handcuff or the case."

I stared at him. "You don't have keys? You got that case through customs and airport security without even opening it?"

"My employers arranged it. They have clout with the authorities."

"Apparently so." I would have pressed for more details, but didn't have time. "Look, I can probably pick the handcuff's lock . . . and I will if that'll save lives. We'll toss the case down to the bad guys. No point anyone else getting hurt over money."

"This isn't about money," Reuben said. "It's about fighting goons like the ones outside. If I manage to make my delivery, criminals all over the world will be in serious trouble."

"You've got evidence against them? Or secrets about criminal operations?" Before Reuben could answer, I waved him to silence. "Never mind. It's too late to explain."

Down in the street, dark figures were climbing from the Explorers: four from each of the four SUVs, making sixteen thugs in all. They wore the sort of black-on-black ski-mask-and-Kevlar outfits that have become mandatory for hoodlums with no fashion sense. Where *do* they buy those clothes? From some charity shop that gets hand-me-downs from Hollywood B movies? Just once, I'd like to face gunmen decked out in tuxedos. Or cashmere.

"One last question," I said to Reuben. "If that attaché case is a delivery, where's it supposed to go?"

He hesitated . . . but he realized if he wanted my help, he had to trust me. "St. Bernward's Monastery," he said, "a long way northeast of here, near the Lithuanian border. It's hard to find—a lot of rough back roads—but if you drive me, I'll show you the way."

I raised my eyebrows, wondering how monks might fit into the increasingly convoluted picture . . . but I knew from experience that monasteries could contain a great deal more than prayers. "St. Bernward's it is," I said. "I'll get you there, Reuben. Now follow me, do exactly what I tell you, and otherwise keep out of the way."

If I'd been on my own, I would have gone upward. One floor up was the old church belfry, raftered with bells and open to the night. I could get outside from there and carefully climb down the bell tower's wall. Once I reached solid ground, I'd vanish into the medieval complexities of Stare Miasto and eventually make my way to St. Bernward's.

But Reuben's presence ruled out such an easy escape. He was a scholar, not an athlete—even on his best day, he couldn't descend a brick wall covered with December ice. His wounds just made things worse. So I had no choice but to escort him out by more conventional means: down through the actual clinic, where unfriendly men who thought that watch caps were fashionable headgear would try to "fill us with lead."

Then again, I've always liked a challenge.

The waiting room where we started was two floors above street level. A single flight of steps led down one floor to an area that held half a dozen rooms for overnight and long-term patients. The next floor down—the ground floor—held treatment facilities, including an operating room and a general examination ward. I knew there was also a small laboratory, run by a gifted medical technician who was so clinically phobic of other human beings, she was unemployable by any traditional hospital. At Jacek's, she fit right in. The staff here were all unfit for normal jobs, whether through mental imbalance, outstanding arrest warrants, or sheer inability to meet minimal standards of social behavior. These were underground people . . . and sadly for them, their untouchable status meant they couldn't call the police when trouble crashed through their thick steel door.

When the crash came, it wasn't loud. All I heard was a muffled thud—probably shaped demolition charges blasting out the lock that kept the door shut. Gunfire came immediately thereafter: gunfire from the attackers and return gunfire from the doorman's MP5 A5. But in a straight-up firefight, sixteen against one, the doorman didn't have a chance.

It was over in five seconds. Silence returned as the echoes of shooting faded.

The doorman was undoubtedly dead. Probably the receptionist too—hit in the cross fire or deliberately shot by thugs who didn't know she was unarmed. I could only hope a few of the attackers got killed or wounded in the process. Much as I like a demanding fight, it's nice to have help whittling down the odds.

Reuben and I hadn't just stood slack-jawed listening to the firefight below us. The two of us hurried down the bell tower steps, with me practically carrying Reuben so he wouldn't stumble. We made it to the floor below without major mishap, at which point I abandoned the stairway. Reuben and I were still a story above the street, but it would be suicide to continue down to ground level by the stairs. The assault teams would surely position a few shooters to pick off anyone coming out of the stairwell.

That route was out of the question . . . at least until I'd reduced the opposition to a manageable number.

We left the stairs and dashed into the corridor. (I dashed; Reuben managed a wobbly shuffle.) As I've mentioned, this level of the clinic housed patients: three windowless rooms on either side, their doorways staggered so that no two were directly opposite each other. (Privacy is important in Dr. J.'s line of work.)

The first room we passed contained an ice-pale young woman with a plasma drip in her arm and prominent bite marks on her throat. Friday nights in Warsaw always produce a few of those. The next two rooms were empty, but the one after that held a man with his leg in plaster, suspended by one of those traction slings one sees in Three Stooges films but nowhere else. The man must have heard the shooting because he asked in Russian, "What's going on?"

"The clinic is being invaded," I told him in the same language.

"By police? Or the Sicilians?"

"Whoever they are, they aren't after you."

"How do you know?"

"Oh. Er."

The man raised a valid point. Reuben might not be the only one in the clinic targeted by gun-toting thugs. This chap with the broken leg, for example—he had the look and aroma of the Russian Mafia, in which case he'd probably committed violence against rival gangsters during squabbles to control Warsaw's underbelly. The Russian man's victims might well seek revenge, especially if they knew their enemy lay helpless in a hospital bed.

But I didn't think Warsaw's local villains would invade Dr. Jacek's. Gangsters needed this clinic; they depended on its services. The premises were therefore regarded as neutral ground, not to be used as a war zone. A single crook might still barge in with mayhem on his mind—criminals are famous for poor impulse control—but a massed assault by sixteen attackers sounded more like out of towners who didn't care if Dr. Jacek remained in business after they were gone.

The rental-car bombers had shown the same attitude—no concern if their actions filled Warsaw with law enforcement agents. My gut instincts told me the bombers and assault teams both had the same target: whatever Reuben carried in his attaché case.

"No time to chat," I told the Russian. "If I were you, I'd pretend to be unconscious. Maybe the shooters will leave you alone." Also, if he was pretending to be unconscious, he'd be less likely to tell the attack squad where Reuben and I had gone . . . but I didn't mention that, for fear of putting ideas into his head.

I dragged Reuben farther down the hall, past another empty room and to the doorway of one where a motionless figure lay wrapped in gauze. No way to tell if the patient was male or female; the only distinguishing feature was a breathing tube protruding from his or her mouth. The tube connected to respirator equipment, complete with a tank of oxygen . . . and there were two additional oxygen tanks for when the first tank ran out. The room also held a waist-high cart loaded with bandaging materials, plus a spray can of disinfectant and a good-sized bottle of rubbing alcohol. I could even see a pair of sharp scissors for cutting lengths of dressing.

"Lovely," I said.

"What?" Reuben asked.

"You're about to get a lesson in wise financial management. We start with a small nest egg." I picked up the scissors. "Then with careful planning and prudent use of our original investment, we make our assets grow." I tossed him some gauze off the cart. "Wrap your head in that, if you please . . . and be quick about it."

Downstairs there were shouts and screams but no further gunfire. Good. I'd worried the assault teams might just kill every person in the clinic . . . but it sounded as if the invaders were merely rounding up captives. They'd gather the prisoners in some suitable location—perhaps the OR, the largest room in the clinic—then some thugs would stand guard while the rest fanned out in search of Reuben. I was glad they'd decided to secure the ground floor before dealing with the rest of the building; the longer they spent down there, the more time I had to prepare.

At last I heard feet coming up the stairs: two men making no attempt at silence or caution. They'd probably interrogated their prisoners enough to know that no one in the building had weapons except the doorman. The invaders also knew that their target, Reuben, was no great threat—he was wounded and not much of a fighter in the first place. If I was lucky, however, the hooligans weren't aware of my own presence. I'd only been seen by the doorman and the receptionist, both of whom had likely been killed in the initial firefight. No one else knew I was here, so no one could give me away, even if threatened at gunpoint.

When the intruders first laid eyes on me, I wanted them to see me as just another patient. To encourage that impression I fixed a wad of gauze across the lower half of my face. Not only did that make me look wounded, it reduced the chance I might be recognized if these thugs had seen my picture in the papers. For clothing, I wrapped myself in a sheet from one of the unused beds. I still wore my normal clothes underneath, but Reuben assured me the sheet hid my ready-for-action outfit. It also hid the scissors, which I'd secured to my thigh with adhesive tape.

Reuben was concealed in sheets, too. Once he'd wrapped his head with medical dressing—only his eyes exposed—I'd ordered him into the empty bed in the second last room from the stairs. The attaché case locked to his wrist made a visible lump under the covers if he lay flat, but if he bent his knees, he could slide the case under his legs where it was reasonably unnoticeable beneath the bed linen. "Good enough," I told him. "Now stay put until I call you."

Twenty seconds later, two ski-masked men emerged

from the stairwell. I'd positioned myself nearby, swaying rhythmically with what I hoped was a dazed expression and muttering plaintively in Polish, "I just took a little, I just took a little, I just took a little . . ."

"You!" one of the gunmen said in English. "Stand still."

I pretended I hadn't heard. "I just took a little, I just took a *little*." Out of the corner of my eye, though, I sized up the men: bulky street beef carrying—what a surprise!— Uzi mini-pistols. Honestly, I have nothing against Uzis, but there *are* other SMGs in the world. When I see some- one carrying an Uzi, I think, *Do you truly know anything about guns, or did you just shop by brand name?* Even homicidal thugs can be fashion victims.

"Don't move!" the other gunman shouted at me. This one spoke Polish . . . not that it mattered, because I kept up my chant of, "I just took a little, I just took a little . . ."

"What's she saying?" the first gunman asked in English.

The second gunman didn't bother translating. "She's high on something," he said. "This place handles lots of junkies." He looked at me with disdain. "Trash."

"Maybe we should shoot her," the first man suggested. "Give her a quick death instead of a slow one."

*Uh-oh,* I thought, *best to discourage such thinking.* I lifted my head and looked at the first man, the one who didn't speak Polish. In stilted English, I said, "Hey, mister, you tourist? You like party, yes?"

My voice was still distant and dreamy, as if I spoke from reflex: a drugged-up gutter girl reciting her spiel, barely understanding what she said. The men, however, under- stood clearly . . . and the second one laughed to the first, "Hey, she likes you."

"She can't even focus on me," the first said. But he could certainly focus on *me*. He eyed the sheet I'd clutched around my body . . . probably wondering if I was naked beneath.

"You like party," I said, staggering up to him. "You like party, I like party, very nice."

Just before I stumbled into him, I opened the sheet.

Then I was tight against him, wrapping the sheet around both of us. With no hesitation—as if he were such a popular chap, women threw themselves at him every day—the man sent his hands a-roaming. When he felt my clothes under his fingers, he must have realized I wasn't as naked as expected . . . but that didn't slow him down. His breath was hot against my neck. Too bad his ski mask left his mouth uncovered.

"Some guys have all the luck," the other man said, turning away. "I'll check these rooms while you're 'busy.'"

"Hey," said the man next to me. That's all he ever got out. I'd grabbed the scissors taped to my thigh and had rammed their tips upward at just the right angle, past the man's ribs and into his heart. Kevlar is fine for stopping bullets, but does nothing to protect against blade weapons. I'd been ready to jam my mouth against the man's lips to silence him if he cried out . . . but he just loosed a sigh and became deadweight, held up by the scissors in his chest as if he were on a clothes hook.

Good. I didn't mind killing the man—he was a killer himself, having helped shoot the doorman—but I preferred not to be kissing him as I perforated his aorta.

I killed a man once while kissing him. It's an experience I'd rather not repeat.

If the other man noticed what I'd done, all he saw were movements hidden under the sheet. He'd assume I was up to something far different from what had actually happened. Besides, he was already heading down the hall to search for Reuben.

Which left me in a quandary. I could grab the Uzi from the man I'd just killed and shoot his partner in the back . . . but that would make too much noise. Gunfire would be heard by the assault teams downstairs, letting them know this mission wasn't the cakewalk they expected. I hoped to avoid that: life is easier when the enemy is overconfident.

The worst-case scenario was if the invaders stopped being sloppy and attacked me en masse. I couldn't stand up to them in a head-to-head shoot-out. For one thing, when Dr. Jacek converted this place from church to clinic, the old skinflint had put up walls of the cheapest plaster-board—the sort that bullets passed through easily. Anywhere Reuben and I took cover, the bad guys could simply shoot us through the walls.

My ideal strategy meant picking off ruffians silently, one by one, like a horror-movie monster stalking teenagers. Gunplay was only a last resort. On the other hand, I had to do something soon. The thug in front of me was closing in on the room where Reuben lay. My arm was also getting tired holding up the man impaled on the end of my scissors . . . and my grip was growing slippery with his blood.

"Hey, you!"

It was the other gunman, speaking in Polish. Luckily, he wasn't speaking to me. He stood in the fourth doorway down the hall, staring into the room that held Mr. Russian Mafia. "I know you're not asleep," the gunman said. "Stop faking."

From where I stood, I couldn't see into the room. Apparently, though, the Russian was following my advice, pretending to be unconscious. The act must have been unconvincing because the Polish gunman strode into the Russian's room. "Do you think I'm stupid? What are you hiding? Open your eyes."

I don't know how the Russian responded . . . but with the Polish hooligan no longer in the corridor, I could deal with my own problems. Quietly, I lowered the dead man in my arms to the floor. I wished I had time to commandeer his Uzi, but it was secured on a shoulder strap; wrestling it free from the man's corpse might take too long, especially since I couldn't afford to make suspicious noises. I contented myself with cleaning my blood-smeared hand on his shirt. Then I left him lying under the sheet. I preferred not to look at my handiwork after the deed was done, no matter how necessary the kill had been.

Glad to get away from the body, I moved soundlessly toward the Russian's room.

The Russian had given up playing possum . . . probably when he felt the muzzle of an Uzi pressed against his skull. At that point, however, the gunman and the Mafioso reached an impasse; the Pole clearly didn't speak Russian, and the Russian showed no sign of speaking Polish. The gunman was now trying English, which didn't strike a chord either. Globalization has a long way to go in the criminal world.

I took all this in with a quick peek around the door-frame. The men were too busy to notice. I might have walked in and rendered the gunman unconscious without too much trouble . . . except for the pistol he held pressed against the Russian's head. The safety was off, and the man's finger was on the trigger. Whatever I did to knock him out—whether a nerve strike, a sleeper hold, or a plain old punch to the jaw—I couldn't be certain his hand wouldn't clench by pure reflex and fire off a round. Not only would that alert his companions on the ground floor, it would probably kill the Russian.

I couldn't allow that. Much as I suspected the Russian belonged to the Mafia, I didn't know for certain. Even if he did, he might not have blood on his hands: a bookie or a fence, deserving jail but not a bullet to the brain.

So I waited . . . hoping the gunman wouldn't shoot the Russian out of pique at the failure to communicate. It was touch and go for a few seconds; but at last the Pole must have realized the Russian wasn't part of the mission at hand. The invaders wanted Reuben Baptiste, not some Moscow Mafioso with a broken leg. "You're wasting my time," the gunman said. He flicked on the Uzi's safety and pistol-whipped the Russian hard across the face. The Russian fell back, blood gushing from his nose. At least he wouldn't have to fake unconsciousness anymore.

Angrily, the gunman came stomping out of the room. As he reached the doorway, he snapped, "Have you fin-

ished with that whore yet?" He turned toward the spot
where he'd last seen his partner and me.

That's when I hit him with a ridge hand across the
throat—a clothesline maneuver into which I put all my
strength.

If that first strike didn't collapse his windpipe, my second one did. I was in no mood to be gentle.

I stashed the corpses under the unconscious Russian's
bed, leaving the first man wrapped in the sheet to avoid
any pool of blood. Lady Macbeth asked, ". . . who would
have thought the old man to have had so much blood in
him?" . . . but that proves Lady M. was an amateur when
it came to violence. Dead bodies can spill *prodigious*
quantities of blood. In a cheaply constructed place like
Jacek's, one must store corpses carefully to avoid leaks
seeping through the floor and out the ceiling below. Blood
dripping from the rafters may delight splatterpunk movie
audiences, but it's undesirable when one wants to be
stealthy.

As I was hiding the dead men, I searched them. They'd
brought precious little equipment with them: no standard
mercenary gear like walkie-talkies or night-vision goggles. Not even an electric torch. They must have expected
this mission to be a complete cakewalk. All they carried
were weapons, which I took for myself—not just the Uzis
but also a Kaybar commando knife in a sheath, which I
slid onto my belt.

To my deep unease, one of the men also possessed a
glittering grenade of a type I didn't recognize. It was the
size of my fist but spherical with a polished exterior that
looked like sterling silver. There were two press buttons,
one on either end. Presumably, one triggered the grenade
by pressing both buttons simultaneously; but I couldn't
guess what happened after that. Did it explode? Was it a
stun grenade, designed not to kill but to bang out a con-
cussion wave strong enough to knock victims senseless?

Could it contain noxious gas, and, if so, would the contents be simple tear gas or something more lethal?

Speculation was pointless. The next time I saw my armorer, I'd ask if he knew what the grenade was. For now, though, all I could do was stash the thing in my pocket. I certainly couldn't *use* it: I didn't know the timing delay—whether it went off in three seconds, five seconds, or longer. I'd feel like an utter prat if I whipped out this fancy grenade, then accidentally blew myself up.

Instead of brooding about the unknown weapon, I prepared a series of surprises for the next round of gunmen who might venture up the stairs. Afterward, I checked on Reuben. He lay in the bed with only his eyes showing beneath his bandages. "How's it going?" he whispered.

"Our initial investment is earning interest," I said, showing him the Uzis. "Soon we'll begin collecting dividends."

I had the guns strapped around my shoulders so I could fire with both hands if need be . . . but such two-fisted shooting is nearly useless, even if it looks brilliant in the cinema. Uzis kick like mules when firing full auto; if I let loose with both at once I'd be lucky to stay on my feet, let alone keep my aim on target. Quite possibly, the recoil would send me flying through one of the clinic's flimsy walls . . .

Hmm. *Hmm.*

"New strategy," I told Reuben. "Stay in the bed but be ready to move at a moment's notice." I might have said more, but I could hear company coming up the stairs.

"Hey," a man called from the stairwell. "What's taking youse guys?" The accent was pure Brooklyn . . . which prompted me to reflect on what a diverse lot these villains were. Traditional organized crime gangs clump together by ethnicity—Colombian cartels, Japanese Yakuza, Chinese triads, and so on. Multiculturalism among criminals almost always means a force of mercenaries: soldiers of fortune from around the world, recruited higgledy-piggledy with no common bond except a greed for cash.

Most mercenaries have some military background and consider themselves professional warriors—la crème de la crème. Usually, though, they're just men who like to play with guns. They may possess skills, but they're too much in love with their own self-image to achieve true crème-dom. The majority have been discharged from regular armies for not following orders, and they turn even more unruly once they go independent. The group I was facing might see themselves as a well-coordinated unit, but when push came to shove, I was betting that they'd respond as egotistic individuals. The primary weakness of mercenaries is that they're dreadful team players.

Then again, I'm one to talk.

The man in the stairwell called, "Hey! What's up?" He received no answer. I could hear him muttering to someone—presumably one or more partners—then he began to ascend.

This thug came up more cautiously than the first two: slowly, listening for trouble. I doubt if he was truly worried—as far as he knew, he and his fifteen buddies faced a single unarmed man—but he must have wondered why no one up here was answering. When the Brooklyn man reached the final step, he stood out of sight in the stairwell and shouted down the hall, "Where are youse guys? Say something!"

No reply.

I'd had time to creep down to the room nearest the stairs. I stood there, back to the wall, the Kaybar knife in my hand. If I was lucky . . .

I was. The man on the stairs was only half a professional. His professional half was smart enough to call to his friends below, "Something's up. Foxtrot and Golf are missing." But instead of waiting for backup, the man's glory-hound impulses propelled him forward: moving slowly, Uzi drawn, as if the pistol were enough to protect him.

It wasn't. My knife, his throat—fill in the blanks yourself.

I didn't have time to hide the body—more people were coming up the stairs. A lot of them. I did take a second to do a quick visual once-over of the corpse but saw nothing of interest. The dead man had been carrying nothing except his Uzi: no radio, no torch, not even one of those strange silver grenades.

Someone spoke unintelligibly in the stairwell, and I knew I had to go. I raced back to Reuben's room. "Get ready to move," I whispered. "We're leaving."

"How? Aren't there bad guys on the stairs?"

"We won't take the stairs."

He stared at me. I said, "Stand back. When I run, follow."

Plenty of noise on the stairs now. Four mercs; maybe more. But before I'd killed the previous one, I'd arranged a vigorous welcome for such visitors.

I'd removed the two spare oxygen tanks from the end room and positioned them on either side of the doorway to the stairs. At the base of one tank, I'd placed the bottle of rubbing alcohol. By the other, I'd set the spray can of disinfectant. The arrangement might look odd to someone peeking out from the stairwell, but not enough to raise dire suspicions. After all, oxygen tanks and the rest were common items in a clinic. The mercenaries would probably assume the tanks were kept by the stairwell for lack of better storage space.

A man appeared in the doorway. I ducked out of sight. Five seconds passed. Then I heard the scuff of army boots as someone scurried out of the stairwell and bolted to the first doorway. The mercenaries clearly planned to advance forward, one man at a time, straight from the team ops' textbook. I waited for boots again, then popped one Uzi around the doorframe and fired.

I didn't have to see my targets—I wasn't aiming at men in motion, I was shooting at the unmoving oxygen tanks. A burst of full auto straight down the hall couldn't help hitting both big metal canisters just standing there. Couldn't help puncturing them either . . . at which point the two steel tanks containing gas under high pressure turned into modest but effective pipe bombs.

This wasn't the sort of explosion that's powered by a flaming detonation. The percussive energy came entirely from oxygen bursting outward with a force of thousands of pounds per square inch. I doubt if it caught fire at all; but then I can't give an eyewitness description. It seemed unwise to stick my head out into a corridor full of (a) gunmen, and (b) shards of flying metal. Still, I heard the tanks rupture with a satisfying bang, followed by rapid-fire thunks as bits of steel blew outward and embedded themselves into anything nearby. That included at least one ruffian, who screamed in astonished agony.

But the hurtling metal fragments were only the start of the chaos. The oxygen tanks were holed and breached but still mostly intact. All the holes were on the side facing me . . . which meant that the oxygen shot straight down the hall at high pressure, like the exhaust blast from rocket engines. In response to Newton's third law, the tanks embarked upon an equal and opposite reaction: bashing their way through the thin wall separating the corridor from the stairs and careening into the stairwell at significant velocity. The stairwell, being part of the church's original bell tower, was stone lined and strong enough to withstand the flying $O_2$ tanks. The tanks clanged furiously within the contained volume, bouncing off anything in their path until all the gas inside had escaped.

I myself have never been struck full force by a jet-propelled oxygen tank. Judging by the shrieks from the men on the stairs, I doubt it's a pleasant experience.

The immediate response was gunfire—shooting at random. The mercenaries weren't sure who'd attacked them, but their first instincts said to spray the world with bullets. They were probably smart enough not to shoot each other; beyond that, all bets were off.

I can't tell you if the bottle of rubbing alcohol got broken at that point, or if it had already been smashed when the oxygen tanks blew. Either way, this was the moment at which the flammable alcohol caught fire amid the pandemonium of hot lead and muzzle flashes.

*Whoosh.* Then *bang* . . . as blazing alcohol spilled across the floor and reached the disinfectant spray can, causing another small-yield high-pressure explosion. Uzis chattered toward the source of the noise; the gunmen must have thought the bursting can was someone shooting from behind them.

I hoped the men would eventually calm down and stamp out the fire—I didn't want to torch the entire clinic. Meanwhile, however, under cover of the uncontrolled gunfire in the hall, I opened up with the second Uzi I held: blasting the back wall of Reuben's hospital room. Half the clip made a ragged polka-dot effect that weakened the cheap plasterboard to the consistency of tissue paper. I sprinted forward, ramming the wall full strength with my shoulder . . . and crashed through into falling darkness.

I landed on hard wooden flooring one story below—not an enjoyable jolt, but I've walked away from worse.

The light from the room above me showed that I'd dropped into the empty sanctuary of the old church. As I'd suspected, St. Anthony the Great had been blessed with more space than Dr. Jacek needed. The worship area was built in the traditional shape of a cross, but the clinic only occupied the cross's vertical part—what architects call the nave. The cross's horizontal piece—the transept—and its top—the apse—were empty and unused . . . like vacant wings of the building if Dr. Jacek ever chose to expand. At present, however, the doctor's clinic was just a walled-off box set in the cross's leg.

Reuben appeared backlit in the hole I'd smashed through the upper story wall. "Get down here!" I said in a harsh whisper. "Can you make it?"

He nodded and crouched, getting ready to jump. I could see him hesitate, probably imagining how his broken rib would lurch painfully under the impact of landing. "Hurry!" I told him. "I'll catch you."

"No. Stay back." It might have been male pride speaking or fear that getting caught would hurt his rib more than landing unassisted. Either way, I accepted Reuben's decision. In the few seconds he needed to summon his courage, I took the opportunity to check my surroundings.

The church had been thoroughly emptied before Dr. Jacek took over. Every pew was gone; the altar had been taken away too, and the pulpit, the lectern, the choir benches. The stained-glass windows had been replaced with sheets of plywood, and I knew the doors were boarded up from the outside. (I'd surveyed the building for escape routes before entering. Doesn't everyone do that?)

Given time I could smash loose a board from a door or window, but it would be a loud, lengthy process—sure to attract unwanted attention. Our best way out was back through the clinic: piercing another flimsy wall, then racing through the ground floor rooms while the main force of mercenaries looked for Reuben and me upstairs. These chaps weren't the brightest sparks on the bonfire; they'd waste quite some time Uzi-dusting empty rooms before they realized Reuben and I had moved on. Meanwhile, I could quietly dispatch whatever sentries were guarding the exit, then leave posthaste.

Easy. Nothing to it.

Reuben landed heavily beside me. He gasped in pain, but straightened up quickly. He stayed upright for three whole seconds before sagging and clutching his side.

"How are you doing?" I whispered.

He straightened up again, trying to pretend he was fine. "Can I take off these blasted bandages?" His voice came out muffled; his head was still sheathed in gauze.

"Feel free," I said. "Catch your breath while I clear the way." I glanced at the hole in the wall above us. "Rest somewhere you'll be out of sight. Make sure that nice shiny attaché case doesn't glint in the dark."

# 3

# WARSAW: THE CLINIC'S LOWER FLOOR

I took a quick tour of the clinic's outer shell: the plaster-board walls that separated the dark church from the well-lit medical rooms. Every few steps, slits of light shone at ankle level—places where electrical outlets had been set into the cheap walls. Wires emerged from the rear of each outlet box. The wires were duct taped to the back of the plasterboard, then ran around to a central junction box where the main electrical feed entered through a wall of the church. If I were a professional electrician, I'd be horrified by the slapdash wiring: exactly the third-rate construction you'd expect in an illegal clinic built in defiance of safety codes. Not being an electrician, I was ready to dance for joy. One good yank on the incoming feed would cut power to the whole clinic. And since I already knew the men hadn't come equipped with electric torches . . .

Nothing promises more good clean fun than shutting off the lights in a building full of high-strung men with Uzis.

First, though, I had to secure a way forward. I listened at the wall nearest the main electrical box: no sounds on the other side. Quietly, I pressed the Kaybar knife's tip to the plasterboard and drilled a small hole at eye level. Peeking through, I saw a room cluttered with test tubes, microscopes, centrifuges, and other such equipment—obviously, the clinic's medical lab. The phobic medical technician was nowhere in sight; since she seldom left her lab voluntarily, I assumed she'd been dragged out by force. The assault teams had indeed taken the clinic's staff as prisoners.

I'd have to do something about that when I got the chance. So much to do, so little time. The story of my life.

I gave Reuben the choice of yanking the electrical feed wire or cutting through the wall with the Kaybar. He chose the wire. He winced as he raised his arms to grab the thick insulated cord, but when I whispered "Go!" he pulled without hesitation. The wire jerked out of the fuse box with a sharp bright *crack*; then the lights went dark, and I began whittling the knife through the wall.

The blackness wasn't 100 percent, but it came close. A few photons feebly crept around the plywood that blocked the church's windows—just enough that I wasn't entirely blind but too little to show anything but the vaguest outlines.

It didn't matter. Cutting the wall went well, though it was hard work. I was constantly tempted just to bash through by brute force, but that would make noise and I didn't want to give away our location. As far as the bad guys knew, Reuben and I were still hunkered down in that room overhead . . . and with the lights out, the men up there would take a long time discovering otherwise.

I could hear them muttering to one another, debating their next move. Some had been injured by bouncing oxygen tanks, so their numbers were moderately diminished. They also knew I'd taken possession of their comrades' Uzis. Correction: they knew *someone* had taken possession of the Uzis. The mercenaries had no idea who their enemy was. With some of their group hors de combat, and the opposition well armed but unknown, the men would likely adopt a wait-and-see attitude rather than charging willy-nilly into the dark.

Meanwhile I continued slicing through the wall. In half a minute I'd cut a hole big enough for Reuben and me to crawl through. I sheathed my knife and started forward. Since we had no lights, I worried we'd make a racket knocking over glassware in the lab, but just as I'd begun to move, a faint illumination sprang to life outside the room's open door.

I raised an Uzi, thinking we were about to be discovered—maybe one of the gunmen had a light after all. But no one appeared. Instead, people gabbled a short distance away, saying in Polish, "Thank God!" and "That's better!" Then a brassy woman's voice said, "See, Stanislaw, that emergency light wasn't a waste of money after all."

It was Jacek's senior nurse—possibly also his wife or his mistress . . . I'd never figured out their precise relationship. Her words suggested that the light we were seeing came from a battery-powered lamp, the sort that turns on when normal power goes out. A conventional hospital might have dozens of emergency lights throughout the building . . . but Stanislaw Jacek, ever the tightwad, had installed only one.

That single light would surely be in the operating room. Anyplace else, a blackout was merely inconvenient. In the OR, light could literally mean the difference between life and death.

"Stay here," I whispered to Reuben. I followed the dim spill of light out of the med lab and up a short corridor to the OR. One peek showed what I'd expected: the staff was here, most of them huddled against the far wall. In the middle of the room, Jacek and two nurses, in green scrubs and wearing operating masks, clustered around the main table where they were working on a patient.

I couldn't see the patient because the operating team was in the way. I couldn't see any mercenaries either. It was possible these people had simply been herded here and ordered to stay put. Perhaps a gunman had watched them for a while; but when trouble erupted upstairs, the man had left to help his compatriots.

*A promising situation,* I thought. If I cleared a path between the OR and the exit, I could get the staff to safety. The patient on the table presented a problem—no way to tell how soon he or she could be moved—but the more people who left the building, the fewer would be in the line of fire if the mercenaries started shooting.

Quickly and quietly, I went back for Reuben. The best place to put him was with the other captives. He'd be less noticeable among them, especially if he could find medical scrubs and a surgical mask to use as a disguise. Yes, we'd have trouble hiding the attaché case on his wrist; but we could cover it somehow so it wouldn't be immediately obvious if a mercenary glanced into the room. Whatever we did, taking Reuben to the OR was better than leaving him in the lab where he'd stick out like a sore thumb.

Or so I thought. I'm not always right. When Reuben and I appeared in the operating room doorway, I held my finger to my lips. "Shhh." The people stayed obediently silent . . . but Dr. Jacek, wearing a rueful expression, stepped back from the operating table to reveal the patient lying there.

It was one of the bad guys. He was getting surgery for a bullet that had shattered his ankle. The man was fully awake and still held his Uzi.

Oops.

I still had two Uzis of my own . . . and within a nanosecond, they were both pointed at the ruffian. To have his ankle mended, the man had removed all Kevlar below his waist; so that's where I aimed my guns. There are times one can't afford to be genteel.

Perhaps my choice of target was what discouraged the man from firing at me. I too preferred not to shoot—the noise would attract attention. So the hooligan and I faced each other in a standoff: gazes locked, guns at the ready, waiting for signs of weakness.

"If you move or shout," I said, "you won't enjoy the consequences."

"Neither will you," he replied. His English had a Scandinavian accent. "I've already been shot once tonight," he said. "I'm not eager for more."

"Shot by the doorman?"

"The scumbag got lucky."

"I doubt he lived long enough to celebrate his luck."

The gunman smiled. "If you want to avoid something similar, put down your guns."

"I could say the same to you."

"You're outnumbered," he said.

"You're outclassed," I replied. "You're also unobservant. While we've been talking, Dr. Jacek has positioned a scalpel directly above your jugular vein."

The gunman's head snapped toward Jacek, and his pistol began to pivot in the same direction. In fact, the good doctor was *not* about to cut the ruffian's throat. For all his quirks, Stanislaw Jacek really did live by the Hippocratic oath—he would never harm a human being, not even a murderous mercenary who'd helped kill the clinic's doorman. But the villain on the table didn't know that . . . and by the time he realized Jacek posed no threat, I was hurtling across the room. The gunman tried to bring his Uzi back to bear on me, but I cleared it away with a crescent kick that knocked the gun from his hands. I tried to follow up with an ax kick—up, then straight down—with the intention of slamming my heel hard onto the shooter's stomach. The man saw it coming and threw himself back off the operating table. My boot made a heel-shaped dent as it struck the table's metal surface but otherwise had no effect.

If I'd had enough clearance, I would have vaulted over the table and landed feetfirst on the man, now sprawled across the OR floor . . . but Jacek and his nurses were in the way. If I took the time to run around the table, the man would have ample opportunity to yell for help; so I dived straight forward, arms out, legs extended, much like the position for leaping headlong into a somersault. Instead of jumping all the way over the table, I let myself land half on, half off: my hips and legs on the tabletop, my upper body hanging over the far edge. I had just enough arm reach to get my hands around the gunman's throat, choking off any cry he might make to his comrades.

It was hardly a ladylike position—my backside up on the table, the rest of me dangling head downward while trying to strangle someone on the floor—but none of the half dozen people in the room showed any inclination to lend a hand. Through gritted teeth I said, "Would someone please stamp on this fellow's face? Or inject him with anesthetic. At this point, I'm not picky."

Under normal conditions, my opponent would have wrenched my hands off his throat within seconds—I had no leverage to hold him down. But he must have been weakened from getting shot, not to mention his jarring drop off the operating table and whatever pain medication Jacek gave him before surgery. All the man's flailing couldn't break my hold. When Reuben started forward to get in on the action, the gunman gave up fighting me and shoved a hand into his pocket. "He's going for a weapon!" I yelled; but no one was fast enough to intercede.

The man's hand emerged from his pocket, holding a spherical silver grenade like the one I'd found on the thug upstairs. "This is not good," I muttered. Still squeezing the man's throat with my right hand, I swatted at the grenade with my left . . . but the mercenary avoided me and pressed the grenade's buttons. With no other options left, I inhaled fast and deep in case the room filled with toxic gas.

But the grenade wasn't filled with poison vapor. Instead, its mirror surface liquefied like mercury, pouring over the man's hands and running up his arms: a thick silver gush that spread over flesh and clothes, coating his fingers, his wrists, his sleeves. A moment before it touched my hand—the one I still held on the man's windpipe—I felt glacial cold from the air in front of the advancing fluid. I tried not to flinch as the silver washed against my skin, bitterly sharp, like instant frostbite. It oozed its way under my grip, forming a frigid barrier between my hand and the man's throat. In a heartbeat, my fingers went numb with cold. I jerked my hand free; the tissue had already turned a bloodless white, and I shook my wrist hard to get circulation flowing again.

Meanwhile the silver spread faster, enveloping the man's

head and running down his body—changing him into a featureless mirrored humanoid, like some computer-generated figure intended to show off software graphics. I saw my own face reflected in its surface; then Reuben appeared beside me in the reflection.

"What the . . . ?" Reuben said, looking at the spreading silver.

"I quite agree," I told him.

Staying atop the operating table, I reached for my belt sheath and drew the Kaybar knife. The mercenary was now encased in silver. The whole process must have taken less than five seconds, though it seemed much longer as I'd watched. Now I hefted the Kaybar and stabbed down hard, wondering how much force it would take to pierce the gleaming surface that covered the man's vitals. I felt the jar of impact as the knife tip struck home . . . then the blade shattered with a bristling crack, like a champagne glass struck with a jackhammer.

Kaybar blades are the finest steel. They never break, ever . . . except, I thought, under several tons of pressure or perhaps when made brittle by being plunged to the temperature of liquid nitrogen . . .

Where my hand had touched the silvery surface, I still felt blistering cold.

Down on the floor, the glossy figure stirred. He rolled over slowly, rising to his hands and knees. Despite the silver sheath's subzero exterior, the interior was obviously still warm enough for the man to survive. He might have been trying to say something . . . but the sound was muffled by the mirror shell.

One of Jacek's nurses, obviously moved by a heroic impulse, stepped forward. It looked like she intended to whack the thug's head with a bedpan. "No," I said quickly. "Stay back. Everybody. Keep out of my way and I'll deal with this. That silvery surface is so cold it's lethal."

"What *is* it?" Reuben whispered.

"Some kind of portable armor," I said, "for absolute emergencies. You saw what it did to the knife . . . and what it will do to your hand if you touch him." I clenched my own hand again, trying to squeeze back some warmth. The skin would definitely blister; even so, I was lucky I'd only made contact while the mirrored barrier was still forming, before it reached its final temperature. Otherwise, my iced-over fingers would have shattered as easily as the knifepoint. "Bullets likely won't penetrate either," I told Reuben. "And who knows what else that shell can resist? Flamethrowers. Acid. You could probably wear it to swim through lava."

Reuben looked at the shining man, still just trying to steady himself on his hands and knees. Inside that protective shell, the mercenary was clearly in bad shape: hurting from his injuries and woozy from anesthetic. He might also have been having additional difficulties. "Can he breathe in there?" Reuben asked.

"I doubt it," I replied. "The air around the shell is unbelievably cold. If any could get inside, it would freeze the man's lungs. No," I said, "that mirror stuff must be airtight. Once you're inside, you only have a minute or so before you began to suffocate. The shell must be designed to dissolve before that happens." I shook my head. "But a minute of absolute safety, no matter what's trying to kill you? Don't ask me how often I've prayed for something like that."

"Look out," Reuben said. "He's going for the gun."

The man was indeed crawling toward the Uzi I'd knocked from his hand. Obviously, the icy armor allowed him to see things outside. But the chap moved as ponderously as a giant tortoise. I couldn't tell if he was being slowed by his protective shell or just from being on his knees after getting shot, operated upon, dropped off a table, and partly strangled. Either way, I had no trouble rolling off the table and grabbing the pistol before the man reached it.

"You want it?" I said. "Here you go." I ejected the ammo clip and emptied the chamber—safety first, always safety first—then swung the butt of the unloaded gun at the man's silverized head. I didn't expect my attack to have much effect, but maybe the more I stressed the glossy shell, the faster it would dissipate.

The Uzi struck with a jarring thud I felt all the way up my arm like swinging a sledge hard into granite. Part of the gun butt fractured. I pulled away fast as the man darted his hand up to grab the weapon. He could have the gun for all I cared. It had no bullets . . . and if the man and I fought over it, I might literally freeze my fingers off.

As soon as the thug seized the Uzi, a coating of frost sprang up around the gun's barrel. I thought, *Didn't I see that effect in a Batman film? Or was it Bugs Bunny?* I enjoyed it more in films than in real life. Three seconds after the man grabbed the pistol, he squeezed and the weapon fell apart in his hand. Fragments of brittle metal showered to the floor like hail.

"So why did the gun go all frosty," Reuben asked, "but the guy himself isn't iced up at all?"

"Reuben," I replied, "this is hardly the time to quibble about physics. That silver stuff looks more like magic than science."

"Even magic has rules. So how does it work? Maybe like a self-cleaning freezer?"

"If you really want to know, we could try an experiment."

The OR had a large double sink where the surgery team could wash the blood-specked tools of their trade after an operation. The sink sported one of those spray attachments, a nozzle on a hose, for aiming jets of water at stubborn bits of human tissue that wouldn't come off the cutlery. I grabbed the hose, turned the water on full, and aimed the squirt nozzle at the mirror-clad hoodlum on the floor.

Instant ice: a white crust froze hard around the man as soon as water came close to his frigid exterior. I had time to think, *Brilliant, we'll immobilize this thug in his own private glacier* . . .

Then: *crack!* The sound reminded me of my last trip to

Antarctica, when a crevasse had ripped open under my feet. The ice that had just solidified around the silver shell exploded outward in a barrage of diamond-like pellets. I shielded my head with my arms, as others in the room screamed. Glass shattered, a nurse fell, and a metal bed-pan clanged like a bell . . . but I suffered only a few modest stings. No worse than getting shot with a dozen BBs at point-blank range.

However, note to self: DON'T SPRAY MORE WATER.

"Huh," Reuben said, "it *is* self-cleaning."

The man began to get to his feet. I'd been afraid of that. As long as he stayed on his hands and knees, people could dodge quickly enough to keep away from him. Once he was standing, however, he'd move faster . . . unless he collapsed from pain when he tried to put weight on his ankle. Such a collapse was unlikely. Before the operation, Dr. Jacek must have anesthetized the lower part of the gunman's leg; furthermore, the armor might serve as a splint to support the damaged leg bones. In the long run, frisking free and easy on a broken tib-fib might leave the mercenary hobbled for life. In the short run, though, he could cause cryogenic chaos, lunging about the OR and giving freezer burn to anyone he touched—not to mention raising such a ruckus that the thugs upstairs would hear. If I tried to intervene, I'd just get gelatoed myself . . .

Unless . . .

Okay. New strategy.

I whipped off one of the Uzis I still had strapped around my shoulders. "Stay down," I told the rising bad guy, swinging my gun at his head, eye level. It wouldn't have hurt him if he'd let it make contact, but reflexes are reflexes: he ducked automatically and—thanks to his ankle—awkwardly. A nanosecond later, I brought the pistol back on a return arc. The man was already off balance and perhaps distracted as he realized, *I didn't need to duck.* When the Uzi came back, maybe part of his mind was saying *Don't flinch* while his combat training shouted

*Dodge! Dodge!* and his ankle chimed in with *Hey, remember me? I'm still broken.*

The upshot was that the man fell down. Sloppily. The impact of his fall did cold, messy things to the floor, leaving sections of the linoleum looking like shattered glass.

The Uzi I'd swung had never actually made contact with the ruffian. I handed the pistol to Reuben. "Take this." I whipped off the other Uzi too. "Here's its brother. If our friend tries to stand, keep clubbing him on the head as long as the guns hold out. Don't shoot, and avoid too much noise. We don't want our chums upstairs coming down to investigate."

"What are you going to do?"

I reached into my pocket and pulled out my own shiny silver grenade. "Fight fire with fire. In an absolute-zero nothing-at-all-like-fire sort of way."

I pressed the grenade's two buttons and waited.

Silver rose ticklishly up my arm, reminding me of being swallowed by a boa constrictor. That may sound unpleasant, but it actually brought back fond memories of the Amazon rain forest where I encountered a dashing man from Her Majesty's Secret Service . . . sorry, can't tell you more without violating the Official Secrets Act. But a boa constrictor featured prominently, so I confess to being distracted as the silver continued to spread. At the very last moment, I remembered to take a deep lung-filling breath; then I was enveloped in airless silence, the mirrored shell muffling all outside sounds.

I tried to inhale a little deeper. I couldn't. As I'd expected, the armor was entirely impervious, shutting me off from the outside air as effectively as it shielded me from bullets. Now I only hoped that my other supposition was correct: that the shell would dissolve on its own in a minute or so, before I began to suffocate. If my guess was wrong and I stupidly smothered inside the silver container, wouldn't my face be red? Or blue, as the case might be.

The armor—or was it a force field?—might have kept

out all air, but it let in light easily enough. I could see as if looking through gray-tinted glass. Reuben was just stepping away from the mercenary, both Uzis reduced to crumbled ruins. Farewell to the last of our firearms . . . but the pistols had served their purpose, distracting our enemy until I was armored up. Now it was my turn to deal with the hooligan: mano a frigid mano.

He began to stand. I let him. Then I punched him in the face.

It was more an experiment than a serious attack. I doubted my strike would penetrate his protective shell any more effectively than the Uzis or the Kaybar knife. Still, one shouldn't take anything for granted. Since the silver barrier stuff had already displayed properties that defied my understanding of physics, I chose to regard it as magic in accordance with dear old Sir Arthur's law. Why not test the nature of its mystic power?

So: up with the fist and out with the fist, full strength into my opponent's nose.

Have you ever wondered what happens when an irresistible force, my armored fist, meets an immovable object, the gunman's armored face? Turns out, the result is an earsplitting bang. By which I mean, *BAAAANNNNGGGG!!* with as many additional exclamation points as you care to append.

The noise was hemorrhagingly loud even with silver muffling my ears. To others in the OR, it must have been deafening: a bona fide sonic boom. I imagined all Warsaw echoing with the thunderclap. Within seconds, half the city would be calling the police to report someone shooting off a howitzer.

So much for keeping quiet. All the gunmen upstairs would come running immediately. So would the MI6/CIA/Interpol agents no doubt investigating a mysterious car explosion near the airport. I fervently wished to be elsewhere before those agents arrived. Otherwise, I'd end up "helping police with their inquiries" . . . then "detained pending further investigation" . . . then "taken into protective custody" . . . and even though the spooks knew I was no criminal, they'd threaten to put me in jail unless I did them "a few little favors." Next thing I knew, I'd be paragliding into Beijing to steal the Sacred Sword of Sinanju or some such nonsense.

No thanks. After that mess in Mauritius, I was sick of playing errand girl. Which meant I had to finish things off fast and vamoose before the Sweeneys arrived.

My first obstacle: the ruffian in front of me. He turned in my direction, putting up his fists as if ready for more sonic-boom boxing . . . then suddenly he dropped his feint and bolted for the door. Coward. Then again, the man didn't have many options left. If I was right, and the silver armor held up only a minute or two before dissolving, my opponent's mirror shell must be close to shutting off. By the time that happened, the thug would want to be else-where—back with his fellow mercenaries. They were his only protection, now that his Uzi was reduced to frozen frass.

I caught the gunless gunman just as he reached the corridor. This time, I didn't punch him—I had no desire to trigger another thunderclap. Instead I thrust my arm around his neck and gingerly pulled back with a basic forearm choke hold. There was still a *whomp* as our silver shells made contact, but much softer than the first time. That could have been because the shells didn't smack to-gether with the pile-driving force of a punch . . . or maybe the silver force fields had blown off most of their energy the first time they collided. Now, they had far less "juice" to power sonic outbursts. Every moment they remained in contact, they seemed to drain each other more. After five seconds, both the mercenary's silver lining and my own winked out with a soft *whoof* of air, like two fires that have burned up each other's fuel.

For an instant, nothing happened . . . but my arm was still bent around the man's neck, pressing in on his throat, and now there was no shell preventing me from cinching up on his esophagus. I did so. The mercenary attempted to respond with a standard escape move—turning his head toward my elbow to reduce the constriction on his windpipe, grabbing my wrist to loosen the grip, and stepping into a lower stance in preparation for a release maneuver—but partway through, his injured ankle snapped from exertion.

Nothing sounds so *meaty* as a leg bone breaking. It's the crack of mortality.

The man would have fallen if I hadn't been holding him around the neck. He ended up dangling from my choke hold, making urgent gargling noises. I could have proceeded to kill him . . . but why? I whispered in his ear, "If I let you live, do you promise to be good?"

He gagged out something I took for a yes.

"Fine." I dropped him to the ground and stepped away. He lay on the floor, gasping. I considered whacking him a few times to knock him out, but the thought of pummeling an injured man into unconsciousness turned my stomach. In his weakened condition, any more damage could kill him. I made do with poking my foot lightly into his ribs. "Help the poor," I said. "Find a cure for cancer. Do something useful with your life so I don't regret letting you live."

The man didn't answer. He might not have understood what I'd said. But he looked so dazed—close to clinical shock—I was certain he wouldn't cause any more trouble.

I turned to Reuben. "We'd better get ready," I said. "The bad guys will be here any moment. Time for our last stand."

We had half a minute to scour the OR for implements of defense. The place had exactly what you'd expect: an abundance of bandages and penicillin but a dearth of firearms, Tasers, and antipersonnel devices. I improvised what I could, then ran to the door as I heard combat boots drawing near.

The corridor outside the OR was just wide enough for a gurney . . . and since we *had* a gurney available, I'd asked a nurse to wheel one out. With its brakes locked, the gurney formed a simple barricade between us and the oncoming horde. It wouldn't stop our enemies for long, but it would slow the first arrivals. We'd also moved the emergency light into the hall to illuminate anyone approaching. Enough light spilled backward that the OR wasn't completely dark, but we could see the gunmen more clearly than they could see us.

Such little advantages were important. The assault force had started with sixteen bad guys. Dr. Jacek said the doorman had killed one with a lucky shot to the head and had disabled another with an ankle shot. The ankle victim was, of course, the man sprawled on the OR floor. I'd eliminated another three scoundrels upstairs, reducing the opposition to eleven less however many had been taken out by flying oxygen tanks. There was no way to guess the number of men who'd charge the OR, but even one hooligan with an Uzi was a serious threat—we had no guns of our own.

Of course, we weren't *entirely* unarmed . . .

I took a position in the doorway. Reuben stood behind me, ready to pass armaments as needed. I saw a ruffian begin sneaking up the corridor and I held my hand out to Reuben. "Scalpel."

"Scalpel." He slapped the scalpel's handle into my palm.

The approaching mercenary had almost reached the gurney. He was farther away than my favorite dartboard in the Fox and Trotter, but I thought I could still hit the bull's-eye.

With light from the emergency lamp shining in his eyes, all the man might have seen was my arm in the doorway, cocking back and throwing. Then he stopped seeing anything at all . . . at least with his right eye. He screamed for a moment, then fell silent.

One down.

I held out my hand to Reuben. "Forceps."

"Forceps."

Surgical forceps come in many sizes. The biggest are huge tongs for gripping a baby's head during difficult births. The smallest are tweezers that can delicately manipulate blood vessels and other tiny tissues. Between those extremes are a multitude of variations. I'd chosen a set like the tongs used to lift hard-boiled eggs out of hot water. With rubber surgical tubing tied between the outstretched prong arms, the forceps made a nice little catapult . . . or what American weaponry catalogs call "a high-powered hunting-grade slingshot."

I held out my hand to Reuben again. "Hypo."

"Hypo."

He passed me a hypodermic syringe of truly prodigious dimensions. I wondered if Dr. Jacek sometimes needed to vaccinate elephants. Despite its monstrous proportions, the needle fit nicely on the slingshot's rubber strap . . . and it flew nicely, too, as soon as I caught sight of another mercenary skulking toward us.

Who knew that syringes were aerodynamic? It shot forward like a javelin, spiking into the bad guy's ski mask and burying itself deep, deep, deep. An instant after impact, the hypo's glass body broke, splashing the man with its contents. I don't know what the fluid was—Dr. Jacek had simply handed me a bottle and said, "Fill the needle with this"—but whatever was in the hypo, it worked a wicked treat. The villain gave a gagging cough, loosed a three-bullet burst into the ceiling, and collapsed like a sack of bananas.

Two down.

The next mercenary tried to learn from his comrades' mistakes. He charged toward the gurney, shooting suppression bursts down the middle of the corridor in an attempt to discourage answering fire.

"Ether," I said to Reuben.

"Ether."

We had a big bottle of the stuff, easy to launch with the slingshot. By reflex, the gunman shot the bottle as it hurtled toward him. The glass broke; the flammable ether inside caught fire from the muzzle flash and continued forward in accordance with the usual laws of momentum.

The hooligan was inundated with a faceful of blazing liquid he'd ignited himself.

Howling ensued. A torch dance.

Three down.

The corridor wasn't wide enough for two, but a pair of mercenaries tried it anyway. They opted for caution; they also opted to pop a few bullets at the emergency lamp, shooting out the bulb.

I'd wondered when someone would think of that.

In the resulting blackness, the gunmen moved forward as silently as they could. Bulletproof vests make stealth difficult, but I gave the men points for effort—they kept the rustling to a minimum. I held out my hand to Reuben and said, clearly and distinctly, "Grenade."

"Grenade."

This was a ruse we'd arranged earlier. Instead of a grenade—which we didn't have—Reuben gave me a cake of antiseptic soap. I counted under my breath, softly but audibly, "Five, four, three . . ."

I threw the soap down the corridor. It bounced off the wall with a thump. Both mercenaries turned tail and ran, causing a ruckus that I augmented by hurling a couple of bedpans I'd been keeping for just this moment. Under cover of the noise and darkness, I leapt from the OR doorway, cleared the gurney that blocked the way forward, and slipped inside the next door along the hall into a room that smelled fiercely of disinfectant.

This was the main examination room. Every patient passed through here for preliminary inspection and treatment. It might have been full of items I could use for bringing down prey, but I couldn't see a thing. I had only one weapon left in my arsenal: a roll of suture cord, used for stitching up wounds. I pulled it out of my pocket. The cord was strong and tough, like high-pound-test fishing line—practically unbreakable. I unwound a length, holding the spool in one hand and wrapping the loose end around a small metal clamp I'd taken from the OR. Holding my breath, I waited.

The pair of mercenaries who'd just run away soon realized there'd been no grenade. "Just a trick," one man muttered. "A lousy trick!" Unwisely, the man stormed back without waiting for his partner; I suppose he was eager to dish out payback on those who'd fooled him. In the dark, of course, he couldn't see. After bumping into the wall once—bumping hard, by the sound of it—he continued forward a little more slowly, dragging his fingers along the wall to keep himself oriented. He must have thought his opposition was still on the far side of the gurney. He had no idea I was inches away, silent and unseen.

I located my target by sound; he was quite the noisy fellow, still grumbling under his breath, "Just a lousy trick!" My ambush silenced the grumbling along with his breath: suture cord circled the man's throat from behind in a cuttingly effective garrote. The thug struggled a bit, but couldn't squeeze out a sound . . . nothing except a soft squirt as the suture cord sliced into his skin.

It was over quickly. Four down. And as I lowered the corpse to join the growing pile by the gurney, I helped myself to the strangled man's Uzi.

A moment later, the mercenary's partner plodded up. He heard me moving in the dark. "Charlie?" he said. "Charlie?"

I could have been subtle; but why?

It's traditional to say SMGs sound like *buddah-buddah-buddah*, but I've always found Uzis are just a loud bright *trrrrrrr*.

Two bursts at head level. *Trrrrrrr. Trrrrrrr.*

Five down.

Ten men—nine by me, and one by the guard's lucky shot—had now been eliminated. The remaining six might all have been injured or worse in the furor upstairs, but there was no way to tell.

I rummaged briefly through the heap of fallen gunmen, searching by feel for useful equipment. I found nothing but Uzis . . . not even another Kaybar. In a way, that was good news. If none of these hooligans had night-vision goggles or even a Maglite, I could breathe a little easier. Even better—sort of—I found no more silver-armor grenades. It would have been nice to get my hands on another, but I took solace in knowing that mirror shells weren't standard equipment for *every* mercenary between me and the exit. If I was lucky, none of the remaining attackers had one of the little silver devils. After all, magic armor force fields must be expensive, right? Perhaps this group of mercenaries could only afford two grenades all told.

Especially since these thugs were clearly second-rate. Or third-rate. Poorly equipped and poorly coordinated. It didn't say much for Reuben that his capture had been assigned to twits. Still, there'd been sixteen of them—quite a few to send after only one man. Whoever commanded this crew might have thought quantity would make up for quality. Or maybe there was more going on than met the casual eye.

I'd think about that later. For now, I had to finish my pest removal. Grabbing another Uzi from a fallen thug, I started quietly forward . . . listening for danger.

If I were a clever mercenary—or even a mutton head with a sense of self-preservation—and if I saw five of my comrades venture down a corridor without coming back, I'd think, *Perhaps going down there myself isn't the best strategy.* Instead, I'd take a position watching the mouth of the corridor and prepare to shoot anything that emerged. On the off chance some of the bad guys had such a glimmering of intelligence, I stopped near the end of the corridor and lowered myself to the floor. Silently, I belly crawled the rest of the way forward. Then I tossed my spool of suture cord into the next room, bouncing the cord off a side wall.

*Tink.*

Immediately, two Uzis opened up on the source of the sound. Immediately, I opened up on the gunmen holding the Uzis. Aiming at the muzzle flashes, I scored shots on both men; but as soon as I'd fired, I rolled away fast from my original position, just in case I wasn't the only one trying to trick the opposition into betraying its location.

Another gun flared in the darkness: *trrrrrrr.* Linoleum fragments stung me, kicked up by a flurry of 9-millimeter Parabellum blasting the floor where I'd been lying a split second earlier. I fired back at the source of this new attack, but the brief light of my muzzle flashes showed the man ducking out of sight behind something big and solid. Without hesitating, I dived back down the corridor, just as another rain of bullets slapped into my previous position.

Darkness and silence returned . . . giving me a chance to sort out what had just happened. The room in front of me was the entry area where the doorman met incoming patients and patted them down. The "something big and solid" between me and the mercenary could only be the doorman's safe: the vault where he stored visitors' weaponry. If I recalled correctly, the vault's walls were four-inch steel that no bullet could penetrate.

The mercenary had taken cover behind the toughest protection in the building . . . certainly tougher than the flimsy walls around me. If the bad guy knew where to fire, he could kill me straight through the plasterboard. Fortunately, he *didn't* know where to fire; and shooting at random would just waste ammunition.

I waited for what I knew would come next.

"Oi!" the man called. "Can we talk?"

His accent was Australian . . . not that it mattered. I didn't answer because the moment I spoke, he'd know where to aim.

"I saw you just now by the muzzle flashes," the man said. "A woman, right? Right? Don't know who you are, but you aren't our target. We're after a sod named Reuben Baptiste. Actually, we aren't after him either—just what he's carrying."

He waited for me to betray myself. I didn't.

"Maybe it's like this," the gunman said. "You're, what, a spy or something? An international assassin in Warsaw on a mission? You see guys with guns, and you think they're after *you*. Understandable mistake. And I don't give a damn even if you *have* killed everybody I came with. More money for me when I bring home the goods."

Did that mean he was the last mercenary standing? Or was it a ruse? No, it was probably true. I'd seen nobody else in the front room . . . and since that's where the stairs to the bell tower came out, that's where the survivors from upstairs would gather.

I tallied up numbers again. If I'd disabled three hooligans with the oxygen tanks—a reasonable possibility—this man was my final opponent.

"I'm willing to let you go," the man was saying. "I'll even sweeten the offer with money. You get me Reuben Baptiste and the boss'll put you on the payroll. He's generous, you'll see. And he's got a good eye for talent. A woman like you, he'd give you a Silver Shield right off."

A Silver Shield? Meaning a shiny force field? Apparently, the silver grenades were only given to lackeys of a certain rank . . . which explained why few gunmen had them. The man talking to me must not have earned his Silver Shield yet; otherwise, he'd just armor up and come for me.

"So what do you say?" the man asked. "Want to join? The boss'll be glad to have you."

I wanted to ask who this boss was. But talking wouldn't get me answers; it would just get me shot.

Once more, I moved quietly to the mouth of the corridor. I lifted both my Uzis judiciously, trying to gauge which one was lighter—which had less ammo left. Probably the one in my right hand. I unstrapped it and tossed it into the middle of the next room.

Instant gunfire. A single three-bullet burst. Of course, the man hadn't meant what he'd said . . . but his impulsive shots lit the room enough to show me everything: a chair where the doorman once sat, the safe, the front exit, the entrance to the stairwell.

"Sorry about that," the man said . . . as if a simple apology could excuse his attempt to shoot me. "I overreacted. But, really, we can work something out . . ."

That was all I heard—I retreated, fast and quiet. Down the corridor, over the gurney, past the OR, back to the hole leading into the church. There was just enough light in the church sanctuary to let me find the spot where Reuben and I had leapt from the upper story. I jumped . . . grabbed the edge . . . pulled myself up . . . and was once more on the higher level, in the patient rooms. Forward, heading for the stairs . . . nearly falling when I tripped over a body but catching myself in time . . . stealthily down the stairs . . . and the last mercenary was still babbling, "Come on, can't we talk? We can work things out . . ."

My whole journey upstairs and down had taken less than thirty seconds; but now I was on the other side of the room. The man taking cover behind the solid steel vault was totally exposed from this angle.

My Uzi went, *trrrrrrr*. Its muzzle flash showed the mercenary wearing a look of utter astonishment as he died.

One final errand: checking the getaway vehicles. I donned the winter jacket I'd left on the entrance room's coat stand and slipped outside.

When I first saw the black Explorers pull up, I'd assumed the mercs would leave a driver in each to allow for fast escape. I therefore flattened myself in the clinic's doorway, inched through shadows, dodged behind a lamppost, crawled across the pavement on my stomach . . . only to find the cars empty, unlocked, with keys in the ignition. It was a miracle they hadn't been stolen; Warsaw is no worse for crime than any other city its size, but leaving brand-new SUVs unlocked in the middle of the night is asking for trouble. Then again, Stare Miasto is supposed to be a no-vehicle zone, so maybe carjackers never visited the district.

I took the keys from the nearest Explorer and locked all the doors before jogging back into the building. "Reuben!" I called. "Let's go."

"The coast is clear?" His voice came from the OR.

"It's clear for now. But the police may arrive any second."

"They'll take their time." That was Dr. Jacek talking. "The police try not to disturb us . . . and when they have no choice, they don't come straight here. They find excuses to take a roundabout route. In case we need time to clean up."

I wondered whom Jacek had to pay to receive such treatment. Maybe no one. Maybe influential people simply told the police Dr. Jacek was not to be raided. The rich and powerful occasionally need discreet clandestine clinics that deal with medical emergencies . . . and such gentry don't like interruptions when they're getting patched up or medicated.

Something clattered down the corridor—something accidentally knocked over in the dark—then Jacek and Reuben appeared. They looked relieved . . . maybe because the crisis was over, maybe just because they could finally see. I was holding the street door open, letting in light from outside. I told Jacek, "Sorry about the mess, Stanislaw. I didn't mean to demolish your surgery, but I didn't have much choice. Of course, I'll pay for the damage."

"Oh yes?" His voice was immediately cheerful. When he sent me the repair bill, I'd likely be paying for plasterboard at mahogany prices.

"One last thing," I said to Jacek. "Do you know the combination to your doorman's gun vault? I'd hate to leave without my pistols."

Jacek *did* know the combination . . . but that didn't help much with the room pitch-black. To get light, we used the dashboard cigarette lighter in one of the SUVs to set fire to a waiting room magazine: a French-language copy of *Life,* dating back to the mideighties. I held the burning magazine as a torch while Jacek fumbled with the combination. The whole process took so long, I almost said, "Never mind, we don't have time." But when I felt the familiar weight of my VADS pistols resting in their holsters, a great weight lifted from my shoulders. Once again, I was ready for anything.

"Let's move," I told Reuben. "The Warsaw police may treat this clinic with kid gloves, but they aren't the ones who worry me." I nudged him toward the door, then turned back to Jacek. "Sorry again, old man. Trouble seems to follow me around."

"Ach, Lara," said Jacek with a shrug, "what's to apologize? For real trouble, you should have been here *last* night."

# 4

# ST. BERNWARD'S MONASTERY: THE INFIRMARY

We passed half a dozen police cars on our way out of town. They were all heading leisurely for Stare Miasto . . . but by the time they dawdled into Jacek's, the mercenary corpses would be gone. The bodies and SUVs would turn up elsewhere—probably in some neighborhood noted for gang violence—and in due course, the authorities would write off the deaths as "drug-related killings."

Though our destination lay to the northeast, I headed northwest on the highway to Gdansk. I was, after all, driving an SUV commandeered from the mercenaries. If it contained a LoJack or some other tracking device, I didn't want to give away our intended direction.

We stopped at the first petrol station/coffee shop along the road. I made a phone call, then settled down to wait. Reuben had something to eat, while I bought road maps of every Polish province. I also took the chance to do a quick web search on St. Bernward using my mobile phone. *Born 960 A.D. in what is now northern Germany. Became Bishop of Hildescheim, 993. Famed for encouraging sacred art in churches, most notably the superbly decorated bronze gates of the cathedral at Hildesheim. Died 1022. Canonized 1193. Now the patron saint of metal workers, architects, and sculptors.* No mention of a monastery in Poland, but that didn't mean much. The Roman Catholic Church has thousands of unpublicized retreats in odd corners of the world, most of them named after saints with no obvious connection to the site or its inhabitants. Whatever awaited us at St. Bernward's Monastery, we'd have to find out for ourselves.

Half an hour later, a man named Krzysztof with terrible teeth arrived to take our Explorer in exchange for an aging Honda Accord. The Accord had seen years of rough treatment, but that was what I wanted: its dents would be camouflage, helping it fit in with other vehicles in the cash-strapped backcountry where we'd be going. Krzysztof assured me the engine was still "strong like tiger" . . . and since he owed me his life (five years earlier, I'd pulled him out of a giant wasp's nest in the sewers of Krakow—don't ask), I was willing to trust him. The car proved peppy enough; not in the same class as a Lamborghini Diablo, but exactly what we needed to trundle through Polish farmland without attracting attention.

Three hours passed uneventfully with Reuben asleep in the passenger seat. His breathing was troubled by gasps that never quite stirred him to consciousness. Once, as we passed through a village with a single streetlight, the mercury glow revealed that his bandages were red with fresh blood. I cursed my stupidity; before leaving the clinic, I should have asked Dr. Jacek for appropriate medical supplies. Krzysztof had left a filthy old blanket in the back of the car, so I ripped off a strip and tied it around Reuben's torso in the hope it would press his dressings tighter against the bullet wounds. Reuben whimpered in his sleep but didn't wake.

I checked a road map. The nearest hospital was hours away. I decided to press on to St. Bernward's Monastery; the monks would surely have a first-aid kit and maybe a full-scale infirmary. Rural monasteries were usually self-sufficient in such matters.

Back on the highway, farmland gave way to snow-packed forests and lakes. In wealthier countries, an area like this would be full of hunting lodges and summer cottages . . . but few in Poland could afford such indul-

gences. Besides, the Soviet Union had operated military
camps here until the Iron Curtain fell. The Red Army had
strongly discouraged Polish families from holidays in the
region. With the Soviets gone, vacationers might now
begin to filter in; but it would take years for a full-fledged
tourist industry to develop.

So nobody lived here but lumberjacks and the occasional recluse. Only a few snowy dirt tracks led into the
woods—mostly logging roads not shown on the map.
Some had signs telling which timber company owned
the land, but the majority just said PRIVATE, KEEP OUT in
Polish.

"Reuben," I called. "Reuben. Reuben!"

He woke only when I shook him hard. "Wha . . . what?"

"We're getting close," I said. "You'll have to tell me
which road to take."

"Oh. Right." He rubbed his eyes as if they wouldn't
focus. His head slipped back against the seat again.

"Reuben. Reuben!"

"Yeah. Yeah. Yeah . . ."

"Talk to me," I said, just to keep him awake. "Tell me
about where we're going."

"I told you—St. Bernward's Monastery."

"What kind of monastery is it?"

He forced himself to concentrate. "It's old. There's been
a monastery on the site for more than a thousand years.
Parts of the original are still standing. It hasn't always
been called St. Bernward's, but—"

"What type of monastery is it?"

"Roman Catholic."

"I guessed that," I said dryly. "But what order of
monks? Franciscan? Dominican? Benedictine?"

"Uhh . . . Dominican."

"Reuben, here's a tip: don't lie unless you know what
you're doing. The Dominican order was founded by St.
Dominic in 1215—eight hundred years ago, not a thousand. But then, you've always been the type of archaeologist who concentrates on true antiquities. I could never

trip you up on prehistoric Mesopotamia, but anything after the fall of Rome is beyond your expertise."

He said nothing. He should have known I was only teasing, but he was too weak to make a retort. "Who *really* lives in the monastery?" I asked.

Reuben sighed. If he'd been stronger he might have told me it was none of my business, but he seemed too tired to fight. "They *are* monks, Lara. And a few really are Dominicans. Also some Jesuits, some Trappists, some Hospitallers . . . some Buddhists, some Sikhs, some Sufis . . ." He sighed. "Nuns, too. Taoists, Jains, Essenes . . . a lot of different types."

I raised my eyebrows. Hospitallers? They were a tiny order whose members hardly ever left Rome. And the Essenes were a Jewish sect who disappeared from history around the year 200. "An eclectic group to find anywhere, much less the backwoods of Poland. Care to tell me what they're up to?"

"They call themselves the Order of Bronze," Reuben said. "The Order is, uhh, quite old."

I groaned. "An ancient society of religious dropouts hiding in the back of beyond? Reuben, how could you get involved with such people? They could be trying to summon some evil elder god . . . open the gates of hell . . . immanentize the eschaton . . ."

He stared at me blankly. I said, "It means bringing about the end of the world."

"No, Lara, these people are all right. They're the good guys. Really."

I rolled my eyes but said nothing. Reuben had always been too trusting. Finally, I asked, "What were you doing for them?"

"Just research. Investigating rumors about bronze statuary."

"What type of bronze statuary?"

"Umm. Er. Oh, here's our turnoff. Turn left down that track."

\* \* \*

Reuben refused to say more. I was too busy driving to argue. The road was light gravel covered with three inches of snow; any moment, I expected the Accord to get stuck in some hollow where the snow had built up too deep. I had precious little room to maneuver around any blockages: snow-hung pine trees crowded on either side, stretching their branches above us. It seemed as if we were driving down a white-lined tunnel into a black unknown. If I hadn't been worried about Reuben's bullet wounds, I might have turned around and gone back . . . but my friend needed treatment, and St. Bernward's Monastery— the Order of Bronze—was the closest place to find clean bandages.

Besides, I wanted to meet these people: to get a feel of who they were. If the Order of Bronze were Satanists or lunatics, I might have to take drastic action to free Reuben from their clutches.

For twenty minutes we drove through the dark. Our Accord bounced over rocks and potholes hidden under the snow, but sounds seemed eerily muted. The snow subdued every whisper . . . even the car's engine. Once, we came to a stretch where the road ran along the shore of a jet-black lake. The water steamed, unfrozen despite the cold—most likely because of underground hot springs—but I couldn't help picturing dark creatures lurking below the surface, ready to grab us as we drove past. I was relieved when we plunged safely in among the trees again . . . then immediately grew angry with myself for indulging in ridiculous fantasies. Usually, I know better than to unnerve myself with pointless imaginings; but there was something about the landscape, the silence, the brooding solitude . . .

I was glad when we broke out of the forest and saw our destination.

The monastery sprawled gloomily atop a low hill. It showed no lights—not a single candle—so the only illumination came from the few stars not obscured by clouds. Fields had been cleared in a wide ring around the monastery's stone walls, but the Accord's headlights picked out nothing but stunted weeds poking through the snow. I suspected the open area wasn't for farming crops; it served as a no-man's-land—a zone with no cover—so intruders couldn't approach the central complex without being seen. Who knew what weapons were trained on our car as we climbed slowly up the rise?

The stone walls, topped with an abundance of razor wire, blocked all view of what lay beyond. When we reached the gates—two slabs of steel more suited to a military bunker than a harmless religious retreat—Reuben said, "Get out of the car. And, uhh . . . maybe you better take off your guns."

I sighed. It wasn't an unprecedented request—I've visited numerous religious institutions, and the doorkeepers almost always demand I leave my weapons outside. For some reason, they believe firearms are out of place in "retreats of peace and solemnity." However, it's one thing to disarm oneself while visiting the Archbishop of Canterbury or the Dalai Lama; it's quite another to drop one's guns at the door of an obscure cadre of possible demon worshippers. The Dalai Lama wouldn't try to cut me open and devour my liver. With the Order of Bronze, I wasn't so sure.

Grumbling, I left my guns in the car. Reuben was already stumbling toward the gates. He was trying to hold up his hands like a hostage at a bank robbery—obviously to show any watchers how harmless he was—but he didn't have the strength to keep his arms raised. Soon he let his hands drop and clutched them to his broken rib. I tried to help but he pushed me away and continued forward.

When he reached the steel slabs, he placed his palm flat on a slight indentation in one of the gates—a concealed fingerprint scanner. Five seconds passed. Then the gates swung back, softly scraping the top layer of snow.

"Leave the car," Reuben told me. "Someone will come for it."

"Someone with horns and a pitchfork?"

"Don't be silly, Lara. The Order are . . ."

He stopped. I waited for him to finish his sentence, then realized he was about to fall over. He'd put up a brave front, but his energy was exhausted. If I hadn't caught him, he'd have toppled face forward onto the road.

I draped Reuben's arm over my shoulders and walked him into the monastery grounds. His breath was ragged with panting; he moved in a semiconscious daze. I let him lean most of his weight on me, and scanned the area in search of anything that might be a medical facility.

Despite Reuben's acting as if people were watching our every move, St. Bernward's appeared deserted. Not a light, not a sound, not a sign of life—nothing but buildings of silent stone, draped with wintry shadows. Our breaths steamed. No one came to greet us or to offer Reuben a hand. After a few moments, I started forward again, ready to kick down doors if that's what it took to get Reuben some help.

There were more than a dozen buildings within the monastery's walls. Most were stone huts—not for people to live in but for the many functions a medieval monastery once performed. There'd be a hut for drying herbs, another for blacksmithing, another for curing leather, and so on.

Four larger buildings were arranged in a square around a central courtyard. One had the look of a chapel, with a round stained-glass window above the entrance doors. The other three had no identifying marks: just chunky two-story buildings made of stone, with narrow windows cut grudgingly into the walls. Those buildings would house the monks and nuns, and provide the usual amenities of cloistered life—a kitchen, a refectory, a library. They might also contain an infirmary . . . so I guided Reuben toward the courtyard. When we got near enough, I called, "There's an injured man here! He needs help!"

Light appeared in the entrance of one of the three anonymous stone buildings: an oil lamp in the hand of a man wearing the black robes of a Dominican monk. He was in his sixties, with short-cropped gray hair and a lean leathery face. His vision was obviously diminished with age because he squinted into the darkness several seconds before spotting us; then he stared disapprovingly for a count of ten before beckoning us inside.

As I propelled Reuben forward, the monk's gaze dropped to the blood-soaked bandages on Reuben's ribs. The man's expression tightened. He stepped back so Reuben and I could get through the doorway. "Down here," he said, leading us along a corridor of damp stone. Twenty paces later, he stopped at a closed wooden door, tapped once, then opened it.

My eyes were flooded with electric light . . . not abnormally bright, but after all the darkness, I was temporarily blinded. Someone eased Reuben's arm off my shoulder. Two dark figures escorted him away and helped him onto a flat surface. As my vision returned, I took in my surroundings: a modern treatment room, as good as Jacek's or better. The temperature was cozy. Two women in their twenties—twins, Japanese, wearing dark brown habits in the style of Zen nuns—stood on either side of Reuben where he lay on an examining table. One woman removed his bandages while the other pressed a stethoscope against his chest.

"Kaisho and Myoko are licensed doctors," said the Dominican monk. His accent sounded Germanic . . . maybe Austrian or Swiss. He stared at me a moment, sizing me up. "I'm Father Emil. You're Lara Croft?"

"Yes."

"Reuben has been urging me for months to talk to you. I suppose he finally contacted you on his own." Father Emil's expression was sour. "I dislike people going behind my back."

"It wasn't like that," I said. "Reuben intended to clear it with you first, but events got out of hand."

"So it would seem."

The woman who'd removed Reuben's bandages walked to a chest-high cistern in one corner of the room. She reached over the cistern's stone wall and dipped a metal pan inside. A moment later, she walked back to the examination table; the pan was now full of water. The water must have been cold, because when she began washing Reuben's wound, he flinched.

"You don't have indoor plumbing?" I asked.

Father Emil shook his head. "The monastery is built on solid rock. No one's ever managed to drill through the stone down to the water table. There's a good well outside on the flats; and in the old days, the monks used to carry up water in buckets . . . but they also built pipes to collect rain from the roof and channel it into that cistern. An infirmary needs plenty of water."

"The water can't be clean," I said.

"We use chemical purifiers. The water becomes undrinkable, but quite good as a disinfectant." He might have said more; but as the doctors washed away Reuben's crusted blood, the nature of his injury became apparent. Father Emil said, "Is that a bullet wound?"

"A clean in and out," I replied. "Reuben got shot . . . and he barely escaped getting blown up at the airport."

"I heard about the explosion. We listen to the news on radio. I knew Reuben was flying in around the same time, and I was afraid—" Father Emil broke off. "But he's here now, and alive. Praise God." The monk gestured toward a corner of the room. "Let's sit and talk."

We walked to a table with two metal chairs—the sort of place a doctor might take notes while patients described their symptoms. Father Emil held one chair for me, then sat in the other. He gave me a piercing look. "What happened, Ms. Croft? Tell me everything."

I was tempted to refuse, to explain nothing until I'd gotten answers to my own questions. What was the Order of Bronze? Why had it hired Reuben to investigate bronze statuary? What was in Reuben's attaché case, and who wanted it so badly? But I decided not to be confrontational . . . at least not until Reuben had been patched up. Besides, if I humored Father Emil he might do me the same courtesy.

"Reuben called me from Athens," I said, "and asked me to meet him in Warsaw . . ."

The story took ten minutes. I didn't bother with details on the fight at Jacek's, but I *did* mention the silver grenade that produced the frigid armor. I couldn't help asking, "Have you heard of such a thing? A Silver Shield?"

"No," Father Emil answered, "but I can check—" He stopped himself. I wondered what he'd been going to say. Where does one go for information on shiny violations of nature? But Father Emil just said, "Please, continue your story" . . . and I proceeded to the end.

When I finished, he sat back with a thoughtful expression. "You have no idea who the mercenaries were?"

"No," I said. "But the Warsaw police will find the bodies and identify them soon enough. Most mercs are ex-military, so their fingerprints will be on file somewhere. Interpol will put out a worldwide alert; they'll have most of the dead men's names by morning. Then hundreds of cops and operatives will start investigating the mercenaries' backgrounds." I shrugged. "By this time tomorrow, the wire services will publish the gunmen's names, mug shots, military and criminal records, all that trivia . . . and none of it will matter, because it doesn't address the real question."

"You mean who hired the mercenaries and why."

"Right. We can hope the employer was sloppy—maybe he left a trail. But these investigations usually hit dead ends: anonymous calls from pay phones, or e-mail addresses registered to the tooth fairy. At best, the authorities will trace everything to some expendable go-between whose corpse is now feeding the fishes." I looked at Father Emil. "Unless the police have extraordinary good luck, they'll come up empty. We, on the other hand, can approach this business from a more promising angle . . . because now you're going to tell me what's in the attaché case and who would kill to get it."

Father Emil didn't answer right away. He stared across

the room at Reuben, watching Kaisho and Myoko fix new dressings over the bullet wounds. "How is he?" Father Emil asked the doctors.

"Stable," the women answered together.

"I'm fine," Reuben said in a wheezing voice. He tried to sit up, but the doctors immediately pushed him back down.

"Lie still," the women snapped. I wondered if their unison was a twin thing, a nun thing, or a doctor thing.

"Take it easy, Reuben," Father Emil said. "There's no reason to exert yourself." He looked at me as if weighing a decision. "Ms. Croft," he said, "the Order of Bronze does not share confidences lightly. However, I believe you are an honorable woman. I also believe you will not be put off. If I send you away without answers, you will cause us a great deal of fuss. That would be . . . most regrettable."

I nodded, trying to keep a straight face. It was hard to tell if Father Emil was just stating a fact or making a veiled threat; but with his German-tinged accent, he sounded like a Nazi mad scientist from some dreadful B movie. *Ahh, mein Liebchen, it vould be most regrettable if I vere forced to use vhips und chains!*

"Quite," I said. "Do let's keep this civilized."

Father Emil gave me another hard stare. Then he reached into his robe and pulled out two metal keys. One key appeared to be normal steel, but the other was brightly polished bronze.

The steel key unlocked the handcuff on Reuben's wrist. Father Emil took the attaché case back to the table where we'd been sitting and slid the bronze key into the case's lock.

Click . . . and the case opened.

Inside the case lay a jumble of papers—maps, computer printouts, scribbled notes in Reuben's handwriting—but what caught my eye was a sealed plastic box the size of an encyclopedia volume.

I'd seen such boxes before. They were tough, padded

containers for transporting antiques. This one was labeled OMÓNIA: a name unknown to the masses but as familiar as Sotheby's to someone in my profession. Omónia Auctions in Athens hosted exclusive sales of antiquities from around the world. Most customers were billionaires; most items sold went unpublicized except among the favored few. I myself had attended the sale of King Tutankhamen's funerary mask—the real one, not the fake displayed for tourists in the Egyptian Museum—and I'd peddled a few of my own finds there too. (Usually, I keep the treasures I fetch from tombs, but some aren't worth the trouble . . . especially the ones that are cursed. I don't mind dealing with mummies coming to reclaim their favorite scarabs, but the farmers around Croft Manor complain if I bring home some ancient amulet that makes their milk cows run dry.)

It took all my self-control not to grab the Omónia box and rip it open. Instead, I let Father Emil take it . . . whereupon he spent a maddeningly long time trying to peel off the tape that sealed the box shut. In the end, he carried it to Kaisho, who spent another maddeningly long time slicing through the tape with a scalpel as slowly as if she were performing brain surgery.

To keep from bursting with impatience, I turned back to the open attaché case. I'd intended to flip through the documents inside . . . but my eye was caught by something else: faint scratches around the lock. I looked more closely. The marks had the telltale appearance of furtive probing. Someone had attempted to pick the lock.

Hmm. Had the man at the rental car agency tried playing locksmith before deciding to chop off Reuben's hand? Reuben had no idea how long he'd been unconscious—the man might have had time to fiddle with the lock. But why? If the man had a knife for severing Reuben's wrist, why mess with the lock first? I supposed the fellow could have been squeamish about hacking human flesh . . . but if so, why was he assigned to the job? Whoever wanted the case had plenty of mercenaries on staff; so why would the task of wrist lopping be given to someone with scruples? And if the rent-a-car man wasn't reluctant to spill blood, why did he waste time tinkering with the lock?

Admittedly, the pick marks might not have been recent. The attaché case looked several years old; it could have acquired the marks earlier in its life. The scratches might not even be pick marks. With the explosion and all the excitement at the clinic, the case could have gotten scraped by accident.

But I was still uneasy. Something wasn't right. I wished I knew what it was.

"Ahh!" said Father Emil. I'd been so distracted by the scratched attaché case, I'd forgotten about the Omónia box. Father Emil had finally gotten it open. He'd put on a pair of latex gloves from the infirmary's supply cupboard and was now holding up the box's contents: a statuette of a man cast in greenish metal.

The man stood ten inches high. His legs were spread as if striding forward. His arms were crooked at elbow and wrist in the classic "walk like an Egyptian" pose. He was naked except for a short kilt and the familiar atef crown of a pharaoh: a high conical headpiece with two ostrich feather plumes and a rearing serpent ornament—the uraeus—facing out above the forehead. When I stepped closer, I saw the metal man's body was inscribed with shallow lines dividing the anatomy into segments. Each arm, for example, was marked with divider lines at shoulder, elbow, and wrist . . . reminding me of childhood dolls that were made of separate pieces jointed together so they could bend into different positions. Unlike my old dolls, the metal statuette had tiny hieroglyphs scrawled across its skin, too small and spidery to read without a magnifying glass.

"Osiris," Father Emil said. I nodded. King Osiris, Lord of Eternity, was one of the foremost deities of ancient Egypt: in charge of both fertility and the afterlife. When pharaohs died, they mystically became one with Osiris . . . which made Osiris the embodiment of all former kings.

Unlike much of the Egyptian pantheon, Osiris looked human—no falcon's head or cat fur—but he still had one distinctive trait. In certain depictions, he was marked with Frankenstein-ish sutures all over his body.

The old myths claimed that Osiris had ruled the other gods with justice and wisdom. One day, however, he was ambushed by his brother Set, who envied Osiris and wanted to seize the heavenly throne for himself. Set chopped Osiris into pieces, then scattered the bloody chunks all over the world. Evil seemed to have triumphed . . . but Isis, Osiris's wife, searched high and low, found all the pieces, and stitched them together again. That didn't bring Osiris fully back to life, but he was sufficiently restored to rule the world of the dead; and in a death-centered culture like Egypt, lording it over the afterlife made Osiris an important member of the pantheon.

Most illustrations of Osiris showed him strong and robust—everything a pharaoh should be. Other representations portrayed him as dead but regal, properly mummified and bearing the symbols of royal office. But a few depictions were like the statuette in Father Emil's hands: a patchwork man made of bits sewn together, with all the seams still visible. Indeed, some heretical versions of the Osiris myth whispered that Queen Isis hadn't yet found all the pieces. She was still traveling the world, searching, searching, searching for the parts that would make her husband whole.

Father Emil handed me another pair of latex gloves. Once I'd put them on, he passed me the statuette. "You're an antiquities expert," he said. "I'd value your opinion, Ms. Croft."

I hefted the small figure in my hands, testing its weight: quite heavy. It looked to be solid bronze, the metal greened with age. The pose and presentation of the statue were consistent with ancient Egyptian style . . . and small characteristics of face and body let me narrow the date to a specific period. "Nineteenth dynasty," I said, "1250 B.C., give or take half a century. At least that's what it looks like. These days, I don't believe any artifact is genuine until I've seen a lab analysis. Counterfeiters are getting too good at forgery."

"Don't be so suspicious," Reuben said from the examination table. "The Order bought that at Omónia. Omónia doesn't sell fakes."

"That's what you were doing in Athens?" I asked. "Attending the latest auction?" Omónia's most recent sale had been two days earlier. I'd been so busy fighting the *Méne* cult, I'd only had time to glance at the catalog. Omónia had been scheduled to sell the collection of a deceased Greek shipping magnate. Some truly stellar pieces were up for bid.

"I didn't go to the auction myself," Reuben said. "The Order sent someone else. But they bought Osiris at the sale, and Omónia guaranteed complete authenticity."

I looked at the statuette again, bringing my eye up close to the metal. It did look genuine . . . but I distrust any artifact I haven't found myself. You wouldn't believe how often "reputable" dealers have tried to swindle me with artificially aged trinkets. I examined the position of the hands, the expression on the face, the tiny imperfections in the bronze that one always encounters in early metal casting . . .

. . . and then I saw it. Something that sent a chill up my spine.

As I've said, the body was divided into pieces, reflecting how Osiris was dismembered by Set. The front and back halves of the statuette's torso were separate hunks of bronze joined in a seam that ran up both sides from hip to armpit. When I looked very closely at the seam, I saw a hair-width copper wire hidden deep within: a wire far thinner than Egyptians could possibly produce in 1250 B.C.

It was an antenna. The statuette had been bugged.

Omónia's experts were far too careful to overlook such an obvious anachronism; and they certainly weren't the ones who'd hidden a radio transmitter inside the statue. But if Omónia hadn't done it . . .

I remembered the pick marks around the attaché case's lock. What if the man at the rental car agency hadn't just *tried* to open the lock but had succeeded? What if he'd replaced the real statue with a counterfeit? Then he'd waited for Reuben to wake, and made a big show of preparing to cut Reuben's wrist . . . when he'd never intended to do any chopping at all.

*That's* why the man with the knife had hesitated. And why Reuben, a not-very-athletic research assistant, had managed to escape from two rough-and-tumble hoodlums. And why the mercenaries I'd faced at Jacek's had been so inept, none of them even carrying a pocket light.

It was all a setup. Reuben was *supposed* to get away intact and bring the bugged statuette here. A Trojan horse. Whoever was behind this must have expected Reuben would call me for help and that I'd successfully help Reuben escape the gunmen. Then we'd deliver Osiris here, and the unsuspecting Father Emil would let us bring the statue past the monastery's big steel-vault doors.

It wouldn't be hard to make a duplicate statue. Omónia published photos of the items for sale. It even allowed registered customers to examine pieces firsthand, weeks or months in advance of the actual auction. That gave plenty of time to create a convincing forgery and to package it in an Omónia box that could be switched for the real one in Reuben's case.

The only question was why. Merely to plant a listening device in the Order of Bronze headquarters? Or was there more inside the statue than a simple radio transmitter?

The metal man was *very* heavy.

I spoke none of my suspicions aloud. The statuette might transmit every sound I made; and hidden somewhere outside the monastery walls, bad guys must be listening. If they suspected I'd seen through their deception . . .

Casually, I crossed the room, the statuette still in my hands. Father Emil said sharply, "Where are you going?"

"Over where the light is better," I said. And where there was a heavy stone cistern containing several tons of rainwater.

One quick toss and the statuette splashed inside.

"What are you doing?" Father Emil cried.

"Everybody run," I said. "Now." I raced to Reuben's side and tried to get him to sit up.

"But . . ."

"If I'm wrong," I said, "I'll fish the statue out again. It's bronze—water won't hurt it. But if I'm right . . ."

Wherever the bad guys were, they realized something was wrong. Either they heard Father Emil shout at me, or the bug in the statuette began to crackle from being underwater. I hoped the water would short out the electronics entirely, but no. In the darkness beyond the monastery walls, someone recognized the game was up and pushed a button.

The false statuette held more than a transmitting microphone. It held a radio-activated bomb.

The cistern exploded in a roar of water and stone. If I'd had another second, I would have thrown myself across Reuben on the table . . . but I was hurled off my feet by the blast, tossed helplessly backward amid torrents of drenched masonry. One fist-sized rock punched me in the stomach, knocking the breath out of me, while others pummeled my arms and legs. Sharp edges of stone gashed my skin; and when I hit the ground, I was barely conscious enough to cover my head with my arms. Smaller rocks clattered around me: pebbles that had been hurtled toward the rafters by the initial detonation and were now coming down like hail. The barrage lasted another long heartbeat. Then heavy silence descended, punctuated only by water pattering onto the cold hard floor.

I stood up slowly: bruised and soaked to the bone. Father Emil moaned on the ground, a wicked slice bleeding on his forehead. The twin doctors, Kaisho and Myoko, lay on the ground too, wrapped around each other in tight protective fetal positions—sisters returning to the womb. I couldn't even tell if they were alive.

There was no such doubt about Reuben. The bronze head of Osiris, blown off the false statuette, had hammered through the top of his skull. Blood poured out of the wound, mixed with slimy dollops of Reuben's gray matter. It oozed onto the table like rising bread dough. Here in an infirmary, with two doctors right at my feet, no miracle of surgery could save him.

I closed my eyes, feeling the sting of tears. Some idiotic voice in my mind said, *At least it was fast.* As if that was any consolation.

A different voice in my mind said, *Someone will pay.* That was no consolation either; but it was an ironclad promise.

# 5

# ST. BERNWARD'S MONASTERY: THE CHAPEL

Kaisho and Myoko were battered but alive. For the next few minutes, they tended their own injuries and Father Emil's . . . but when they tried to do the same for me, I refused their coddling. I wasn't badly hurt, and I couldn't bear the thought of sitting still while someone painted my cuts with iodine.

Instead, I went outside to steady myself in the cold night air . . . and to listen for any sound from whoever triggered the bomb. The murderer couldn't be far off—radio detonators seldom have much range—but I heard nothing: just the wind. I pictured the killers sitting in a car in the nearby forest. The instant the bomb was set off, they must have raced away into the blackness.

Cowards.

I stood there for several more minutes. Just breathing. Looking at the stars. Making no noise. Thinking of a time when Reuben and I got kicked out of the National Diet Library in Tokyo for laughing too loudly at an inept translation of the Pnakotic Manuscripts. And another time we were trying to decipher a set of Mayan inscriptions, when Reuben—the idiot!—read them aloud and summoned a swarm of locusts into my study. And another time he tried to make beer from an ancient Babylonian recipe but didn't bother sanctifying the brew kiln first, so anyone who drank any began speaking in Enochian . . .

When I finished thinking of all those things, I dried my eyes and went back inside.

"Tell me everything," I said.

Father Emil looked up. He was sitting at the table where we'd had our earlier chat. A bandage wrapped whitely around his forehead; the doctors were dabbing antibiotics on a long gash up his arm. His robe was spattered with blood. I didn't know if it was his or Reuben's. Reuben's body was now covered with a sheet. Father Emil had already promised to transport it back to Reuben's family. I would make sure he kept that promise.

"Tell me everything," I said again. "What does your Order do? Why would someone want to blow you up? Who killed Reuben and where do I find the person responsible?"

Father Emil glanced at Kaisho and Myoko. They both shrugged, as if to say *do what you think best.*

"All right, Ms. Croft," Father Emil said. His gaze flicked to Reuben's shrouded corpse . . . then he closed his eyes and turned away. "I'll tell you what I can," he said. "But in exchange—"

I cut him off. "No exchange. Just tell me who killed Reuben. Otherwise, I take it out on you."

"Ms. Croft," the monk said, "you aren't the only one here who was Reuben's friend. I've known him for years; he's helped our Order many times. Reuben will be in my prayers every day for the rest of my life.

"But," Father Emil went on, "the Order of Bronze has been attacked. As chief administrator, I must put the Order's safety ahead of personal grief. Don't think I'll jeopardize our secrets for the sake of vengeance." He locked gazes with me a moment. Then he lowered his eyes. "There's so much at stake, Ms. Croft. Do you know what that statuette was?"

"A fake," I said. "The original was stolen from Reuben at the rent-a-car agency."

"I believe you're right," Father Emil replied. "Which

means some enemy has the real Osiris. That's a fearsome blow to the Order."

"Why?"

"The statuette is a map. The hieroglyphics engraved on Osiris's body—the *real* Osiris—are coded directions toward the location of . . . certain items."

"What kind of items?"

"Powerful artifacts: dangerous in the wrong hands. Now that the killers have the statuette, they can find those artifacts before we do. Unless . . ."

He let his voice trail off. I asked the obvious question, though I guessed the answer. "Unless what?"

"Unless," Father Emil said, "you can retrieve the items first, Ms. Croft."

I came close to punching Father Emil in the face. I'd been in this position many times: a map stolen, a treasure to be found before the Forces of Evil got hold of the Mystic MacGuffin.

*Please, Ms. Croft, sign up with us and save the world.*

I didn't want to save the world. I just wanted to do something for Reuben. But after the urge to lash out subsided, I realized I shouldn't pass up this opportunity. If the real statuette was a map . . . if Reuben's killers would follow the map in search of the mysterious "items" . . . if Father Emil could help me reach the target destination before the killers . . . then I could catch the murderers when they showed up. And that was something I dearly wanted to do.

"All right," I said. "I'll listen to your pitch. No promises, but I'll listen."

Father Emil gave me a sour look—he was good at sour looks. But he was astute enough to realize I wouldn't commit myself further until he'd told me the truth.

He pulled his arm away from the doctors and stood up. "Follow me, Ms. Croft. I'll take you to the head of our Order."

We went back into the night. The temperature was falling . . . or perhaps I was just more sensitive to the cold.

Reuben was dead. I felt tired.

We crossed the courtyard toward the darkened entrance of the chapel. Father Emil stopped at the door. "Before we go in," he said, "let me ask you, Ms. Croft, have you heard of Roger Bacon?"

"An English scholar," I said. "One of the early lecturers at Oxford, back in the twelve hundreds. Some people consider him the first true scientist. He insisted you shouldn't believe anything till you tested it experimentally."

"He was also a Franciscan monk," Father Emil said. "And a member of the Order of Bronze."

"Really," I said, "how interesting." But in my head, I muttered, *Dear, oh dear, oh dear.* If Father Emil was telling the truth, his precious Order dated back to the Middle Ages . . . and my past dealings with medieval secret societies had never turned out well. Then again, the good father might simply be wrong. The Order of Bronze wouldn't be the first quasireligious organization to claim deep historic roots when it was actually whipped together by poseurs pretending to represent ancient mystic traditions.

"And have you heard," Father Emil continued, "about Roger Bacon's bronze head?"

I nodded. "Supposedly, Bacon built a man's head of bronze. Stories claim it could talk and predict the future."

"And what do you think of that?"

I hesitated. In a profession like mine, one can never be sure when odd tales are mere empty folklore or the gospel truth. As it happens, however, I'd done a little research into Bacon and his bronze head. With a start, I realized I'd done so after a conversation with Reuben several months earlier. He'd casually mentioned the head, and I'd been interested enough to look it up in a few reference books.

Father Emil was still waiting for an answer. I decided to be wary. "Bacon might have made a simple clockwork," I said. "A windup head that could open and close its mouth . . . maybe blink its eyes. More likely, it's just an old wives' tale. Talking bronze heads were common in medieval superstitions—like UFOs and scrawny gray aliens are today. Pope Sylvester II reportedly kept a bronze head in a back room of his basilica. So did St. Thomas Aquinas. Further back, bronze heads were associated with the Greek philosopher Agrippa, the Roman poet Virgil . . ."

"You don't believe such stories?" Father Emil asked.

"Considering all the bizarre things I've seen in my life, I never rule anything out. But when bronze heads show up all over, one suspects they're just a standard fictional motif—as if medieval historians felt they had to invent stories about bronze heads whenever they were writing about clever men. *He was a bright fellow, so of course he must have owned a talking bronze head.*"

"It never occurred to you that all those people might have owned the same head?"

My mouth opened for a sarcastic retort . . . but a dire suspicion struck me and I stopped myself. Father Emil waited for me to speak; when I didn't, he nodded to himself and opened the chapel door.

Lights blazed into life a moment after the door opened. The sanctuary was full, not with religious paraphernalia but with electronic equipment: computers, printers, big-screen monitors showing everything from satellite photos to fingerprints, and dozens of humming black boxes whose purpose I couldn't identify.

In the middle of this high-tech array sat a single man-like figure on a chair that looked like a steel throne. The man himself was also metal: a gleaming figure of rich copper-bronze.

For a moment, I thought the figure was just a statue—a brazen idol the Order worshipped. Then the bronze man shifted to face me and said in a grating voice, "Lara Croft." He stared for a full ten seconds . . . then blinked and turned away.

I'd faced the impossible many times: living dinosaurs, shambling mummies, giant insects, ancient gods. I was long past the point where I could be shocked by the uncanny. My response to this living metal man was more like . . . acute disappointment.

It's hard to explain. I wished the universe were better behaved. I don't mean I wanted my life more tame or predictable—heaven forbid. But I felt as if the world had gotten drunk and vomited on the dinner table. Violations of science didn't shake me, but they left me wishing for better. Why did the world keep breaking its own rules? Couldn't it show better manners?

I suddenly felt bone tired.

Father Emil placed his hand on my shoulder and eased me across the threshold. I let myself be led inside. The bronze man took no notice. Colored pixels from monitor screens reflected distortedly on his polished metal skin.

He wore no clothes but was smooth and sexless . . . like the Oscar figurines given out as Academy Awards. Unlike Oscar, however, the bronze man's head had the conventional elements of human features: eyes, nose, ears, mouth. Not that any of these were entirely normal. The eyes, for example, were unmarked orbs of metal with no pupils or corneas. The mouth had mobile lips capable of forming expressions, but inside there were no teeth or tongue. The nose looked standard enough at first, until I noticed that the nostril openings were covered with a fine wire mesh. As for the ears, they had no openings at all— they seemed to be present for the sake of appearance, aimed at giving a vestige of humanity to a creature who had little else in common with *Homo sapiens*.

Had Roger Bacon once looked upon this inhuman face? Was the metal man old enough to have known Thomas Aquinas and Virgil? But the stories only talked about a bronze *head,* not a full bronze body . . .

Wait. I hadn't noticed at first, but the bronze man was missing his left leg. The "flesh" of his left hip was black where the leg should have been attached—an ugly puckered black, unlike the mirror finish of the rest of his body.

Unbidden, the name "Osiris" rose in my mind . . . particularly the legends that some of the god's dissected body parts had never been found.

"Are you the god Osiris?" I asked the metal man.

He said nothing; he didn't even look in my direction. Eventually, it was Father Emil who answered my question.

"Bronze is the source of the Osiris legend; but of course, he's not a god."

"What is he?"

"We don't know." Father Emil gazed at the man of bronze, the monk's expression unreadable. "Members of our Order have proposed many theories about Bronze's origin. Virgil thought he might have been built by the Roman god Vulcan. Agrippa suggested Bronze was a demon summoned by Atlantean sorcerers. Thomas Aquinas thought Bronze was a golem made to work on the Tower of Babel. More recently, we've considered he might be from outer space or perhaps an android transported back through time from our own future." Father Emil gave a rueful smile. "Feel free to offer your own guess. Every generation invents new paradigms. Do you think Bronze is a collective hallucination made tangible by human belief? Or perhaps we're all living inside a computer simulation, and Bronze is a glitch in the operating system."

"What does Bronze say he is?" I asked.

"He won't answer. Those who believe he's a robot think he's been programmed not to give out information on his background. Those who believe he's magical say he won't talk about himself for fear someone learns his true name." Father Emil shrugged. "I don't think Bronze himself knows where he came from. He's . . . well, he's not all there, is he?"

"You're referring to his missing leg? What happened to it?"

"A lot of Bronze's backstory is sketchy," Father Emil said. "I can tell you what little we know . . ."

\* \* \*

According to Father Emil, the metal man called Bronze dated back long before the start of recorded history. No one knew where he came from, but in 8000 B.C.—give or take a few centuries—Bronze was attacked by an unknown assailant and chopped into pieces . . . just as Egyptian myth said Osiris had been. The resulting bits of bronze anatomy were scattered around the globe by someone the myths referred to as Set.

That should have ended Bronze's mysterious existence. It didn't. The bronze body parts remained "alive" and indestructible. Even when thrown into volcanoes, the pieces refused to melt. Father Emil believed the original Bronze was an assemblage of distinct components that could be separated but not destroyed. The ears, for example, could be severed from the rest of the body using an ordinary knife. However, no known force could reduce the ears further—like atomic particles that might be disconnected from other particles but couldn't themselves be split.

The body parts couldn't even be lost. Throw them into the deepest ocean, and somehow they'd make their way back to land. They might be swallowed by some bottom-feeding eel who'd then be swallowed by a squid who'd then be swallowed by a whale who'd then wash ashore with bronze fragments in its belly. The process might take decades, but always the body parts resurfaced.

It was part of their magic . . . or if you preferred scientific explanations, it was a programmed function of the nanotech—or whatever—that made up the metal man. Even in pieces, the high-tech/sorcerous components displayed an ability to make astonishing comebacks.

They also displayed raw power. Wherever the body parts came to people's attention, shamans and priests, magi and monarchs recognized the pieces as potent talismans. High priestesses wore them as amulets; chieftains carried the bronze fragments into battle or placed them in shrines where blood was spilled in sacrifice. Wizards found ways to draw energy from the metal chunks—prodigious amounts of energy, used in arcane rituals that could make humans immortal or twist humble animals into monsters.

Was it mystic enchantment or radioactive mutation? Father Emil couldn't say; but it worked. Much of the magic performed in bygone days could be attributed to scraps from the man of bronze.

Naturally, these mighty bronze talismans were prized in the ancient world. They were also kept fiercely secret. In time, though, word leaked out . . . until one night on neutral ground, the Greek oracle from Delphi met with Persia's high priest of Zoroaster and the two hesitantly showed each other the sources of their power: a bronze skull and a bronze eye. When the two metal pieces were brought into contact, they fused seamlessly. The result was more mystically powerful than the two separate pieces and supposedly bestowed greater material blessings on the cultures involved.

Thus was born the Order of Bronze—a secret society of people from different religions, devoted to tracking down more bronze bits and uniting them into a whole. By the first century B.C., as the Roman Republic became the Roman Empire, the Order finally assembled the complete head. That was when Bronze gained his voice; when enough of his spirit—or his logic circuitry—was restored that he could finally speak.

His first words were, "I must fight evil." Through the ensuing centuries, he'd cared about nothing else.

He was only sporadically active: the bronze head sometimes went dormant, neither moving nor speaking for years. Then it would suddenly awake, demanding to be told of "evildoers" who had not been brought to justice. The members of the Order would brief the head on whatever evil deeds they knew about—anything from major wars and royal assassinations to street crime and spouses cheating on each other. The bronze head would listen . . . sometimes asking questions, sometimes assigning people to obtain more information or to bring back evidence to be examined . . . and in the end, Bronze would explain what had to be done to "achieve justice."

He had, for example, laid out foolproof plans for the murder of mad Emperor Caligula and the removal of Emperor Valerian (who sponsored a vicious pogrom against innocent Christians in the third century A.D.). Often though, Bronze ignored large-scale problems and spent his time tracking down sneak thieves or merchants who shortchanged their customers. He had a knack for finding the guilty party, no matter how confused the evidence might be; in Roman times, Bronze was even thought to be clairvoyant. Father Emil, however, had a more mundane explanation. He believed Bronze relied on standard forensic science—fingerprints, DNA, etc.—which would have seemed like magic at the time.

Bronze occasionally managed feats of analysis that were still beyond the capacity of twenty-first century technology. He could break any code—even modern computerized encryption—and could often predict a felon's actions with uncanny accuracy. No doubt, the metal man just extrapolated from past patterns of behavior . . . but it was easy to see how the bronze head had gained a reputation for prophecy.

I interrupted to ask, "So he's basically a mechanical Sherlock Holmes?"

"That's an oversimplification," Father Emil replied. "One could equally suggest he's an agent of divine justice created by long-forgotten gods: a spirit of vengeance made manifest. But," the monk went on, looking a little sheepish, "you're not the first to perceive Bronze as a glorified RoboCop."

Father Emil continued his story, describing how the Order of Bronze had devoted itself to two activities: helping Bronze apprehend evildoers and procuring the remaining pieces of bronze anatomy. Reassembling the body parts went slowly, hindered by difficulties of travel and lack of information—in days of yore, an expedition might take decades chasing rumors of a magic bronze artifact in the jungles of Southeast Asia, only to find that the stories were hokum. But once the Industrial Revolution created telegraphs and steamships, the process of reclaiming bronze fragments sped up . . . to the point that Bronze was now almost entirely restored.

With each new body part, Bronze increased in strength and intelligence. His periods of dormancy grew shorter; he worked almost constantly, tapping into the data banks of Interpol and other law enforcement agencies. The Order could no longer track everything Bronze did. He was constantly e-mailing Scotland Yard and the FBI, offering psychological profiles of suspects or forensic analyses of obscure evidence. Bronze operated under dozens of different identities, pretending to be police officers, criminology consultants, and even secret informants. This chapel contained the most sophisticated forensic analysis equipment in the world.

I interrupted again. "So why didn't it detect the bomb in the statuette?"

Bronze snapped his head toward me. "Because you didn't bring the statuette to me. Did you?" His voice actually sounded angry. "Father Emil boasts of the power of my equipment. He's wrong. The generators that provide this monastery with electricity may be state-of-the-art, but to me they're unbearably inadequate. My best sensor devices can only guarantee safety within this chapel. The rest of the monastery grounds are only lightly scanned . . . and the statuette bomb was well enough disguised that it wasn't detected. If you'd ever brought the bomb within range of my high-security grid, things would have turned out differently. But you didn't."

"So you're saying it's my fault?" I asked.

The bronze man didn't answer. He'd turned away again. I took a step toward him, but Father Emil placed a hand on my arm. "No, Ms. Croft. Bronze is correct. We should have submitted the statuette to a detailed scan. We let our concern for Reuben's injuries override normal security precautions."

"I thought we *were* being scanned," I said. "All that fuss at the gate . . ."

Father Emil shrugged. "Our sensors at the gate are not as sophisticated as the ones here in the chapel. As Bronze said, we don't have the resources to scan every millimeter of the grounds in fine detail. Only this chapel is truly secure."

"So Bronze makes sure he's good and protected, but the rest of the Order just take their chances?"

"It's not like that," Father Emil said. "For one thing, this is the first time in recent memory we've been attacked. The Order's secrecy keeps us safe. And of course, Bronze keeps watch for potential threats. Under any other circumstances, the bomb would never have been allowed inside the walls. But not even Bronze is perfect."

"He's made that abundantly clear."

I took another step toward the metal man, sitting smugly in his chair like a king on a throne, but once again, Father Emil restrained me. "Please, Ms. Croft. Don't distract Bronze from his work. At this moment, he might be ferreting out a serial killer in Amsterdam, arranging the downfall of a corrupt business executive, or thwarting the latest computer virus."

"You mean you don't know what he's up to?" I asked. "If he really is stopping serial killers and corporate crooks, then hip, hip, hurrah. But how do you know that's all he's doing? What if he's burning witches and stoning adulterers? What if he's overthrowing governments that pass laws he doesn't like? He's over ten thousand years old. His morality predates the Dark Ages. Don't you think he needs to be watched?"

"Bronze has an infallible sense of justice," Father Emil said. "Our Order wouldn't support him if he didn't."

I was too flabbergasted to answer. How could Father Emil think a machine was infallibly just, when no two people on the planet could agree what justice was? What about actions that were perfectly acceptable in one culture but crimes in another? Whose morality did Bronze follow? If he was the original Osiris, might he believe in ancient Egyptian ethics, where commoners were executed for looking a king in the face? Did Bronze consider that justice?

But there was no point debating the issue with Father Emil. The monk was a true believer: a faithful member of the Order. Which brought up a pertinent question. "Why monks and nuns?" I asked. "I can see how your Order might start from religious priesthoods—people who considered the bronze pieces were sacred relics—but things are different now. Assuming that you're a devout Dominican . . ."

"I am," Father Emil said.

". . . then how does Bronze fit with your churchly duties? Dominican vows don't say anything about helping androids track down criminals."

Father Emil smiled thinly. "Dominicans have always served justice. You might recall, we were the ones in charge of the Inquisition. Those were ugly times, but my predecessors found it useful to have a bronze bloodhound tracking down sinners."

Outraged, I said, "The Inquisition used Bronze to find heretics?"

"Yes . . . though he refused to go after harmless people who simply disagreed with church doctrine."

"The Inquisition killed a lot of harmless dissenters, Father."

"Yes, but Bronze didn't help with that part of the Inquisition's activities." Father Emil suddenly grinned. "It annoyed the inquisitors no end. Bronze absolutely refused to participate in 'defending the faith.' But, Ms. Croft, there were plenty of heretics who weren't harmless: murderers and violent insurgents. As I said, those were ugly times. Bronze helped inquisitors clean up a great deal of viciousness—including corruption within the Inquisition itself."

"How did inquisitors get along with other members of the Order—the Buddhists, Essenes, and all? 'Defenders

of the Faith' weren't noted for cooperating with 'hea-
thens.' "

"There were unfortunate incidents," Father Emil admitted, "but Bronze himself dealt with the culprits. Bronze
wanted the Order to embrace different creeds—'for balance,' he said—and those who couldn't coexist were expelled. Eventually, my Dominican predecessors decided
they couldn't let Bronze become the sole property of
'pagans' so they learned to behave themselves. They
arranged for this monastery to become Bronze's permanent home, and they made sure Bronze always had a Dominican in his retinue. I am their latest representative; and
I fully believe I'm doing God's work, helping Bronze any
way I can. Buying him equipment. Serving as an interme-
diary with police agencies. Hiring people like you to find
Bronze's missing pieces. Call me old-fashioned, but isn't
it righteous to punish the wicked?"

Spoken like a true spiritual descendant of the Inquisition. Father Emil didn't question Bronze's goodness or
wisdom . . . and I'd be wasting my breath trying to persuade him otherwise. Besides, I knew nothing about
Bronze; maybe he *was* as pure and noble as Father Emil
thought. It didn't matter. I was only here for one reason.

I strode to the bronze man and rapped sharply on his
chest with my knuckles. It was like knocking on a solid
metal statue: no hollow echo, just a dull thunk. "Hey,
you," I said, "if you know so much about crime, you
should know who killed Reuben. You've had a full five
minutes to look into it, right? So who made that bomb?"

Bronze lifted his gaze to meet mine. "Lancaster Urdmann." Then he turned away as if he found me boring.

Lancaster Urdmann. I barely stopped myself from
choking at the sound of his name.

Urdmann embodied everything that had given the
British Empire a bad name: a sweaty, arrogant man who
flaunted his upper-class breeding and despised all foreign
"wogs." He'd made a dirty fortune selling guns to mob-
sters and terrorists, then "retired" to a more genteel life—

trafficking in stolen antiquities, blood diamonds, ivory from freshly killed elephants, and other such plunder.

Recently Urdmann had taken up smarmy social climbing, winning public attention by donating priceless jade carvings to the British Museum. No one in the fawning museum crowd knew that Urdmann had stolen the carvings from a placid Sri Lankan retreat, slaughtering dozens of peaceful worshippers in the process. Urdmann had painted *Down with the Government* slogans at the scene of the crime, making it look like the massacre was committed by local rebels; but in my brief stint as errand girl for the CIA, someone at the agency had told me about an intercepted phone conversation in which Urdmann bragged of how easy it had been to kill the "little brown blighters."

Repugnant man. Most galling of all, he called himself a "tomb raider" and fancied himself an expert on ancient treasures. I grudgingly admitted he had a decent knowledge of archaeology . . . but that just made it worse. Instead of finding lost artifacts on his own, he stole them from defenseless monks. Urdmann was no tomb raider; he was nothing but a murderer and thief. Two hundred years ago, his kind plundered Asia and Africa, shooting native people for sport. As far as Lancaster Urdmann was concerned, not much had changed.

"How does Urdmann fit into this?" I demanded. When the bronze man didn't answer, I turned to Father Emil. "Do you know anything?"

"I know Urdmann bid on the Osiris statue. Our agent at the Omónia auction gave me a complete report. Mr. Urdmann was apparently most upset when our Order outbid him."

"Urdmann has always been a poor loser." In fact, Lancaster Urdmann must have been furious at losing the auction—furious enough to steal the statuette that he believed was rightfully his and plant a bomb on the Order as payback for the insult. Urdmann couldn't stand being beaten. "But why did he want Osiris in the first place?"

"As I said," Father Emil answered, "the statuette is a

map: a map telling where the pieces of Bronze can be found. It was created by a secret order of Egyptian priests dedicated to Osiris—people who knew that, contrary to the usual myths, Osiris had never been completely re-assembled. They spent years performing divinations, casting spells, having dream visions until they determined precise locations for each missing body part. We know their predictions were accurate, because they recovered several fragments themselves.

"Unfortunately for the priests," Father Emil went on, "most of the bronze pieces were too far away to retrieve—in the Far East, Northern Europe, the Americas, Australia. It was 1250 B.C.; no one from Egypt could possibly travel so far. The pieces that *were* within reasonable distance belonged to other powerful cultures . . . like Assyria, Mycenae, and Babylon, who wouldn't give up their sacred treasures without a fight. Eventually, the Egyptians might have acquired additional fragments despite the difficulties; but they ran afoul of more orthodox priests, who preached that Osiris had already been fully restored. The priests who made the statuette were denounced as heretical and executed by royal decree. All their possessions, including the statuette and the bronze pieces they'd found, vanished into the pharaoh's treasury."

"If that happened around 1250 B.C.," I said, "the pharaoh was Ramses the Great."

"Correct," Father Emil replied. "The statuette was stored in one of the temples Ramses built during his reign. It was stolen sometime afterward, disappeared for many centuries, and finally turned up again in 1622. By then, Egypt had been conquered by the Ottoman Empire, and the statuette was presented as a gift to the local viceroy. It stayed with the viceroy's family for many years until they fell on hard times and had to sell it. From there it passed through the hands of various collectors until it ended up at the Omónia auction."

"Where Lancaster Urdmann tried to buy it," I said. "Do you think he knew what it was?"

Father Emil shrugged. "I don't know. Our Order works hard to keep Bronze's existence a secret. But there were so many bronze pieces, and the pieces were so powerful . . ." The monk sighed. "Legends abound, Ms. Croft. They're usually dismissed as folktales, but the stories are out there: whisperings about strange bronze body parts possessed of mystic energies."

"And Urdmann is such a power-mad thug," I murmured, "he'd want such things for his own."

"Even if Urdmann didn't know about the bronze pieces beforehand, he'll learn about them soon enough. The inscriptions on the Osiris statuette explain the whole story. They're in code, but a good Egyptologist could decipher them."

"Urdmann knows his stuff," I said. "He'll probably decode it on his own. And if he can't figure it out, he's rich enough to hire people who can. As soon as Urdmann realizes he's found a map, he'll use it to track the remaining bronze pieces."

"Exactly," Father Emil replied. "Which is where you come in, Ms. Croft."

"You want me to find the missing parts before Urdmann does."

"Yes. Our Order will pay your expenses, plus a generous finder's fee. We have ample financial resources."

"How do monks and nuns acquire ample financial resources?"

Father Emil smiled. "Bronze knows we need funds to operate. From time to time, he uses his predictive powers to suggest profitable investments . . . and over two thousand years, Ms. Croft, the revenues build up significantly."

*Lovely,* I thought, *an agent of divine justice who gets rich from gaming the market.* I had nothing against making money by guessing at good investments; but if Bronze had high-tech/mystical superintelligence, it seemed like shooting fish in a barrel. Still, it's no crime to be smarter than everyone else. "If Urdmann has the real statuette," I said, "aren't we out of the game? We've lost the treasure map. How can we find the missing pieces?"

"We were close to finding them, even before the Osiris went up for auction," Father Emil told me. "Reuben had been researching the problem off and on for years. The statuette would have given precise positions, but even without that information, Reuben had narrowed the locations down. You shouldn't have trouble finding what we want."

I sighed. "All right. What parts are missing, and where are they?"

Father Emil pointed to the man of bronze. "As you can see, he's missing the left leg. It will be in three parts: the upper leg from hip to knee, the lower leg from knee to ankle, and finally the foot."

"The toes aren't cut off separately?"

"No. The toes *can* be cut off—we, uhh, tried that as an experiment with the right foot—but the evil Set didn't bother. With the rest of the body in so many pieces, he must have decided that cutting off the toes was a waste of time."

Note to self: evil gods are lazy and slapdash . . . but then, that's exactly what mythology said, wasn't it? Evil gods were constantly being tripped up by their own careless mistakes, misinterpreting prophecies, or underestimating the abilities of heroes. "Who *was* this Set anyway?" I asked.

"We don't know," Father Emil said. "Probably just some Stone Age criminal Bronze tried to apprehend . . . a bandit who snared Bronze in a booby trap, or an evil king whom Bronze was trying to neutralize. All it would take was a bit of bad luck—getting caught in a rockfall or surrounded by too many opponents to fight off—and Bronze could be immobilized long enough to get chopped up. Mind you," Father Emil added, "the chopping-up process couldn't have been easy. Some parts can be cut off readily, but others are practically impossible to sever by conventional methods. I have no idea how Bronze's head was originally detached from his torso. We tested it a few decades ago during one of Bronze's dormant periods. Nothing we had could make the slightest dent. Perhaps the mysterious Set had some kind of magic at his disposal."

"But even if Set magically sliced Bronze up, how could anybody from the Stone Age scatter bronze body parts all around the world?" I asked. "You said pieces ended up in the Far East . . . Northern Europe . . . the Americas. No one back then could possibly travel so far afield."

"No single person did," Father Emil replied. "The pieces were probably scattered among the tribes in a small area, and over time, those tribes dispersed outward. If Bronze was dismembered in 8000 B.C., the pieces had thousands of years to be carried elsewhere . . . and of course, fragments thrown into the sea might wash up on the other side of the ocean, especially if they got swallowed by migratory whales."

I thought about that. Given enough time, nomadic tribes and marine mammals might transport bronze body parts far beyond their starting point. Still, I wasn't convinced. Some instinct told me the truth was more complex than Father Emil believed.

I glanced at the bronze figure sitting in his steel chair . . . a metal man watching monitors, analyzing data in search of "evildoers." What was he really? If we put this bronze Humpty Dumpty back together again, would I regret it?

*Worry about that later,* I told myself. My foremost priority was dealing with Lancaster Urdmann. If the best way of catching up with Urdmann was hunting bronze pieces, I'd go to where one was hidden and wait. "Where are these pieces you're looking for?" I asked Father Emil.

"You'll retrieve them for us?"

"I'll do what I can."

He held out his hand. I shook it. Bargain sealed.

# 6

# SIBERIA: THE PODKAMENNAYA TUNGUSKA RIVER REGION

Twenty-four hours later, my teeth were being rattled by a decrepit Mi-28 Havoc helicopter flying over Siberia. The land below was snow-smacked wilderness—lots of trees, a few outcrops of granite, and vast stretches of bog/swamp/lake that were frozen ten months of the year. The sun crouched tepidly on the horizon, working its way up to subarctic dawn. In December at this latitude, the feeble light would last less than four hours before subsiding again into darkness. Weather reports said the day would be clear and windless with temperatures low enough to make a brass monkey sing soprano.

I had on a new cold-weather outfit, well insulated for heat but not so bulky that it would slow me down. It's nice to know a Paris couturier who's willing to work with advanced thermal-locking polycarbonates and who can cut R-factor-18 fabric on the bias. What I liked most about the suit was its reversible outer layer—white on one side for blending into snowy backgrounds, black on the other for after-dark ops. I'd spent time practicing quick-change maneuvers: zipping and unzipping until I could switch from black to white in under thirty seconds.

Speaking of reasons to get in and out of clothing . . . piloting the chopper was my longtime friend, Ilya Kazakov: ex-cosmonaut, ex–air force captain, ex–aeronautics engineer, ex a lot of other things that are none of your business. Now aged a dashing forty-five, Ilya had abandoned space-program life and retired to his native Siberia, where he worked as a bush-pilot/guide. If anyone asked why he lived a thousand miles from nowhere, he'd invent some story about hiding from the CIA . . . or a Mafia vendetta . . . or a jealous husband.

But I didn't believe such excuses. Deep in his soul, Ilya was a brooding Siberian mystic—never at ease in the city, always searching for something no man or woman could give him. When he wasn't flying customers across the tundra in his armored copter gunship, he hunkered down alone in his log cabin, where he read morose Russian poetry and filled thick journals with Reflections on Life. I wouldn't be surprised if he held long conversations with reindeer or danced naked under the northern lights; but perhaps I'm just fantasizing about that. Ilya was a big handsome man . . . and as I remembered vividly from an evening in St. Petersburg, he was an *excellent* dancer.

I'd contacted Ilya the previous day, calling him directly from St. Bernward's Monastery. According to notes in the metal attaché case, Reuben Baptiste had traced Bronze's thigh to central Siberia—specifically a region near the Podkamennaya Tunguska River—and nobody sensible ventured into the Siberian wilds without Ilya Kazakov as guide. In fact, when I talked to Ilya, I learned that he'd served as escort for Reuben a few weeks earlier. The two men had flown across the virgin pine forests, landing at native encampments to talk with elders and listen to folktales. Kazakov had served as Reuben's translator, and therefore knew something about what I was chasing: the biggest thing to hit Siberia in recorded history. Literally.

"Just over that rise," Ilya told me, "you'll see the edge of the blast radius."

Given so much snow, I doubted I'd see a thing. But when the Havoc crested the hill, I found Ilya was right. Even after a century, no one could mistake the devastation.

On the morning of June 30, 1908, something over

Siberia went boom. The force of the blast equaled fifteen megatons of TNT: comparable to the A-bomb that leveled Hiroshima. Seismographs around the world registered what was called the Tunguska event; but the site was so remote, twenty years passed before scientists arrived to investigate. They found half a million acres of forest flattened by the explosion—a circle thirty miles across wherein every living thing had been crushed and scorched.

Surprisingly, the ground at the heart of the blast had suffered little damage. In particular, there was no impact crater . . . which argued against the easy explanation of a meteor strike. No human had been within fifty miles of the epicenter, but distant hunters reported seeing a fireball on the horizon, followed by an earthquake and gusts of hot air strong enough to knock people off their feet.

The cause of the destruction was never established. Conspiracy theorists claimed it had been a flying saucer crash or a nuclear detonation thirty-five years before the Manhattan Project. Even respectable scientists proposed far-fetched theories: for a while, some thought it had been a miniature black hole piercing the Earth at close to the speed of light. More cautious researchers suggested a comet fragment had disintegrated high in the atmosphere with a titanic burst of energy . . . but the evidence was still disputed. All anyone knew for certain was that something tore a million trees up by the roots and charred a million more into black burned-out husks.

Almost a century later, the damage below our copter was still obvious. Scrub and spindly birch trees had sprung up amid the fallen pines, but they didn't come close to filling the mown-flat swath of forest. This close to the Arctic Circle, nothing grew quickly—not even the bacteria and fungi usually responsible for rotting wood. In a tropical jungle, trees begin to decay even before they're dead . . . but here in the far north, thousands of toppled pines remained intact long after their demise. Most had simply dried out and shriveled like driftwood. Where the wind blew strongly enough to clear away snow, bark-stripped trunks lay like parched bones on the thin Siberian soil. Elsewhere, the trees were vague lumps under drifts of white: corpses beneath a vast shroud.

Every one of those corpses pointed toward the heart of the devastation. They'd all been knocked back, instantaneously pushed down and outward so their roots aimed directly at the source of the blast. Scientists could easily pinpoint the epicenter; but all they'd found in that heart of darkness was a boggy marsh, fed by the nearby Tunguska River and two small lakes.

No crashed alien spaceship. No secret lab run by Nephilim. Nothing but otters and minnows, with wolves, hares, and foxes occasionally coming to drink. The scientists took photos and soil samples, interviewed tribespeople who witnessed the event from afar, scratched their heads wondering what really happened, then hurried home before some unexpected blizzard trapped them for months in the icy armpit of nowhere.

None of the investigators thought to ask the natives about a remarkable fact: not a single human had been killed in the blast. Why had there been no hunters—not one—in a huge region filled with game? Why no reindeer herders letting their animals graze beside the river? Why no fur trappers, no berry gatherers, no herb-seeking grannies, no fishing parties, no loggers, no amorous couples searching for privacy—nobody nearer than fifty miles on a pleasant morning in June? Wouldn't people spread across the countryside, making the most of the brief Siberian summer?

Unless, of course, local tribes avoided the area for reasons they didn't mention to strangers.

"Look there, Larochka," Ilya said. "Someone's camping at ground zero."

He was right. Four tents squatted at the edge of the epicenter's marsh: blue vinyl beehives perched on the bright white snow. No one came out to look at us as the rattletrap

Havoc flew overhead. "Seems like nobody's home," I said. "Do you know whose camp it might be?"

"Not locals," Ilya replied. "The tents are too fancy and expensive."

"Maybe visiting hunters?"

"It's the wrong time of year; most animals are hibernating. Might be curiosity seekers—they come now and then, thinking they'll find a piece of the comet or whatever it was. But even crazy tourists know better than to visit Siberia in December. Besides, I'm always informed when company's coming; every outfitter from Moscow to Vladivostok sends people to me because I'm the best guide in the district."

"How much does that cost you?" I asked.

Ilya grinned. "This is the new Russia, Larochka—all is open and honest. We no longer bribe each other for the privilege of fleecing rich foreigners." He looked down at the camp. "On the other hand, if some outfitter neglected to inform me of a lucrative business opportunity, I should learn who it was so I can correct any flaws in my marketing outreach."

In other words, he'd paid under the table for exclusive rights to this territory, and he wanted to find out who was making deals behind his back. "So you're going to land?"

"Just to look around. See what outfitter's name is on the equipment."

"All right, Ilyosha. But let's be careful."

I said that from habit, not because I anticipated trouble. In all likelihood, the camp belonged to the sort of people Ilya expected: curiosity seekers touring the site of a famous explosion. Who else could it be?

Not Lancaster Urdmann. He'd stolen Osiris only the previous day. How could he decipher the coded hieroglyphics, arrange a Siberian expedition, and still arrive in Tunguska ahead of me? True, he'd gotten a head start: he'd taken the statuette from Reuben before I landed in Warsaw—and the time I spent driving to the monastery and back added several hours more—but could Urdmann decrypt ancient writings so quickly? It seemed far-fetched, even if he had a team of skilled Egyptologists already assembled.

Besides, the statuette gave locations for dozens of bronze body parts all over the world. Urdmann wouldn't know which parts had already been retrieved by Father Emil's Order; he'd waste considerable effort chasing after segments that were no longer where the hieroglyphics said. It might take weeks for him to get around to Siberia.

But he'd come here eventually—I had no doubt. Urdmann might be vile, but he wasn't a total fool. He must have heard of the Tunguska explosion; and when the ancient inscriptions told him a chunk of Osiris was hidden on this site, Urdmann would choose this as one of the first locations to investigate.

Which is why I'd come here. Lancaster Urdmann would show up, and sooner rather than later. I expected to wait less than a month before he arrived . . . and I'd spend that time well, living in a tent or a cave and deciding exactly what to do with Urdmann when he got here.

Ilya set down the Havoc on a patch of level snow just behind the camp. As we got out, I saw we weren't the first to land a helicopter in that spot. Five paces away, the snow was dented by the skid rails of another chopper the same size as ours . . . probably another Havoc. Old Soviet copters weren't hard to acquire—you could buy them officially from the cash-strapped Russian military or unofficially from a chap named Sergei who ran a strip club in Novosibirsk—but the majority of Havocs were purchased by third-world nations to beef up their air defenses. The remainder went to large corporations, especially companies that did business in war zones. Ilya's Havoc was the only gunship I knew of in private hands, and it was a special case: "a gift from the grateful Russian people" for reasons he'd never explained. I didn't know whether Ilya had stolen the aircraft, blackmailed some top official, or gotten it fair and square as payment for secret services on behalf of the motherland. Frankly, I preferred to remain in ignorance; the truth was bound to be less interesting than the scenarios I imagined.

Ilya noticed the tracks of the other copter too. As he bent to examine the marks, I asked, "Anyone you know?"

He shrugged. "Mining companies sometimes fly Havocs. They come here occasionally to prospect."

I looked around at the snow covering the area: only a few inches of white, but it would make life difficult for anyone looking at rock formations, taking drill samples, and all those other things prospectors do. "Wouldn't it be smarter to come in summer?" I asked.

"Yes," Ilya said. "Prospectors know better."

"So we're back to curiosity seekers?"

"Who knows?"

He headed toward the campsite, walking easily on the hard-packed snow. When he got to the nearest tent, he reached toward the entrance flap; but I stopped him.

"Not yet," I said. "Better safe than sorry."

He raised his eyebrows in question. Once more, I thought through my arguments why this couldn't be Lancaster Urdmann's camp—why it didn't make sense that he'd beaten me here. But if these tents *did* belong to Urdmann, he was just the sort to prepare for intruders.

"Back up," I said. "Let's try an experiment."

We retreated a dozen paces. Ilya wore the look of a man humoring a woman's whim. I picked up a handful of snow, made a snowball, and threw it full strength at the entrance flap of the nearest tent.

*Boom.* Or rather *boom, boom, boom, boom,* as all four tents detonated simultaneously.

"Well, well, well," I said. "Mr. Urdmann has developed a definite fondness for explosives."

Ilya picked himself up off the snow. Unlike me, he hadn't been ready for fireworks; he'd dropped to the ground from sheer startled reflex. He dusted himself off and said, "You have rough friends, Larochka."

"Not friends, Ilyosha," I told him. "Definitely not friends."

And definitely unexpected. How could the loathsome Urdmann have reached Tunguska before us? Even if he'd had a top Egyptologist ready to translate the statuette's hieroglyphics, why go to Siberia first? Why not start the hunt for bronze fragments someplace warmer and easier to reach? Did Urdmann know exactly which body parts were missing?

Maybe. The Order of Bronze could have tipped their hand. If they'd been too aggressive in acquiring bronze pieces, a dealer like Urdmann might have noticed. He may have started doing research . . . asking questions . . . laying out bribes and threats . . . perhaps trying to identify members of the Order . . .

If Urdmann *had* found a member of the Order, he wouldn't hesitate to use extreme measures to wrench out the truth—kidnap the target; use torture, drugs, whatever. Once he'd learned what he wanted, he'd kill the poor victim and dump the corpse where it would never be found.

So Urdmann might have known about Bronze before he got the statuette. I could imagine the arrogant blackguard, bloated monster that he was, sitting in a private jet with his mercenary lackeys, waiting to hit the runway as soon as they learned where the missing leg parts were.

Which is how he reached Tunguska first. Even so, he didn't have much of a head start. A few hours at most.

"Our enemies have to be close," I said. "Wherever the bronze thigh is, Urdmann camped here because it's ground zero. Then he coptered to the actual site. We can use the Havoc to search—no, wait, that's a bad idea."

"What's the problem?" Ilya asked.

"Urdmann used to be an arms dealer," I said. "Guns mostly but also weapons with more kick."

"You mean surface-to-air missiles?"

I nodded. "Urdmann might have brought shoulder-mounted heat seekers to shoot down unwanted visitors.

He enjoys blowing things up. Can the Havoc withstand rocket fire?"

Ilya shook his head. "I get nervous around children with peashooters."

"So we'd best stay on solid ground." I took a breath and scanned the surrounding area: frozen bog, trees, stone. "It shouldn't be hard to spot Urdmann's chopper. It can only set down on clear terrain, and I doubt if Urdmann would bother with camouflage nets." I looked around again. "We'll head up there," I said, pointing to a nearby hill. "It's high enough to give a good lookout point . . . especially if I climb a tree for a bird's-eye view."

"Always so energetic," Ilya muttered. "Why not just wait till this fellow comes back to camp?"

"If he gets the bronze thigh, he might fly straight home— Urdmann's too rich to care about losing a few tents. And he probably heard his booby-trap bombs go off. Sound carries a long way in this wilderness. If he knows someone else is nearby, flying home fast makes sense. Then we'll have to pursue in the Havoc . . . and what if Urdmann's copter is faster than ours?"

"It probably is," Ilya said. "Rich men can afford all the maintenance needed to keep a chopper running well. Me, I can barely pay to keep my ship in the air."

*Now he tells me,* I thought. Aloud, I said, "So let's avoid flying chases. We have to find Urdmann before he gets off the ground."

With purposeful stride, I headed back to the Havoc. Ilya followed, his expression turning gloomy. "Larochka," he said, "you're sure this isn't just an excuse to try your new toys?"

"What do you have against toys?"

He didn't answer. Broody Siberian mystics shy away from frivolities . . . which is why Ilya disapproved of my lovely new snowmobiles.

We'd attached the two sleds to the Havoc's external landing rails. The copter's interior might have been big enough to hold them, but hauling them out would have been a night-mare. Snowmobiles may look lightweight when they're roaring over jumps and moguls, but they're brutishly heavy devils . . . especially the high-performance models. And I *always* choose high performance.

I'd named my new darlings *Powder* and *Puff*: both white, both beautiful, both gifted with the horsepower of a cavalry brigade. They had no make or model number—I'd sweet-talked the manufacturers into giving me experimental prototypes after I drove for their company in the Transalaskan marathon. (I won but missed setting a new record by 3.8 seconds. Tsk.) This was the first time I'd taken my sweethearts out in untamed conditions, and I was looking forward to it immensely.

"So which do you want?" I asked Ilya. "*Powder* or *Puff*?"

He looked dubiously at both machines. "What's the difference?"

"*Powder*'s guns are 45s; *Puff*'s are 9 millimeters. Do you like imperial or metric?"

"They have guns?"

"Of course, they have guns. What's the point of snowmobiling without guns?"

I pressed a button on *Puff*'s dash. Metal covers slid back on the snowmobile's bonnet, and a pair of Ingram MAC-10s leapt into ready position. "You aim with trackballs near your thumbs on each handlebar." I demonstrated; the guns responded smoothly, stabilized by an advanced gimbal system with internal gyroscopes. "Not perfect for targeting," I admitted, "but if you've played enough video games, you'll soon get the hang of it. Each gun has thirty-two rounds in the clip . . . and you can't reload while driving, so don't squander shots. Only bring out the guns when you need them," I added, pressing the button again so the SMGs retracted into their housings. "Otherwise, they'll clog with snow, and that would be bad."

"The kind of bad where the gun barrels get plugged and explode in your face when you fire?"

"Yes, that kind of bad. Avoid it."

Ilya shuddered. He looked like he'd rather remain with his beloved Havoc than bounce about the countryside on *Powder* or *Puff*. Like many pilots, Ilya felt no qualms riding miles aboveground in shaky aircraft, but he deeply distrusted land vehicles. Still, he wasn't a man who'd let a woman go off on her own . . . so he slouched over to *Powder* and gazed gloomily at her controls.

"They're easy to drive," I said, tossing him a safety helmet. "Just like motorcycles, except they're *supposed* to skid."

For some reason, he didn't find that reassuring.

We drove up the hill at a restrained pace, Ilya on *Powder,* me on *Puff*. Both of us had good reason to take it easy. Ilya knew nothing about snowmobiles; as a topnotch pilot he soon grasped the basics but wasn't satisfied with simple competence—he wanted to be *good*. I could see him experimenting with the sled: first trying modest little maneuvers, then gradually adding more challenge as he got the feel of the controls. I, too, had to take my time . . . not to get used to driving but to learn the tricks of the terrain. Ilya's years in Siberia let him instantly discern fallen trees beneath the snow, but I had a dozen close calls nearly smashing *Puff*'s front runners before I could distinguish harmless snowdrifts from lurking deadfalls.

Five minutes later, we topped the rise and halted to survey the land. The sun still hadn't cleared the horizon—it moved like a sleepy old woman reluctant to get out of bed—but there was light enough to see untold miles of trees, ice, and long shadows. Ilya got out binoculars—the snowmobiles had small storage trunks which we'd filled with useful equipment—and he searched for signs of Urdmann's copter. I crossed to the other side of the hill and did the same.

After a preliminary visual sweep, I lowered my binocs and let my ears take over from my eyes. The world was coldly silent: no leaves to rustle on the winter-stripped birches, no birds cheeping, no insects buzzing, not even a whisper of wind. Just my own heartbeat . . . the crinkle of my clothes as I shifted my weight . . .

Then a distant scream, an animal's roar, and the *trrrrrrr* of Uzis firing. At this distance, the guns sounded like the purring of contented cats.

Ilya came charging through the bush, manfully keen to protect me though the guns were a mile away. The noise of his approach made it hard for me to pinpoint the noises of battle. I waved him to silence, but it was too late; the fight lasted only a few seconds. Still, I had a general bearing on the commotion. "There," I said pointing northwest. "Somewhere over there."

Ilya squinted in the indicated direction, but trees hid whatever we might see. "What do you think it was?" he whispered.

"Something attacked Urdmann's party. Maybe a wolf or a bear."

Ilya shook his head. "I know every noise local wildlife makes. That roar wasn't a wolf or a bear."

"Maybe a Siberian tiger?"

"None within a thousand kilometers. Their range is far to the east."

"Well, whatever the animal was, it's dead. Otherwise, Urdmann's men would still be shooting."

"Unless the creature got them all."

"Such a cheerful man you are." I patted him fondly on the arm. "Let's go see what type of carcasses are bleeding on the snow."

I'd been close when I suggested the roar came from a tiger . . . but it wasn't Siberian, it was saber-toothed: a massively muscled beast with tawny fur, a huge feral head, and incisors like eight-inch bayonets. Conventional science claimed the last such cat died ten thousand years ago . . . but this one had been killed within the past ten minutes, shot dozens of times from several different directions.

Despite voluminous gunfire, the saber tooth had taken out two men before it fell. Their bodies lay nearby: one with his throat obliterated, the other with his chest raked to ribbons by lethal claws. Both men were dressed like the mercenaries in Warsaw but with thick padded parkas over their black-on-black outfits. The dead men's parkas were in tatters—shredded by the saber tooth's attack and spilling blood-spattered goose down into the drifting air.

Ilya barely glanced at the human corpses. His eyes were on the cat, as if he feared it might spring back to life. I felt the same apprehension—I wasn't sure the beast was dead until I'd given it several hearty shoves with my boot. Once we'd both accepted that the tiger had shuffled off its mortal coil, Ilya let himself relax . . . slightly. "I thought these things were extinct."

"So did I," I replied. "I thought the same about T. rexes till I met one in the Himalayas." I gave the saber tooth one last nudge. "Odd that Urdmann didn't take the head as a souvenir. He's the sort of man to hang big game on his wall."

"Maybe he couldn't afford the time. Urdmann must know we're nearby—with the helicopter, the exploding tents, and the snowmobiles, we've made enough noise to be heard halfway to Irkutsk. So the man decided to move on quickly before we caught up with him."

"No," I said. "Urdmann wouldn't let our presence cheat him of a trophy. If he ran off, he had some urgent reason to get away."

"Like what?"

Very, very close to us, something trumpeted like an elephant. I was certain Siberia didn't have elephants . . . but once upon a time, it had something similar.

"Quick," I said. "Back to the snowmobiles."

I'd just got my engine started when the mammoth crashed out of the forest.

I know modern elephants quite well. I've ridden domesticated ones, and I've—carefully—befriended a few in the wild. I've also examined specimens of ancient elephant ancestors: prehistoric mammoths and mastodons, some just skeletons, others with their woolly hides intact and their tusks lovingly polished by museum conservators. Well lit and well posed in well-researched displays, mammoths seem noble, dignified beasts . . . dangerous if angered but with an air of tragedy that overwhelms any imminent threat.

Such romanticized notions get hastily revised when a great hairy monster gallops at you like a hirsute city bus. The mammoth in front of me was big—bigger than anything I remembered from museum dioramas. The beast was fast too, storming across the snow at a ground-shaking sprint. Most of all, it was utterly crazed with rage: its black eyes wild, its mouth spilling froth, its voice a maddened bellow. Few creatures ever plunge to such bottomless fury; animal anger is brief—a moment's lashing out after which the beast flees or reverts to a formalized show of ferocity that intimidates without drawing blood. Predators pouncing on prey are seldom angry at all. Their kills are dispassionate . . . or if there *is* an emotion, it's the straightforward pleasure of catching a meal. Lions aren't mad at gazelles, they're just hungry.

But the mammoth hurtling down on us wasn't after food. It wasn't protecting its young, defending its territory, or venting any other natural instinct. One look at its frenzied expression convinced me the creature was driven by pure burning hate. It wanted to kill Ilya and me simply for the satisfaction of snuffing out lives.

Beneath me, *Puff*'s engine roared on all cylinders. I cranked the throttle and jolted away, checking over my shoulder to make sure Ilya had gotten *Powder* started too. If we could outrun the beast, there was no point in killing it . . . and surely my supercharged snowmobiles had more speed than an antique elephant in need of a currycomb. Besides, friends give me grief for the number of endangered creatures I've killed—though I swear I do so only when I have no other choice—and I didn't want to gun down the sole mammoth seen by human eyes since the Pleistocene epoch. That might be sufficient grounds to get me tossed out of the Royal Society. Again.

So I chose flight over fight: accelerating away with snow spewing wetly behind me. Ilya cursed as he got half my plume in his face. He steered quickly out of the spray just as the mammoth loosed an ear-piercing blare that sounded more like a mechanical air horn than noise produced by a flesh-and-blood throat. I looked around, thinking I'd see the mammoth trumpeting in frustration because it couldn't keep pace with *Powder* and *Puff*. Instead, the mammoth kept thundering forward, deliberately altering course a step so it could trample one of the dead bodies lying in the snow, then putting on a burst of speed to get back on track, only a stone's throw behind Ilya's sled.

As the beast ran, it *changed*. The crude coarse hair on its lower body withered like grass in a bonfire. Its burdensome trunk shortened, no longer low to the ground but ending at knee height, where it interfered less with galloping. Worst of all, the animal's heavy tree stump legs grew sleek . . . brown . . . metallic . . . *bronze*.

"Dear, oh dear, oh dear," I muttered. What had Father Emil said about Bronze's scattered body parts? That they had arcane powers, including the ability to twist humble animals into mutants. Long, long ago, this beast might have been a genuine mammoth . . . but after millennia of living too close to the bronze thigh, the creature was a warped monstrosity—no more a mammoth than I was. How on earth could Father Emil be sure Bronze was a force for good when the detached bronze bits produced such abominations?

On the bright side, however, if this was no longer a real mammoth, the Royal Society wouldn't mind me shooting it.

We'd first met the mammoth in a clearing beside one of the region's small lakes. Ilya and I raced along the edge of the lake, where the ground was clear of fallen trees. I'd purposely stayed off the lake itself—its surface was frozen and dusted with snow, but I had no clue if the ice was thick enough to hold the combined weight of me and half a ton of turbopowered *Puff*. Now, however, I mentally crossed my fingers and veered hard left. One fierce bounce at the edge of the beach, and I was skittering across the lake. Ice cracked beneath the sled like the back stairs at Croft Manor, which have creaked up a storm since 1532 . . . but those stairs are perfectly solid and so was the ice, groaning in protest but holding firm.

Back on shore, the bronze-legged mammoth checked its pace for a heartbeat, deciding whether to pursue Ilya around the edge of the lake or go after me. In the animal's moment of hesitation, I swung *Puff*'s rear end in a dough-nut spin across the ice until I was facing the mammoth head-on. My hand went to the button on *Puff*'s dash. The MAC-10s lifted their eager little noses and clicked girl-ishly into place.

"Hey, Dumbo," I told the mammoth. "See if this helps you fly."

The MAC-10s packed enough kick to push *Puff* a full foot back across the ice. I contented myself with a three-round burst from each gun, which I thought would be ample to turn the mammoth into worm food. All six shots were on target—how can one miss a yobbing great pachy-derm?—but the results were less decisive than I wished. Four of the bullets simply vanished into the thickets of hair, having no visible effect; whatever damage they caused was hidden by the creature's pelt and showed no sign of disrupting anything vital. The two remaining bullets struck the mammoth in its now-bronze legs and ricocheted harm-lessly away with the clang of a temple gong.

"That was disappointing," I said. But my shots still had a result: they convinced the animal to chase me rather than Ilya.

It pounded across the beach and onto the ice, feet ham-mering the frozen whiteness with the rumble of kettledrums. I watched, hoping the ice might give way or the beast's bronze legs would slippy slide out of control on the slick surface. No such luck—the mammoth's metal toes dug in like skate blades, providing traction as the animal barreled toward me. Briefly, I contemplated the possibility of a prehistoric mammal competing in the world figure skating championships, doing sit spins and triple axels . . . but there was no time for whimsy as the creature bore down upon me.

I gunned *Puff*'s engine and sped off, taking advantage of the lake's flat straightaway with no fallen trees to dodge. *Puff* zoomed from zero to sixty in better time than many automobiles on dry pavement; too bad the blasted mammoth matched me speed for speed. In fact, I could hear it gaining on me, the clamor of bronze feet growing louder by the second. I had to resist the urge to look back over my shoulder to see how close the beast was. At the rate I was going, I couldn't afford to take my eyes off the road.

*All right,* I thought, *if velocity isn't the answer, let's try maneuverability.* I heaved to my right in the tightest turn possible, nearly rolling the sled but barely hanging in by leaning hard into the curve. The mammoth was a blur of bronze as I came around and shot past it. For a split second, I was close enough to smell its musty hair, damp with snow, clotted with well-aged dirt. Then I was racing back the way I'd come, with the mammoth receding.

*Ha!* I thought . . . momentarily. But I hadn't lost my pursuer, nor had I tricked it into tripping over its feet as it wheeled in my new direction. The infernal creature had much faster reflexes than you'd expect in an elephantine herbivore. If real Ice Age mammoths had been so quick, our great-great-ancestors would have never hunted them to extinction.

Speaking of extinction, it was time to devise a new plan before I myself went the way of the dodo. Ilya was too far away to help—I'd left him behind in my first top-speed rush across the lake, and, first-time driver that he was, he'd fallen farther back as the chase continued. He just couldn't manage high-velocity craziness on ice . . . though he was doing his best and coming my way as fast as he could. In the meantime, I'd have to deal with Mr. Mad-and-Hairy on my own.

If I couldn't outrun or outweave the beast, I decided to retry my earlier tactics: 9-millimeter rounds, served piping hot. I'd try to hit something vulnerable; the eye is a perennial favorite, though I've also had success firing into wide-open mouths. Sometimes a bullet's easiest route to the brain is through the soft palate.

So I swung around once more, curving sharply to bring *Puff*'s guns to bear before the mammoth got too close. A burst from the left gun tracked across the beast's front—one bullet ricocheting off bronze, two more striking meaty targets without effect—then the right gun took over, one bullet hitting flesh, one clanging on bronze, and one flying aimlessly off into chill air. Tsk. But see how accurate *you* are when firing full auto from a snowmobile spinning in doughnuts over glare ice.

None of my shots dampened the mammoth's bloodlust. None even slowed it down. Growling, roaring, trumpeting, the monster hurtled forward. Ice cracked with every footfall, yet the frozen surface was just too thick to break under the creature's weight. Of course, if I could persuade the monster to pound over the same patch of ice several times, weakening the crust with every transit . . .

Okay. New strategy.

I revved *Puff* again and surged away . . . in the nick of time, because the mammoth was bearing down rapidly. Too rapidly. Something flicked past my ear as I bolted: a long shaggy trunk, grabbing for my head, missing by inches. I dodged quickly—left, right, left—barely keeping out of reach. *Puff* couldn't muster enough speed to propel me away. Even evasion was getting iffy, as the mammoth became less and less easy to fool with feints. Its trunk swung again, and I ducked . . . not quite fast enough. The trunk brushed the top of my driving helmet; and even that glancing contact felt as strong as a bludgeon to my skull. Helmet or no, a direct hit might be enough to knock my head clean off my shoulders. Desperately I twisted *Puff*'s throttle, trying to squeeze more acceleration from the overtaxed engine before the trunk took another swat . . .

. . . and suddenly guns fired off to my left, round after round after round. Ilya had arrived, riding in like the cavalry. I didn't turn back to see his bullets strike home, but they were obviously enough to divert the mammoth's attention from me. The pounding bronze feet sprayed a shower of ice shavings as the beast rerouted its charge toward my friend.

I heeled *Puff* around as fast as I could and saw the mammoth racing toward Ilya, trunk whipping, spittle streaming. Its path would take it back over a region of ice that was already heavily gouged from a previous passage of the creature's metal feet. "Opportunity knocks," I muttered under my breath; but I barely heard my own voice over the mammoth's bellowing and the sound of Ilya's MAC-10s chattering. A moment later I added to the din, driving *Puff* hard, off on an angle, till I had a clear shot at the damaged ice. I held my fire till the mammoth was almost upon the crack-fractured surface. Then I pressed the trigger buttons, blasting both guns at the ice an instant before the great heavy beast ran walloping onto the target area.

Splish splash.

With all the noise of gunfire, snowmobile engines, and maddened animal cries, I didn't actually hear the ice break. Nor did I hear the eruption of frigid water as a multiton pachyderm plunged in an involuntary cannonball, sending a tsunami into the air. I could see it all clearly though: the mammoth thrashing to stay afloat despite the mass of its flesh and the even greater weight of its bronze legs; the trunk flailing to grab some support from the ice surrounding the hole but finding the grip too slippery; the beast's sodden hair dragging it downward that much faster; and at the end, a look of sad resignation stealing into the animal's eyes just before it sank into the depths.

Dark cold water. Not a good way to go. I shivered and looked away.

Two minutes later, all was silent again: the chilly stillness of the north. Ilya and I had driven back to shore, with me trying not to imagine the frigid black drowning that awaited if we hit thin ice.

We automatically turned off the sleds once we were safely on land. The quiet sifted into us as the noise sifted out. I let myself exhale. "Hope there aren't more of those monsters about."

"If there were," Ilya said, "they'd be here by now. We made enough ruckus to attract anything that might be interested."

"Too right." I scanned the trees surrounding the beach. "Surprising that Urdmann hasn't showed up . . . or at least sent a few men to see what we're up to."

"If they'd seen the mammoth, they'd keep their distance." Ilya glanced back toward the lake, as if he expected the beast to come bursting out of the ice. "What *was* that thing? I've visited this area dozens of times and never seen anything like it."

I shrugged. "The bronze thigh we're looking for—it can supposedly change normal animals into . . . nonnormal animals. Apparently, that means big bronze maniacal mutants."

"Do you know where the thigh is?"

"Reuben never got an exact location—just that it was hidden near the center of the Tunguska explosion." I glanced at Ilya. "You were Reuben's translator when he visited the local tribes. You should know more about this than I do."

Ilya shook his head. "Reuben was fluent in Russian; so were most of the people he interviewed. I never sat in on Reuben's conversations except when he met with nomads who only spoke obscure native languages."

"But you still must have picked up bits and pieces."

"All I heard were folktales: myths that this area was inhabited by evil shamans who lived underground. But underground means caves, and this part of Siberia has none. It's either swamp or solid granite. The rock has niches big enough for bears to curl up in winter, but no caves that reach any depth. That requires a different type of geology."

"On the other hand," I said, "Urdmann is here. And the mammoth was here. And the 1908 explosion was here. The source of such oddities must be well hidden or it would have been found by now. Tunguska has been visited by scientific expeditions, curiosity seekers, hunting parties . . . lots of people. They'd notice anything strange lying out in the open."

"They'd notice a big killer mammoth too. Not to mention that saber-toothed tiger. But I've never heard reports of such creatures."

I thought for a moment. "Suppose the folktales Reuben gathered were true. Suppose shamans *did* live in a cave system here, even if caves don't occur naturally in this terrain. Suppose the shamans harnessed the bronze thigh's powers to *dig* caves . . . and to preserve Siberia's last mammoth and saber-toothed tiger by turning them into monsters. Both mammoths and saber tooths survived here up to the end of the last Ice Age, or even later. They only died out when humans hunted them to extinction. But suppose the shamans kept one mammoth and tiger alive with the bronze thigh's magic, holding the animals as pets underground until Urdmann came along." I looked Ilya in the eye. "If a door was sealing the cave entrance, Urdmann might have opened it and let the animals out."

"Losing two men in the process," Ilya said, nodding thoughtfully. "That suggests the door should be close to where we found the tiger's body."

"Let's go back and look around." I climbed back onto *Puff.* "There were plenty of tracks in the snow. If we can't follow the trail of a mammoth back to its source . . ."

"I can follow a mouse across bare stone," Ilya said. "I can track a flying chickadee by its wing currents. I can trace the thoughts of insects and the spoor of a speck of pollen drifting on the wind . . ."

Which was typical Ilya nonsense, but we still found the caverns without difficulty.

# 7

# SIBERIA: THE TUNGUSKA CAVERNS

Close to the spot where the saber-toothed tiger had been killed, the lake's edge blurred into frozen marsh. Frostbitten reeds, brown and withered, poked brittlely out of the ice. Some had been trampled by Urdmann and his team; the men's tracks were easy to follow into the swamp and up to a hummock of stone that jutted waist high above the bog's ice surface. The hummock itself, blown bare of snow, showed no footprints . . . and no footprints exited on the other side.

"Interesting," Ilya said. He bent closer to the rock, looking for traces of Urdmann's passage. His eyebrows lifted in surprise. "There's a seam in the granite." Ilya straightened up. "This stone must be a cap—like a trapdoor over the entrance."

I looked at the hummock: a rock slab four paces wide and twelve long. "It must weigh tons," I said. "Too heavy to lift by sheer muscle power. Let's search for some hidden opening mechanism."

In my tomb-raiding travels, I've encountered many concealed locks. Some were diabolical to find: you needed the Sacred Eye of This or the Holy Hand of That, and if you held them in the proper place at noon on the summer solstice while singing a perfect B-flat and standing barefoot in a bowl of crushed garlic . . . some giggling child would walk up and show you the secret entrance that local kids had known about for untold generations. This time, however, I thought we wouldn't have such trouble. If Lancaster Urdmann had found the lock, how well hidden could it be?

Still, Urdmann possessed one major advantage over Ilya and me: he had the statuette. Its hieroglyphics had sent Urdmann straight to the cave entrance. If the statue also told how to find a lock that was otherwise impossible to locate . . .

"Over here," Ilya said. "This is it."

I kicked myself mentally for letting my mind stray. Ilya was pointing at a shiny gleam on the rock: a thumb-sized circle of bronze embedded in the gray stone. "A push button?" he asked.

"One way to find out." With the toe of my boot, I tapped the bright metal. The top of the hummock pivoted horizontally on some unseen axle, swiveling ninety degrees to reveal a shaft sloping downward.

The opening was easily big enough for a mammoth and saber-toothed tiger to come charging out. Perhaps the tiger came first, and Urdmann—ever the avid hunter—gave chase. He'd lost two men killing the beast . . . but before he could take the cat's head as a trophy, the mammoth showed up in all its trumpeting fury. Urdmann and his team fled into the caves, closing the trapdoor behind them before the mammoth could follow.

At least, that was one possible scenario. When I found Urdmann, I'd ask what really happened . . . provided I could restrain myself long enough from killing him.

Before going underground, Ilya and I assembled equipment from the packs on the sleds: the usual adventuring gear—lights, ropes, night-vision goggles, etc.—and of course, appropriate weaponry.

I was carrying my two VADS pistols. VADS stands for Variable Ammunition Delivery System, a voice-activated wonder that let me "call my shots" (so to speak). If I wanted normal ammo, I just had to ask. I could also order up silver bullets—more necessary than you might think—explosive rounds, incendiaries, and even a few blanks . . .

in case I wanted to make a show of force without causing injury. Consider the oft-used expedient of firing a round into the air to get a mob's attention. Any bullet shot straight up comes down again with almost the same velocity. Each year, a few unlucky victims die from free-falling bullets plunging into their skulls . . . which is why I load a blank or two in every clip to avoid such contingencies. Blanks are also good for faking deaths—your own or someone else's—or for easing the monotony of an archaeological dig; a gun with blanks can serve as a starter pistol for a foot race or as a prop for an around-the-campfire production of *Hedda Gabler*.

Ilya, on the other hand, disdained fancy high-tech weapons. He carried one of his country's most popular gifts to the world: an AK-47 assault rifle. The rifle was officially outdated, replaced by the more modern AK-74 . . . but Ilya was a traditionalist, and, besides, AK-47s were easier to come by on the back streets of Omsk. Ilya also carried a beautiful katana that his great-grandfather had picked up in 1905 during the Russo-Japanese war. The sword was a masterpiece of samurai weapon crafting—perfectly balanced, sweet in the hand, and as sharp as the first breath of winter. I coveted it profoundly. If Ilya hadn't been a friend, and if the sword hadn't been his treasured family heirloom, I would have found some way to make it mine, either by buying it outright or by challenging him to a high-stakes poker game when we got back to civilization.

For now, I contented myself with a single wistful glance as Ilya slid the sword into an over-the-shoulder sheath on his back. Then I gave myself a *down-girl* shake and said, "Are you ready?"

Ilya shifted the weight of his pack a little. "All right. Ready."

"Then let's go. We have business underground."

Together, we began our descent.

The tunnel downward was nothing like a natural cave. Its walls reminded me of the stonework in St. Bernward's

Monastery: rough cut but regular, clearly the work of humans hewing out chunks of rock. What had they used to dig? Primitive mining tools couldn't possibly make headway through solid granite, let alone create the extensive mammoth-sized shaft that stretched before us. This underworld domain must have been excavated by the power of bronze—a power whose magnitude disturbed me every time I saw evidence of its work. Whether Bronze was supernatural or ultrahigh-tech, his body could produce gobsmacking amounts of energy. If one small body part could pierce Siberian bedrock like a dagger through flesh, how much more could one expect from the reassembled whole? How dangerous might our bronze Humpty Dumpty be when he no longer needed all Father Emil's horses and all Father Emil's men to put him back together again?

But I had more immediate concerns: Lancaster Urdmann and his crew. Urdmann knew he had company on his heels. He might well have set booby traps or an ambush to slow us down . . . so I had to focus on the present and keep my eyes open for trouble.

Ilya and I carried electric torches, but the tunnel had its own weak illumination. At first, I couldn't tell where the faint light came from; I needed a full minute to realize that the glow was all around, reflecting off a thin sheen of ice coating the rock walls. The ice was no more natural than the walls themselves: it didn't melt at all when I breathed warm air on it, and a close look showed it was perfectly faceted like an insect's eye, with millions of tiny flat surfaces slanting in all directions. Human hands couldn't have shaped such intricacy, nor could any human science preserve the ice's form so perfectly year after year through every freeze and thaw. The smallest beam of light (from our torches, from the open entrance behind us, from sources farther below) bounced from facet to facet, diffusing far and wide. The glow wasn't bright, but the tunnel was never completely dark—a netherworld dusk of thready gray propagated by fun-house mirrors. With every step forward, my eye was caught by flickers of motion nearby . . . my own reflection, broken to pieces, following us just out of reach.

To conserve our torch batteries, Ilya and I turned off our lights soon after we began our descent. Dim light persisted around us. The slope of the tunnel was gentle, our footfalls soft. The temperature increased as we went downward, though the ice on the walls remained hard frozen. Maybe the warmth was just my imagination—caused by the utter lack of breeze in that enclosed space or by the adrenaline in my veins as I waited for some sudden attack.

The shaft slanted downward a hundred paces before it leveled out. At the bottom, we came to a junction where the tunnel split in three: one route continued directly ahead while two others angled off on either side. We scanned the floor for hints of which way Urdmann went but found nothing useful—the gray rock showed no tracks. "Keep going straight," I decided. Urdmann struck me as the sort who'd bull in one direction as far as he could go, unless he had good reason to detour. Ilya shrugged and started forward again . . . then stopped as he caught sight of the tunnel wall.

Like the walls of the entrance tunnel, it was encrusted with faceted ice; but beneath the frozen veneer, a mural had been painted on the stone. The style reminded me of ancient cave art from places like Lascaux and Altamira: pictures that originated long before the development of familiar visual conventions.

The artists—definitely more than one, with varying degrees of skill—had produced a profusion of images (animals, people, the sun, abstract designs) with no obvious organization. Some figures were crammed tightly together; a few even overlapped, such as a scarlet man with a spear who'd been painted diagonally across an orange reindeer. Other elements stood in isolation, perhaps to give them special status. One solitary form was clearly a mammoth with tusks, a trunk, and crude shocks of hair. Another was a blob of brown portrayed in otherwise empty space, as if no one dared draw anything near it. Under other circumstances, I would have had a hard time guessing what the blob was . . . but I had no doubt it was a life-sized depiction of a chunky bronze thigh.

"The colors are all so bright!" Ilya said. "I've seen photos of Stone Age art. Even the best preserved are faded."

"The coating of ice must have kept these pristine. Not to mention there's mystic power in the air. It might have helped people create more vivid paints in the first place."

I walked slowly along the wall, thinking how many archaeologists would sell their firstborn for such a spectacular find. Like most art of its type, the mural paid tribute to the sacred glories of the Hunt: people with knives and spears stalked various species of game or gathered in celebration as they butchered the kill. A few human figures had animal characteristics—a man with antlers, for example, and a large-breasted woman whose hands had elongated fingers ending in claws. These would either be shamans wearing special costumes—an antlered headdress, a claw-studded glove—or tribal gods imagined to have both human and animal traits.

As I continued forward, however, the pictures changed. The style grew more sophisticated: fewer images drawn at random angles, a greater attention to small details. People were no longer painted as single-color silhouettes; they had light brown skin, dark brown clothes, and white eyes with black pupils. The animals changed from recognizable types—mammoths, deer, bear, wolves—into more alien forms. Creatures with reindeer heads sported long snakelike necks attached to bulky torsos. Bristle-haired cats had too many legs. Shapeless things waved tentacles. Disembodied mouths floated in the air, gnashing icicle teeth.

The people changed, too: the farther I went along the mural, the fewer *Homo sapiens* I saw. Each humanoid figure had some gross deviation, from bird beaks to forked tails to heads with faces both front and back. I had the unpleasant suspicion these weren't just flights of fancy. They had the look of pictures painted from life.

Ilya obviously felt the same. "Does this mean the people became freaks?" he asked. "Or just that their stories got wilder? Maybe at first they drew themselves hunting . . . but after a while, they might have gotten bored with pictures of everyday life and started drawing fantasies—fairy tales full of ogres and demons."

"That's what traditional archaeologists would say. They'd tell you that over time, true-to-life representations must have fallen out of favor and artists turned to works of imagination. But you don't really believe that, do you?"

"No." Ilya made a sour face. "Their drawings remained true to life. The people who lived here turned into horrors. At least some of them did."

He pointed to another section of the wall. Mutated humanoids were shown devouring a normal man—biting into his arms as he screamed in agony. Nearby, more mutants were . . . no, I shan't describe it. I shan't describe *any* of the atrocities depicted in that part of the mural. The world is depraved enough without me adding to the mess. Just take it on faith the paintings showed monstrosities behaving monstrously. No further details will be supplied.

Sickened, I turned from the pictures. Ilya joined me, looking as if he might vomit. "Did these fools summon demons?" he asked. "Did they open hell itself?"

I shook my head. "No telling what really happened . . . but I can guess. The shamans who used the bronze thigh as a talisman spent too much time in its presence. Over the years, it changed them. Their lives were extended, but their bodies and minds became so twisted . . ." I shook my head again. "There were other people down here, too: normal people. The shamans used them as playthings. From time to time, the shamans might have ventured to the surface for more victims. That would explain why local tribes have stayed well away from this area for many centuries— they didn't want to get caught. In the end, the shamans must have run out of innocents to mutilate. They needed other ways to amuse themselves."

"Such as?"

I forced myself to return to the mural. It continued for some distance—each pace representing an unknown length of time, centuries or even millennia, from the Stone Age all the way to . . . who could tell? I saw shamans facing hideous beasts, probably of their own creation: repulsive hybrids—part mammal, part reptile, part nothing on Earth. Sometimes the shamans fought these creatures; sometimes they coupled with them. After a while, it was difficult to distinguish the shamans from the horrors they constructed.

Near the end came the war. Previous sections of the mural had been painted in lurid detail by shamans proud of their perversions. They'd depicted exact patterns of blood spatter in loving portraits of mutilation. But the final pictures on the wall had the look of hurried sketches: one grotesque shaman stabbing another in the eye; two shamans hurling fire at each other; a shaman impaled on spikes at the bottom of a pit, while another stood by laughing; six shamans arranged in a circle with a lump of bronze in the center . . .

"They fought over the thigh," Ilya said.

I nodded. The shamans had exhausted all sources of prey, then turned on themselves. I could imagine them, mutated lunatics, fighting face-to-face or setting traps, killing one another, then sneaking to this mural to record their "triumphs." They didn't have time to paint details; just a few fast daubs to commemorate some victory over an opponent, then they'd scurry away for fear of getting caught by other enemies.

"There's one thing missing," I said. "The final battle. They couldn't paint that one because nobody survived."

"You're thinking of the explosion?" Ilya asked.

"The great Tunguska blowout. The last blast of the war."

"But the explosion didn't happen in these caves," Ilya said. "It detonated many kilometers up in the sky."

I pointed to the wall—the picture of six shamans poised around the bronze talisman. "What if the last six survivors agreed to a final duel? A contest of power, winner takes all, with the thigh as the prize. Can you picture them flying, high in the air, ready to loose all their might on one another? They'd probably leave the thigh here where it would stay safe underground . . . and where it would be out of reach in case someone tried to grab it for an energy boost. But the shamans themselves could have opted for a gigantic airborne Armageddon."

"And their clash caused the explosion," Ilya said, "annihilating them all."

"They may have been so deranged they *wanted* annihilation. A fifteen-megaton suicide pact."

"Leaving the bronze thigh behind in their underground bunker?"

"We'll see."

I turned away from the mural. As I did, gunfire sounded in the distance, echoing and reechoing off the tunnel walls.

"The shamans left more than the bronze thigh," Ilya said. "I've got a feeling that the mammoth and saber tooth were only the start of the welcoming committee."

"It'll be a shame," I said, "if they rip Urdmann to pieces before I can kill him myself. Come on."

Ilya and I slipped deeper into the caves.

The tunnel had dozens of side passages—probably leading to sleeping quarters, latrines, and all the other facilities an underground society needs—but the main shaft continued straight ahead, still lit with its ice-reflected glow. Ilya and I pressed forward another five minutes until we came to the scene of the fight we'd heard: another dead mercenary, another dead creature, both bleeding the ground slick.

The creature had the size and build of a bear, but its face was insectlike—some breed of black fly, with huge scarlet eyes above a dripping sucker mouth—and its forelegs ended in snake heads rather than paws. It must have walked upright, with serpent mouths hissing as it reached to grab prey. I could imagine it lurking out of sight in a nearby side passage, then storming out with a roar when the mercenary came within striking distance. The bear thing's right-hand fangs had pierced the man through both cheeks, like double spikes rammed into the flesh; then the left-hand fangs had ripped out the man's throat. Other mercenaries had shot the monster, dropping it in its tracks . . . but that was too late to save the injured man. Urdmann and his team had simply moved on—though I imagine they were much more wary when they came to other side tunnels.

I was wary myself. First, I put on my night-vision goggles; the tunnel's dim light was adequate for simple walking, but perhaps it was time to see farther into the shadows. Then, keeping well away from the bear-fly-snake in case it wasn't as dead as it seemed, I started forward again with my nerves on high alert.

My precautions were wise but not wise enough—I should have kept my distance from the mercenary, too. As I passed his corpse, his hand darted out and caught my ankle. Before I could react, he yanked and pulled me off balance, toppling me to the floor. My goggles went flying and smashed against the tunnel wall. As for me, I hit hard on one shoulder, not able to do a proper break fall because the grip on my leg didn't let me move freely. A second later, the man grabbed me with his other hand too, clutching my ankle and squeezing so hard I felt bones grind against each other.

I shot him in the face. It didn't make a bit of difference.

The man had looked dead before—half his throat was missing, and he'd been lying in a pool of his own blood. Now, he was *definitely* dead; my bullet blew away enough of his skull to give new meaning to the term "scatterbrained." Yet the grip on my leg didn't lessen. In fact, the dead man pulled me toward him, hand over hand, dragging me closer with his bloody fingers.

Note to self: the bronze thigh didn't just produce monstrous animals, it made zombies too.

I fired at the man again. Generations of movies had assured me the living dead would cease to be a nuisance once their gray matter got minced. But two point-blank head shots didn't slow my attacker at all—he continued to paw my leg as if crawling up a rope. So much for believing Hollywood. Instinctively, I kicked the zombie with my other foot . . . as if a kick would work where bullets didn't. No. But I could slam my boot heel down on the zombie's fingers, a target I didn't dare attack with my guns for fear of shooting myself in the leg. As my boot struck home again and again, I heard the pleasing snap of undead metacarpals.

The zombie's grip eased. At first, I thought it was because of my knuckle-crushing footwork. Then I saw that one of the arms clutching me was no longer attached to the dead mercenary's body. Something glinted as it slashed in the darkness . . . and the other arm came loose too, sliced off at the shoulder. I looked up to see Ilya holding the katana. He contemplated the zombie as a butcher might size up a side of beef before deciding where to cut next. After a moment, Ilya swung the blade again . . .

I was pleasantly surprised that chopping up the zombie actually seemed to disable it. Too often in movies, undead arms keep working even after they're detached from the body. But perhaps there was something in the steel of Ilya's century-old sword that gave it power against monstrosities—some samurai magic that worked where bullets didn't. I was thankful for whatever little advantages we might have.

I was also thankful the dead man had already shed most of his blood. Otherwise, my nice white snowsuit would have been ruined.

Several sword chops rendered the cadaver sufficiently discontiguous that it posed no further threat. Partway through this dissection, the zombie fell still. I couldn't tell whether it was now irrevocably dead or just in a sulk at being carved up.

As Ilya cleaned off his sword blade, he said, "Life is full of the unexpected, Larochka, whenever you're around."

I picked up my fallen night-vision goggles, looked at

them for a moment, then tossed them aside again. They
were shattered beyond repair. Tsk. "Life is *always* full of
the unexpected, Ilyosha," I said. "These caves have been
here for centuries. The monsters too. I didn't make them."

"But you opened the door."

"It's good to open doors. Better than tiptoeing past for
fear of what's behind."

Ilya smiled softly and put his hand on my cheek. "We
each tiptoe past *some* doors, Larochka. We just pick different ones to avoid."

Without another word, he turned down the tunnel and
walked quickly away.

A short distance onward, we came to the heart of the underworld: a vast cavern larger than Wembley Stadium, its
walls terraced, its ceiling more than ten stories high above
its floor. Like Wembley, the layout was oval; our tunnel
entered at one end, halfway up the wall, then split into narrow paths and walkways that ran the circumference of the
place, connecting to all the terraces.

The light was the same feeble dimness we'd seen in the
tunnel—too faint to show us the cavern's far end. But I
had no doubt the bronze thigh was down there. This chamber felt like a cathedral. In the years before the shamans
went mad, the people of the tribe must have come here to
worship: to behold the bronze talisman, to bow down before it, and to watch as their fellows were killed in sacrifice.

A steep ramp led to the cavern floor. I started down but
stopped when I saw Ilya wasn't following. He'd gone
along a side path to the nearest wall terrace; I trotted back
and found him on one knee. "Dirt," he said, touching the
ground. "Not rock." He dug his fingers into the earth and
let bits of soil trickle out. "Feels like humus. Good and
fertile. Smells rich too. I'd like some for my vegetable
garden."

"No, you wouldn't. This soil has been mutating for millennia. It would only grow Venus flytraps. Or triffids."

"Still . . ." Ilya looked around the cavern, his gaze slowly taking in the terraces. Each was a flat ledge jutting from the rock wall. The ledges varied in size from a few feet square to patches twenty or thirty yards long. They all appeared covered with a fair depth of soil above the underlying rock. "I think they were gardens," Ilya said. "The people may have used these terraces for cultivating crops."

"There's not enough light," I said. "Maybe you could grow mushrooms, but nothing that photosynthesizes. Unless . . ."

My eye had been caught by an irregularity in the terrace's wall. When I investigated, I found an expanse of sewn-together animal hides hanging on spikes driven into the rock. Some of the hides had mangy bits of mammal fur; others had scales, like snakeskin; a few felt like tree bark. Considering how long these skins had been down here, they should have rotted to dust ages ago; but just as the mutant mammoth had been kept alive for thousands of years, the patchy animal hides must have been preserved by the wonders of bronze radiation.

At the seams where one skin was sewn to another, ghosts of light oozed through from the other side. Not what you'd expect from something spiked against a solid rock wall. I grabbed one edge of the hanging and pulled. The hides tore away from the spikes that held them. Light flooded out from behind—not powerfully bright but hard on the eyes after spending so long in semidarkness. Both Ilya and I lifted our hands to block the glare.

After a moment, I peeked through my fingers to get a better look at what I'd uncovered. It resembled a window . . . not glass but some translucent material that acted as a lens: perhaps the same material that served as "ice" on the walls of the tunnels we'd just left. The lens gathered light from beyond, illuminating the terrace garden where we stood. The light only shone on a part of the area; but the lens was mounted in an adjustable wood frame that allowed a degree of movement. I shifted the focus until light covered all of the terrace—a perfect greenhouse for whatever once grew here.

"Where does the light come from?" Ilya asked.

"The surface," I said. "The sun. It may seem bright to our eyes, but it's only winter daylight. Heaven knows how the sunshine is collected; maybe through cracks in the rock. Every stone outcrop for miles around might hide gaps that funnel light into underground channels . . . like prehistoric fiber optics. Surprising what you can do with high-tech ultrasorcery."

"High-tech ultrasorcery?" Ilya made a face. "Please, Larochka, don't babble." He let his eyes roam over the dozens of other terraces lining the cavern. "I suppose they all have light sources, too?"

"Probably. You were right about the people using these terraces for crops. They could grow practically anything down here . . . especially in summer when days are twenty hours long."

"But why would they cover the lenses?" Ilya nudged the animal-skin blackout curtain with his foot. "This place would be much more cheerful if they let in the sun."

"Once the shamans went mad, they wouldn't want 'cheerful.' And maybe light caused them pain. There's a long mythological tradition that light injures evil beings. In my line of work, one learns to respect long mythological traditions."

"If we had the time," Ilya said, "I'd go around this cavern, pulling down all the curtains I could find. Let the light in."

"We might do that after we've dealt with Urdmann. I'm always game for unveiling ancient ruins . . . but first things first."

We returned to the ramp and descended to the cavern's floor. Still no sign of Urdmann. I thought I heard whispers from the far end of the chamber, but it might have just been a breeze. It might also have been the sound of monsters sliding softly toward us.

Rather than walk across the middle of the cavern, Ilya and I kept to the gloom along the wall. Urdmann's men would be watching for us . . . and this group wouldn't be like the bunglers in Warsaw. The thugs who invaded Jacek's were handpicked to fail; they had to let Reuben escape with the booby-trapped statue. The thugs with Urdmann now, however, were apparently top-drawer, as evidenced by the fact that they hadn't cut and run despite the monsters they'd encountered. They'd also have top-drawer equipment—probably including night-vision goggles. Since my own goggles were broken, all I could do was creep forward, wondering if my body heat was glowing a bright green in somebody's infrared sniper scope.

Several times we came to side tunnels leading off the main cavern. Ilya and I passed each one cautiously, watching for hungry bear-fly-snake things. We saw nothing . . . but three-quarters of the way along the cavern, we came to a tunnel where we *heard* something: a bubbly crackle, like bacon in a frying pan when it starts to spit. Whatever made the noise, I didn't want to meet it; I glanced at Ilya and could tell he felt the same. We stepped up our pace to a trot. That might make it easier for Urdmann's thugs to spot us, but they seemed the lesser of two evils.

The bacon-fat sound didn't fade behind us. It continued at the same volume, as if the source of the noise was following on our heels. When I glanced behind, I saw nothing. That didn't reassure me. Either our pursuer was keeping low to the ground and hiding in the shadows . . . or else it was truly invisible. Neither possibility filled me with buoyant good cheer.

Then—as if things couldn't get worse—something in front of us went flash-*crack*. A sniper rifle. Ilya staggered, then dropped to the ground. I joined him an instant later. "Are you hit?" I whispered.

"My leg. Damn."

I reached toward him, intending to probe his injury, but he pushed me away. "You deal with our other problems. I can patch myself up with my first-aid kit . . . but not if something is trying to eat me."

I lifted my pistols, pointing one forward toward the unseen sniper, one back toward the bacon-fat crackle. A moment later, someone called from up ahead. "Lara, dear, how lovely to meet you again."

I kept quiet. Why give away my position? But it didn't matter. "Come now, Lara, don't be shy. I can see you perfectly well with my night-vision scope. You cut a distinctive figure, even wearing a parka. The least you can do is say hello."

I still held my tongue. If Urdmann wanted chirpy conversation, I'd do my best not to give it to him. Besides, I couldn't afford to get distracted with talk; the crackling thing behind us was getting closer.

"All right," Urdmann said with a theatrical sigh, "if you won't be civil . . . you should know that I've got what we both came for. The bronze thigh. It was sitting right here on a pedestal. It's rather pretty—still brightly polished after all these years. I can see my reflection in it . . . handsome chap that I am."

He paused. I could imagine a smirk on his porcine face as he waited to see if I'd answer. When I didn't, he went on. "You probably think the only way out is back the way we came in . . . which would mean I'd have to pass you in order to leave."

The thought had crossed my mind.

"But guess what?" Urdmann said. "The shamans who built this place made a special escape route direct to the surface. They must have feared getting trapped down here—perhaps if they used the thigh to create something they couldn't handle. Those shamans may have been lunatics, but they were masters of self-preservation." He laughed. "I am too. I have no macho need to tangle with you, Lara. I'll just quietly take my leave. You tend your wounded friend and follow when you're ready."

He laughed again, pleased with himself. Urdmann knew I'd never abandon Ilya . . . and with Ilya's wounded leg, we couldn't possibly move as fast as Urdmann and his men. They'd reach the surface far ahead of us; they'd race to their copter and get away long before we could pursue.

"Farewell, Lara, dear," Urdmann called. "Rule Britannia, and God save the queen."

I could hear the sounds of people on the move: our enemies scrambling up the escape tunnel. It occurred to me Urdmann may have deliberately shot Ilya in the leg rather than trying for a kill—if Ilya was dead, there'd be nothing to slow me down. And, of course, Urdmann wouldn't just shoot *me;* he wanted to humiliate me first, to pay me back for previous indignities I'd heaped on him. Besides, if I was dead, Urdmann wouldn't have the fun of gloating to my face.

*One more score to settle,* I thought. *One more debt to repay, you arrogant toad.*

"How are you doing?" I asked Ilya. All this while he'd been packing his wound with bandages. I still didn't know how badly he'd been hit, and he was doing his best to hide it from me. He'd turned away to treat himself; I couldn't tell if his secretiveness came from modesty, male pride, or damage so severe he didn't want it to distract me. Under other circumstances, I'd have smacked him and taken a look for myself . . . but the bacon-crackle sound was so close, I decided I better deal with it before I checked Ilya's injury. I took a few steps toward the noise . . .

A piece of the floor rose up: featureless, black, and floppy, like a silhouette cut from tar paper. Its cloth-thin shape was humanoid but embellished grotesquely with reindeer antlers and a tail that reminded me of the saber-toothed tiger's. Bacon-fat sounds sizzled within its dark folds. With a jolt, I realized the noise was the creature's voice, so degraded it no longer sounded like words. The hiss-spit-crackle was all that remained of a language older than fire. Without doubt, I was facing the last of the shamans—one that somehow had survived the Tunguska blast, though now so withered it had literally become a walking shadow.

"Stay back," I said, raising my guns. If the murals we'd seen had told the truth, this shaman must have committed many murderous atrocities; but there was no point shoot-

ing him in cold blood if he kept his distance. Besides,
would bullets faze a flapping shadow who'd lived through
a fifteen-megaton blast? Better to try intimidation first,
rather than resort to violence.

But I'd wasted my breath. The shadow shaman stretched
out his fluttering hand . . . and I knew if that blackness
touched me, I'd regret it. I fired both guns point-blank into
the thing's body. Simultaneously, I used the recoil as im-
petus for a back flip, up, over, and down feetfirst several
paces away.

In the dim cavern glow, the dark figure wavered like
water. Then it released a flurry of crackles, like a bonfire
when dry twigs are tossed in. I feared the sound was
laughter: my bullets had passed through the shaman
harmlessly. How can you shoot a shadow?

"Silver bullets," I said. You can never be sure if silver
bullets will work against a particular type of creepy
crawly, but they're always worth a try. The VADS instantly
delivered the ammo I asked for. Too bad when I fired, the
silver rounds had no more effect on the shadow than normal lead.

"Larochka," said Ilya, not far away. "Take the katana."

I spun my guns back into their holsters and Ilya tossed
me the sword. "Please tell me," I said, "that a hundred
Japanese priests blessed this blade when it was forged and
gave it the name Shadow Slayer."

"Don't know," Ilya replied. "Great-grandfather looted it
off some dead guy's corpse."

"Then we can't say it *isn't* named Shadow Slayer." I
turned to the shaman. "You hear that?"

The darkness crackled. I charged.

One good thing about shamans who've lived in a hole
for millennia: they know bugger all about swordplay. The
last time my opponent had tangled with outsiders, pointy
sticks were the peak of military technology. The shaman
surely realized my katana was a weapon—I held it like a
weapon as I sped to the attack—but this throwback to
primitive hunters had no experience facing sharp, swing-

ing steel. He raised his shadowy hands in an attempted defensive posture, but his guard wouldn't have stopped a mosquito. With a feint and a twist and a back cut, I evaded his block and delivered a perfect killing stroke. My blade slashed through his neck with a whisper like silk on silk.

It didn't decapitate him. I saw no effect at all; the flapping darkness remained unbroken, as black as a mine at midnight. But perhaps Japanese priests *had* blessed the sword against evil, or those old tales were true about cold iron harming supernatural beings. The shaman shrieked as the steel sliced through. He staggered back, then shrieked again. This time the cry came from anger, not pain. Howling in outrage he came at me, his hands clawing the air with murderous fury.

I dodged and swung the katana again—another killing swipe, this time to the body. Any other foe would have been disemboweled; the shaman screamed but kept coming, driving his flimsy frame forward onto the blade like paper impaling itself on a spike. A split second later, his outstretched hand raked my left shoulder . . . and although he was nothing but shadow, his fingers gouged my parka, tossing up goose down in surprised white clouds before stabbing my flesh.

Unlike my howling enemy, I didn't scream in pain. *Never let the other fellow know you're hurt.* Blood gushed down my arm from finger-sized holes pierced deep into my deltoid; but I backed off fast and took time to smile before weaving my sword in a sweeping *S* through the shadow man's torso. He screeched and retreated, no longer giving his bacon-fat laugh.

For another few seconds, we sparred with each other. I could rely on practiced technique: good footwork, trained reflexes, and a wealth of sneaky tricks acquired in the kendo schools of Kyoto. Maybe I couldn't compete with top Japanese sword masters—maybe—but I could outfight, outthink, and outmaneuver a bronze-wraith bumpkin who hadn't mixed it up dirty since the Stone Age.

On the other hand, expertise only went so far. Each

strike with the katana made the shaman wail in agony, but I never caused tangible damage. When my opponent chose to grit his invisible teeth and plow forward despite the pain, all I could do was back off. I could merely hurt the shaman; he could *gut* me.

Okay. New strategy.

I scrambled back to put a few yards between me and the bad guy, then panted loudly to give the impression I was running out of breath. I also flexed my wounded shoulder with many groans and winces, doing my best to portray a woman stiffening with pain—too bad that wasn't completely an act. In short, I put on a show to suggest I was weakening. The shaman barreled forward to take advantage of my failing strength. I hesitated, then fled: aiming my feet for the nearest ramp up the side of the cavern.

The shaman pursued, snuffling like a pig after truffles. Inwardly, I rejoiced. Ilya was virtually defenseless on the cavern floor: unable to run and armed only with bullets. If the shaman had headed for my friend, there was little I could do to intervene. Fortunately, the shadow man only had eyes for me. I had hurt him; I had assaulted his dignity; I had *defied* him. After centuries of ruling the subterranean roost—butchering unmutated humans for pleasure, always having his own way—the shaman saw me as a rebellious peon who must be made to suffer.

So he chased me. I ran. To the garden terrace above us—which happened to be a large level patch, almost a small field rather than a mere garden. What had once grown here? Wheat? Rye? Barley? Likely some kind of grain . . . but whatever had thrived here in ages past was long gone now. No light meant no plants.

At the rear of the terrace, another patchwork of animal skins had been staked to the wall. I ran across the bare earth, fast but not *too* fast. I wanted the shaman close on my heels. If I got too far ahead, and if he saw what I intended to do, he might retreat. Then again, if my new strategy didn't work . . . did I really want the shaman within spitting distance behind me?

No time for doubt. The shaman traveled almost as quickly as I did. He didn't run—he glided over the ground like a legless ghost. Without looking back, I could tell how close he was behind me; he'd started the bacon-fat crackle again, laughing at my efforts to escape.

You'd think an ancient spellcaster sadist would have more brains. How had this shadow thing lasted so long if he couldn't tell when he was being played? Then again, maybe *I* was the fool. Maybe the shaman wasn't afraid because he knew he was in no danger.

Only one way to find out.

As I reached the wall I swung my sword, slashing at the skins that hung there. The sharp katana cut a gash across the pelts. Sunlight flooded forth, gathered by the lens on the other side and focused all around us.

The shaman shrieked. This time the sound wasn't pain, it was fear.

I swept the katana again, slicing off more of the animal hides that held back the light. More sun poured in. The shaman reversed course and fled, making a squirrellike chitter as it fled the brightness. "Too late," I said. One more swing of the sword and the lens was completely uncovered. I shifted the lens in its frame to bathe the shaman with channeled sunbeams.

You know what happens to shadows at daybreak: they're dispelled by rosy-fingered dawn. Most shadows don't give earsplitting screams as they vanish, but apart from that, it was the same old, same old.

I jogged back to Ilya. He was still in one piece and had bandaged his bullet wound. "I heard the screams," he said. "Glad to see they came from shadow man rather than you. What did you do?"

"I enlightened him," I said . . . then regretted it. As a peer of the realm, I should hold myself to a higher standard than bad movie gag lines.

Ilya put his arm around my neck, and I propped him up as we crossed the cavern. A few times his bad leg gave out and he lost his balance, clutching at me for support. When he grabbed my injured shoulder, it hurt. A lot. The cave's weak light wouldn't allow a good look at my wounds, but I could see feathers from the ripped parka sticking to the dark grit of my blood. Feathers had likely been driven into the punctures, too—a fine way to bring on infection. But something told me we didn't have time to deal with my injuries. The sooner we got back to the surface, the happier I'd be.

The cavern ended in a crude stage area—an expanse of stone several feet higher than the rest of the cave's floor. This would be the tabernacle: the shamans' unholy of unholies, where they kept the bronze thigh and committed their greatest atrocities. In the middle of the space stood a plain stone pedestal the height and shape of a birdbath. It must have been the bronze thigh's resting place.

Not anymore. The pedestal was empty.

A tunnel opened at the rear of the tabernacle: the escape route Urdmann had mentioned. He must have been standing in the tunnel's mouth as he spoke to us—probably with his sniper rifle propped against the surrounding stone. But the opening was empty now; Urdmann and his men had scarpered.

From the cavern's main floor, Ilya and I approached the raised area with caution. I couldn't believe our enemies had simply fled without leaving a nasty surprise: a booby trap on the ramp to the tabernacle or something in the escape tunnel. Lancaster Urdmann was not the type to make a peaceful exit. I kept a keen watch for trip wires and electric-eye triggers as we climbed to the shamans' sacred dais.

Nothing. But as I placed my foot on the stage, something went *woomph* in the escape tunnel. I pushed Ilya down and threw myself on top of him . . . but nothing further happened. Nothing but Ilya's profane protests that (a) he wasn't some frail old granny who needed me shielding his body, and (b) would I please get off him because I was hurting his %*$#&! leg.

I rolled off my friend and stood up. The escape tunnel's

mouth was now blocked with tumbled ice and snow: a thick barricade of it, freshly fallen from above.

"Oh, very nice," I growled. "He's shut us in with an avalanche." The *woomph* must have been an explosion set off by Urdmann as he left the tunnel: an explosion that dropped a load of Siberian winter to seal off the shaft.

"Don't fret, Larochka," Ilya said. "We can make it back the long way. I can't move fast, and we may meet more monsters, but . . . oh."

His last word caught my attention. I turned and saw where he'd been looking. At the far corner of the tabernacle, in the shadows against the rock wall, an electric device had begun to blink atop a stack of what looked like gray bricks.

"That's a bomb, isn't it?" Ilya whispered.

I nodded. The bricks were plastic explosive: maybe C-4, maybe one of the new military-grade plastiques circulating on the black market. Whatever it was, I was sure the stack contained enough firepower to bring the cavern down around our heads.

"Ilyosha," I said, "how good are you at disarming bombs?"

"Never tried it," he replied. "So who knows? I might be brilliant. How about you?"

"My preferred technique is running like mad to get out of the blast radius. But since that would involve abandoning you . . ."

Ilya didn't bother arguing. He knew I wouldn't leave him . . . even if there was enough time to do so, which I doubted. Urdmann would have set the bomb's timer for only a few minutes—long enough to let us agonize over our predicament but not long enough to defuse the bomb or get ourselves clear.

Still, maybe I *could* defuse the bomb. If I was lucky. In movies, you just had to cut the red wire . . . or was it the green? I walked carefully forward, hoping the great mound of explosives didn't have a motion sensor to set it off if I got too near.

A piece of paper lay folded on the stack. I debated touching it—a demolitions expert might have rigged a trigger that went off when the paper was moved—but if Urdmann had left me a note, he wouldn't want to kill me before I'd read it. Urdmann liked to gloat . . . and this note was his chance to say *Ha-ha, Lara, I beat you.*

Nothing went boom as I opened the message:

> *Lara dear,*
> *As soon as you drew near, the warmth of your lovely body triggered this bomb's detonation sequence. You now have ten minutes to live. What a pity I'll never know how you chose to pass the time.*
>
> > *All my best wishes,*
> > *Lancaster Urdmann, O.B.E.*
>
> *P.S. If you get out of this alive, let's meet for a return engagement in the Sargasso Sea.*

"O.B.E.?" I squawked. Who on Earth had Urdmann blackmailed to get an Order of the British Empire? He must have held a gun on the queen's favorite corgi. Or maybe he was just lying about the O.B.E. so I'd spend my final minutes in anguish. "That does it," I said. "We're getting out of here *now*."

I glanced at the guts of the bomb, but it was a snarl of electronics with nothing that cried out *I'm the deactivation switch*. Urdmann would surely have put in false circuits, touch-sensitive triggers, and all kinds of other tricks to discourage tampering. The moment might come when I'd be desperate enough to yank out wires at random on the off chance I'd get the right one. But not yet.

Instead, I looked around the cavern, searching for means of escape. We'd passed all those side tunnels as we walked along the cavern's edge; who knew where they led? Possibly into private living quarters for the shamans: dead-end crawl spaces whose only way out was back the way we'd come. If we went down a tunnel and the bomb went off, the cavern would collapse, trapping Ilya and me in a lightless hole until we ran out of air, water, food, or all three. Not good. Or perhaps the cavern would turn out to be the lair of more monsters, in which case the end result would be the same, only quicker. But what else was there? As I gazed upon the cavern, all I could see was dark unforgiving stone . . . and of course, light from the two terrace lenses we'd uncovered . . .

Hmm.

"Ilyosha," I said, "drag yourself to the escape tunnel. Watch for traps but get ready to leave."

"What about the avalanche blocking the passage?" Ilya asked. "You think the warmth of your smile will melt the snow away?"

"Close." Without waiting to explain, I ran for the nearest terrace.

At the back of the terrace, another lens had been covered with hides to shut out the light. My katana blade went *snicker-snack,* and sunshine flooded in . . . or as much of a flood as one gets from the near-arctic sun in December. I grabbed the lens's frame and aimed the light straight at the escape tunnel. Two more seconds to focus—three cheers for arcane devices that defy the laws of physics—then I stepped back to judge my handiwork.

A beam of sun illuminated the mouth of the escape tunnel like a theater spotlight. Ilya, lying near the opening, blinked at me through the glare.

"Does it feel warm?" I yelled.

"A little," he replied. I couldn't tell if he was just humoring me or if the lens really was focusing the sun like a magnifying glass, heating up the blockage of snow between us and the outside world. Only one way to find out: more light, more sun, and—I hoped—more heat.

I ran from terrace to terrace, uncovering lenses and aiming them at the barrier of snow. When I'd done a dozen terraces on the lowest level, I pulled myself up to the next highest tier and repeated my rounds. One by one, beams of light converged on the frozen wall that sealed off our escape; one by one, the heat sources accumulated, combining their thermal strength. Ilya was forced to crawl back from the tunnel mouth: first, to remove himself from the increasingly toasty brilliance of the lenses, then to avoid the meltwater and toppling chunks of ice that fell from the hole once the weight began to loosen.

Meanwhile, I kept an eye on my watch. Urdmann's note said the bomb would go off in ten minutes. Under other circumstances, that might be a lie—Urdmann would cheat for cheating's sake, promising ten minutes but setting the detonator for nine. Or two. In this situation, however, I believed he'd allow the full time. He wanted to prolong our suffering; he wanted to savor the thought of us wallowing in despair till the very last moment. If anything, he'd let the clock run a little longer . . . maybe ten minutes and ten seconds, so we'd have a brief moment of false hope that the bomb had fizzled. Then *boom* and the end of all things.

So I gave myself nine minutes. Nine minutes of racing from terrace to terrace, setting up lenses. Then a final dash to the escape tunnel, where dozens of light beams converged with blowtorch intensity. The blockage was almost clear . . . but we had no more time to wait. Over Ilya's protests, I picked him up in a firefighter's lift and threw myself at the opening.

Ice in front of me, fire behind: a blast of heat as we entered the area where the lens lights merged. I slammed against the frozen obstruction, smelling acrid fumes as my parka smoldered. Then the cold gave way and I stumbled up a steep, shadowed tunnel. Clouds of steam accompanied me: melted snow that had flash evaporated under the focused beams. I blundered fog blind up the tunnel; the barrage of light receded behind me, but the heat didn't. Near-boiling mist soaked my face, obscuring my vision and slicking the stone under my feet. If I slipped, off balance with Ilya's weight, we'd both hit hard on the rock— maybe even tumble down the slope, back into the fierce burning light.

And the explosion.

We were nearing open sky when the bomb went off. All my complaints about jungle-hot steam seemed trivial in the face of the skin-searing fireball that burst up the shaft behind us. It threw Ilya and me the last few paces, tossing us out onto oozy mud that had melted under earlier gushes of heat. Even so, the flaming eruption that reached the surface could only have been a tiny fraction of what ripped through the cavern below. It was no fifteen-megaton blast—nothing to make seismographs dance around the world—but the ground beneath us shuddered, and I dug my fingers into the mud to hold on.

Nearby, the frozen lake cracked. Its flat sheet of ice collapsed; Urdmann's bomb must have ruptured the cavern's roof under the lake. A slurry of mud, ice, and near-frozen water gushed down into the caves, filling them after all these years: blotting out the murals and all other traces of the underground civilization. Perhaps some vestiges would survive—I'd pass the word to archaeologist friends who might like to mount an expedition—but I doubted there'd be much to find. Any remaining mammoths, saber tooths, and other monsters would be drowned in the deluge . . . nibbled by fish and reduced to gnawed bones, just like all the other prehistoric carcasses that turn up each year in Siberia.

Another Tunguska enigma.

I helped Ilya to his feet. Slightly burned, our parkas in tatters, we started back to the copter.

# 8

## THE SARGASSO SEA: ABOARD *UNAUTHORIZED INTERVENTION*

Two days later—give or take a few hours lost to time zones, jet lag, and the international date line—I stood on the deck of the good ship *Unauthorized Intervention,* tossed by the North Atlantic.

According to maritime registries, *Unauthorized Intervention* was a private yacht owned by Lord Horatio Nelson-Kent, Viscount of Aylsford, retired rear admiral of the Royal Navy. According to Lord Horatio, the ship was a man-of-war, loyally serving the Crown whether the Crown liked it or not. *UI* sailed the world in search of trouble—pirates to hunt, atrocities to quash, shipwrecked sailors to rescue—crewed by thirty stalwarts like Lord H. himself: ex–Royal Navy or ex–Royal Marines, retired but still fighting the good fight.

Don't get the wrong impression. These weren't old fogies spending their twilight years pretending to be heroes. *Unauthorized Intervention*'s crew were hard, experienced men in their fifties or slightly more, tougher than most young bravos half their age. Each had his own reason for leaving the regular services, but none did so out of frailty. Some were put off by the military bureaucracy; some had grown tired of "personality conflicts" with younger officers; some couldn't stand "those idiot politicians" who'd "never worn a uniform" but were now "forcing changes down everyone's throat"; some had simply grown bored with routine and had shopped around for a change.

Lord Horatio enlisted them all in a new type of service: his private go-anywhere commando squad, "protecting Her Majesty's interests" on land and sea. If such a team had been assembled by Lancaster Urdmann, they'd just be malignant thugs, looting and wreaking mayhem wherever they could get away with it. Lord Horatio, however, was a grand old man in the finest English tradition. Like Churchill, like Nelson, like leaders all the way back to Arthur, Lord H. was a military genius who clung to the noble code of "doing the right thing." Also like Churchill and the rest, he was a swooping mad eccentric who might do anything on a whim . . . such as saying, "Of course, Lara, it sounds like a good bit of fun," when I asked if he'd sail me into the most haunted part of the Sargasso Sea.

*Sargassum* is a brown seaweed that floats on the ocean's surface, most notably in a swath of the Atlantic that starts in the Bermuda Triangle and reaches halfway to Africa. This is the Sargasso Sea: more than two million square miles of water calm enough for *Sargassum* to accumulate. Early sailors worried the sea might have places where weeds grew so thick they could trap passing ships, but individual *Sargassum* plants seldom clump together. They just waft loosely like leaves on an autumn pond.

Still, the Sargasso Sea has its share of doomed vessels. Any ship that goes derelict on the Atlantic—whether the crew dies of thirst, starvation, storm, disease, inept navigation, or any of the other dangers that have plagued mariners since humans first plied the waves—gradually drifts toward the Sargasso. Currents carry things to the region, then peter out . . . as if the Sargasso were a nexus of ocean flows, a magnetic place that attracts all loose flotsam. Some call it the graveyard of the seven seas; but from the deck of *Unauthorized Intervention,* it looked and smelled more like a sewage dump.

Night was falling as I gazed over the waters. This close

to the equator, the sun set quickly—a big change from Siberia, where dawn lasted two hours and dusk the same, with no time in between. I turned to say as much to Ilya, who sat nearby in a deck chair . . . but he'd fallen asleep, thanks to powerful painkillers prescribed by a doctor in Alaska. (For reasons known only to global airline schedulers, flying by way of Anchorage worked out to be the fastest route from Tunguska to Bermuda, where we'd boarded *Unauthorized Intervention*.)

I watched Ilya breathe for a few moments, then bent to make sure he was all right. If I'd had my way he'd be resting in some hospital, but he absolutely refused. He wasn't the sort to stay quietly behind while I followed Urdmann's taunting invitation to a "return engagement in the Sargasso Sea." Even if Ilya was too injured to take an active part in the hunt, he wanted to be close when Urdmann went down. Reuben had been Ilya's friend too . . . and there was also the matter of the bullet Urdmann had pumped into Ilya's leg. I'd decided I had no right to stop Ilya from coming along. Besides, *Unauthorized Intervention* had medical facilities as good as any army field clinic. I straightened the blanket over Ilya's legs and silently assured myself he'd get all the care he needed.

"He'll be fine, my dear," Lord Horatio said. He stood on my opposite side, watching the sunset: a grizzled leather-skinned man in a dark gray uniform that blended into the twilight. I'd known him all my life—he'd taught me to tie bowline knots when I could barely walk—and since I'd turned twenty, every year on my birthday he gave me the greatest gift he could imagine: yet another invitation to become the first female member of *Unauthorized Intervention*'s crew. Each year, I had to say no . . . with a kiss on his wind-rasped cheek and a whispered, "Thank you, but I can't. Not now. Not yet." Though I'd visited the ship several times—a few days in Hong Kong, a week near the Falklands, an unplanned two hours when we happened to run into each other on Krakatoa—I'd never taken part in one of Lord H.'s "quiet little operations."

Not until now. Now we were headed into dangerous seas: where the Sargasso intersected the Bermuda Triangle. Last known location of the bronze man's lower leg.

Once upon a time—400 B.C. or earlier, according to Reuben's notes—the leg had been a secret treasure of Carthage. The city's priesthood had used their bronze talisman more cautiously than the shamans of Tunguska; Carthage chose a look-but-don't-touch approach that saved them from Siberian-style degeneration. Still, the leg's influence gave its owners an advantage over their neighbors. In the course of a few centuries, Carthage grew from a small North African town to a major Mediterranean power: a rich city-state, one of the greatest trading ports of its day, with outposts reaching from the Middle East to Spain.

Too bad for Carthage it shared the region with another rich city-state, equally adept at trading and expansion: the feisty Republic of Rome.

The two cities began battling each other in 264 B.C., at the start of what's called the First Punic War. The fighting continued off and on for more than a century until in 146 B.C., Rome finally came out on top, crushing its enemy's army and navy. To make sure Carthage never caused trouble again, Roman legions demolished the city and scattered the people; but the night before Rome's scorched-earth invasion, Carthaginian priests loaded their most sacred treasures onto a fast trireme and sailed off under cover of darkness.

One of those treasures was the bronze leg, pulsing with arcane power. Perhaps that fluky power was what allowed the galley to slip past the Roman fleet blockading Carthage's harbor . . . but even magic has its limits. The treasure ship was spotted during its escape and pursued westward by a Roman patrol. The chase stretched for hundreds of miles, all the way to the Strait of Gibraltar and beyond into the Atlantic. Finally a storm arose, during which the Romans lost their quarry . . . and that was the last anyone saw of the leg for more than a thousand years.

In 1710, a half-drowned pirate washed ashore on Florida's Dry Tortuga islands, claiming that he and his men had sighted a genuine trireme in the midst of the Sargasso Sea. The galley floated at the center of a gridlocked flotilla of ships, some many centuries old. Naturally, the pirates investigated, thinking the ships might contain treasure . . . but they never got close enough to find out. When they came within a few hundred yards, the pirates were suddenly mobbed by "haunts": walking corpses like the zombie mercenary who'd attacked us in Siberia.

The pirates, being sensible men, turned their ship around and raced off as fast as they could. Not fast enough. One of the attacking haunts set fire to the pirates' powder magazine, filled with twenty barrels of gunpowder for the pirate ship's cannons. *Kaboom.* The only survivor was the man who'd reached the Tortugas—a chap blessed with admirable luck, not only getting thrown clear of the explosion but waking up afterward amid wreckage that included a lifeboat, half a barrel of drinkable water, and some not-too-green dried beef. The supplies had kept him alive long enough to get back to civilization, where he told his tale to anyone who'd listen.

That was when his luck ran out. The night after washing ashore he died "under mysterious circumstances." Some people said the haunts finally caught up with him. More likely, a gang of civic-minded Floridians returned the pirate to the sea, this time with weights around his ankles. In those humorless times, before Errol Flynn gave piracy an air of swashbuckling romance, drunkenly admitting you were a pirate could severely shorten your life expectancy.

But without the pirate's tale-telling, Reuben Baptiste would never have discovered the leg's whereabouts. How could anyone guess that a Carthaginian galley last seen off Spain would end up near Bermuda, almost all the way across the Atlantic? And even if we knew that, how would we find a single galley in the two-million-square-mile Sargasso?

No matter how much we knew, without the exact location from the Osiris statuette, we were still searching for a needle in hundreds of square miles of haystack. The galley could have drifted a long way from its position in 1710 . . . and that was assuming the galley was still afloat. Derelict ships eventually sink, worn down by weather and waves. Any normal galley from 146 B.C. would have gone to the bottom long ago. Only the power of bronze mumbo jumbo could have preserved the Carthaginian ship into the 1700s . . . and how much longer could the bronze energy work? The waterlogged galley might now be lying in Davy Jones's locker, far out of anyone's reach.

As if reading my mind, Lord H. patted my arm. "Don't worry, child. This won't be a fool's errand. The sea's getting ready for something big." He inhaled deeply through his nostrils, sniffing the air. "Some nights, you can smell it on the wind."

"Smell what?" I asked.

"Change. As if the sea has made a decision. Time for things to come together."

He turned his eyes to the horizon, where the last red of sunset was fading. "The ocean's so vast, my dear, it's rare to cross paths with anything out here. Most naval battles take place near known harbors or along well-used shipping lanes. On the high seas, off any standard route, ships have trouble finding each other. In a thousand square miles of ocean, you're lucky if there's one other vessel . . . and how likely is it you'll sight each other in all that great area? But sometimes . . . some nights . . ." He sniffed the air again. "Once in a while, the sea decides it's time for a bit of fun."

"You mean we'll find the Carthaginian treasure ship? Or will we find Lancaster Urdmann?"

Lord Horatio took one last sniff. "Sometimes," he said, "the sea likes a *lot* of fun."

Five minutes later, we intercepted an encrypted radio signal. Its source was almost exactly where we expected the galley to be.

* * *

"It's no code I've ever seen, Captain."

The radio man was called Amps. Everyone on *Unauthorized Intervention* had a nickname like that: short, snappy, and twee. Amps was built like an aging sumo wrestler, huge as he sat at his radio console on a too-small chair; but his oversized head had oversized ears—the better to hear you with, my dear. Like most encrypted signals, the transmission he'd picked up sounded more like random static than anything intelligible. Amps's highly trained ears, however, recognized it as a coded message. The only problem was deciphering what the code was.

"Does anyone on board have experience breaking codes?" I asked.

Lord Horatio gave me a pained look. "We *all* do, dear. And we keep several dozen computers in the lower hold, programmed with thousands of decryption algorithms . . . many of which are supposed to be top secret."

Amps nodded. "If anyone found out what we can decode, MI5 and the NSA would have right massive coronaries . . . not to mention the World Bank and the RIAA. Considering the work *Unauthorized Intervention* does, it's handy to understand what the opposition says to each other. But this code we've picked up—it's new. Fits none of the usual patterns."

"Can you pinpoint the source?" I asked.

"I've got a line on it," Amps replied. "Can't triangulate to get a precise point, but I know the direction it's coming from."

"Thank you, Amps," Lord H. said. "Send the coordinates to the bridge, if you please, and ask the helm to set course on that heading."

"Aye, aye, Captain."

"Also raise the ship's readiness level to Precaution Three." He glanced at me. "We're assuming the signal came from your Mr. Urdmann?"

"That's a safe bet," I said. "I wish I knew where he acquired fancy new cryptography gear."

I wished I knew a lot of things about Urdmann: not

just where he was getting his high-tech equipment—particularly the Silver Shield force fields—but how he'd tracked the bronze leg to the Sargasso. The Osiris statuette was made in 1250 B.C.: long before Carthage rose and fell. Long before the treasure ship fled from the Romans and ended up in the Bermuda Triangle. The statue couldn't possibly have been inscribed with the bronze leg's current location . . .

. . . unless the statuette's makers were more clairvoyant than I thought. Perhaps their prophecies had focused on where the bronze pieces would actually be recovered, not where the pieces happened to be in 1250 B.C. When I thought about it, that made sense. If you were a seer scrying for an arcane talisman, asking *Where is the object now?* wasn't as good as *Where will the object eventually be found?* If, for example, a bronze fragment was currently at the bottom of the sea, knowing its exact location didn't help. What you wanted was where it would finally wash up.

So maybe the statuette *did* tell Urdmann the leg's present location, not where it had once been. And the villain was on the scene now, sending secret messages to someone.

To whom? An unknown partner? A partner who might be the source for supercold silver shells and bleeding-edge encryption techniques? If so, I longed to know what Urdmann was saying.

"Are you *sure* you can't decrypt that message?" I asked Lord Horatio.

He pursed his lips. "I might get in touch with a chap I know in Whitehall; he has access to MI6's code-breaking supercomputers. But security agencies monitor everything so tightly, it's almost impossible to sneak processing time unnoticed. If this was some major terrorist threat, the risk might be justified . . . but I'm reluctant to ask my friend to jeopardize himself over a little bit of bronze." Lord H. gave me a look. "Didn't you do some work for the CIA? Maybe you could—"

"No," I cut him off. "I won't ask them for help. They're just gagging for an excuse to get their hooks into me again."

Lord Horatio shrugged. "You have friends all over the world, my dear. Don't you know some keen young mathematician who's a dab hand at breaking codes and is dying to do you a favor?"

I was about to say no . . . then I mentally smacked my forehead at overlooking the obvious. "Amps," I said, "can you set up a radio link to Poland? A place called St. Bernward's Monastery."

Before I'd left St. Bernward's, Father Emil had scribbled down phone numbers, web addresses, radio frequencies, etc. for getting in touch with the Order of Bronze. I handed the list to Amps. In thirty seconds, he'd established a secure audio link with the man of bronze himself.

"Yes?" came the metallic voice.

"Father Emil says you're good with codes. What do you make of this?"

Amps played back the signal he'd picked up: a white-noise gush that reminded me of surf washing onto the gravel of Brighton Beach. "Did you get that?" I asked when the playback finished.

No answer. I repeated my question. Still no answer. I looked at Amps, but he murmured, "Our link is still open. Your friend must be too busy to talk—probably feeding the message into a computer. There's no way human ears can understand encrypted transmissions."

I was tempted to say Bronze's ears weren't human . . . but I hadn't shared that part with *Unauthorized Intervention*'s crew. Lord H. knew the story, but as far as Amps and the others were concerned, this was just about precious antiquities. I'd told them Urdmann had killed a friend of mine in connection with a hunt for ancient treasure; they accepted that as justification enough for our trip into the Sargasso. Like good soldiers, they cared more about the enemy's capabilities than the reasons behind the operation. I'd provided all the details I could, including the possibility of facing monsters and the undead. None of the crew showed surprise at the notion of walking corpses . . . but then, this was the sort of ship that often sailed into strange waters.

Twenty seconds passed before Bronze finally spoke. "Where did you pick up this message?" There was something sharp in his grating voice . . . a surge of emotion. Could an android feel excitement?

"We're in the Sargasso Sea," I said. I read Bronze our current coordinates from the GPS on Amps's control panel.

"Who sent the coded signal?" the metal man asked.

"We think it was Lancaster Urdmann."

"Lancaster Urdmann," Bronze repeated. He spoke the name as if it was a puzzle he keenly wanted to solve. Back in the monastery when I'd talked with Bronze face-to-face, he'd told me Urdmann was responsible for the bomb that killed Reuben; but after that, Bronze seemed to lose interest. He'd behaved as if Urdmann was just another criminal, a routine villain to bring to justice. Now, though . . .

"Who are Urdmann's associates?" Bronze asked, his harsh voice tense.

"All I've seen are run-of-the-mill mercenaries," I said. "But you're the one who reads Interpol files. They must have a full dossier on Urdmann. Who do they say are his cronies?"

"No one who'd know that code."

"What's special about the code?" I asked. Bronze didn't answer. Father Emil had warned that the android could be closemouthed. "Look," I said, "we'll be facing Urdmann in the near future. If you know something that will help us . . ."

No answer. Finally, I sighed. "Can you at least tell us what the coded signal said?"

"Yes," Bronze replied. "The message reads 'Requesting intervention against bogeys at . . .'" He gave a set of coordinates not far from our own location. Amps jotted them down.

"Is that all?" I asked. "Nothing about the nature of the bogeys? Or what constitutes an intervention?"

"That is the complete message," Bronze replied. "Please keep me apprised of any further signals. Signing off."

"Oh no, you don't," I said. "If you recognize the code, tell us where it comes from, who uses it, what we might be up against . . ."

But Bronze had disconnected. No matter how often Amps tried to reestablish the link, we got no answer.

Night on the ocean can be black as tar . . . especially when the stars vanish one by one behind slow accumulations of cloud. The darkness increased when *Unauthorized Intervention* turned off its running lights—Lord H. preferred a stealthy approach. We'd gone to total silence, even shutting down our active sonar and radar. Our passive receivers still functioned, so we'd hear other ships shooting beams our way . . . but our ship's muffled engines and wooden hull made us difficult to pick up. With no lights on deck, we'd be practically undetectable until we were atop our quarry.

Or at least that was the theory. We hadn't counted on the sea starting to glow.

Dim phosphorescence is common at sea. A ship's wake can glow a faint blue green, thanks to billions of microscopic plankton shining slightly as they're churned to the surface. But this was different. At first, I thought my eyes were playing tricks: imagining light that wasn't there, perhaps in response to the extreme blackness. The farther we went, however—the closer we got to where Urdmann had called for "intervention"—the more we could see that the ocean emitted a soft turquoise luminance: an eerie aqua luster that lit everyone's face from below. It reminded me of a party I'd attended in Beverly Hills, where the only light came from bulbs underwater in the swimming pool . . . the same blue-green underlighting. It also reminded me of a certain Pacific island lagoon where I'd faced, and killed, the nightmarish horror of a risen *Méne*. I tried to keep my thoughts on the Beverly Hills party. What with all the Hollywood types in attendance, it had been almost equally vicious but a lot less bloody. While the crew went about their business, Lord H. and I stood at the rail staring into the depths.

The water was full of glimmering turquoise eels.

Eels come every year to the Sargasso. They arrive by the millions to lay eggs, which will later drift back toward land and, through a complex life cycle several years long, mature into fresh-water eels in the rivers of Europe and North America. I had no idea if December was the usual spawning season, but I doubted it was common for eels, even in breeding frenzy, to shed light like long fluorescent tubes.

"Are they supposed to shine like that?" I asked.

Lord Horatio shook his head. "Some types of eel lumi-nesce, but not the species in the Sargasso."

"Then we must be near the bronze leg. The presence of android body parts changes animals in odd ways."

"So it seems." Lord H. glanced at me. "I confess I doubted your story, dear girl. I've seen queer things in rough parts of the world, but I still thought you might be exaggerating." He looked at the eels again: a vast shoal of them lighting the water as far as the eye could see. "This is no exaggeration."

"It will get worse," I said, "the closer we get to the leg." I went to Ilya, still in his deck chair, and poked him to wake up. "Time for you to head inside. Things may turn nasty soon."

Ilya stood—refusing my help—and hobbled toward the bridge. "Have we spotted Urdmann?"

"We think so," I said. "He's close."

Lord H. nodded. "About an hour to the coordinates in the message."

The ship sailed on, its engines muffled; *Unauthorized Intervention* had special audio bafflers for silent running.

Eels teemed around us, slithering through the floating *Sargassum*. If I'd lowered a bucket on a rope, I could have pulled up a dozen glowing wrigglers . . . which is why I didn't do such a stupid thing. Why would I want a bucket of eels that looked like they'd eaten plutonium?

Dark shadows appeared in the distance: lightless bulks floating on the ocean. Lord Horatio handed me a pair of binoculars. "Ladies first," he said—probably because he knew my eyes were decades sharper than his, but he didn't want to admit it.

I took the binocs and scanned the horizon. Even with light from the eels, I was hard-pressed to make out details. Shadowy forms lay low in the water. Here and there, bits protruded above their surroundings: a mast . . . a smokestack riddled with rust holes . . . a winged figurehead. Ships from all ages of history had congregated into a gridlocked mass, their hulls pressed against one another, debris from one craft toppling onto the decks of its neighbors.

As we drew nearer, I began to identify individual vessels. A coal-powered steamer from the early 1900s. A Viking longboat, the carved wooden dragon on its prow glaring at me in a silent snarl. A tall ship from the Napoleonic Wars, cannon on its decks, dangling moss on its yardarms. A Nazi destroyer emblazoned with swastikas. A modern supertanker almost submerged, with only a bit of its hull above the surface . . . and who knew if its hold was empty or filled with floods of oil?

"What do you see?" Lord H. asked. I handed him the binoculars and let him look. "No haunts in sight," he murmured. "Do you think they're invisible?"

"Those pirates in the 1700s saw them clearly enough. But the haunts didn't attack until the pirate ship got close. Maybe they're hiding belowdecks. Or in the water."

"That's not a comforting—" He stopped. Our position at the rail was only a few steps from *Unauthorized Intervention*'s bridge. A crew member had just come out through the bridge's hatch. "Captain, we've detected a yacht on the far side of the derelicts. They're projecting both sonar and radar. Amps thinks it's the ship that sent the coded message."

"What's the ship doing?"

"Lying still. We can hear its engines idling, but it isn't moving."

"They must be waiting for that 'intervention against the bogeys.' " Lord H. looked at me. "What do you think?"

I asked the sailor, "How far is the yacht from the derelict ships?"

"Half a mile."

"Maybe it's hanging back far enough to keep clear of the haunts. Maybe this intervention can neutralize the undead."

"What could do that?" Lord Horatio asked. "One of those firefighting planes flying over and dumping holy water on the zombies' heads?"

"Holy water is for vampires," I said. "Against zombies you use salt." I smiled. "Get a priest to bless salt water and you've got the best of both worlds."

"Heaven knows we have enough salt water," Lord H. replied. "But the only priest on board got himself defrocked for killing a parishioner. It's rather a funny story—"

"Save it for later," I said. "For now, why not anchor at the same distance from the derelicts as the other ship? Wait to see what happens."

"A capital idea," his lordship said. He turned to the man from the bridge. "Make it so."

"Aye, aye, Captain."

We went into the bridge to wait.

I've never been good at waiting. I considered asking Lord H. if he had a Jet Ski so I could just scoot in and fetch the bronze leg; but getting the leg was secondary to getting Urdmann . . . and getting Urdmann meant dealing with however many mercenaries he had on his ship. Did I really want to drive up to Urdmann's vessel on a big loud watercraft, making a target of myself for both mercenary sharpshooters and haunts? No. Nor was I likely to succeed by approaching Urdmann stealthily underwater—not with a thick mass of glowing eels making swimming difficult. Best to play it cool . . . at least until we knew what the expected "intervention" was.

When the intervention came, it arrived fast and furious.

"Incoming!" cried a lookout. "Missile from the southeast!"

Urdmann's ship was west of us—completely the opposite direction—so where had the missile come from? But there was no time to answer that question. The missile streaked toward us like a meteor.

"It's painting us with radar," Amps called. "No . . . wait . . . it hasn't locked on. Either it didn't detect us, or we aren't the target."

"No countermeasures," Lord Horatio ordered. "Maintain silence. All hands brace for impact."

Neither he nor I were seated—the small bridge only had chairs for crew members who needed them—but there were grab bars fastened to the walls for just this kind of contingency. I seized the nearest in a death grip and whispered to Lord H., "Do you think the missile will hit us?"

"Even if it misses, this could be a rough ride. A good-sized explosion might throw up waves—"

Before he could finish, the missile burst in the atmosphere, high above the flotilla of abandoned ships: not with a thunderous bang but with a gentle pop that reached our ears several seconds later. By then, tendrils of silver mist were showering onto the derelicts below. They fell like streamers on New Year's Eve, some dropping onto the derelicts' decks, others reaching all the way down to the ocean. Each thread had the vaporous consistency of fog . . . yet the fog didn't disperse on the breeze. Within seconds, the area was draped with ghostly silver filaments—an umbrella radiating out from the point where the missile went off. It reminded me uncomfortably of that lethal jellyfish called the Portuguese man-of-war, which floats placidly on the sea surface, but out of sight underwater, it reaches venomous tentacles a hundred feet in all directions.

"What *is* that stuff?" a crew member murmured. "A chemical weapon? Nerve gas?"

"No nerve gas I've ever heard of," another man said. "Neurotoxins are designed to spread, not stay in coherent strands."

"Maybe the stuff is sticky," someone else suggested. "Like a spiderweb."

"Captain," Amps said, "the yacht has revved its engines. It's moving toward the derelicts."

"So Mr. Urdmann isn't afraid of that stuff." Lord H. turned to me. "What do you think, my dear?"

I said, "If Urdmann is going in, we should too. Otherwise, he'll grab the leg and run."

"What about the, uhh . . ." Lord H. gestured toward the umbrella of silver threads.

"They must be the intervention. A defense against the haunts."

"So you hope."

I smiled and drew my pistols. "If not, there's more than one way to stop a zombie."

Lord Horatio sighed. "Very well. Action teams prepare for a sortie . . . and load up with silver bullets."

Our party numbered ten, plus Lord Horatio and me. The men carried chunky OICWs:—Objective Individual Combat Weapons—from Alliant Techsystems, combining the firepower of both an assault rifle and a grenade launcher.

Technically speaking, the OICW didn't fire actual grenades, but 20-mm burst shells—big explosive rounds that detonated above a target, showering the neighborhood with frag—but enemies in the blast radius wouldn't notice much difference between bursters and grenades. Not for long, anyway. Heaven knows how Lord H. got his hands on such guns. Last I heard they were only in the prototype stage, still testing the fire control system: laser range finder, night-vision sights, and targeting computer all in one. Urdmann's prissy little Uzis would seem like toys compared to a full-fledged OICW. I, of course, had my usual pistols and a commando knife in a belt sheath, while Lord H. carried a Walther PPK. Everyone knows the PPK is small, outdated, and underpowered . . . but so are Scotch terriers, and who isn't fond of Scotties?

Ilya made a token effort to accompany us, but allowed himself to be dissuaded—he knew he was in no condition. The Carthaginian galley lay at the center of the derelict mass; reaching the treasure would require jumping from ship to ship, and Ilya's injured leg wasn't ready for such exertions. "No way you're coming with us," I told him. "It's bad enough we have Lord H."

"What do you mean by that?" his lordship asked.

"You're the ship's captain. You ought to stay here."

"When Sir Francis Drake attacked a Spanish galleon, do you think he stayed with the ship? No. He boarded the quarry beside his men."

"He had to," I said. "Otherwise, Drake's men would fill their pockets with the best Spanish treasures and by the time Drake joined them, he'd only get leftovers. One would hope that's no longer the case."

"Well," said Lord H. with a sheepish smile, "a wise commander tolerates a *little* plunder . . . just to keep up morale."

"And the captain is right there fighting with his men. For shame, my lord."

"Lara," he said, "who's the one who calls herself a tomb raider? Do you have permission forms from the pharaohs you've robbed? *This authorizes Lara Croft to pry golden scarabs from my cold mummified hands.*"

I laughed. "Touché. But let's keep priorities straight. Lancaster Urdmann first; looting the dead, second."

"Of course, my dear. We're professionals."

# 9

# THE SARGASSO SEA: CROSSING THE FLOTILLA

We didn't bother lowering a boat. The pilot simply nudged our nose against the closest ship of the packed-in flotilla. It happened to be a steamship, Canadian, pre–World War I: low enough in the water that our commando team could jump from *Unauthorized Intervention* to the steamer's deck.

As soon as we did, the haunts appeared.

There's a gray area between zombie and skeleton: a stage of decomposition where most flesh has withered but traces still cover the bone. Crispy hair dangles down sunken cheeks, swishing past empty eye sockets. Arms look anorexic, devoid of meat; chests are merely ribs and skin, so tightly wrapped it seems as if a pinprick would pop the epidermis like a balloon. Throw in tatters of clothing—ripped, ragged pants or unbuttoned shirts flapping in the wind—and you've got the haunts that rattled out to greet us.

They came from deck hatches or out of inner cabins. One clambered up a ladder from the sea, *Sargassum* seaweed around his neck and a glowing eel drooping from one eye hollow. Most of the haunts were unarmed, but a few had simple weapons: a fire ax, knives, clubs of rotting wood. The commandos beside me sprayed every attacker with bullets. Bone chips flew as abundantly as shell casings. The skeletal haunts showed no sign of dying, but with their legs shot out from under them, they ceased to be threats.

Then a haunt wearing a captain's hat emerged from the bridge carrying a pistol. I fired the instant I saw him; he fired simultaneously. My shot would have punctured his heart, if he'd had one. As it was, the bullet passed through his chest cavity, leaving a modest hole but no other visible damage. His own gun did more damage—the rusty thing blew up in his hand, taking off his lower arm.

The loss made no difference. Captain Haunt continued forward, holding out his stump as if it still gripped the pistol. I lifted my own gun, preparing to shoot again, when the captain thing brushed one of the misty threads still hanging in the air—the dangling strands of silver that had come from the "intervention" missile. For a moment, the undead man continued forward as if nothing had happened; then the haunt shriveled, its skin and bone shrinking like melting ice. The haunt made its first and last sound, a gasp filled with overwhelming sorrow. A heartbeat later, it was gone—no corpse, no dust, no residue, just the captain's hat dropping to the deck.

*Unauthorized Intervention*'s commandos were quick to take the hint. With the butts of their OICWs, they shoved legless haunts toward the nearest foggy threads. The undead fought back, biting at the gunstocks—breaking off teeth from their decaying gums—but our squad had no trouble keeping clear of the gnashing attacks. Haunt after haunt went into the misty silver . . . and each disappeared with the same sad sigh, as if overcome by profound regret. The sound was disturbing, like somebody weeping in whispers when you can do nothing to help.

Lord Horatio seemed similarly unsettled. "Terrible business," he murmured as our comrades dealt with the haunts. "If the poor beggars had just left us alone . . . Why did they try to attack? Weren't they just sailors? Before they died, weren't they ordinary decent men? Normal blokes. Chaps who'd share a pint with strangers in foreign ports. Why would death make them ready to kill us?"

I shrugged. "Some cultures think the soul is made of different pieces that separate at the moment of death. The good pieces—the intelligent kindhearted ones—proceed to some afterlife reward. The rest are cold and hostile: all the cheap angry impulses that don't deserve to go to heaven. A corpse has to be buried properly to tranquilize the leftover evil. If you don't perform the proper rituals . . . if you leave dead men to rot in the middle of the sea . . . the remaining evil festers. Eventually, it gets strong enough to raise the body as an undead thing full of hate."

"Do you really believe that?" Lord Horatio asked.

"Sometimes," I said. "The world's a mishmash, isn't it? Just when you think something's only superstition, you discover otherwise. If I start to believe some monster is fictitious, I soon find one chewing my ankle. If I take it for granted there's no such thing as a mummy's curse, the very next day I have to fend off some nutter in bandages. But if I say, *All right, fine, every legend is real,* the next eldritch horror I meet is just a mundane hoaxer dressed up to scare the tourists. What's sham? What's genuine? I'm no longer surprised when myths come true, but I get tired sorting things out."

Lord H. looked at me a moment . . . then he leaned in and kissed me on the forehead. "Don't be downhearted, girl. There's a line between true and false, even if it's hard to find." In a softer voice, he added, "We all get tired. We simply don't let it stop us. Stiff upper lip and all that. The greatest gift of our British heritage is how deep we can live in denial. Thriving at pressures that would crush a bathysphere."

He gave a grandfatherly wink, then turned abruptly toward the men. "All right, lads, if you've finished playing with these nuisances, might we please get back to work?"

"Aye, aye, sir!" Ten voices clear and steady.

"Very well," said Lord H. "Forward march."

* * *

We didn't actually march; we *proceeded*. The commandos moved forward in brisk military style: hurrying dramatically from niche to niche, never more than two men on the move at any moment, so the rest of the squad could stand ready to give covering fire. Lord Horatio and I trailed behind, trying to keep a straight face. Hollywood had ruined my ability to appreciate this sort of disciplined maneuvering. Even in moments of tension—and we were, after all, on the dark, high seas with malicious zombies around every corner—I couldn't help recalling every mediocre war movie where the same type of scene had played out. I expected to hear background music or those cloppy echoing footsteps that sound-effects departments always superimpose over people trying to move quietly.

In reality, the men of *Unauthorized Intervention* made almost no noise at all; their boots barely whispered and their gear was packed to prevent the smallest rattle. The only disturbance they couldn't avoid was the occasional creak of aged deck planks under their body weights . . . and such missteps were usually hidden by innumerable other creaks caused by wave and wind. Even in calm weather, old ships make an unholy racket.

And some of these ships were *ancient*. The Carthaginian galley was the oldest, but over the years, the bronze leg's power had attracted dozens of other vessels. You'd think that the ships would be clustered by age, with the earliest in the middle and later ones accumulating at the outer edges like the rings of a tree. Not so. Currents slowly swirled the flotilla so that the ships shifted positions over time. Our group clambered from that early-twentieth-century steamer down to the Viking longboat I'd seen earlier, then up the side of a wooden schooner that I guessed dated from the sixteen or seventeen hundreds. Foolishly, I let myself breathe a sigh of relief once we'd passed the longboat; I'd been so worried about an attack from ax-wielding undead Norsemen that I didn't think about what might wait for us on the schooner next door.

It had been a slave ship. Its hold had contained more

than two hundred Africans crammed into an overcrowded hell. On an average slaver voyage, 10 to 20 percent of the living cargo died from disease, starvation, heat prostration, and asphyxia. On the last voyage of *this* ship, some unknown disaster had far surpassed the average. Every soul on board had perished—cargo and crew—before the bronze's arcane influence raised them again.

Death had erased the social barriers between people above decks and below. Padlocked hatches lay smashed open, releasing the skeletal slaves to mingle with their rotting masters. White-skinned and black-skinned haunts stood shoulder to shoulder on the schooner's deck, as if time had brought brotherhood and forgiveness. But there was no forgiveness in those hollow-pitted eyes. As the first of our squad swung over the railing, hundreds of undead attacked.

Five seconds of carnage ensued. Bursts from ten OICWs in assault-rifle mode. Explosive and incendiary rounds from me. We mowed down a horde, most of whom were slaves: men and women . . . naked, lice ridden . . . hideously emaciated. Did their gauntness come from the natural withering of death or from weeks of starvation while still alive? It made me gag to massacre these blameless victims, and to do it face-to-face—some of the people within arm's reach—as if I'd become a slaver myself, heaping new indignities on innocents. Shooting black legs off black bodies and trying not to retch.

Five seconds only. Then with some vestige of intelligence, those who were still intact realized they couldn't stand against our gunfire. They stopped in their tracks as if trying to decide what to do next.

Fractured body parts surrounded us: shot-off limbs, heads, torsos, heaped up like a knee-high rampart between us and the haunts. Most of the parts still twitched. Hands reached blindly for something to attack, while mouths bared rickety grimaces of cracked yellow teeth. Two dozen zombies were out of the fight; two hundred or more remained. Just waiting for an opening.

Two of our own men were down . . . not dead but battered by the mob's front line. The men had been clubbed, punched, kicked, before the rest of our team could rescue them. Someone was already binding their wounds. Someone else was signaling *Unauthorized Intervention* on a laser comm link, requesting a stretcher crew. Lord Horatio's men would evacuate the wounded in brisk, orderly fashion.

But that wasn't our most pressing problem. We stood at the slave ship's rail, surrounded by a half ring of haunts who kept their distance but still seemed eager to spill our blood. They blocked our only route forward. We had the option of retreating: going back to our own ship and sailing around the flotilla's edge until we could approach at a new angle. But that would waste time, while Urdmann and his lackeys raced to grab the treasure. Besides, the moment we tried to withdraw, the undead would attack again—I had no doubt of that. More carnage. More chance that we'd take casualties.

Did we have an alternative? Three or four zombie-killing strands dangled onto the slave ship's deck like foggy rigging ropes. They'd likely obliterated a few haunts when they first appeared, but now the undead knew to keep their distance. How could we force hundreds of shambling corpses into those few strings of silver?

A man on my right cleared his throat. "Captain," he said to Lord H., "should we use burst shells?"

His lordship shuddered. He must have been picturing what bursters would do to the naked people. Men and women sliced by shrapnel. A repugnant possibility. A dangerous one, too—like using grenades in close quarters. Perhaps some of our squad could fire bursters at the rear half of the undead crowd, while the rest of our men gunned down the front; but it would be the stuff of nightmares, a cold-blooded atrocity. The weaponless, defenseless haunts looked too much like real slaves. None of us wanted the image of their deaths on our conscience.

And yet, what other option did we have?

"All right." Lord Horatio sighed. "I suppose we have to—"

He was interrupted by the deck heaving violently beneath our feet. I kept my balance by grabbing the ship's rail. Most of our squad did the same, but the haunts—slow to react with their deadened brains—toppled like dominos. Some fell against misty threads of silver and disappeared from the world. The rest ended in a muddle, arms and legs tangled, fighting to regain their feet.

Before they managed to do so, a huge form rose in front of the schooner's prow, like a whale surging up from the depths: as big as an obelisk five stories high, draped with *Sargassum* and glowing a faint blue.

Not a whale—a giant eel. Yet another monstrosity created by living too close to a chunk of bronze.

For several seconds, the eel stared down as if trying to understand what it was seeing. Its head turned slowly, scanning the deck. To have grown so large, the eel must have lived many years near the bronze leg . . . but it gazed at the haunts as if it had never seen such creatures before. Maybe it hadn't; maybe it had spent its whole life underwater and this was the first time it ever stuck its head above the surface. It might have preferred to live at a particular depth and pressure—so deep it had never been aware of the upper world. Then it heard the blasts of our gunfire and had been drawn to the noise or, perhaps, to the bits of zombie that had fallen over the sides of the ships to sink into the depths like dry fish food trickled into an aquarium.

Now the eel leaned in for a close look. "Hold your fire!" Lord Horatio whispered. "No sudden movements, no hostile acts. Do not provoke it. Do not—"

Like lightning, the eel struck. Whatever its species, it was carnivorous—its mouth, lined with sword-length teeth, enveloped three haunts in a single bite. It lifted them off the deck, their legs kicking feebly between the monster's lips; then the eel tossed its head back like someone gulping a vodka shooter, and the haunts disappeared down its gullet.

I swear the eel took a moment to reflect on the taste: rolling the flavor of undead *Homo sapiens* in its mouth to see if it liked the meal. It did. It wanted more. With another lunge it thrust toward the deck, its maw open to snatch as many haunts as it could swallow. I thought, *Maybe we should reconsider that whole hold-your-fire strategy* . . . then *boom!* The eel slammed down.

In its eagerness, the animal had misjudged its strike—it had engulfed a mouthful of prey but had thrust too far and smashed its snout on the deck. The schooner bucked like a bronco under the impact; even with my grip on the rail, I was nearly tossed overboard. I flew up and over the side, the force almost ripping me free . . . but I held on fiercely and ended up hugging the rail in both arms, my feet dangling over waters that teemed with small glowing eels.

I threw myself back onto the right side of the rail, only to see there was worse to come. When the eel had crashed down, it broke through the age-weakened deck planks, plunging snout first into the cargo holds. Its head was now stuck in the hole it had made; it fought to release itself, shaking the ship as it struggled. Zombies, slow to catch their balance, were thrown off into the sea as the schooner quaked. More were crushed as the eel's body—now lying flat on the deck—writhed wildly in its efforts to escape. Those of us from *Unauthorized Intervention* were out of the path of the eel's frantic throes—at least so far. But some of our team had already been hurled overboard, and the rest of us would go the same way or get squashed unless we escaped fast.

I looked around. We had four commandos left, plus Lord H.; the rest, including the wounded, had already been flung off by the eel's thrashing. I prayed they'd survived. In time, they might be picked up by a rescue party—there was likely one on the way—but for now I had to rescue myself.

"Okay," I muttered. "New strategy."

A rope slapped up against me: a piece of the rigging knocked loose by the commotion. Taking a deep breath, I let go of the rail and grabbed the rope instead, jumping as high as I could. I started swinging like a pendulum . . . and I scrambled farther upward for fear the low point of my arc would smack me into the deck. Following the great swashbuckler tradition, I swung across the width of the schooner—above the haunts' heads and the giant eel— straight into the ratlines of the ship next door, a sturdy Spanish galleon. The galleon wasn't perfectly stable, being rocked by waves from the nearby eel. Still, I wasn't in immediate danger of being propelled into the ocean or worse. I deemed that a great improvement.

Lord H. and the commandos saw my escape. The eel's crazed frenzy had torn loose plenty of ropes besides the one I'd just used. In fact, the beast's struggle was wreaking havoc on everything: the schooner's rigging, its yards, the tattered bits of sailcloth still attached to the masts. Our men had their choice of a dozen untethered ropes as lines flew in all directions. Grabbing a length of hemp as it whipped past was no easy feat, but the men of *Unauthorized Intervention* were experienced sailors. Within seconds, they'd all followed my lead and were perched with me in the comparative safety of the galleon's shrouds.

Not a moment too soon. Showing monstrous strength, the eel bore down and slowly lifted upright. Its head was still jammed through the deck. As the eel straightened up, the schooner came with it, stuck on the creature's head like a hat. The few haunts remaining on deck plummeted into the sea as the ship turned completely upside down. It seemed as if the eel struck a pose for a second—its body upraised, wearing the schooner like an awkward fedora. Then the eel and slave ship plunged beneath the waves, vanishing into the depths.

"Well," said Lord H. beside me, "that's something you don't see every day."

# 10

# THE SARGASSO SEA: ON THE CARTHAGINIAN TREASURE SHIP

We reached the Carthaginian galley with no further difficulties. True, we had to shoot more haunts and sweep them into the Misty Tendrils of Doom . . . but there were no more giant eels, and the zombies came at us in manageable numbers: no more than a handful at a time.

My greatest challenge was keeping a straight face as we crossed the Nazi destroyer. I mean, really: do other people keep running into undead storm troopers? Am I the only woman being stalked by the Third Reich? Where does one go for a restraining order? When I visit my club in London, I freely describe my run-ins with yetis, T. rexes, and wraiths—other members can sympathize. But if I talk about Nazis, there's only laughter or embarrassed silence. "Lara, dear, aren't you past that yet? Nazis are so mid–twentieth century. You've got to move on."

I decided the next time I went to my club, I'd pretend the Sargasso Nazis were really Satanist skinheads from a drug cartel—opponents I could discuss without feeling ridiculous.

Our shooting undoubtedly let Urdmann know we were in the neighborhood. Urdmann's flunkies had firefights of their own—from time to time, we heard the *trrrrrrr* of Uzis blasting unknown targets. I caught myself imagining Urdmann being eaten by a giant eel . . . but no matter how much I liked the idea, it wasn't something I hoped for. In a world where Unreason reigned, having Urdmann disappear into an eel's stomach didn't guarantee the villain would be gone forever. I had to put down the mad dog myself, as permanently as possible.

I also had to retrieve the bronze leg. If I left the thing here, it would only cause trouble: more undead, more giant eels—and how long before some luxury cruiser with hundreds of passengers wandered into the danger zone? Better to procure the leg myself. I could then hand it over to Bronze. Once the parts fused with the rest of the android, they seemed to stop harming their surroundings. At least, Father Emil and the rest of the Order showed no signs of mutation. Perhaps detached bronze parts leaked energy at random, but reconnection put them safely under the metal man's control.

We jumped to the treasure galley's deck from an adjacent pleasure yacht—an overglossy wooden craft from the 1950s that had been occupied by middle-aged businessmen zombies in ragged velour smoking jackets and bikini-clad undead party girls. I was glad to put such tackiness behind me . . . and glad I'd have a chance to find the leg before Urdmann arrived. "Lord Horatio," I said, "could you and your men wait on deck for the enemy? Set up whatever ambush you like. I'll go below and get the leg."

"On your own, my dear? Permission denied. At the very least, the leg will be guarded by undead Carthaginians. And what if you come up against a giant barracuda or a fire-breathing killer whale?"

"Fortunately," I said, "giant barracudas and fire-breathing killer whales can't fit in the hold of a trireme. I mean, look at this thing."

The galley wasn't imposing. It was about as wide as a city bus, and twice as long, with tightly packed seats along both sides, arranged at three different heights. One man and one oar per seat . . . with precious little space for either. A wooden carport-style roof ran above the rowers' heads—not to protect them from rain but from arrows that might shower down upon them. The roof also offered a place for fighters to stand if the ship was carrying troops to board other vessels.

Apart from the roof and the rowing area, there wasn't much to the ship. On the bow was a battering ram at water level, intended to smash holes in enemy boats. At the stern was a small poop deck, home to the man who held the rudder and the chap who banged the drum that kept the oarsmen synchronized.

The only way to go belowdecks was a hatch in the poop. I expected it led to a storage area just big enough to hold a few days' food and water. Galleys like this weren't meant to carry cargo; they were fast attack ships, built for speed and ramming. In a typical naval invasion, you sent your triremes ahead to deal with enemy defense vessels and maybe to establish a beachhead. Then, when the way was clear, you could move in your main troop carriers and all your cargo boats hauling supplies.

Since galleys were designed for speed, a trireme didn't have much below the waterline—just the bare minimum required for stability. They had none of the amenities we usually associate with seagoing vessels: no kitchen, no infirmary, no sleeping quarters. Most nights, a trireme put into shore and the men set up camp on land. If that wasn't possible, rowers slept in their seats while officers bunked wherever the deck had room.

Considering this lack of space, I expected the galley's "treasure vault" would be nothing more than a wooden chest stuffed into a cubbyhole. Any guards protecting the loot would be crammed into an area no bigger than an airplane's washroom. Dealing with them would be like shooting fish in a barrel.

I explained all this to Lord H. He glowered but didn't intervene when I went to the poop-deck hatch. First things first: I drew a pistol and attached a silencer to keep noise to a minimum; Urdmann knew by now he had company, but why ruin all chance of surprise by giving away our exact position? Once I was ready, I knelt, gun in hand, and drew the hatch open.

No flurry of arrows flew up from below—just a sharp briny smell, intense enough to be noticeable despite the general saltwater odor of the ocean. Water sloshed in the dark beneath . . . not unusual for a vessel like this. Wooden ships always leak a little; the lowest level inevitably has bilgewater, no matter how hard the crew pumps or bails. If it's only an inch or two, the boat is doing fine.

Cautiously, I turned on a Maglite torch I'd brought with me. The space below was as small as I'd thought: adequate for a two-person sauna, but not much else. A foot of water slopped on the floor, moving as the galley rode the waves. Beyond that, the cubbyhole was empty—not a single box or barrel and certainly no haunts or monsters. So where was the bronze leg?

I grabbed the edge of the hatch, preparing to lower myself. Lord H. gave me a don't-you-dare look. "It's clear," I said. "Honestly. Not a thing in sight."

"Not a thing in sight doesn't mean clear," he replied.

"I'll be careful," I told him, then jumped down before he could say more.

A lot of vile things can hide in a foot of dark water . . . but nothing snaked around my ankle or tried to chew my toes. The worst danger seemed to be gagging on the stale salty air—a thick unpleasant stink. I wrestled my queasy stomach under control and shone the light around to see if there was some concealed niche not visible from above.

There was: a floor-level panel in one wall, almost hidden by the water. Two thousand years earlier, it would have been hard to detect—designed to match perfectly with the rest of the bulkhead. Time and the sea had made the panel easier to spot; the wood had bulged and the seams were no longer the exact fit they'd once been. I got a pry bar from my pack—all archaeologists carry brute force—and popped out the panel with a minimum of unladylike exertion.

Behind was a long dark crawlway. It ran the length of

the trireme, too far for my torch beam to show what lay at the other end . . . but I assumed the Carthaginians had built a secret treasure chamber at the far end of the ship. That's where I'd find the bronze leg.

To get there, I'd have to creep on my back or my belly, nearly submerged in seawater, breathing only the foul-smelling air at the top of the passageway—air that regularly disappeared when the wave-rocked ship rolled beyond a certain angle. Anywhere along the way, sea life in the water might make my life difficult. Even ordinary jellyfish could plague me with stings, the usual ocean predators could take a bite out of me, and if I met some kind of mutant . . .

I sighed. At least there wasn't space for a fire-breathing killer whale.

"Need some help?" Lord H. called down.

"Thank you, no. This is a one-person job." I doubted if any of the commandos could even fit in the shaft to the vault; they were big tough men, substantially larger than the average Carthaginian circa 146 B.C. Modern nutrition made us giants compared to our ancient ancestors. Even *I* might find the going snug . . . and, please, no churlish comments about my personal proportions.

I decided to travel on my back. That would make it easier to breathe: just stick my nose up into the airspace. It also meant I'd enter the treasure room faceup instead of with my eyes turned down toward the floor. I liked that idea; if anything tried to attack me, I'd see it coming.

On the other hand, there's a reason why babies creep on all fours rather than sliding on their backs. The human body can travel on hands and knees a lot easier than the other way up, especially in confined passageways. That was something I'd learned the hard way on spelunking expeditions, nearly getting stuck on several occasions. But the passage through the trireme's belly wasn't a cave formed by natural processes, with all the resulting constrictions and twists. This passage was built purposely to let priests worm their way to the treasure room; it might be claustrophobically narrow, but it still ought to be navigable. I crossed my fingers that the high priest had been some fat old man who told the shipbuilders to give him plenty of clearance.

Bilge sloshed around me as I lowered myself to the floor. The water temperature was tolerable—this part of the Sargasso benefited from warm equatorial currents—but I was instantly soaked to the skin. Tsk. My clothes would end up with unsightly salt stains. How embarrassing.

With pistol in one hand and Maglite in the other, pushing my little backpack ahead of me, I threaded myself into the passageway arms first. Reluctantly, I turned the light off; much as I liked to see my surroundings, the glow might alert undead guards of my approach. Better to make my way stealthily. At least I didn't have to worry about being absolutely silent—with the creak of the ship and the splash of the sea, any noise I made would be lost in the general hubbub.

I thrust my way into the darkness, propelling myself by leg power: the soles of my feet on the floor, pushing backward. Once I was fully inside the passage I could only bend my knees halfway, making it impossible to get a really good shove. Luckily, I didn't need much strength. The water wasn't deep enough to float me off the floor, but it buoyed me sufficiently to take most of my weight. Featherlight, I walked myself down the lightless tunnel, willing my brain not to think of all the things that could go wrong.

The worst part was trying to breathe. The piercing salt stench stunk so badly, I breathed through my mouth instead of my nose . . . but with the blackness of the shaft and the rolling of the waves, I had difficulty telling when there was actually enough air to grab a good inhalation. I ended up spluttering on several occasions when I timed the ship's movements incorrectly. Salt water in the lungs is nasty; it burns like a fist of hot coals.

But slowly I slid toward my goal, still pushing my backpack ahead of me. Though I couldn't see, I could gauge my progress by touch: wooden ribs ran across the shaft's roof every foot and a half—that distance the Egyptians called a cubit. I counted sixty cubits before a change in the water echoes told me I was nearing the passage's end. This was the bow of the boat, home to the trireme's greatest weapon: the ship-smashing battering ram. In Carthaginian times, most such rams had been clad with bronze for strength and puncturing power . . . but it would have been normal bronze, not the arcane stuff I'd come here to fetch.

First my backpack, then my hands slipped out into open air: the treasure vault. Time for a dramatic entrance. Never letting go of my gun or Maglite, I hooked my hands on the edge of the passage's mouth and pulled with every ounce of muscle. I scooted out of the hole like an auto mechanic on one of those trolleys used to get under a car's chassis . . . or perhaps more accurately, like someone zooming headfirst down the last stretch of an amusement park waterslide.

As I popped out I flicked on the torch, holding it at arm's length from my body just in case. That proved to be a wise precaution. Something slashed down, aiming at the light: a thick green metal blade. I let go of the torch and rolled away. Water surged around me, slowing my movement, but I managed to bring up my pistol and fire. *Phut, phut*—the sound of silenced bullets. My shots were so wild I missed my opponent, but muzzle flash succeeded where my aim had failed. The flash was substantially reduced by the silencer, whose job was to decrease the speed of gases erupting from the gun; but even a stifled flash was bright to a haunt who'd spent two millennia in darkness. My opponent screamed like he'd been stabbed in the eyes and flailed out wildly with his weapon.

He was still targeting the Maglite. It had fallen in the water and was now casting wavery beams through the bilge. Its light showed a small chamber the same size as the one at the stern—a chamber I now shared with an undead man in green-rusted helmet and breastplate. He wore nothing but the armor; any other clothes he'd possessed must have rotted centuries earlier. His body was rotting too, especially his lower legs, which were in constant contact with the sea. The flesh down there was a wet puffy white, like that of a drowning victim's. It looked ready to burst.

The haunt moved stiffly on those bloated legs. His weapon was a cross between an ax and a sword, a cleaver that looked able to chop me in two despite its coating of rust. The haunt never got the chance. I shot the cleaver out of his hand . . . by which I mean I shot the hand itself, which snapped off at the wrist. Two more bullets (*phut, phut*) into the zombie's knees—the puffy flesh spewed ooze—and my opponent toppled into the water. It took me a few moments to find the cleaver he'd dropped . . . a few more moments to detach the undead hand from the cleaver's handle . . . then a very unpleasant thirty seconds to cleave the guard into a sufficient number of pieces that he ceased to be a threat.

Only then did I begin searching for the bronze leg. It wasn't much of a search. The treasure vault was smaller than my closet—smaller than my butler's closet, smaller than my butler's valet's pet basset hound's closet—and its only feature, besides chunks of dead guard, was a water-soaked chest attached to the bulkhead. Under other circumstances, I would have teased open the lock using delicate laboratory instruments . . . but with Urdmann on his way I couldn't waste time, so I just had a go with my pry bar.

Final score: Pry Bar 1, Chest nil. The lid cracked open on rusted hinges, revealing a pile of . . . the usual antique glitter.

Gold. Jewels. Engraved scroll cases. A gem-encrusted saltcellar. Two ruby scarabs, probably pilfered from a pyramid. Assorted amulets with Phoenician inscriptions, sacred to various gods.

No bronze body parts.

The leg's apparent absence may have fooled a dim-witted burglar, but I was an old hand at this game. I felt around the floor of the chest, found the false bottom, and tugged it out.

Here was the genuine treasure: reliquary boxes containing holy hunks of flesh; a mummified monkey's paw— let's not think about it—a bottle containing a writhing black tentacle—let's *really* not think about it—and a length of greenish bronze shaped like a lower leg.

I took out the bronze. It was heavy: dead weight. Thickly tarnished. I half expected it to glow in the dark or to give off some other hint of power.

Nothing. No light, no special heat.

Hmm.

In Siberia I'd never gotten close enough to see the thigh, but Urdmann had said it was still brightly polished. He'd bragged he could see his reflection. Scoundrel though he was, Urdmann had no reason to lie about such a thing. So why was the Tunguska bronze as clean as a mirror, when this one was coated with corrosion? Could this be a decoy to throw off looters—a counterfeit made of ordinary bronze, so thieves wouldn't search for the real thing?

I looked around the compartment, scanning the walls carefully. Yes. Another hidden panel in the forward bulkhead. Even after two thousand years, it was almost impossible to see. I could discern it under the Maglite's glare, but someone whose only light was a flickering torch might never locate it.

"Tricky fellows, those priests," I said. I shouldered my backpack and once more went to work with the pry bar.

The panel opened into a hole through the forward bulkhead. A second panel covering the far mouth of the hole opened into the outside air.

When I stuck out my head, I was only a few feet above the waterline—right at the bow of the ship. Beneath me, the galley's battering ram jutted through the waves, slopping in and out of the sea as the boat rocked. The ram was covered in bronze, as was normal for its time . . . and I laughed as I realized where the priests must have hidden the real bronze leg.

Any ships rammed by *this* trireme would get hit by more than they bargained for. But then, I expected the ship's crew were under strict orders not to ram anything—the priests didn't want to risk losing their most prized possession.

I dragged myself out of the bulkhead hole. Maneuvering none too gracefully, I lowered myself onto the ram and straddled it like a seesaw. It moved a bit like a seesaw too, up and down, first inching above the water, then a short way below. I shinnied along the ram, gripping tight to the slick wet metal and grimacing against the sprays of salt water splashing into my eyes. The seesaw motion of the ram increased, the farther out I went . . . but I reached the end safely enough.

"So far so good," I muttered. "But could this *be* any more Freudian?"

Clinging to the beam with my thighs, I bent over and felt around the ram's underside. Sure enough, my groping fingers found an anomalous hunk of metal beneath the ram's tip. The moment I touched it, I felt a spark: not electrical, but a surge of adrenaline that zinged through my veins like fire. The sensation didn't feel dangerous; it didn't feel, for example, like alien bronze mutagens rearranging my DNA. The best I can describe it is that I was struck with a burst of *recognition*—like seeing Picasso's *Guernica* for the first time in person when you've seen it so often in photos, or catching sight of a friend's face in some remote corner of the world where you didn't expect to know anyone. The touch of the bronze leg was warmly familiar . . . something I'd known all my life and hadn't realized I was missing.

I said, "Well, that's bloody weird, isn't it?"

Briefly, I wondered how I'd detach the leg from the ram. The Carthaginian priests must have fixed it in place as securely as they could; the last thing they wanted was their precious treasure falling off into the sea. I pictured myself hacking at the leg with my pry bar, trying to break through ancient solder or whatever the priests used for glue. But

I'd reckoned without the bronze leg's magic and its instinct for getting back home. When I gave an experimental pull to see how firmly the leg was attached, it came loose as easily as a plug sliding out of a socket.

"Thank heavens," I said, "at least that's one thing I don't have to fight for."

I should know not to say such things. With a geyser of water, the bronze leg's most formidable guardian rose from the sea.

Remember how I'd hoped the Carthaginian high priest had been some fat old man? Be careful what you wish for . . . especially when it might mean a fat old man—a *grotesquely obese* old man—who's mutated into an eel.

The transformation was incomplete. The priest's torso remained recognizably human, with blubbery arms and belly. But the monster's lower body was eel-like from the hips down—wet and yellow, smeared with slime—and his head had the look of an oversized moray: gills, beady eyes, and a mouth of stiletto teeth. Despite this metamorphosis, the eel priest still wore his sacred headdress, a tall miter reminiscent of an Egyptian pharaoh's crown. It remained in place with a chin strap that dug deep into the flesh of the moray's jaw. Picture the cap of an organ-grinder's monkey . . . if the cap was wet with seaweed and the monkey was a homicidal fish.

I shouted, "Let's talk about this!" in Phoenician, the language of ancient Carthage . . . but the priest didn't seem in a mood for negotiation. Guardian monsters never are. Just once I'd like a crypt thing to say, "Okay, luv, slip me a fiver and I'll take an early coffee break, wink, wink, nudge, nudge." Instead, the great eel hurtled toward me as fast as a torpedo. My response went *phut, phut,* each bullet striking home; but my shots, whether in the flabby human torso or the moraylike head, bounced off like pebbles on granite. I swear one of my slugs phutted straight into the priest's squinty little eye. It didn't even make him blink.

Nothing I hate more than bulletproof monsters . . . though cilantro comes close.

I ran out of time before I ran out of bullets. The eel priest descended upon me, striking snake style in an attempt to bite off my head. From my seat on the ram I rolled backward, pushing up hard in a reverse somersault that reminded me of gymnastics class back at Gordonstoun Boarding School. I ended on my feet, just like in my first balance-beam routine . . . whereupon I intended to retreat, doing a tumbling run if necessary, back along the ram to the main body of the ship. With a bit of luck, I could scramble up the galley's prow and onto the upper deck.

But luck wasn't mine at that moment. The eel priest's attack missed and kept going—slapping the ocean's surface with the force of an overweight prankster doing a cannonball off the high platform. The resulting eruption of water smacked me with bludgeoning impact, knocking me off the ram in the middle of a roaring tsunami. I plunged helplessly into the sea . . . right onto the priest's home turf.

Small eels writhed around me: blue-glowing millions, perhaps trying to keep their distance from the landlubber in their midst but unable to stay clear because of their brothers and sisters crowding close. They didn't bite, as I'd feared. But their slimy bodies pushed in on me, not just cramping my movements as I tried to tread water but lighting me brightly on every side . . . all the better for the eel priest to find me. He'd vanished after his big splashdown; I half expected he'd grab me from below, like a bad remake of *Jaws*. But the masses of smaller eels, not just near the surface but several fathoms deep, impeded the priest as much as they did me. Perhaps, too, some part of the creature's brain still thought like an air breather rather than a denizen of the sea. Whatever the reason, he decided to attack on the surface again. He broke from the ocean some twenty yards to my right and looked around quickly in search of me. When his eyes met mine, his toothy mouth turned up in an eelish version of a grin.

This time when he charged, I didn't bother shooting. Treading water, I holstered my pistol and drew my commando knife from its belt sheath. It was a knife very much like the Kaybar I'd taken from the mercenaries in Warsaw. I had no idea if it could penetrate the eel priest's hide any better than bullets, but it was worth a try. If that didn't work, I still held the bronze leg in my other hand; maybe I could ram the chunk of metal down the eel's throat and choke it to death. (Except, of course, that eels breathe through gills, not windpipes. I put that out of my mind as the priest bore down on me.)

Once again, the monster reared over my head before making its darting strike. Apparently, the priest preferred show over subtlety—an occupational weakness. At the instant he started his downward attack, I surged forward through the water, not trying to get away but moving in close: so close he'd have to bend double to reach me. He wasn't quite flexible enough . . . and a moment later, I'd wrapped my arms around his eely body, well below the human portion of his anatomy.

I've ridden angry mustangs; I've ridden rodeo bulls; I've ridden maddened buffalos, panicked giraffes, and elephants in heat. But imagine something stronger than any three of those animals . . . then remember an eel is slippery with slime and able to dive underwater.

I pretty much had my work cut out for me.

At least I had a solid grip—not just my arms but my legs circling the priest's slippery self. My nose was pressed tight to the monster's skin; it stank of rotten mackerel, like Billingsgate fish market on a hot day in summer. *Euu.* I'd be doing the world a favor by sending this freak to his final reward.

But my knife wasn't up to the task. I tried; I tried with all my strength. Hugging the eel with one arm, I stabbed as hard as I could at the greasy yellow flesh. The blade skittered off, not gouging the slightest furrow. I made several more attempts—fast jabs, slow thrusts; the knife's tip, then its edge—but the eel had a hide like an M1 tank. No chance of gutting this fish unless I found a more vulnerable part of its anatomy: perhaps its human abdomen or its wicked tooth-filled head. If I slipped the blade through its gill slits . . . but before I could test that approach, I had to get within striking distance.

No sooner did I start to climb the eel's body than the monster plunged underwater. It submerged fast and hard, blue fingerling eels glittering in a blur past my eyes. I had no choice but to give up my grip: the priest thing had gills and could stay down indefinitely; I had lungs and couldn't. Letting go near the surface was better than ending up hundreds of feet below, clinging to a monster I couldn't hurt and wondering where my next breath would come from. Still, I hesitated a fraction too long. By the time I pushed away from the priest, we'd descended far enough to get past the school of glimmerlings . . . into the dark beneath the smaller eels, where the priest had more freedom of movement.

He turned the instant I released him: his long body snaking around, a shadowy sinuous form I could barely make out by the dim light glowing above. One look at his speed told me I'd never make it back to the surface in time—he could swim far faster than any mere human. Instead of trying to get away, I jackknifed down to meet him. New strategy: jam the bronze leg between his teeth so he couldn't bite me, then hack away with the knife ad lib.

I almost didn't make it. The water slowed me so much, I nearly didn't get the bronze leg between me and the eel's snapping jaws. I'd pictured putting the leg right across the monster's mouth, like a bit between a horse's teeth; as it was, I only got an inch of bronze into place on one side of the gaping maw before the teeth chomped down.

Urban folklore says that when people with metal fillings bite tinfoil, you can sometimes see sparks. My mutant priest had no fancy dental work, but the flash of light when his teeth snapped the bronze was brighter than a swimsuit photo shoot. I floated there blinded, brazen after-images dancing on my retinas. When my vision cleared, I was still nose to nose with the eel priest . . .

. . . but he wasn't quite so eel-like as before. His moray head had shifted back to something semihuman. The jaw was shorter, the eyes larger, the gills a little like ears.

Which seemed like a positive development. And since the priest was no longer munching on the bronze leg— he'd let go in shock at the blazing flash—I cocked back my arm and swung the leg to whack him right between the eyes.

Another burst of light: bronze in color. The monster changed again in the direction of *Homo sapiens*. His long yellowed tail shriveled to half its length. His snout became a nose. His conical hat fit better.

*This is brilliant,* I thought. *The bronze giveth and the bronze taketh away.*

So I cudgeled him with the leg, clubbing at any target within reach. A dozen blows later, my opponent was re-duced to his original self: a blubbery man, naked except for a fancy hat, unmoving in the water. I couldn't tell if he was dead—possibly dead for twenty centuries—or just passed out from the shock of restoration. Either way, I took pity on the poor sod and dragged him behind me as I swam to the surface.

Turns out I didn't save the priest's life, even if he still had life in him. A split second after we reached open air, something went *crack* from the direction of the trireme. The back of the priest's skull splattered across the water, courtesy of a high-velocity bullet. I plunged back under the ocean before something similar happened to me. Ei-ther the chaps from *Unauthorized Intervention* were get-ting gun happy or Lancaster Urdmann had arrived.

And if Urdmann could shoot at me from the trireme, that was bad news indeed. It meant Lord Horatio et al. had been taken out of the picture while I was fighting monsters. I didn't know how Urdmann and his thugs for hire could defeat a crack commando team, but that didn't matter. My companions were either dead or taken hostage, and I could guess what Urdmann wanted as ransom.

I looked at the bronze leg and thought, *If you've got any mojo to spare, now would be a good time to toss me a miracle. Remember, I'm on your side. I'm trying to get you back to your bronze daddy.* Which wasn't entirely true, since I still had my doubts about putting Humpty Dumpty together again; but at least there was a chance I might help, whereas Lancaster Urdmann was definitely a lost cause. *He'll put you on display,* I told the leg, *between a stolen Rembrandt painting and the head of an illegally poached elephant. Wouldn't you prefer to avoid that? So why not whip up some magic or highfalutin nanotech or whatever it is you do?*

No response. The leg remained inert. *All right,* I mentally grumbled, *make me do all the work.*

Scowling at the leg's obstinacy, I swam toward the trireme.

I surfaced under the galley's prow, hidden from the deck by the curve of the hull. The first thing I heard was Urdmann: "Lara, dear, I apologize for my man's shooting at you. He'll be punished, of course. It was inexcusable."

*Because,* I thought, *if the man had killed me, the leg and I would sink to the bottom of the Atlantic.* But I didn't say that aloud. I just tried to gauge Urdmann's position by the sound of his voice. He gave me plenty to work with. For another full minute, he kept calling—things like, "Lara, Lara, can't we discuss this like civilized people?" It was almost enough to goad me into an angry retort . . . but I held my temper and my silence. At last, Urdmann said, "All right, Lara, dear, by now I'm sure you've surfaced somewhere and are hiding close enough to hear me. Let's get down to brass tacks. You've got something I want; I've got something you want." He paused. "Say something, Lord Horatio."

Nothing happened for a moment. Then there was a sudden groan: Lord H. in pain.

"Your friend is alive," Urdmann said. "And I have no desire to kill him. All I want is the bronze."

*Oh, please,* I thought. This standoff was bad enough; why make it worse reciting movie clichés? I promised myself then and there, if I ever found myself on the other side of a give-me-the-MacGuffin-or-the-old-guy-gets-it routine, I'd come up with sparkling new dialogue.

As it was, however, I was stuck in my usual role: holding the treasure while somebody else held the gun. My bargaining position ranked somewhere between wretched and nonexistent. I had the passing thought, *Wouldn't it be fun to see the look on Urdmann's face if I told him to get stuffed, then just ran off with the leg?* But that wasn't an option. Neither was bargaining in good faith—Urdmann had no good faith in him.

So it was time once more for a new strategy.

First: reconnaissance.

With the bronze leg zipped into my backpack, I silently climbed up the trireme. The bulkhead had plenty of handholds—the boards were warped, with ample space between them for my fingers and toes. Given the many unseaworthy gaps, the galley couldn't possibly be staying afloat naturally. Only the bronze leg's preserving influence kept the ship on the surface.

The three-tiered area where the rowers once sat was empty, so I continued up to the flat roof over their heads. Soon I was perched just below the top edge; I lifted my head to survey the situation.

Urdmann wasn't immediately visible. Eight of his thugs were. Four had surrounded Lord Horatio. He was still alive and sitting up, blood streaks on his face. His men lay scattered around the roof deck. None was moving. I doubted they'd be left unguarded if they'd had any drop of life in them. All those good men gone—I cursed Urdmann under my breath.

The four remaining thugs stood beside the hatch where

I'd first gone below. Urdmann was likely down in the hold . . . which was just as well. If he'd been anywhere in sight, I might have lost control and pumped a few bullets into his face, thereby endangering Lord Horatio. As it was, I had a less emotional decision to make: Could I dispatch eight mercenaries fast enough to make sure none shot Lord H. first? It was a ticklish question, especially considering that my pistols and ammo were soaked from a considerable time underwater. Misfires were a definite possibility.

Tough call. As I deliberated, the trireme rolled on the waves. Perhaps it was just a fluke of the sea or perhaps the bronze leg grudgingly expended a pinch of energy on my behalf . . . but at that moment, the galley was lifted by a particularly powerful swell. As the deck tilted, the body of one of the dead commandos slid a few feet my way—dragging with him the OICW still strapped around his neck.

*Okay,* I thought. *I can work with that.*

The movement of the ship wasn't cooperative enough to bring the OICW right to me. I'd have to cross a short distance without being noticed before I got my hands on the gun. After that . . . a burst round over the poop deck would go off like a grenade, giving the four men back there something to occupy their minds. Preferably bits of shrapnel.

I couldn't do the same with the mercs around Lord H.— not without fragging his lordship, too—but the OICW was also an assault rifle that could fire quite a few rounds in the time the thugs took to recover from surprise. I gambled that my enemies' first instinct would be to turn their Uzis on me rather than Lord Horatio. They'd find me a difficult target: much more so than a wounded man sitting in the open at point-blank range. If I was lucky they'd never think to put a gun to his lordship's head. The first thug who tried would be the next to fall.

But before that could happen, I had to reach the OICW. Once I did, I had to disentangle the gun from its previous owner, wrestle it into firing position, and sight up the burst shell targeting computer before any of the bad guys spotted me.

Nothing to it.

"Lara!" Urdmann called from the hold. I nearly jumped out of my skin, thinking I'd been seen . . . but it was just another round of taunting. "I'm running out of patience, Lara. We really have to talk. Or perhaps you want me to carve souvenirs off your friend? Maybe an ear or a finger? What do you think, Lara?"

I thought he was a gasbag who loved his own voice. But Urdmann's blather distracted his men, who seemed to be listening to their boss rather than watching for me. Even better, torturing Lord Horatio seemed to capture the mercs' fancy. Two of them slung back their Uzis and rummaged in their pockets, presumably searching for implements of torture. By then, I was already belly crawling across the deck, hoping I blended into the night's shadows.

"Lara!" Urdmann crooned, "I know you're out there." My arms sprouted gooseflesh with the foolish dread that he could see me . . . but, no. The thugs didn't notice me either. I reached the OICW without being ripped apart by bullets. My knife cut the strap that attached the gun to the fallen man. Carefully, I raised the weapon and put my eye to the scope.

Have I mentioned I'd never actually fired an OICW? I've explained that the guns were prototypes—not the sort of weapon I could buy in a Surrey hunt shop. When I first came aboard *Unauthorized Intervention* in Bermuda, Lord Horatio had talked me through the OICW's features . . . but it seemed like bad manners to fire any rounds while we were still in Castle Harbour. Later, at sea, I had other things on my mind—like catching up on sleep before we reached the haunted flotilla. So I knew, in theory, how to work the laser sights, the targeting computer, the range finder, the safety release, the fire-mode selector, the electro-optical day-night viewer with patented blah, blah, blah . . .

Oh, to heck with it. I aimed and pulled the trigger.

A 20-mm round has a wicked recoil and a bang like the birth of a universe. Microseconds later, the burst shell exploded acceptably close to the poop deck: an air detonation three feet above the mercenaries' heads. Don't ask me what the shell was made of—steel, lead, Teflon, who knew?—but the hail of fragments lacerated the men beneath with the efficiency of an abattoir. I couldn't tell if the shrapnel barrage got as far as Urdmann in the hold, nor did I have time to brood about it. The four thugs standing around Lord H. were out of the burster's blast radius. They needed to be put down fast before anything regrettable happened.

OICWs can't fire full auto: just single bullets or two-round bursts. I switched to assault-rifle mode, thumbed the switch for two at a time, and blasted away. The first two shots disappeared who knows where as I tried to get a feel for the weapon—how much it kicked, how high it climbed between shots, how hard I had to squeeze my trigger finger. I was lying stomach down on the deck, which gave me decent stability against recoil . . . but the ship was still rolling on the waves, which didn't help my aim.

Even so, I took out two of my four remaining targets before they could react. Head shots were the only sensible choice; the men would be wearing Kevlar or some other type of armor, so bullets to the body were a waste. I was trying to draw a bead on the third man when he threw himself down and rolled. I fired a burst anyway but missed him. Then I was rolling myself, spinning away from my previous position just before a flurry of Uzi rounds chewed up the deck where I'd been.

The corpse from whom I'd taken the OICW wasn't so lucky. He got caught several times by the Uzi, his body jerking under each impact. Ghoulish though it was, I benefited from the dead man's flopping—the motion was enough to catch the fourth merc's eye, and he fired at the flailing corpse rather than me. I pulled my trigger to gun down the thug while he was still shooting the cadaver . . .

. . . and that's when I learned I was out of bullets.

Ladies and gentlemen, boys and girls, this is the risk you run in borrowing another person's firearm. When I took the OICW from the dead man, I didn't know how many rounds he'd already used, blasting haunts, giant eels, and Urdmann's rent-a-goons. Too many, as it turned out. Moreover, I had no replacement clips for a lightning-quick reload; any spare ammo was back with the corpse, and I'd put a lot of distance between him and me. In a perfect world, my evasive moves across the deck would have brought me, by sheer coincidence, within easy reach of another dead commando and another OICW . . . but in this vale of tears, dice crap out, roulette wheels come up double zero, and you can never draw to an inside straight when you need it. All I could do was continue my desperate roll as Uzi muzzles swiveled toward me. If the trireme had been a few feet wider, I'd be telling this story by Ouija board.

Fortunately, the Carthaginians hadn't opted for spacious sailing. Before the last two mercs could fire, I reached the edge of the deck and rolled over the side. Bullets sizzled through the dark . . . possibly killing some very surprised eels in the waters below, but missing me completely. Me, I just clung by my fingertips, dangling above the drop— a position that I seem to end up in with astonishing regularity.

Good thing I've trained extensively to handle such situations. I let go with my right hand and drew one of my regular pistols from its hip holster. With a one-armed chin-up, I lifted my head and shoulders back to deck level.

The good news is that despite so much time underwater, my pistol discharged its first bullet perfectly. One shot fired, one mercenary down: removed from the fight with an extreme headache.

The bad news is that the fool pistol jammed when I tried to shoot the final thug; and however skilled I might be at dangling maneuvers, unjamming a waterlogged gun at rapid speed while hanging off the edge of an ancient galley is a titch beyond my limitations. In another second, the last man would have shot me . . . but he didn't have that crucial second.

*Whomp!* A fist to the jaw. *Thud!* Another to the stomach. *Crack!* A knee to the face when the merc bent over from the gut punch.

The gunman dropped and Lord Horatio turned to me, dusting off his knuckles. "Got him, my dear," Lord H. said with a smile on his bloodied face. Then he collapsed in a heap, passed out from the effort.

I was heaving myself back onto the deck when a figure emerged from the hold. It had to be Urdmann—the tiny hold was scarcely big enough to hold his porcine body and anyone else—but the villain was now encased in silver.

With everything that had happened since Warsaw, I'd forgotten about the Silver Shields. My mistake. As soon as I saw Urdmann armored in a mirror-surfaced force field, it answered a number of questions that had plagued my mind.

How had Lord H. and his commandos been beaten by Urdmann? The mercenaries must have been wearing Silver Shields, impervious to anything *Unauthorized Intervention*'s men could dish out. Even though the mirror protection lasted only a few minutes, the mercs would have ample time to take Lord H. prisoner and kill everyone else. Our side would have been helpless.

After winning the battle, why had Urdmann hidden below but left his men on deck? The mercenaries were bait—for me. Urdmann knew exactly what I'd do: come in with guns blazing, killing everyone in sight. The arrogant blackguard waited in the hold for my arrival. When he heard the shooting begin, he activated another Silver Shield, delayed to let the armor surround him, then came up to greet me. Now here he was . . . untouchably cold, immune to gunfire, and no doubt smirking in triumph beneath his glossy shell.

At least he couldn't make a speech; with impregnable armor muffling his voice, nothing came through. He could still send a message, however. Moving at a run, icing the damp deck with every footfall, he got to the fallen Lord H. before I could. Urdmann lifted a foot above Lord Horatio's head, threatening to stomp down with freezing impact. Unless . . .

"All right!" I snapped. "I take your meaning."

Urdmann held out his hand. I pulled the bronze leg from my backpack and handed it to him.

In contact with the silver shell, knife blades went brittle, guns fell apart, and human flesh withered to white. The leg, however, suffered no ill effect as Urdmann's fingers closed gently over it. Urdmann didn't suffer either. I'd hoped a surge of bronze energy might shrivel him on the spot or turn him into an eel; at the very least, I wanted the leg to dissipate the force field so Urdmann and I could duke it out, mano a mano. But the leg just nestled into Urdmann's silver hand like a bird in its nest.

Speaking of birds, Urdmann flipped me one. Then, not stopping for a cheap shot at Lord H. or me, he sprinted in the direction of his own boat.

I was tempted to follow. His force field would last only a minute. If I was there when the shield went away, I could pound Urdmann's smug face into eel food.

But the moment Urdmann jumped from the trireme to the next vessel—a World War II patrol boat—the galley's hull gave a groan. As I'd feared, only the bronze leg's magic kept this ship afloat. Now that the leg had departed, two thousand years' worth of leaks were opening. If I abandoned the unconscious Lord H. to pursue Urdmann, Britain would lose a viscount to the Sargasso. If I ran after Urdmann with Lord H. slung over my shoulder, I'd never catch the villain in time.

The most humiliating part was that Urdmann must have planned it this way. Protected by the Silver Shield, he could have killed Lord H. . . . but he'd left the lord alive to handicap me.

"Blast you!" I shouted at Urdmann's retreating back. "This isn't over! I'll . . . I'll . . . I'll think up some less hackneyed dialogue and crush you the next time we meet!"

Beneath me, the galley was sinking. On the deck, four commandos lay dead. I reminded myself this was not some game of one-upmanship.

Good people had died. Lancaster Urdmann was still alive.

That appalling situation must be remedied.

# 11

# CAPE YORK PENINSULA, QUEENSLAND: THE PENNABONG RIVER

When you think of Australia, the first thing that comes to mind is the outback: the vast semidesert filled with sheep, kangaroos, and venomous beasties. But Australia is larger than the continental United States and has wide geographic diversity. In the far northeast, Cape York Peninsula—called the Tip—encompasses mountains, swamp, dry lands, and thick stands of tropical rain forest . . . all barely inhabited. Untouched wilderness stretches for hundreds of square miles: no roads or permanent villages, just a few Aborigine camps.

A handful of visitors come every year for rugged expeditions into the highlands or jungle, but even the most adventurous stay away from the Tip in December. That month marks the start of the Australian summer *and* the local monsoon season. North Australia's monsoon rains are more irregular than the near-constant downpour of India; but when the rains finally come, they do so in abundance. Rivers flood, and the land turns to boot-clogging muck.

It wasn't actually raining beside the Pennabong River—in fact, it was sunny enough to merit my darkest sunglasses—but we'd suffered a deluge the night before and our camp had become a pig wallow. Ilya, Lord Horatio, and I sulked in our tents, inventing excuses for not venturing outside. The Sargasso was two days behind us. *Unauthorized Intervention* was ten thousand miles away, transporting the bodies of fallen comrades back to Britain. Lord H. had anguished whether to stay with his ship or to help me deal with Lancaster Urdmann. His crew had made the final decision: "Go get the bastard, Captain."

So here we were in Queensland. The morning was already steaming hot. My view out the tent flap showed not one, not two, but three crocodiles smiling on the far bank of the river. An equal number likely lived on the near bank, but they were hiding in hopes of catching some leg of Lara for lunch.

Speaking of legs, somewhere up the Pennabong lurked the final bronze fragment: the missing left foot. I told my companions, "I shudder to think what bronze mutation will do to crocodiles."

"Ah, Larochka," said Ilya, "don't worry about giant mutant crocodiles. Those are too obvious . . . too *expected*. The bronze foot will set its sights higher: giant mutant spiders and snakes, dripping with weapons-grade venom."

"Indeed," said Lord H. "Rude of the Australian government not to let us bring in rocket launchers. But maybe Teresa will have some."

"Not a chance," I said. "Teresa might own a cheap hunting rifle, but more likely, she'll just have a tranq gun."

Teresa Tennant was a zoologist I'd met years earlier in the outback. At the time, she was surveying reptile species around Alice Springs; I was being fed to some of those same reptiles. (Long story short: a Cambodian war criminal was hiding on a cattle station. He had several jade artifacts not rightfully his. He also had a fondness for dumping intrepid archaeologists into death traps. The death trap he chose for me featured tiger snakes, an unusually lethal type of cobra. Teresa had previously tagged several snakes with radio trackers; she showed up to see why they'd all chosen to congregate in an abandoned tungsten mine. High jinks ensued.)

Now Teresa's herpetology survey had moved to Cape York. Though she'd been working in a different part of the Tip, she was close enough to where we wanted to go that she could reach us in reasonable time. When I'd contacted her, she said she had all the equipment we'd need to go in country and she'd be happy to serve as our guide. Now we were waiting for her at the agreed-upon rendezvous. It was hot, wet, and sticky . . . the waiting got on my nerves . . . and I found myself wondering why I hadn't chosen a job that conducted its business in air-conditioned offices.

A cockroach the size of a ferret poked its head into my tent. "Oh, push off," I snapped, and kicked it out the door.

Teresa arrived just before noon. We heard her approach long before she came into sight: a white noise that grew to a hum, then a roar. Overcome by curiosity, we slogged our muddy way to the riverbank to see what was coming toward us.

It was an airboat: one of those wonderful watercraft with a huge fan mounted behind the driver's seat. This was the superdeluxe size, with room for four people and even a small amount of space to store equipment. It was loud, dangerous, and calling my name.

*"Bogemoi,"* Ilya muttered. "That's worse than a snow-mobile."

"Buck up, old chap," Lord H. replied. "At least it won't be Lara driving. This Teresa is surely a sensible woman who'd never trust Lara with . . ."

His voice trailed off.

Five minutes later, I was gunning the airboat's throttle, wondering how fast this bad little tyke could go. I took back every sullen thought about Cape York, mud, and jobs without air-conditioning.

Teresa didn't quite give me a free hand at the airboat's helm. She sat beside me on the driver's seat. The look on her face said she might wrestle the controls out of my grip if I got too carried away.

In any such wrestling match, she stood a good chance of winning. She wasn't tall but was wide and muscular:

seven-eighths Aborigine, very dark, dressed in khaki safari gear. Teresa was one of the many Aborigines who combined modern and traditional lifestyles. She possessed a Ph.D. from the University of Sydney but spent most of her time in the untamed wilds. I had no idea what part of the country she considered home; she'd lived in every state and territory, spoke a dozen different Aboriginal dialects, and seemed comfortable in any environment from desert to jungle to downtown Brisbane.

Teresa was more than just smart and adaptable. Somehow she'd also become rich—not rich as in owning the ten biggest skyscrapers in Melbourne, but rich as in buying an airboat with cash if she thought it would come in handy. When she bought the boat, she also picked up four pairs of ear protectors to block out the din of the fan. Even better, she'd purchased top-of-the-line equipment, with short-range radios in the ear sets and sweet little button microphones like the ones pop singers wear when they're pretending to sing at concerts. The earphones and mikes let us talk without shouting, despite the gale-force winds blowing behind us.

We'd traveled some distance upstream—the river fat and swollen, the banks snarled with driftwood from recent flooding—when Teresa finally asked the burning question. "When do you explain why you're here? Or are you just going to keep playing mysterious. 'Ooo, can't talk on the phone—never know when the line's tapped.'"

"Ooo," I said, "can't talk on your little radios. Never know when someone is listening."

"The sets have a range of fifty feet, Lara. Unless we're passing some croc with a scanner, privacy is not an issue."

I laughed, then launched into a lengthy account of all things bronze and bestial. At the end, Teresa sat back and looked at our surroundings. The river—more of a creek by now, given how far we'd traveled while I told my story—was the width of a two-lane street, with trees growing up to the banks on either side. No birds or animals were visible; the noise of the airboat's fan sent them fleeing. While the sun was still high enough to shine down hot on the water, the forest lurked under its own green shadows.

"You really think your piece of bronze is here?" Teresa asked.

"Reuben's notes say the foot lies up the Pennabong River."

"Lara," Teresa said, "*nothing* lies up the Pennabong River. I have maps and aerial photos of the entire Tip. This area is pure wilderness—not even a tribal campsite."

"That's a good sign," I answered. "The Pennabong is a perfectly good freshwater river. Why doesn't anybody live here? What do the locals know that we don't?"

"Perhaps that the fishing is bad. Or there are patches of quicksand. Or aggressive army ants. Lots of perfectly natural things could persuade people to give the Pennabong a miss. Cape York has plenty of other rivers . . . and it's not like this region has millions of people fighting over every inch of land."

"You're being too rational," I told her. "When it comes to hunks of bronze, rationality doesn't apply. For example," I said, pointing into the forest, "what do you make of *that*?"

I brought the airboat to a halt while Teresa and everyone else looked. In the shadows of the forest, draped with vines and moss, stood a stone statue ten feet tall. Half of that height was the statue's head: square featured with deeply sunken eyes, a long sloping nose, and prominent chin. I recognized the artistic style immediately, and so would anyone who's ever subscribed to *National Geographic*. The statue was a *moai*—an exact duplicate of the famous stone heads of Easter Island.

Except that Easter Island was eight thousand miles to the east, with no obvious connection between there and here.

"What in the world is *that* doing here?" Teresa exclaimed.

"It's likely a marker," I said, "saying either, *You're in the right place, welcome!* or *You're in the wrong place, go away!* Don't you just hate ambiguity?"

"Statues like that aren't Australian. The people on Easter Island were Polynesian."

"Didn't Polynesians trade with the Aborigines?"

"Once in a while," Teresa said. "It was rare—both groups were habitually unfriendly to strangers. But Polynesians did visit the Tip now and then. And you could just barely get an outrigger canoe up the Pennabong this far."

"But not much farther." I pointed upstream; the river ahead continued to narrow until it disappeared around a bend.

Teresa nodded. "Maybe that statue means *Here's the best place to get out and walk.*"

"I know a hint when I hear one," I said.

Landing the airboat was easy: I turned off the fan and the current pushed us into shore. Lord Horatio leapt onto the bank and tied a mooring rope to a tree using some seafarer's knot whose history he explained at torturous length. Teresa jumped after Lord H., while I helped Ilya clamber out; the bullet wound in his leg was healing, but he wouldn't be competing in track and field events any time soon.

Once we were all on solid ground, I let Teresa lead the way to the statue. She was the natural person to put in front, because she knew this type of country better than the rest of us. More important, she carried a Crocodile Dundee–style machete; the tropical undergrowth was so thick, we never moved more than three steps without stopping to hack at the foliage. I would have taken my fair turn chopping greenery, but I preferred to keep my pistols in hand. Lord H. had his Walther PPK and Ilya his AK-47. Teresa made snide remarks about what Freud would think of so much firepower . . . but she hadn't seen the woolly mammoth or the giant eel.

By the time we reached the statue, we were sodden with sweat from the heat and sticky green juices that dripped on us from plants cut by the machete. I gingerly touched the statue's carved stone. Nothing happened; it was just normal rock. The statue's creators had probably cut stone from the inland mountains and floated it down the river on a raft.

"Did you know this would be here?" Teresa asked.

"Reuben predicted the possibility, based on a combination of Polynesian and Aboriginal legends."

"What kind of legends?"

I had Reuben's notes in my backpack, but I didn't bother getting them—I remembered the gist. "Long ago in this region, the Ancestors held a gambling match with the Python. The snake lost everything he owned, and eventually he had nothing left to wager except his feet. He bet them too, and lost . . . which is why snakes no longer have legs. The Ancestors kept one of Python's feet for their own purposes, but they gave the other foot to human beings. A village of Aborigines kept the foot as a sacred object for many years. Then they foolishly boasted about the foot's mystic power to Men from the Sea, who stole the foot for themselves."

"In other words," said Teresa, "your android's bronze foot came into the possession of a Cape York Aborigine tribe. The tribe used the foot's powers in some flashy way that attracted the attention of Polynesian sailors. Eventually, the Polynesians mounted a raid to seize the foot."

"Exactly," I replied. "But even though the Polynesians grabbed the foot, they couldn't get it home. Every time they tried to leave in their canoes, they'd run into ghosts or monsters and have to turn back. Eventually, the Polynesians decided their gods wanted the foot to stay in Australia. They established a permanent Polynesian settlement on the Pennabong River, where they built the foot a shrine."

Teresa made a face. "That must have gone over well with the locals. Thieving strangers steal your great talisman, then try to steal your land too."

I nodded. "The Aborigines declared war on the Polynesian invaders. It was low-key to begin with—just skirmishes in the jungle. Meanwhile, the Polynesians sent canoes across the Pacific, all spreading the same message: *We've got this wonderful treasure but the mean old Australians want to take it.* Holy men and women from many islands made pilgrimages to the shrine. They built a temple and carved *moai* statues as tributes to the gods."

"Which came first?" Teresa asked. "The *moais* here or the ones on Easter Island?"

"*Moais* started here. The ones on Easter Island were copies, made much later. Some priest or priestess probably visited the Pennabong temple, then went home and created duplicates. Not full-size, just miniatures—carvings that were passed down from one generation to the next, with a story saying the originals were much larger. Eventually some Easter Islander decided, 'Hey, let's sculpt big ones again so we can really impress the gods.'"

Teresa glanced at the stone statue . . . and at the vines, leaves, weeds, and moss clotted around it. "Doesn't seem as if the gods found this one impressive. It looks completely ignored." She idly lifted a vine with the tip of her machete. "No surprise the statue doesn't show on aerial photographs."

"The temple is likely in similar condition," I said. "Completely overgrown. It's been centuries since the Polynesians did all this. In their heyday they had a good-sized community, with everything centered around the bronze foot. But they never came to terms with the Aborigines. When outrigger canoes sailed up or down the Pennabong, there'd be surprise attacks. The priests at the temple struck back with 'strange magics' . . . but unfortunately for the Polynesians, things backfired on them. The Aborigines told Reuben a lot of vague stories about 'creatures sent by the Ancestors to drive out the foreign invaders.' After what we saw in Siberia, I think I can guess what happened. The priests had learned how to exploit the foot's power, and they used it against any native Australian who caused trouble. In the long run, though, no one who plays with bronze radiation can keep it under control.

Eventually, it gets out of hand . . . and, presto, you get
monsters. The mutants in this region killed as many Polynesians as Aborigines. Destroyed almost everyone in the
settlement. People told Reuben a few surviving priests
sealed themselves into the temple . . . and it became their
tomb."

Silence fell as the others contemplated that thought.
Then Ilya whispered to Lord H., "Lara likes the word
'tomb,' does she not? Do you think she uses it because
'temple raider' doesn't sound nearly so respectable?"

I gave him a dirty look. Teresa laughed. With a flick of
her machete, she sliced through the vine she'd been toying
with. "Enough jabber. If there's a temple near here, we
should start searching for— What's wrong?"

She was staring at me. I was staring at the vine she'd just
cut. One end had dropped down to dangle in front of me,
close enough that I could see it more clearly than before.
"Back to the boat," I told the others. "Now."

"What's wrong?" Lord Horatio asked.

"That's not a vine. It's a spiderweb. Run."

The benefit of having a zoologist companion is that
when you're attacked by giant spiders, she can tell you
their Latin name. I don't recall what the name was—just
that this species was highly venomous, even at normal
size.

These monsters were *not* normal size. The first one that
dropped from the trees looked as big as a Clydesdale, with
equally hairy legs. Its fangs reminded me of the saber
tooth in Siberia except that the saber tooth had clean white
ivories, while the spider's fangs dripped with frothy black
fluid. The stuff looked like Guinness but probably wasn't.

Four obsidian eyes glinted above the spider's fangs. I
popped off a shot into their midst on the off chance I'd hit
something vulnerable. Even at these magnified dimensions, however, the spider's brain was probably as small as
a walnut and equally difficult to hit. Furthermore, creatures so low on the evolutionary ladder don't rely on gray

matter as much as we lofty mammals; if I puréed the spider's brain with bullets, the beast might keep on coming—legs, teeth, and claws working purely on reflex. Still, I might get lucky and take the brute down. If I didn't, I was buying time for my companions to get back to the airboat and rev up the fan.

Normal bullet. Bang. No effect.

Silver bullet. Bang. No effect.

Incendiary. Bang. No obvious damage . . . but the flash of fire in the spider's face provoked a built-in reflex. The monster backed up a step with an instinctive fear of fire. In doing so, the spider bumped into the *moai* statue—bumped into it hard. The statue rocked on its base: a base that once must have been solidly rooted but had been unbalanced by centuries of monsoons, tunneling insects, and other destabilizing factors. If I pushed it in the right direction, the statue would squash the spider like a . . . spider.

Just one problem. Mr. Eight-Legs-and-Fangs stood between me and the statue. How could I reach the *moai*? How could I get behind the statue and find enough leverage to topple it onto the spider before I became an arachnid's appetizer?

"Hey, ugly," I said, taking off my sunglasses. "Catch."

I lobbed them high in a lazy arc. As I'd hoped, the sight of them triggered some hunting instinct in the spider's poor excuse for a cerebellum. It lashed out a foreleg, trying to spear my specs with the single dagger-length claw on the end of its foot. I waited until the animal's attention was entirely focused on the glasses. Then I ran forward, up one of the spider's other legs, using its squishy body as a springboard and jumping up high to grab the *moai*. My arms wrapped around the statue's head, level with its nose.

For a moment, the *moai* and I nearly fell the wrong direction, away from the spider. I threw my body weight backward, pulling to correct the giant carving's imbalance. We still might have gone over the wrong way if not for a conveniently located tree branch that caught the top of the statue's head and prevented us from tipping too far.

Almost immediately, the statue rocked back like a pendulum reversing its swing. I heaved as hard as I could, using my weight—top-heavy on the stone pillar—to increase the *moai*'s momentum. Below me, the spider hissed and snapped at my leg as the statue leaned over. I could tell exactly when the leaning reached the point of no return: the statue tilted, tilted, tilted, then suddenly started its plunge. I leapt aside as the heavy stone fell, but I didn't jump far enough—I wasn't crushed under its massive weight, but when it slammed down on the mutant arachnid, I was close enough to get caught in the splatter.

*"Euu,"* I said. "Spider spew. Gross."

I was wiping off vile-smelling juice when something thudded heavily to the ground behind me. I didn't even bother to look—it was exactly the sort of thump you'd expect if a second horse-sized spider had dropped from the trees on the end of a web. I threw myself to one side half a second before a sharply clawed foot stabbed through the air where I'd been standing.

"Speedy devil, aren't you?" I muttered. Most natural spiders aren't rapid-attack predators; the whole point of spinning a web is to save you the trouble of outrunning prey. But this mutant was quick enough to become a nuisance. Even worse, I didn't have room to maneuver: the undergrowth hedged me in. I couldn't fight my way through the greenery fast enough to escape my new eight-legged foe . . . and the spider was blocking the only clear path to the boat.

One consolation: Teresa, Lord Horatio, and Ilya weren't trapped in the same situation. They'd reached the boat and were preparing to cast off. Teresa started the engine, while Lord H. released the mooring rope and Ilya pumped careful rifle shots into the spider's back. So far, he'd scored a zero on the shoot-something-vital scale, but at least he was giving the spider something to think about. Each time Ilya plugged a bullet into the beast's body, it squealed angrily and forgot it was trying to eat me. The spider would begin to turn as if it wanted to see what had caused it pain;

then it would catch sight of me again and think, "Food!" It would turn back to me, drool a pint more venom, and try to ram a claw through my gut . . . until the next bullet, the next distraction, and the cycle would start again.

"This is getting tiresome," I muttered. "New strategy." I raised my voice. "Ilya! Hold your next shot until I tell you!"

"What are you going to do?" he asked.

I didn't have time to answer. The spider was gazing at me with hunger in its four beady eyes. Before it did anything I'd regret, I lifted my pistol and fired at the strand of webbing on which the spider had descended. I hit the web exactly where I wanted: at a point just above the spider's head. The bottom of the strand jerked wildly, shot free from the spider's spinnerets. "Ilya!" I yelled, "shoot now! Get its attention!"

*Blam!* The AK-47 flashed. I didn't see where the bullet went, but the spider squealed with more than its usual outrage. As the beast whirled in fury toward Ilya, I made my move: running forward, bounding up the nearest hairy leg, and jumping from there to the loose web strand. I clutched it and swung, letting my momentum carry me far past the monster. At the farthest point of my arc I let go, dropping with only a slightly bone-cracking jar onto the trail below.

The spider, despite its physical speed, had a mental speed slower than paint drying. By the time it figured out what had happened, I was nearly to the airboat, shouting as I ran, "Get moving! Go!" I jumped from the bank to the airboat's pontoon and Teresa gunned the fan to full. As it happened, the boat was still pointed upstream, heading deeper into the interior; I didn't care, as long as we put some distance between us and the mutant web spinner.

The boat moved. The spider did too . . . faster. It raced down the trail with every indication of chasing us to the ends of the earth. Ilya growled, "How can that thing move so quickly? Where's the square-cube law when you need it? And haven't I heard there's an inherent limit on the size of spiders because of their crude respiratory systems?"

"Stop being a physics nerd," I told him. "Where's your katana?"

"If guns don't stop the spider, why should—"

"Give me the blasted sword!"

He bent toward me. The katana was stored in an over-the-shoulder sheath that left the pommel just behind Ilya's head. I grabbed it and drew the weapon just as the spider vaulted from the shore.

The airboat bucked as the spider's weight struck, nearly throwing us all into the river. The monster had jumped at us from behind, so it landed on the wire mesh that enclosed the boat's fan. I had visions of a Cuisinart encounter between the arachnid and our fan's whirling metal blades; but the protective mesh held, at least for the moment. The spider began clambering over the fan housing, venom dripping from its fangs. When the creature's head poked up within reach, I swung the katana with all my strength at the monster's furry neck.

Always thinking like a zoologist, Teresa wanted to keep the spider's decapitated body as a scientific specimen; but the carcass weighed so much, our boat could barely move under its mass.

I let her keep the drooling severed head, provided she put it into a plastic rubbish bag so I wouldn't have to look at it. Sometimes, spiders give me the creeps.

# 12

## CAPE YORK PENINSULA, QUEENSLAND: THE TEMPLE

With both spiders dead, we could have gone back to the *moai* and searched for a path to the temple. However, where there are two spiders, there are likely more. We decided to stay on the boat, traveling farther upriver and hoping we'd catch sight of the temple without hiking under web-laden trees.

So: deeper into the interior. At times, the Pennabong grew so narrow I wondered if we'd get through; but it always widened again, until we reached a spot where it opened into a marsh. "Not good," Teresa muttered . . . and thanks to the radio mikes, we all heard her clearly.

"Do you think we'll run aground in shallow water?" Lord Horatio asked.

"No," she said. "Airboats are perfect for swamps. But, uhh . . ."

"What's wrong?" I asked.

Teresa winced. "This is an ideal environment for crocodiles."

*"Bogemoi!"* Ilya growled. "Or should I say crikey!"

Actually, when the giant crocodile showed up, it turned out to be a *good* thing. We were having a beastly time finding the temple—it might have been anywhere in the swamp, half sunk into the mud and hidden by centuries of overgrowth. The crocodile was like a huge guard dog, posted at the nexus of mystic energy and showing us exactly where to go. All we had to do was get past a carnivorous reptile the size of a train car.

We first saw it from a distance. It was hard to miss—a colossus lying in the shallow water. The croc may have been trying to lurk in the manner of its normal-sized cousins with just its eyes showing above the surface, but an animal ten feet high can't hide in six inches of water. It stood out like the Sphinx above the desert. We stood out just as much; the noise of our fan was so loud, every creepy crawly in the swamp knew where we were. But the croc made no move toward us. Its instincts said to wait until prey came close. Crocs are pouncers, not chasers.

"So what do we do?" asked Ilya. "If our bullets didn't work on the spiders, we haven't a prayer against that thing's hide."

He was right. The leathery skin of ordinary crocs can resist low-caliber bullets; the monster in front of us could likely withstand antitank munitions. To play for time while we pondered our next move, we got out binoculars and checked the croc for vulnerabilities. Perhaps like certain fictitious dragons, our adversary would have an implausibly convenient weak spot in the armor over its heart.

"Nope," said Ilya. "The plating seems solid everywhere."

"It's built like a warship," Lord H. agreed. "The good news is I can see a stone building near its belly."

"That looks like the temple, all right," I said. I couldn't see much with a croc the size of a brontosaurus blocking my view, but bits of gray stone were just visible behind a bank of bulrushes. That was undoubtedly where we had to go. The only difficulty was clearing the way.

"Maybe we can try an experiment," I said. "Take us in slowly, Teresa. Straight toward the crocodile's mouth."

"You're going to dive between its jaws, crawl down its throat, and crush its beating heart with your bare hands?" Ilya asked.

"Let's call that Plan B," I said.

"What's Plan A?" Teresa asked.

"Capitalizing on our available assets."

"Ah, good," said Lord H. "Lara's acting coy and cocky." He settled back comfortably in his chair. "She's thought of something clever that will briefly terrify us but ultimately save the day."

"Yes," said Ilya, also sitting back and affecting an air of composure. "We never have anything to worry about once Lara gets an inspiration." He crossed his arms like a Disneyland tourist waiting for a show to start. "Too bad we don't have popcorn."

I glared at the men, then waggled a finger at Teresa before she started in on me too. "Just drive," I told her. "I'll do the rest."

Ilya got out his canteen and took a long loud slurp. Lord H. lit a pipe. Both put on expressions of avid interest.

"Oh, for heaven's sake," I grumbled. But I took their mockery as a show of confidence.

The crocodile watched as we slowly approached. Just another lazy reptile basking in the sun. Each of its teeth was as long as Ilya's katana.

"Are we close enough yet?" Teresa whispered.

"Not quite," I replied.

Ilya shifted in his chair. "Larochka wants to wait till she sees the whites of its eyes."

"Crocodile eyes don't have whites," Teresa told him.

"Well then," Lord H. said, "this could get awkward."

"All of you, shush." I gauged the distance between us and the croc. Half the length of a football pitch; call it sixty yards. "Closer," I said. "Closer."

Teresa gave me a look but eased the airboat ahead. We were moving up a clear stretch of water with reeds on either side. I couldn't tell if there was enough water beneath the reeds to let us veer sideways or if we were stuck going straight forward.

Fifty yards. Forty. The crocodile watched. Its eyes seemed brightly interested. I waited for signs of movement; if anything happened, it would happen quickly. But the sun was warm and the croc showed no signs of hunger.

It was simply curious about the buzzing water insect coming its way.

At thirty yards, the croc opened its mouth—maybe preparing to chomp us, maybe just yawning. It was my perfect chance.

The giant spider's head lay beside me, still in its plastic rubbish bag. I ripped open the bag, taking care not to splash myself with the creature's black, foamy venom, and booted the head down the crocodile's gullet: a perfect goal kick if I say so myself. The reptile blinked in surprise, then swallowed—the proverbial poison pill.

There were lots of unknowns in what I'd just done. How much venom remained in the dead spider's glands? Would it affect a giant mutant crocodile? If so, how fast? Might the poison simply leave a bad taste in the crocodile's mouth, perhaps provoking the animal to attack? What if the croc *liked* the taste and came after us in hopes of more?

"Okay," I told Teresa, "maybe we should just back up . . ."

The crocodile lifted its head and roared—a thunderous sound of agony. It took two rapid steps toward us, each stirring heavy waves that struck the airboat hard. Then the croc's head slapped the river's surface with a force that sent gushers of water flying. For a moment, I was blinded by the spray. When I could see again, the croc had gone absolutely rigid: stiff from head to tail like a huge plastic toy. Its eyes were closed. Foamy black fluid leaked from one corner of its mouth.

Lord H. favored me with a light round of applause. He was absolutely soaked from the croc's dying splash—we all were. Carefully, he tapped the sodden contents of his pipe onto his palm. He looked at the wet remains, then muttered, "Ah well . . . filthy habit anyway." He dumped the damp shreds over the side and put his pipe away. "Shall we proceed to the temple? I believe the way is clear."

Teresa took a deep breath. We all did. Then she throttled

the boat forward. As she drove to the temple, she stayed well clear of the crocodile's corpse.

Many pretechnical civilizations have left impressive religious structures: pyramids in Egypt and Mexico, the Parthenon in Athens, temples in India and China and other parts of Asia. Polynesians constructed their share of holy monuments, but almost nothing has survived to the present. Blame it on the typhoons, tsunamis, and other disasters that plague the Pacific, not to mention property damage caused by small-scale raids and large-scale wars. The upshot is that we seldom think of the South Seas as the site of architectural wonders. Little remains for travelers to see except bare foundation platforms and tumbled stonework.

But the Pennabong temple was entirely unharmed. It had survived centuries of equatorial rains, spring flooding, and being used as a giant reptile's backrest. No doubt the bronze foot's high-tech/magic power contributed to the temple's preservation, but the architectural style also helped. The overall design was simple: just a single-story stone building shaped like a diamond. No towers to fall over, no grand staircases to collapse. The place was only six feet high, low enough to the ground that tropical storms would pass over without doing much damage. The stonework looked solid—each block fitted perfectly to its neighbors, despite the reeds and other greenery trying to push their roots into crevices. Marsh plants surrounded the temple on all sides and had even seeded themselves on the roof—excellent camouflage for hiding the building in aerial photos. But the temple remained intact, resistant to the forces of nature.

The temple's only entrance lay at one point of the diamond shape. Five *moai* statues stood in a semicircle around the door as if guarding it. These weren't like the ten-foot-high *moai* in the jungle; these only came up to my shoulder and were just heads, not bodies. The entrance itself was a low-set opening blocked by a slab of stone. As

Reuben's notes said, the priests locked themselves in when their monsters got out of hand. Unfortunately, the notes gave no hints on how to get the door open.

Ilya gave the slab a tentative push. It didn't budge. He put his shoulder to it and shoved with all his strength. No good.

"Too bad *Unauthorized Intervention* is so far away," Lord Horatio said. "We have a demolitions chap who could take out that stone as easily as blowing your nose."

Teresa came back from walking a circuit around the temple's exterior. "I don't see any other way in. Of course, there might be a secret door covered by all these weeds . . ."

I shook my head pityingly. "You people have no instincts for advanced archaeology."

"What do you mean?" Teresa asked.

I went to one of the stone heads ringed around the door. I got a good handhold in one of the eye sockets and gave a yank. The head pivoted easily, turning on a concealed axle in its base. "See?" I said. "It's a Neolithic combination lock. Turn all five heads in their proper respective directions and the door will open by itself."

"What are the proper directions?" Teresa asked.

Good question. We tried all five heads facing the door. Then all five heads facing out. Then three facing in and two facing out. Then three facing out and two facing in. Then a number of arrangements with some degree of symmetry and various combinations of the four cardinal points of the compass. Nothing. After fifteen minutes of wrestling the heavy stone statues, Ilya said his bullet wound was hurting so we all took a break. "Are you sure this is what we have to do?" he asked.

"Absolutely," I replied. "If there's one thing I know about archaeology, it's that ancient priests *loved* this kind of puzzle. It must have driven ancient architects barking mad." I patted one of the stone heads. "Normally, one doesn't have to waste time with trial and error. There's usually some carved inscription saying, *I am he who faces the rising sun* or *All eyes must look toward the sacred star.*"

"I haven't seen any inscriptions," Teresa said.

"Neither have I. For once, we've found a culture that didn't print the combination right beside the lock. But if we persist . . ."

It took another half hour to find the correct setting. As far as I could see, the proper arrangement of heads was entirely random . . . as opposed to some simple positioning that looked good but was easy to guess. Had the bronze foot helped its owners comprehend basic security precautions? Or had the Polynesians figured things out on their own, as a smart way to shut out hostile Aborigines? It didn't matter. Once we got the right variation, the slab in front of the doorway slid open with the usual grating sound of stone on stone.

Success. Finally.

"All right," I told the others. "You wait out here . . ."

Howls of protest from my friends. I cut them off. "I can handle whatever's inside by myself. What I can't handle is going into a stone building with only one exit, then finding Lancaster Urdmann and a dozen sharpshooter mercenaries aiming at the door when I'm ready to leave."

"Lara, dear," said Lord H., "you could let *one* of us come with you—"

"No. I want all three of you standing guard. Hide yourselves, with plenty of room to maneuver. Urdmann probably has more Silver Shields. You can't fight anyone armored like that . . . but you can wait a minute till the armor dissolves, and then it's a level playing field." I looked at them all. "That's what I need you to do. Make sure Urdmann doesn't box me in while I'm getting the foot. And for heaven's sake, don't get taken as hostages! Stay out of sight, and run if anyone comes at you wearing a shiny force field. Especially you, Teresa. Ilya and Lord Horatio are a match for any mercenary, but you . . ."

"Me?" She gestured with her machete. "I've wrestled more crocs and won more bar fights than a Pommy girl like you can imagine. Don't treat me like I'm the weakest link."

"Fine," I said. "Go forth and be strong. But be careful too."

With that, I turned on my electric torch and entered the waiting temple.

The roof was just high enough that I didn't have to walk bent over. I crouched a bit anyway. The temple's dank atmosphere nurtured fuzzy black mold all across the ceiling, and the last thing I needed was spores of mutant fungus getting into my ponytail.

But that was a minor consideration. As soon as I came through the front door, I knew I had more serious concerns. The entrance vestibule was small, barely the size of a closet. Three passageways sprouted from it, leading deeper into the building. None of the corridors had a handy inscription saying, *This way to the bronze foot;* they seemed as close to identical as Stone Age building techniques could achieve.

I sighed. This place had *maze* written all over it.

One recommended technique for navigating mazes is to put your hand on the wall, then start walking. Never take your hand off the wall. In the majority of mazes, this approach ensures you'll eventually explore every corridor, while always keeping the option of turning around and retracing your route without getting lost.

There are two downsides to this strategy. First, traversing the entire length of every corridor means you have to face every trap and monster the labyrinth holds. You stumble across every treasure, but you also blunder into every threat. Second, the hand-on-the-wall approach can be defeated if the maze designers know about it. One can easily create layouts that send wall huggers in a big devious circle, eventually leading them back to the starting point without ever entering the vault at the labyrinth's center.

Personally, I prefer to deal with mazes by not playing the game. I head straight toward the middle, bashing through any walls that get in my way. (The guards at Hampton Court still have me under a restraining order.) But the full-speed-ahead approach isn't an option in a building with stone-block walls. I'd have to use a more controlled algorithm: something methodical and thorough.

Drat. That didn't sound like much fun. "Hey, foot!" I shouted. "You want to be found, yeah? So why not give me some help?"

I waited. Nothing obvious happened. And yet . . .

I turned off my torch. Dimly, the left-hand corridor was lit with a ghostly bronze glow.

"Ta," I said, and started in the highlighted direction. It was only a few minutes later I realized I'd made the same mistake as dozens of shamans down through the ages: I'd invoked bronze energy for my own convenience without worrying about possible side effects.

Oops.

The bronze glow led me through the expected maze of twisty little passages. Nothing attacked. No eldritch horrors lurked in the shadows. I didn't even have to avoid scythes swinging out from the walls or spiked pits opening beneath my feet. It was enough to make a girl feel neglected. But I pushed on regardless, until a furious racket broke out up-ahead.

*Bang, bang, bang, bang, bang.* Unmistakably, the sound of gunshots. In the middle of this Stone Age temple, persons unknown were engaging in an anachronistic firefight.

Had Lancaster Urdmann got here ahead of me? We'd seen no signs of his presence. The temple's stone door had been shut; the giant crocodile on guard duty had seemed sleepy and undisturbed. I'd noticed no tracks, no boat, no sentries. And the gunfire ahead of me wasn't the *trrrrrrr* of Uzis but rapid single-round shots. Probably pistols: autoloaders, not SMGs. Such weapons weren't Urdmann's style—he preferred the sloppy overkill of full-auto blast ups. So who was shooting whom? And why?

The gunfight lasted at most ten seconds. During that

time I raced forward, trusting that the shots would cover any sounds I made. As I came to a corner, a bullet nearly parted my hair—it spanged off the wall in front of me and went zinging down the corridor, bouncing three more times before exhausting its momentum. I threw myself back, expecting more shots . . . but none came. That last bullet had been an accidental ricochet, not aimed at me.

Then silence. The firing stopped. I waited, my back against the wall, holding my breath as I listened. The bronze glow around the corner seemed very bright. The sound quality around the corner seemed different too— not the cramped atmosphere of narrow passageways, but something more open. I suspected I'd reached the center of the maze: the room where the foot was kept. Someone with a gun was in there. I heard the familiar spring-loaded sound of an ammunition clip being ejected and a new clip getting shoved in to replace the old one.

Carefully, I peeked around the corner. The first thing I saw was a corpse—a bony brown-skinned man with an elaborate headdress, his face demolished by bullets and his legs shot off at the knees. *Zombie priest,* I thought: one of the Polynesians who'd locked himself into this temple. He'd died of thirst or starvation, then had come back un-dead, thanks to the power of bronze.

As I watched, a figure appeared and nudged the priest with a booted foot, making sure the corpse was truly dead. I recognized the boot. I also recognized the bare leg, the hip holsters, and the stylish-but-functional leather shorts. I even recognized the pistols and ponytail. The only thing I didn't recognize was the glowing bronze sheen that cov-ered her: like a layer of copper paint coating the woman's skin, clothes, and even her guns.

A bronze rendition of me. Metallic Lara. *Hurrah,* I thought. *I've got an evil twin.*

Well, why not a Lara look-alike? The bronze body parts seemed to like making new versions of nearby life-forms. Now that I thought about it, I *had* invoked the foot's power for help navigating the labyrinth. Perhaps that was considered an invitation for the foot to duplicate me. Or perhaps the foot had just decided to cause some mischief. Whatever the reason, I was now facing a bronze version of myself, complete with my favorite pistols: my beautiful voice-activated VADS. They could blow me to bits in the blink of an eye . . . and my bronze-coated double was likely just as good a shot as I was.

She was also likely bulletproof. Most bronze mutants were. If I tried to shoot her and my bullets bounced off, I'd lose the one advantage I had: the factor of surprise. My doppelgänger didn't know I was here . . . so I'd get one chance, one split second, to catch her off guard.

Too bad. I wished I could start with a peaceful approach. After all, she was *me.* Sort of. She might be willing to talk rather than shoot; she might be a rational human being. Well, a rational *something,* anyway. But so far, every bronze mutant I'd met had been 100 percent homicidal. The mammoth, the eel things, the spiders, the undead—all had attacked on sight. This Lara was likely the same.

So I couldn't risk making nice with my double. I had to put her down. Quickly. If I allowed her time to react, she'd start shooting. That would be bad. Whatever type of ammo she fired at me, I knew I wouldn't like it: silver bullets, incendiaries, explosive rounds, plain old lead . . .

Suddenly, I smiled. My lovely VADS pistols were keyed to the sound of my own voice.

I holstered my guns. Then I whipped around the corner and charged my evil twin. As I did, I shouted, "Blanks!"

Time flows oddly during a fight. Sometimes it runs impossibly fast; sometimes it crawls in slow motion. Often it seems to do both simultaneously—a sluggish blur of flashing moments.

Flash 1: My first view of the scene. A room the size of a modest study. The bullet-ridden bodies of three priest zombies sprawled on the floor. In the center of the room stood a stone altar holding the bronze foot.

Flash 2: Lara Croft the second. "Dark" Lara. She raised her guns as I raced toward her. I don't think she realized what I'd just yelled. I dearly hoped the VADS voice sensors were quicker on the uptake.

Flash 3: The pistols went off—all sound and no fury. My armorer once called me a fool for wasting space on blanks in my ammo clips. That shows why *he's* just an armorer, and *I'm* the famous tomb raider.

Flash 4: Dark Lara called for normal lead bullets at the same time I yelled "Blanks!" again. The VADS hadn't been designed to handle two versions of my voice simultaneously shouting contradictory orders. I didn't know what it would do . . . but that didn't matter, because by then, I'd reached my target. She hadn't had time to fire.

Flash 5: My duplicate tried to dodge. I'd assumed that's what she would do. Her head ducked to one side, but the ponytail trailed out behind, making a convenient target. I grabbed it.

Flash 6: I swung with all my might . . . holding on to the ponytail like a handle, flinging Dark Lara toward the altar. If she'd been human, I might have snapped her neck. As it was, I simply hurled her bodily into the bronze foot, releasing her ponytail at the point of maximum momentum.

Flash 7: Bronze woman met bronze toes at high speed. When they connected, something made a sharp hissing sound . . . like a high-pressure steam pipe gushing its contents. The noise didn't come from the foot, which was flying through the air, knocked off the altar by its collision with Dark Lara. The foot struck the wall with a metallic clang and clattered to the floor. But the hissing continued, fierce as an angry cat.

Flash 8: My twin turned around. When I'd sent her speeding across the room, she'd struck the altar and hit the foot with her chest. Now I could see her torso was missing: an empty black void that was leaking away with that piercing, furious hiss. As I watched, the void expanded—creeping upward and downward, consuming my double's body. It was like seeing a cinema reel that's gotten stuck in its projector, where the heat of the light melts the celluloid film. The image on the screen starts to disintegrate at the point of greatest brightness; the melting spreads slowly but increasing in speed; then with a rush, the entire picture eats itself, leaving only bright emptiness.

The same thing was happening to my bronze double. I wasn't surprised—the Sargasso eel priest had shrunk as soon as I'd struck him with the bronze leg. Then again, I'd been forced to batter him repeatedly to whittle him down to size. Dark Lara began to dissolve from a single crashing contact. Perhaps she'd been created so recently, she was still unstable. Or perhaps the difference was that the eel priest had originally been a flesh-and-blood human being, while my evil twin seemed to be nothing but a bronze creation, conjured out of thin air.

The priest had once been real. Dark Lara wasn't. Easy come, easy go. The black void spread up her throat to her face, moving faster with every heartbeat. At the end, it bubbled outward in a rush, going, going, gone. Nothing was left of the bronze woman—not a hair, not a scrap of cloth. Just the echo of the hiss, reverberating down the stone corridors.

Then, even that faded away.

I picked up the foot. It had struck the wall so hard, the pinky toe had broken off. Hmm. But then, Father Emil had mentioned the toes could be severed from the whole. Whoever chopped up Bronze simply hadn't bothered, as if doing a thorough job was too much work. I retrieved the toe from the floor and set it back in place on the foot. The body parts instantly rejoined: a perfect mend, with no sign they'd ever been separated.

"Wish I could do that," I muttered. Foot in hand, I started back toward the temple's exit.

I didn't get lost on my way to the door, nor did I run afoul of any perils I missed on the way in. But when I got to the entrance, I had a sense of foreboding—enough that I stopped a few steps short of the doorway rather than going outside. From the shadows, I peeked around the corner of the doorframe. Nothing looked amiss: just heat haze and water and marsh plants, plus the ring of *moai* heads still turned in the directions I'd left them. The afternoon was quiet . . . in that almost-*too*-quiet way.

Of course, it was supposed to be quiet. If Urdmann and company hadn't showed up yet, Teresa, Lord H., and Ilya would be hunkered down unseen among the reeds. If our enemies had arrived, my friends would be working on a suitable ambush . . . in which case I just had to wait till the shooting started, then join the fun.

I waited. Watched. Listened. Insects chirped, buzzed, hummed. Birds tweeted, twittered, cheeped. Occasionally, something went plop in the swamp—a frog jumping into the river or a fish breaking the surface to gobble a passing bug. Nothing appeared out of place.

Then a gas grenade dropped to the ground in front of me.

I had a split second to decide: out or in. If I ran out the door of the temple, I'd lose my sheltered position; I might get some cover from the *moai*s, but I'd still be exposed to gunfire from a lot of directions. If I headed back into the temple, I'd be safe from getting shot, at least temporarily . . . but I'd also be bottled up. Not good. The gas grenade proved that Urdmann had brought chemical weapons—tear gas, nerve gas, mustard gas, who knew?— and I had no defense against such things. If I fled into the temple, Urdmann could lob a few gas canisters through the doorway, wait for the vapors to spread through the poorly ventilated passages, then come in for me once I was incapacitated. The temple offered nowhere to hide, no safe air pockets for me to breathe. So I really had no choice, did I?

I dived in a somersault over the grenade. When I landed I thrust out my right foot, kicking the not-yet-triggered grenade through the temple doorway. Better for the gas to be mostly contained inside the temple than to have it fill the air around me . . . especially if the grenade contained some fast-acting lethal toxin like sarin or tabun. I somersaulted again in between two *moai,* just as the grenade went off. A sickly yellow smoke coughed out of the temple door, but most of the payload stayed within. Good.

But I shouldn't congratulate myself too soon. Another grenade landed several paces away from me. This time I saw where it had come from—the roof of the temple. Urdmann and his thugs must have climbed up there, then just waited for me to come out. I had no idea what had happened to my friends; probably gassed, just like I would be if I didn't get away from the second grenade. My only hope now was to run for the river and vanish into muddy water. With luck, I could make it to cover under the swamp reeds. Then while Urdmann searched for me—and he *would* search for me, if only to get the bronze foot—I could pick off his men one by one.

First, though, I had to escape the gas. I took a deep breath; I wouldn't be able to do that once the second grenade went off. Then, with my pistols set for explosive rounds, I rolled to my feet and sprinted toward the water. I fired back at the temple as I ran. No one was visible back there—Urdmann's thugs must have been lying flat on the roof—but my shots would force them to keep their heads down. My tactics seemed to work, because no one up there tried to shoot me . . .

Two steps from the river, something stung me in the neck. I had time to turn my head . . . time to see the man with the rifle, hidden in a camouflaged shooting blind among the bulrushes . . . time to raise my pistol and fire at him . . . then my muscles went limp. The last thing I remember is plunging facedown into the water.

# 13

## LOCATION UNKNOWN: A MANSION

I woke in a four-poster bed—a voluminous thing with profusely carved woodwork and far too many flounces in its canopy. The room was dark, lit with a faint ruby light. Floral perfume pervaded the air. I breathed the subtle scent for several seconds before nausea swept over me. Fortunately, a nightstand with a porcelain washbasin stood beside the bed. I emptied my stomach into it, though I didn't have much to retch up. A long time must have passed since my last meal.

The side of my neck still stung. I probably had a bruise. Tranquilizer darts sound ever so harmless, but in practice, they're usually brutal. Think of a hypodermic needle slammed into your flesh with enough force to bury it up to the hilt. Remember that the syringe is filled with some chemical so virulent it knocks you out in seconds. No wonder I felt sick.

But I wasn't dead. Urdmann apparently wanted me alive. Why? The obvious sordid reason suggested itself. Have I mentioned that my clothes were missing? All I had on was a filmy white shift I'd never seen before. And when a woman wakes up wearing unfamiliar lingerie in a bed that looks like it was designed for Marie Antoinette, it's hard not to suspect the worst.

I didn't think anything had happened yet—I felt sick but not used. Besides, Urdmann was the sort who'd want me awake: aware of what was going on. The only surprise was that I hadn't been tied or handcuffed to the bed. If I'd been captured to serve as a pleasure slave, leaving me free was asking for trouble. Even an egotistical brute like Urdmann had to realize I'd fight to avoid becoming his harem girl.

First things first: look for weapons. I found a towel on the washstand and wiped off my mouth as I scanned the room. In the same way the name Marie Antoinette had popped into my mind as soon as I saw the bed, the rest of the room brought to mind French royal decor before the revolution—ruffles everywhere, too much silk brocade, and scrollwork carvings on every square inch of wood. Perhaps the poor of Paris hadn't revolted for liberty, equality, and fraternity but in pursuit of uncluttered design and less crewelwork.

The only source of illumination in the room was a low-watt bulb with a pale red lampshade. The rest of the place brooded in darkness. Two large windows—both made impassable by strong iron bars—showed a black night sky and a greener-than-green lawn lit by security spotlights. As I watched, guards with Uzis strolled past on a sidewalk at the far end of the grass. The guards wore short sleeves and the sidewalk was overhung with palm trees, suggesting a warm, even hot, climate. My room, however, was pleasantly cool. It didn't take me long to spot an air-conditioning vent in the shadows along the far wall. While I was looking around, I also checked for security cameras watching me. I didn't see any . . . but cameras can be so tiny these days, I wouldn't know for sure unless I checked every inch of the walls and ceiling. It didn't seem worth the trouble. Better to concentrate on more productive activities.

By now, my queasy stomach had settled. I was still far from my best—I felt hungry, shaky, dizzy—but I'd collected myself enough to stand. The world stopped spinning after a few seconds. When I thought I could walk without falling over, I went to the nearest of the three doors that exited from the room. It opened onto a self-contained bathroom with sink, loo, and a claw-footed tub. I decided not to look a gift horse in the mouth; I used the facilities quickly, splashing cold water on my face until my head cleared. There was a mirror over the sink . . . and yes, the tranq dart in my neck *had* left a bruise. Otherwise, I was none the worse for wear.

Back in the bedroom, I tried the next door. It led to a walk-in closet that looked like it had been stocked by a movie studio's costume department. Gowns of all descriptions hung from the racks: not just Marie Antoinette–style hoopskirts and petticoats but Elizabethan stomachers, Roman stolas, and Greek chitons; Chinese cheongsams and Japanese kimonos; Indian saris and Turkish kaftans; even an assortment of strapless black cocktail dresses, some vintage, some contemporary. Add to that scanty undergarments; impractical stockings; two dozen pairs of shoes—all either high heels or flimsy slippers; a powdered wig bigger than a Christmas turkey; and enough bracelets, anklets, necklaces, belts, etc. to accessorize a goth senior prom.

My own clothes were nowhere in evidence. Neither were any other garments with an ounce of durability or freedom of movement. I have nothing against fancy finery in the right time and place—but the right time and place is race week at Royal Ascot. I seriously considered remaining in the sheer-nothing nightie rather than hampering myself with frills-and-froufrou frocks; but that might be a mistake. One should never underestimate the value of pockets . . . or a belt where one can hang a knife sheath . . . or dark clothing when one is trying to hide in shadows.

Besides, escaping this place was a high priority—right after feeding Lancaster Urdmann his own entrails and rescuing my friends if they were also being held prisoner. I'd definitely need clothes once I got away. The tabloids write enough rubbish about me already. Can you imagine what they'd say if I was caught trying to hitchhike back to civilization in nothing but knickers? LUSTY LARA IN LECHEROUS LINGERIE! PERVERTED PEERESS SHOWS EVERYTHING BUT SHAME!

As quickly as I could, I assembled an outfit I could live with: the best-made of the black cocktail dresses, ripped off above the knee so I could run in it; another black dress torn lengthwise down the middle and tied around my neck . . . for use as a cloak if I needed to hide my pale face and shoulders in the dark; the three least glittery belts, one around my waist and two across my chest like bandoliers, strapped tightly enough that I could tuck small objects under them for safekeeping; and a pair of black slippers, not on my feet, but under my belt. I was perfectly comfortable going barefoot, but the slippers, turned toes downward, could serve as belt pouches.

The final element of my ensemble was the sturdiest necklace on the rack: a silver chain as thick as my little finger. I tugged it a few times to make sure it was strong. With luck, it would stay in one piece if I needed to garrote someone with it. In the same spirit of improvisation, I removed a pillowcase from one of the bed pillows and tossed some heavy gold bracelets inside. I knotted the pillowcase down near the bottom to hold the bracelets in a single hefty lump. When I swung the result, it didn't feel quite as deadly as a medieval flail but it would certainly be an effective blunt instrument when whipped full force at someone's skull. It was strong enough to be used several times before the fabric broke—hurrah for 800-count bed linens.

I considered making other weapons. With my pillowcase bludgeon I could break the bathroom mirror, making shards of glass to use as daggers. I'm not superstitious about mirrors. When you've been hexed by Atlantean sorcerers and ancient Babylonian wizards, inanimate sheets of silvered glass lose their power to intimidate. But smashing the mirror would make noise; so far I'd avoided that. Any guards outside my door—and I assumed there *must* be guards outside my door—might not know I was awake. My ideal scenario entailed eliminating the sentries without raising an alarm, grabbing any weapons they carried, then playing things by ear. If I couldn't accomplish that with the armaments I already had, extending my arsenal was a waste of time.

Still . . . I went to the bed and grabbed a pillow in case I needed to muffle an enemy's cries before I induced more permanent silence. *Good enough,* I said to myself. *Time to go.*

I examined the final door—the one leading out of the room. Soft light shone around the frame . . . enough that I could check between the door and its jamb to see what was holding me in. I saw no extra bolts or padlocks on the outside, not even a simple hook and eye. The only thing keeping the door shut was its normal latch.

Slowly, very slowly, I tried the doorknob. It turned all the way. Unlocked. A shiver went through me as I wondered what that meant. Why on earth would Urdmann leave me free to roam? Was he *that* confident? Or was he planning some awful surprise I couldn't see coming?

Only one way to find out.

Left hand on the doorknob. Pillow under my left arm. Pillowcase flail in my right hand. Garroting necklace hung on my belt. I whipped open the door and hurled myself outside, expecting to find guards to pummel.

No one. An empty corridor: ornate in the style of a two-star hotel that's trying too hard to earn another star. Rose-shaded lamps hung on the walls but far enough apart to leave long stretches of shadow in between. Either Urdmann liked dim mood lighting or he was tightfisted with his electricity bills.

More doors like mine lined the corridor. I looked through the keyhole of the closest. Lord Horatio lay unmoving in a bed identical to the one where I'd awakened. However, his door was locked. I considered kicking it in, but decided against it. Like me, Lord H. must have been drugged into unconsciousness; he'd be difficult to wake until the drug wore off. Even if he were fully conscious, how much experience did he have sneaking around silently? And with him in tow I couldn't clamber over rooftops or play many of my other favorite games.

No, I decided, I wouldn't try to revive his lordship yet. I'd scout our surroundings first. Learn what Urdmann was up to. Maybe get my hands on *real* weapons. Then I'd come back for my friend.

Quickly, I checked other nearby rooms. Teresa and Ilya were on the opposite side of the hall from Lord H. and me. They both seemed deeply unconscious too. I'd leave them alone for the moment. At least they weren't in some torture chamber, with Urdmann holding a gun to their heads. "Do what I command, dear Lara, or your friends will suffer."

But why not? Why no duress and ultimatums? I hated when villains like Urdmann acted uncharacteristically. What was going on?

At the end of the corridor, a grand spiral staircase led downward: heavy marble stairs, with cupped wear patterns where many feet had trod. The stairway might have been centuries old . . . which suggested the house was old too. I filed that away in my mind and proceeded downward.

A door was open at the bottom of the stairs. I peeked inside. A man stood in a pool of light, painting at an easel. All I could see was the man's back, but I knew he wasn't Urdmann. The painter's body was hidden under an artist's smock, but I could tell he weighed five stone too little to be Lancaster Urdmann, O.B.E.

The canvas he was working on faced my way: a portrait of a sleeping woman, nude. There was no model posing for the painter to paint. Instead, he kept glancing at a side table which apparently held a photo as reference. So far, the painted image only showed the roughed-out contours of the woman's body—her face was a blank pinkish oval, waiting for features to be added. But I could guess who the subject was. Someone had snapped pictures of me while I was unconscious, and now this arrogant prat thought he could turn me into some grande odalisque for the next Salon.

Judging by the rest of the room, I wasn't the first woman to receive this treatment. The walls were covered with other paintings—literally covered, with nary a square inch of open wall. Dozens of canvases, large and small, abutted each other like some mathematical tiling problem . . . and every one of those pictures portrayed a female nude.

The artist showed no prejudice in his subjects: the paintings depicted women of many ethnicities—light skin, dark skin—long hair, short, of all physical builds and coloration. Most looked to be under forty years old . . . but not all. The older women were painted just as lavishly as the younger—maybe even with fond generosity. But I wasn't in a mood to think *What a nice chap this artist is, so receptive to all feminine beauty!* My thoughts were more along the lines of, *You rancid exploitative pig, I'll have your guts for garters. And not* nice *garters!*

The only question was whether to cudgel him immediately into unconsciousness or take some less drastic approach. If I could overpower him without knocking him out, I might force him to spill useful information: where we were, what Urdmann was up to. On the other hand, I didn't know if I could really fight the painter to a standstill when my best weapon was a pillowcase. This man might be smaller than the porcine Urdmann, but I doubted he'd be an easy mark. The painter was six feet tall, and his gloved hand was rock steady as it held the paintbrush. That took muscle control. Besides, the man's loose smock could easily conceal weapons—a knife or pistol slung at the hip. What really decided me, though, was the cad's sheer cheek, thinking he had the right to paint me in the buff. If he'd been painting a landscape or flowers in a vase, I might have hesitated to bash in his skull. As it was . . .

I stole silently across the floor. The painter didn't hear me coming. He didn't hear me wind up with pillowcase, or swing it as hard as I could at the back of his head. I daresay he heard the *crack!* as the business end connected with his cranium . . . but I wasted no time waiting to see how he reacted. An instant after he staggered from the blow, I had my necklace garrote around his throat, twisting it tight with my right hand. My left held the pillow over his face. Whatever sounds he made were lost in the pillow's embrace.

The man never really struggled. I assumed he'd been knocked unconscious by my first attack. I held the smother choke anyway, counting to a hundred before letting him go. When I did, he slumped to the floor . . . just as I expected he would.

What I didn't expect was the look of the pillow I'd held over the man's face. As I pulled it away, I saw its white surface had been smeared with tan-colored smudges. Makeup . . . the fellow was wearing a layer of foundation that had rubbed off on the pillow.

I gazed down at the man: my first good look at him. Where the pillow had come into contact, his cheeks and forehead had been wiped clean of makeup. Beneath the cosmetic tan surface, his skin—his *real* skin—was shiny metallic silver . . . as bright and polished as the silver serving trays in Croft Manor.

As I stared, the man's eyes opened. He smiled. "Ah, mademoiselle. You're awake."

Startled—reflexively trying to silence him before he called for help—I lifted my bare foot and stomped his face. It was like slamming my heel onto concrete. Whatever metal the man was made of, he was as solid as a stone statue.

Or perhaps a bronze one.

The light dawned in my mind. I didn't attack again. If this silver android could withstand choking, smothering, and a full-strength stomp, why waste my energy searching for other ways to subdue him? Maybe if I found my pistols, I'd try again. Until then, there was no point.

Besides, I was beginning to realize this was a setup. My door had been left unlocked so I'd do exactly what I did—come down the stairs and sneak into the first open door at the bottom. The metal man had been waiting, secure in the knowledge I couldn't hurt him.

"All right," I said. "You've got me here. What do you want?"

The man smiled and rose to his feet with easy grace. "I wish merely to talk, mademoiselle. What else should a gentleman do with a beautiful woman?"

He cocked one eyebrow as if inviting me to suggest something. "Oh, please," I said in disgust. "Spare me the innuendo. Who are you, what are you, what's your master plan?"

"Ah." He leaned comfortably back against a heavy wood table that held his collection of paints, brushes, and other art supplies. "Who am I? I have gone by many names, but with you, mademoiselle, I shall not use false pretense. You may call me Silver."

With a theatrical gesture, he swept the sleeve of his smock across his face. I think his intention was to take me by surprise: to wipe off his makeup and reveal the silver beneath. He didn't seem to realize I'd already blotted away his artificial coloring with my pillow. I gazed at him and thought, *You're not as smart as you think.* That made me smile.

If Silver was disappointed with my response to his dramatic revelation, he hid it well. "What am I?" he went on. "Surely you can guess. You know my bronze counterpart, do you not? You're employed by his devoted Order. So you must have surmised your bronze leader and I share a similar nature." He gave me a coy look. "But I am more handsome and charming."

"Sorry," I said, "but I've never pictured myself being charmed by an android."

"An android?" He made a face. "Is that what you think I am? An assemblage of wires and transistors? A mere automaton?"

"What would you prefer to be called? A golem? An elemental? A nanotech swarm impersonating the Tin Woodman?"

"Mademoiselle," Silver said, waggling his finger at me as if speaking to a naughty child. "All these labels you suggest simply show your ignorance. Your language has no word for what I am."

Actually, I suspected English had a number of perfectly good words for what he was . . . though they were words I was too well-bred to use. "Let's try this then," I said. "Are you magical or simply high-tech?"

He sighed. "Again, mademoiselle, your question betrays the abysmal state of your knowledge. I am magical, I am high-tech; I am both, I am neither. I am my glorious self: a mystery you could never fathom."

"So I don't suppose you'll tell me where you're from either. Outer space? Mount Olympus? The future?"

"Suffice it to say," Silver answered, "Bronze and I hail from the same place. You might call us cousins . . . though with different personalities. Diametrically opposed."

"You're evil and he's good?"

Silver laughed. "I'm a witty, delightful companion. Bronze is a self-righteous stick-in-the-mud."

"Bronze seems programmed for law enforcement. What are you programmed for?"

Silver laughed again. "Vivacity!"

I looked around the room at the nudes Silver had painted. "Vivacity with women?"

"I have a gift in that direction. I love women; women love me. And unlike Bronze, I am fully equipped to give a woman exquisite pleasure."

*Ah,* I thought. Bronze was a cop, and Silver was a gigolo: a mechanical or mystic pleasure thing designed to keep women happy. Well, why not? As soon as humanity learns to build lifelike robots, someone will get rich selling beautiful female automatons to lonely men. Why not an attentive male robot/golem/joy toy for lonely women?

"Now what other questions did you ask me?" Silver said. "Ah, yes. What's my master plan? Mademoiselle, I *have* no master plan. I merely enjoy life. I take pleasure in all things." He laughed. "Were you afraid I had sinister ambitions? Perhaps to rule the world? I could have done that ten thousand years ago . . . but it would have been too much bother. Rulers need armies. And tax collectors. And humorless viziers who keep badgering you to make decisions. How tedious! How *aggravating*! Do I seem like someone who seeks responsibility?"

He threw his arms wide in a look-at-me gesture. I barely noticed; I was too busy thinking, *Ten thousand years ago?* That was when Bronze was broken into pieces—Osiris chopped up by Set, his evil rival. "You were Set," I said. "The one who split Bronze apart."

Silver let his arms drop, perhaps annoyed that I wasn't letting him lead the conversation. "Alas, mademoiselle," he said, "dealing with Bronze was unpleasantly necessary. He made himself a nuisance: always getting in the way. No sooner would I establish myself as the benevolent deity of some tribe—an easy thing for one who is indestructible . . . all I had to do was kill anybody who wouldn't submit—but whenever I settled down, Bronze would appear and I'd have to flee. Sometimes I barely escaped. It was terrible! Maddening! So in self-defense, I was forced to treat Bronze, as they say, with extreme prejudice."

"Because he was chasing you." I had a *eureka!* moment. "Because you aren't supposed to be here. You're a fugitive from . . . wherever. And Bronze is a bobby sent to bring you back."

"True," Silver said. "But I am not a criminal, mademoiselle. I'm a tragic victim of boredom. Where I came from, ahh . . . everyone was *serious*. It hadn't always been so. Once upon a time, my people knew how to enjoy the good life. *Très amusant,* every day. But then . . . I don't want to think about it. Let us simply say the party ended. So I left."

I wondered if he was talking about genuine disaster. The collapse of an alien civilization. The Greek gods turning their backs on humanity. A future society mutating itself from human beings into antlike conformity. Or maybe Silver had been laid low by something more trivial: the unstoppable march of progress. Perhaps playthings of Silver's type became obsolete as new models came on the market. He'd ended up unwanted in some attic or bargain basement.

The actual cause didn't matter. Silver had fled from his home to Earth. Bronze was sent to retrieve the renegade, but somehow Silver had turned the tables on his pursuer. Bronze had fallen into a trap; Silver had chopped the policeman into component parts and scattered the pieces all over the planet. Then . . .

"After you sliced Bronze up," I said, "why did you scatter the pieces? Why didn't you hold on to them and keep them from being reassembled?"

"Oh, please, mademoiselle . . . why on earth would I shackle myself to those lumps of metal? What a dreary existence I'd have, constantly worrying about Bronze and dragging him around with me! Let me assure you, I dumped the chunks of his carcass as fast as I could, then settled down to *enjoy* myself. I sought out beautiful women. I established charming venues where I could pursue the greatest pleasures. Palaces . . . private retreats . . ."

"Orgiastic cults?"

"A few." He gave me a knowing look. "I've enjoyed so many diversions, mademoiselle—all you can imagine and more. I have lived many lives, under many names: Casanova . . . Don Juan . . . the Marquis de Sade . . . a thousand others you wouldn't recognize. Name a lover from history; it was probably me. I've always been able to pass as human. My vast repertoire of skills includes a comprehensive knowledge of cosmetics: powders and ointments I can manufacture in order to disguise my true nature. I'm able to make many other things too—everyday items where I come from but astonishing marvels to your unenlightened civilization. Whenever I need cash to pay for my creature comforts, I toss together some trinket I can sell for millions."

"Such as," I said, "a cold silver force field that's packaged in a small grenade?"

"Exactly so," he replied. "I've provided Mr. Urdmann with a number of Silver Shields in thanks for his services.

He's been a useful business partner. Whenever I raise cash by selling my interesting little curios, Mr. Urdmann handles the transaction. He has a flair for squeezing high prices out of miserly bidders."

"So Urdmann works for you?"

"Indeed. He and I met some years ago when we were both trying to sell armaments to the same genocidal dictator. You knew Mr. Urdmann practiced the weapons trade, yes? He realized my wares were superior to his, so he attempted to eliminate me before I hurt his business." Silver shrugged. "Arms dealers take the phrase 'cutthroat competition' much too literally. But when Mr. Urdmann tried to cut mine, he discovered I was not as human as I seemed. One thing led to another, and in the end, my would-be killer agreed to become my sales agent."

"Nice of you to be so forgiving," I said.

Silver made a dismissive gesture. "Holding grudges is hard work. I can't be bothered. Besides, Mr. Urdmann saves me a great deal of annoyance. I despise the world of commerce . . . all that haggling and attention to detail. Too dreary. And the people you meet, mademoiselle! Altogether unsavory."

"Would it help if you didn't sell weapons?" I asked. "If you sold, oh, medicines or better ways to feed the hungry?"

Silver shook his head. "I have lived among your people for ten thousand years, mademoiselle. War is where the money is. Curing the sick? No. The sick are desperate, but they are seldom rich. Feeding the hungry? No. The hungry are hungry because they are poor. They cannot pay me enough to support my lifestyle. So I must cater to the wealthy . . . and wealthy people only want two things: to keep what they have and to acquire more. Ultimately, that means they must command brute force. People in possession of fortunes, mademoiselle, may spend millions on fine wines or lovely houses . . . but those are extras, not essentials. What matters most is firepower. The rich will pay almost anything for personal security. So why would an entrepreneur sell anything but guns?"

I gazed at him, pondering what he'd just said. How often must Silver have given the same speech . . . in a Parisian salon, a Victorian financiers' club, a Babylonian market? His argument wasn't entirely wrong—arms dealing is a lucrative business, and there's never any shortage of people wanting weapons—but it didn't take a genius to recognize these were self-serving rationalizations from a creature who valued his own indulgences over human lives. Silver was a thoughtless, soulless machine who'd bought himself beautiful expensive things—like this beautiful expensive house and the beautiful expensive women shown in his paintings—but who'd done so by delivering misery to those beyond his beautiful expensive walls.

The android didn't care who he hurt. No remorse. One more thing occurred to me. "You're the one who set the bomb," I said. "You're the one who booby-trapped the false Osiris statue."

"Certainly," he replied. "A nice ploy, if I say so myself. I only recently learned that my bronze counterpart was close to being reassembled. Over the past few years, the Order of Bronze has discreetly asked art collectors if they owned rare bronze antiquities. One such collector was a lady friend of mine. When she mentioned mysterious monks asking about ancient bronze body parts, I began inquiring into the matter. It took time, but I ferreted out the truth—just a few weeks ago. Imagine how I felt when I learned I'd have to prevent my old adversary from becoming whole, or I'd end up on the run again."

"So you planted the fake statue on Reuben. The one with the bomb that killed him."

"Yes, Mr. Baptiste took the bait completely." He spoke as if Reuben's life meant nothing. "It was one of my most perfect schemes."

"It wasn't perfect, it was ridiculous," I said. "Risky, overelaborate . . . how could you be certain Reuben would

survive the car bomb? How could you be certain he'd escape from sixteen mercenaries?"

Silver waved his hand dismissively. "My man didn't
trigger the exploding car until he saw Mr. Baptiste had
moved outside the direct area of the blast. As for the mercenaries in the clinic, Mr. Urdmann assured me you'd be
on the scene and would have no trouble shooting them to
ribbons with your clever little pistols."

"I wasn't wearing my pistols! The doorman confiscated
them. I had to face sixteen men completely unarmed."

"Really?" Silver gave me a look. "I wonder if Mr. Urdmann knew that would be the case. He dislikes you so
much." Silver laughed. "That's just like Lancaster, isn't it?
Telling me you'd be perfectly fine, while secretly hoping
you'd be killed. But you triumphed anyway, didn't you?
And my plan worked out splendidly."

"It didn't work out at all. You killed Reuben and didn't
kill Bronze."

"True. But I came close. Let me tell you something,
mademoiselle. Bronze is an extremely clever fellow, but
he has a weakness. He's stodgy in his thinking. Plodding
and methodical. He cannot conceive that anyone would
be such a fool as to use risky impractical tricks instead
of good solid strategies. Flamboyant schemes flummox
him—why would anyone do anything so wild and hare-
brained that there's only a small chance of success? It
makes no sense to him. It's beyond his programming."

"Programming?" I latched on to the word. "I thought
you and Bronze weren't robots."

Silver laughed. "*I'm* not a robot. Bronze, on the other
hand . . ." Silver laughed again. "Bronze isn't a robot either, but, my oh my, he can be robotic. Which is why I did
what I did. If I'd tried anything straightforward, he would
have seen it coming. As it was, I nearly got him. Not a bad
first attempt, if I say so myself. And, of course, I had nothing to lose. My man had already stolen the real statuette,
so it didn't matter if none of the rest worked out."

"Why did you need the statuette?" I asked. "Didn't you already know where you'd scattered the bronze pieces?"

"I knew where I'd dumped them ten thousand years ago. I had no idea where they'd gone after that. Do you think I'd bother to keep track of them down through the centuries?" He wrinkled his nose in disdain. "I'm a lover, not an antique collector. But once I learned Bronze was almost restored, I decided I'd better send Mr. Urdmann to recover the last few pieces. Now that I have them, I'll have to find someplace safe to keep them." Silver sighed like a beleaguered saint. "But Bronze is still too whole for my liking. That's what I want to discuss with you, mademoiselle: how we can do each other a favor."

I resisted snapping back some retort. Better to let the scene play out. Let Silver make his proposition—I could guess what it would be—but on the slim chance he might surprise me, I'd see what he had to say. "What kind of favor?" I asked.

"You work for the Order of Bronze, mademoiselle. Return to their headquarters in Poland. Take with you a device I've made. A bomb. Eliminate my enemy."

"Why do you need me?" I asked. "If you know Bronze is in Poland, why don't you deal with him yourself? Send in your own assault team."

Silver shook his head. "There's no point trying a straightforward attack. I told you, mademoiselle, Bronze is a clever fellow . . . in his plodding uninspired way. That monastery of his has cameras in the woods and sophisticated weapon defenses. He'd see an assault team coming and blast it to pieces. But you, mademoiselle, would be welcomed as a friend. You'd be admitted freely through the gates and straight into Bronze's inner sanctum."

"And I'd be carrying a bomb."

"Yes!"

I shook my head. "It would never work. Bronze's inner sanctum, as you call it, has top-notch bomb detectors. Bronze told me so himself. The bomb that killed Reuben got past the front gate but not much farther. It would have been noticed long before it came close to Bronze himself."

"Possibly," Silver admitted. "But that was a crude radio-activated device. Since then, I've developed something much better." He smiled smugly. "I beg you to remember, mademoiselle, Bronze and I come from the same place. We both have knowledge far beyond anything you can imagine. His knowledge deals with sniffing out danger and capturing malefactors. But mine . . ." Silver smiled broadly. "I modestly claim expertise in not getting caught. I've sneaked through many a window that jealous husbands believed were perfectly secure. I've purloined many a pretty bauble right under the watchful gaze of plodders like Bronze. In other words, mademoiselle, Bronze may believe his cold stone chapel is entirely safe behind its firewall of bomb detectors . . . but every armor has chinks. I have produced a masterpiece, mademoiselle: a bomb undetectable by anything Bronze may devise. It produces no radio signals of any kind. It contains no metal. X-ray scans will reveal nothing of interest. It's so perfectly sealed that none of the explosive chemicals within can leak out and be detected. And the trigger mechanism, mademoiselle! That is the best of all. It senses . . . oh, you might call it a sort of aura, a radiance, an emanation that our kind emits. As soon as Bronze gets close . . . kaboom!"

"And if I'm there, I go kaboom, too?"

"No, no," Silver said, patting my cheek. His hand was soft and warm, not metallic at all . . . but I gritted my teeth to keep from punching him in the face; it would just bruise my knuckles. "I wouldn't want you injured," Silver assured me. "Besides, it takes more than physical force to damage creatures like Bronze and me. It takes ethereal energies."

"You mean magic?"

Silver made a face. "Such an imprecise word. Humans use it for so many different things—some real, some imaginary. Let's just say Bronze is held together by several types of bonds, some of which are stronger than others. A conventional bomb, no matter how powerful, cannot affect Bronze's fundamental structure. It might blow off his fingers and toes, which are only loosely affixed . . . but even a nuclear blast couldn't detach his head. To truly rip Bronze apart, you need a device that adds special disruptive energies to an ordinary explosion. The energies weaken the cohesion between Bronze's component parts. The explosion then does the rest."

He patted my cheek again. "It doesn't have to be a large explosion, mademoiselle. Just enough to break bonds that have been made fragile by the accompanying emanations. You could easily survive such a blast if you were, oh, several meters away and behind some cover."

"That's what you say." I glowered. "But wouldn't it be convenient if I were killed in the same explosion that got Bronze?"

"Not convenient at all!" Silver said. "I want you to survive . . . if only to prevent Bronze's allies from reassembling his pieces immediately after the blast. I would, of course, have forces standing by to help you. They'd have to stay back far enough not to be detected by Bronze's sensors, but they'd rush in as soon as the bomb exploded. You'd just have to stave off the Order of Bronze for a minute until reinforcements arrived. After that . . . I'd shower you with my gratitude."

Speaking of showers, I'd need one after this was finished—to wash off the feel of his touch. "So basically," I said, "you want me to turn traitor in exchange for cash."

"Money could be supplied," Silver said, "but you already possess a fortune. I doubt if you hunger for wealth the way many others do. Surely though, you hunger for other things. Adventure? Romance? If you chose to work for me, those could be supplied. In abundance."

He waited for me to say yes. I didn't. "All right, mademoiselle," he said with a shrug, "let us ponder what else you might care for. The greatest archaeological treasures of all time? How about those?"

"What treasures?" I asked.

"Almost anything you name. I've lived on this world ten thousand years. I've been god to many peoples, king to many more. I can tell you the locations of a hundred undiscovered tombs. Do you want to know the location of Excalibur? The ring of the Nibelung? The lost gold of the Inca? Once Bronze is out of the way, I'd share everything I know."

He waited again. I said nothing. Finally he sighed. "I'd hoped to avoid crude threats, but I *do* hold your friends prisoner. If you want them released, you'll cooperate. And it occurs to me, I can offer one more inducement. Do what I ask, and I'll let you kill Lancaster Urdmann."

"Just like that?" I said. "You'd turn him over to me?"

"Willingly," Silver replied. "I would even allow you the use of facilities I have in my basement: facilities where you could spend as long as you like in ending Mr. Urdmann's life."

"In other words, you have a torture chamber on the premises."

He nodded. "Its resources would be at your disposal."

"To kill your 'trusted' business partner?"

"Mr. Urdmann has been useful," Silver replied, "but he's not irreplaceable. You'd be a much more satisfactory associate, mademoiselle. You're more intelligent, more controlled, and more lethal than Mr. Urdmann will ever be. You're also exceedingly more beautiful . . . and I am a man who appreciates beauty intensely."

"You're not a man at all," I said. "You're a monster." I took a deep breath. "You say you'll let me kill Urdmann; and I do want to kill him, the way I'd kill a rabid dog. But if Urdmann is a dog, *you're* his master. You're the one who's truly responsible for Reuben's death . . . and for the deaths of Lord Horatio's men too. Do you think Urdmann's death would satisfy me so thoroughly that I wouldn't want to kill you? And do you think I'm so witless I'd work for a creature who betrayed his lieutenant on a whim?"

"Not a whim," Silver protested. "Destroying Bronze is more important to me than anything else in the world. But if you remove Bronze's threat hanging over my head, I would have no reason to betray *you*. I would be safe . . . and grateful. Very, very—"

"Oh shut up," I said. "You're a lying pig who'll say anything. All you've accomplished with this talk is to make me think better of Bronze. I used to doubt the wisdom of reassembling a supernatural RoboCop; but if he's here to drag your sorry carcass back to some android lockup, hallelujah and how do I help? You're a worthless, conscienceless parasite who's caused nothing but trouble since the day you came to Earth. I assume it's the fault of your programming—you're *supposed* to be a shallow wastrel—but that doesn't mitigate the damage you've done. The sooner Bronze catches you, the better. I just hope I'm there to see it."

For a moment, Silver stared as if he couldn't believe I'd resisted his charms. A real man might have seethed at my rejection; but after a few seconds, Silver just shrugged. He wasn't programmed for furious outbursts—a pleasure bot, even a totally amoral one, would be designed to have an even temper.

He'd also be long on patience—seducers have to be. Silver would always give a woman a chance to change her mind. I was counting on that.

"Guards," he said . . . not raising his voice, just speaking as if they were in the room with us. Half a second later, they were: running in from the corridor and through two side doors. Eight men—three with Uzis, two with Tasers, two with tranq guns, and one with handcuffs and leg irons. Only the last ventured within arm's reach of me; the rest stayed well back, weapons ready, until I was thoroughly manacled.

Silver came forward and caressed my chin. "Mademoiselle," he said, "I shall not take no as your final answer. Once you have thought this over—especially the danger to your friends if you do not cooperate—I'm sure you will choose more prudently. In the meantime . . ." He gave a dramatic sigh. "I allowed you to wake in a lovely bedroom to show you my generosity. But as I have mentioned, this house has less amiable accommodations."

He turned to the guards. "Take her to the dungeon. Do your best to make her uncomfortable."

# 14

# LOCATION UNKNOWN: THE CELL

They didn't actually torture me. They just disarmed me, marched me to the cellar, removed my chains, and locked me in a holding cell where I could contemplate my fate. Hours or days or weeks later, when Silver thought I'd be more pliable, he'd begin the next phase of "persuasion"— probably torturing Teresa, Ilya, or Lord Horatio right before my eyes.

It was all entirely predictable . . . which is why I'd refused Silver's offer. If I'd said yes, he would have whipped me onto a private jet and flown me straight to St. Bernward's Monastery. Mercenaries would have flown with me, partly to attack the Order of Bronze after I'd set off the bomb and partly to make sure I didn't try any funny business. Meanwhile, my friends would be held prisoner here, wherever "here" was, to be tortured or killed if I disobeyed orders.

A bad situation no matter how you looked at it. Better to let myself be thrown into the dungeon. That way, I remained close to my friends. I also might find a way to escape. If worse came to worst, I could always say yes to Silver later . . . but only after I'd exhausted other alternatives.

Besides, there was a chance Bronze would arrive on his own. Silver had slipped up: in the Sargasso Sea, he and Urdmann had communicated using an encryption method unknown to current technology. It must have been some coding technique Silver learned back "home." Bronze had recognized the code as soon as we asked him to translate the message—that's why the metal "detective" had been so excited. Now Bronze would focus his resources on Lancaster Urdmann, trying to find out how Urdmann had learned the code. The RoboCop android would track Urdmann's every movement, calling in favors from law-enforcement agencies all around the world. It was only a matter of time before someone found a lead that connected Urdmann to Silver . . . and more time before someone sifted through enough data files to locate Silver's hideout.

Silver wouldn't keep a low profile. I'd only just met him, but I knew his type. He'd spend money like water, leaving an audit trail that Bronze could eventually follow. Soon enough, an armed task force would arrive to catch Silver once and for all.

Not that I intended to wait for rescue like a damsel in distress. I allowed myself a moment to daydream: imagining myself breaking out of the cell, sneaking upstairs, finding the bomb Silver wanted to use on Bronze, blowing Silver to pieces using his own "ethereal energies."

Yes. That would be nice. I set about making the dream a reality.

My cell was spartan: stone block walls, a stout wooden ceiling with eight-by-eight beams running across it, a bare cement floor with an open drain in the back, and a single door made from iron bars. I'd seen similar setups in castles dating to the 1500s.

There was, however, a modern touch: the lock on the door was electronic, controlled by a swipe-card and keypad arrangement on the opposite wall. Even if I somehow got hold of a security card, the swipe receptacle was too far away for me to reach from the cell. I also didn't know the numeric key code. When I'd been locked in, a guard stood directly in front of the keypad as he entered the code, making it impossible for me to see what numbers he punched in.

I could see no security cameras spying on me. The room

outside my door was almost as barren as my cell; blank walls, another cell—empty—and a solid steel door leading away. I'd seen what lay beyond that door when I was escorted down here: a wine cellar filled with racks of dusty bottles, plus a staircase ascending to the main floor. If there really was a torture chamber down here, I hadn't seen it . . . but then, the wine cellar's racks had blocked my view of much of the basement.

With nothing else to do, I began a careful investigation of my cell—on the off chance I'd find some vulnerability to exploit. I was still searching when the door to the outer room opened.

"Lara. Fancy meeting you here."

It was Urdmann. He had a gun.

The gun was a gawky-looking thing: an LEI Mark 2 pistol, similar to a Ruger Mark 2 but with an extended barrel. I happened to know the barrel served as an excellent silencer. The pistol had an international reputation as an assassin's weapon; its caliber was small—it only shot .22s—but it was very quiet and acceptably lethal when fired point-blank into the heart or skull. No sensible killer would use the LEI Mark 2 at long range or against a moving target—it just didn't have the stopping power. But for shooting an unarmed victim locked in a tiny cell? The gun was perfect.

"Hello, Lancaster," I said. "Here for a visit?"

"No. This is business."

He closed the door behind him. Just the two of us together. Old chums having a chat.

"What kind of business?" I asked.

He gave me a nasty smile. "I took the liberty of eavesdropping on your conversation with my employer. I heard what he offered you." Urdmann checked the pistol to make sure there was a bullet in the chamber. "Silver is a double-crossing bastard: always has been, always will be. I expected he'd invite you to take my place. He's told me plenty about his past; and in the stories, his second in command is always a beautiful woman. I should feel honored to be an exception—my skills and connections are so good, he hired me even though I'm a man. But Silver can never resist a pretty face. I've already killed four women he was grooming to replace me. You'll be the fifth."

"And Silver keeps you on, even though you execute his women?"

"I get him other women," Urdmann said. "Ones without brains but with all the physical charms Silver could desire. In other words, women who don't threaten my position. Silver has such a short attention span, he can't hold grudges. If I kill one of his favorites but find him somebody else, he forgets there was ever a problem."

"He might not be forgiving this time." I'd moved to the back of my cell, but was uncomfortably aware that wouldn't be good enough. I had no room to dodge, and Urdmann was standing far enough from the door that I couldn't reach him. I didn't even have anything to throw; the guards had divested me of everything except the improvised clothing I wore. "The other women you killed," I told Urdmann, "weren't as valuable as I am. I have connections with the Order of Bronze. Silver cares more about neutralizing his bronze enemy than anything else in the world."

"I'll say I was only protecting him." Urdmann gave me a look. "No one really believes you'll join Silver's team. You're too much the hero—too noble by half, defending the realm and its outdated virtues. Few people ever *believed* in those virtues, Lara . . . certainly not the people who built the British Empire by killing every wog who got in the way. But there were always a handful of blue-blooded toffs so out of touch with reality, they insisted on acting *honorably:* like knights of the bleedin' Round Table."

Urdmann raised his gun and sighted at me along the barrel. "That's you, Lara: a deluded knight. You'll never sign up with Silver—not really. You might make a show of playing along, but you'll double-cross us as soon as you can. Even Silver knows that. He just hopes if he keeps you

alive, you'll give him a shag to pretend you're on his side."
Urdmann rolled his eyes. "Look at it this way, Lara. If I
kill you now, I'm saving you from that indignity."

"A better way to do that would be setting me free." I
looked Urdmann in the eye. "Onetime offer, Lancaster.
Let me out right now, and I won't kill you. You're scum,
and you deserve to be put down like a dog . . . but it's obvious Silver is the greater evil. Whatever role you had in
Reuben's death, I'm willing to let you off the hook because Silver was the one in charge. Just this once, I promise not to hunt you down if you'll open this door."

He looked at me a long moment . . . then laughed. "I
admire your audacity, Lara, but your bargaining position
is nonexistent. In a moment, your life will be too. Good-
bye."

Urdmann pulled the trigger.

Though I had almost no room, I tried to dodge anyway.
The pistol gave a *pock* sound and something burned into
my upper arm. At least it didn't pierce my brain or aorta. I
was preparing to dodge again when the door to the wine
cellar flew open.

Urdmann half turned to face the door. A gun went
off outside, far louder than the silenced pistol. Urdmann
jerked as if hit by a heavy impact and tried to lift his gun.
Another shot rang out from the wine cellar. Scarlet splashed
across Urdmann's stomach. He grunted and opened his
mouth in surprise. A third shot caught him right in the
chest. More scarlet spilled onto his shirt. He fell.

Three guards entered, Uzis drawn. The one at the front
of the formation pointed to Urdmann's body and told the
other two, "Get him out." The two guards scowled but
grabbed Urdmann's arms and dragged him away.

"He tried his trick once too often," the remaining guard
said, more to himself than to me. "That arrogant son of a
bitch *always* guns down Silver's women. This time, the
boss posted us to keep watch."

I said, "Wish you'd watched . . . a little better . . ." I toppled over, smacking the floor hard.

* * *

Here's what the guard must have seen: I was down on the ground, on my side, unmoving, clutching a blood-stained hand to my chest.

Here's what I hoped the guard didn't see: the blood had come from my arm. Since I was lying on the injured side, the wound wouldn't be visible. I definitely could feel it—yes, indeed, I felt it as it pressed the hard cement—but as a connoisseur of Grievous Bodily Harm, I could tell this gunshot was as mild as they come . . . "just a graze," as they say in Hollywood Westerns. I couldn't even feel a bullet embedded in my flesh. It had only brushed past me and flattened itself against the cell wall.

But the guard didn't know that. He'd come through the door after Urdmann fired. All he saw was my blood-damp hand pressed against my heart.

"Damn!" he shouted. He fumbled with the security system: the swipe card and keypad. The electronic lock on my cell door went *click* . . . but I didn't move until the guard rushed in and turned me over on my back to see how badly I was hurt.

Never let it be said I'm an ingrate. The guard had apparently stopped Urdmann from killing me. He even showed concern I might die . . . though that may have been more on his own behalf than mine. Silver had commanded this guard to keep me safe; there'd be serious punishment if I gave up the ghost. But even if the guard was mostly worried for his own skin, I bore him no ill will.

So I put him down gently. As he bent to check my wound, I lifted my legs and locked my calves around his neck: an application of the sleeper hold once popular in wrestling. The essence of the technique is to block the carotid arteries so blood stops flowing to the brain. Squeeze too long, and the effect is fatal . . . but if you time it right, you can knock someone out in under ten seconds.

Not surprisingly, the guard went for his Uzi. My hands were free; I grabbed him and we tussled over the gun. It wasn't much of a fight—my blood choke leg hold soon made him dizzy. Then it made him unconscious. I relaxed my grip as the man slumped out cold on top of me.

Usually, I disdain the cliché of dressing in a guard's uniform during a prison break. It seldom fools anyone, and you almost never get the right size shoes. Other apparel can be made to fit, approximately, with enough tucking or loosening of seams; but shoes have to be a decent match for your feet or they're just more trouble than they're worth.

This time, however, I made an exception. The clothes I had on—my assemblage of hastily altered frocks—had ripped and split shamefully just in my light scuffle with the guard. They'd never stand up to the sort of action I might encounter later. Better to dress myself in the guard's kit, no matter how badly it fit. Besides, the unconscious man wasn't *grotesquely* larger than me; his outfit bagged around my body, and I had to roll up his trouser cuffs more than six inches, but it could have been worse. And the boots were only a few sizes too big. I stuffed them with scraps of my former clothing—swatches ripped off the little black dress—until my feet stopped slopping about in the boots' cavernous interiors.

Clothes weren't all I removed from the guard's body. I also took his Uzi, a ring of keys, and his security swipe card. The card wouldn't help much on its own—the security system needed both a card and a keyed-in code—but people have a silly habit of writing down codes in places they think no one will ever look. If I was lucky, I'd find one. If I was even luckier, I wouldn't need it.

I left the guard in my cell. The door automatically locked when I shut it. When the guard woke up he might holler for help, but I deemed the cell area adequately soundproof. Eventually some patrol or jail keeper would come down here and find I was missing, but by the time they raised an alarm, I hoped my friends and I would be long gone.

* * *

The wine cellar was empty. No blood on the floor where the guards had dragged Urdmann away. Perhaps Urdmann hadn't been fatally wounded; but at that moment, I didn't especially care whether he was dead or alive. Silver was more of a blight than Lancaster Urdmann could ever be: ten thousand years of villainy. I'd have to find a way to put the android down.

But not immediately. Though Silver wouldn't hesitate to lie, I believed what he'd said about his metal body being difficult to damage. I couldn't hurt Silver with any weapons that might come easily to hand; so rather than waste effort, now was the time to run. I'd get Teresa, Ilya, and Lord H. to safety. Then I'd go back to Bronze and see if he could arm me with something that would take the sparkle out of Silver's day.

Quietly, I climbed the cellar steps. No one was visible when I reached the main floor. For the benefit of watching security cameras, I put on a confident guardlike stride and walked down the corridor toward the stairs that led to the bedrooms.

The door to Silver's art studio, at the base of the stairs, was still open. I couldn't help glancing inside as I passed. The room was empty—Silver must have given up painting for the night. On a sudden impulse, I entered the room.

People say art reflects the artist's soul. I wanted to know my enemy. Not that the pictures told me much. As I've said, they were all female nudes—painted with an odd combination of precision and excess. Every portrait conveyed a photographic degree of accuracy, yet none of the pictures struck me as quite believable. The women all seemed to be *gushing* toward the viewer . . . as if Silver painted paramours who all wordlessly gave the message *I want you, I need you, I love you!* All these women were "gagging for it," as the cruder girls at Gordonstoun used to say. I suspected that was more Silver's fantasy than the unvarnished truth.

In disgust, I began to leave . . . but something on the far wall caught my eye: a canvas showing a pale young woman from an era when fashionable ladies never exposed themselves to strong sunlight. One edge of the painting was a smidgen out of alignment with its neighbor—a hint of recent disturbance. I checked and found exactly what I suspected. The frame was hinged to swing out. Behind was a metal door: a wall safe.

I smacked myself on the forehead. Of *course,* Silver would have a safe hidden behind a painting—it was the oldest trick in the book. The safe was old too: probably as old as the house, with its dusty wine cellar and aged marble stairs.

If the safe had been more modern, I would have left it alone. I know better than to tamper with high-tech computerized locks that trigger an alarm if you look at them sideways. But this was an ordinary combination lock, with a big brass dial that ran from 1 to 60. I gave it a spin. I could hear tumblers tumbling. It almost embarrassed me to take advantage of such a poor defenseless security mechanism—it was probably state-of-the-art back in the 1800s but now it had become a pathetic pushover. Thirty seconds later, I had it open.

Inside was a bronze leg: complete. Thigh, calf, and foot joined into a single whole. I thought of the mutating power in any single bronze body part and shuddered at how much there must be in three combined. Enough to make a dozen evil twins or to turn me into a demented bronze platypus.

But nothing happened. I told myself, maybe when several pieces joined together, the energies they emitted were more controlled. Maybe the pieces were less . . . how shall I put it? . . . less *angry* now that they weren't entirely separate from their fellows. They were calmer once they had company. Whatever the reason, I felt no immediate threat from the leg. Hesitantly, I picked it up.

Unlike when I touched the leg in the Sargasso, I felt no surge of energy. Maybe that only happened the first time one came in contact with supernatural bronze. Yet I *did* feel the stirrings of memory. Déjà vu. As if this hunk of bronze were a childhood friend whom I hadn't thought about in a long time. How could that be? How could . . .

Remembrance rose in my mind. My father's study. It had been off-limits for harum-scarum little girls who couldn't be trusted around Ming vases or twelfth-century tapestries. One day I sneaked inside anyway and found something strange on my father's desk: a life-sized finger made of bronze. I was daring myself to touch it when my father caught me—he *always* caught me—and for once, he didn't lecture me on obeying rules. "Ah," he said, "you found that. Well, have a good look, girl. You certainly can't damage it, and this is your last chance to view a family heirloom. I was about to ship it off."

"What is it?" I asked, picking it up.

"A keepsake from an ancestor. Lord Roger Croft—in the navy during the Napoleonic Wars. He was lieutenant on a ship that captured a French man-of-war . . . one that was carrying treasures the French had stolen from Egypt. In those days, the crews got to keep a percentage of booty from any ship they captured; and the captain took a fancy to a bronze hand found in a French treasure chest. As a joke, he broke off the fingers and gave one to each of his subordinate officers. Kept the fingerless palm for himself. Shocking by today's standards, of course. Enough to give an archaeologist a heart attack. But those were different times."

Father took the finger from me and held it up to the light. "It's been in our family ever since. Considered a good luck charm. I have to admit, all the ship's officers who shared the bits of bronze have had remarkable descendants . . . as if some magic influence produced extraordinary children. The captain's name was Greystoke. The officers were Holmes, Quatermain, Templar, Bond, and of course, our own Roger Croft."

He looked at me as if the names should mean something. They didn't; I was too young. "Well, girl," he said, "it doesn't matter. We Crofts are extraordinary enough. And I've just had a letter from some priest in Cairo who's trying to repatriate Egyptian treasures: antiquities plundered by Napoleon and others. This priest says our finger is part of a statue of Osiris they're trying to reassemble. He offered quite a fair price to buy it back. I'm reluctant to part with a family heirloom . . . but it *is* stolen goods, and we ought to do the right thing."

I never saw the finger again. Father must have sold it to the priest—obviously a member of the Order of Bronze. The finger returned to its rightful owner, and I forgot all about the incident.

Until now. I looked at the metal leg in my hands, and realized my fears about being mutated by bronze radiation might have come decades too late. Bemused, I wrapped the leg in unused painting canvas so it wouldn't be recognizable. I tucked the resulting package under my arm, then went up to rescue my friends.

Ilya's door stood nearest the stairs. It was locked . . . but I tried the keys I'd taken from the guard and found one that did the trick. To avoid unwanted disturbances, I locked the door behind me after I went inside.

Ilya lay unconscious in the bed. His breaths were deep and regular . . . a good sign. I was about to begin drastic measures to wake him when I heard a noise in the hallway: someone jangling keys. I slipped into the adjoining bathroom, leaving the door open a crack so I could see. The hall door clicked open and a guard entered, wheeling a small cart. The cart held medical equipment, including a collection of hypodermic needles.

*Aha,* I thought, *Ilya's getting a visit from the doctor.* This would be the man assigned to keep my friends out cold until Silver needed them. Nice of this chap to arrive at such a convenient time . . . but it also made sense that someone would check the prisoners on a regular basis. Anesthetics can be finicky: too little and the patient wakes up; too much and the patient dies. Maintaining the proper balance takes frequent monitoring.

The guard took out a stethoscope and laid it against

Ilya's chest. He leaned over Ilya's body to do so . . . and unfortunately for the "doctor," he had his back to me. I took terrible advantage of his vulnerable position—the man was too busy listening to Ilya's heartbeat to hear me sneaking up from behind. A brief unpleasantness ensued, involving my fists and the guard's kidneys, groin, and face. It ended exactly as you'd expect: me with my knuckles stinging and the guard not feeling much of anything.

Shaking the tingles out of my hand, I checked the contents of the doctor's cart: syringes for all occasions, labeled to avoid any mix-up. MAN 1, SEDATIVE, MIDNIGHT. MAN 1, SEDATIVE, 4:00 AM. MAN 1, STIMULANT, IF NEEDED. Also a set of needles for MAN 2 and WOMAN. I got the feeling the injections had been prepared in advance by a skilled anesthetist, and the guard I'd just knocked out was merely a "night nurse" following orders. Perfect.

I got the stimulant for MAN 1 and injected it into Ilya's arm. While the drug took effect, I took advantage of supplies on the medical cart to bandage my wounded arm. The graze from Urdmann's LEI Mark 2 was as superficial as I'd hoped; it throbbed with pain but wouldn't slow me down. *Nice shooting, Lancaster,* I thought. *Couldn't have done less damage if you'd tried.*

Once I'd patched myself up, I searched the room. The closet held nothing but Ilya's clothes from Australia—Silver didn't provide fancy wardrobes for his *male* guests. The android only cared about women.

Ilya groaned as he struggled up to consciousness. I went back to the bed and urged him to the washbasin before he was sick. He was *very* sick. I felt torn between the desire to play Florence Nightingale—to coddle him as best I could—and the desire to allow him the dignity of pulling himself together on his own. (*Lara, one mustn't intrude* . . . all that stiff-upper-lip nonsense.) In the end, I made do with, "Are you sure you're all right? Okay then, I ought to wake the others." I wasn't sure if I was being cowardly or considerate, but I grabbed up the MAN 2 and WOMAN stimulants, and beat a hasty retreat.

The scene played out much the same with Lord Horatio and Teresa. I realized I'd had it easy when I woke up—yes, I'd felt wretched, but whatever sedative I'd received, Silver let it wear off gradually so I'd come around on my own. My friends didn't have that luxury: their bloodstreams were battlegrounds where sedative and stimulant fought, inflicting untold collateral damage. All three of my companions looked dreadful . . . as bad as zombies, and I'd seen a *lot* of zombies. But their hearts still beat strongly— I checked. Slowly, they regained control over their stomachs, bowels, etc., and began to show signs of life.

Meanwhile, I busied myself with practicalities . . . like recounting my conversation with Silver and keeping watch for guards. No guards appeared; the house was silent. The "doctor" guard had worn a digital watch that moved from 2:31 A.M. to 2:48 while my friends droopily recovered. Through the window, I watched pairs of guards stroll the outside walkways, but it seemed as if no one patrolled inside the house. Good.

I had one other practicality to deal with: arranging clothes for Teresa. Silver had filled her closet with the same frivolous garments he'd supplied for me. On the one hand, I had to give the android credit for consistency—he apparently wanted *all* women to dress like taffeta trollops. On the other hand, I had a devil of a time kitting up something Teresa would actually wear. Pity she was entirely the wrong size to wear the uniform from the guard in Ilya's room. Eventually I got her into a frock that was frilly and pink but long enough to satisfy the dictates of modesty, plus a cheongsam overtop to cover the frock's meteorically plunging neckline. Under other circumstances, Teresa would still have walloped anyone who dared suggest she wear such an outfit . . . but she was drained enough from her drugged stupor not to put up a fight.

2:52 A.M. by my newly acquired watch. With me scouting ahead, our party made its way to the house's ground floor. All clear. I nodded to the others and started along the main corridor.

My plan was simple. With so many guards keeping watch outside, we didn't have a chance of passing them unseen. I could have done it myself, but not with three still-nauseous people in tow. Therefore we'd leave more openly: find a garage, steal a car, drive like mad fools into the night.

If the house had an attached garage, it would likely be on one end or the other of the main floor. I led my friends toward the nearest end of the corridor. Voilà—the room on the end was a vestibule with an assortment of coat hooks, shoe mats, and a rack of labeled car keys. Beyond was a spacious garage filled with exactly the sort of vehicles you might expect Silver to own: some sporty little numbers— a Porsche 911 GT2, a Ferrari 612 Scaglietti, an Aston Martin V12 Vanquish—the mandatory Rolls-Royce Phantom limo, and an equally mandatory Hummer H2. All, of course, were colored silver.

The only surprise was a massive red Oldsmobile 88 roadster dating back to 1957. It had all the classic accoutrements—tail fins, miles of chrome, a V8 engine—with no modern distractions like seat belts or power steering. But the car didn't look like a trophy vehicle. You know what I mean—an automobile kept in mint condition and put on display like Wedgwood china. Silver's Olds was battered and scratched . . . missing its hood ornament . . . equipped with modern Michelins instead of vintage whitewalls. I wondered if it was a recent acquisition; perhaps Silver amused himself by restoring old cars, and this was his latest project.

Then I noticed the license plate: Brazilian. Specifically, the state of Rio de Janeiro. All the cars had similar plates. That told me where I was, and explained why Silver kept the giant not-too-nice clunker in his fleet. We must be on an estate near the city of Rio. This Olds was Silver's non-descript town car, for times when he wanted to cruise around without drawing attention. Most Latin-American cities have plenty of such big old cars. I could imagine Silver driving the Olds along downtown strips or on beachfront roads, ogling Brazilian beauties as if he were just another Rio resident.

"So which car do we take?" Teresa asked.

"Larochka will steal a sports car," Ilya answered with his usual air of resigned gloominess.

"The sports cars can't seat four people," Lord H. pointed out.

"Larochka will squeeze two of us into the trunk," Ilya said.

"Oh for heaven's sake," I told him, "we aren't taking the sports cars. We're taking the old Olds."

"Why?"

"Because the others are too noticeable. Silver surely has contacts in Rio: gang members and other criminals. If we drive a Rolls or Aston Martin into the city, we'll be spotted instantly. But the Olds will blend in with traffic. Practically invisible."

Ilya looked at the Olds for a moment, then turned back to me. "Besides," he said, "you won't mind ruining the paint job if you have to smash through security gates or bash other cars off the road."

I smiled. "There is that." I tossed him a set of keys, then threw other keys to Teresa and Lord Horatio. "Unlock all the other cars. Open the bonnets and remove something vital from the engines. We don't want anyone chasing us in a Porsche 911."

"You can't fool me," Ilya said. "You'd *love* a car chase against a Porsche 911."

"True," I admitted. "But I won't be driving. You will."

"Me?" Ilya said.

"I know you don't like cars. But you were a fighter pilot. You have superb reflexes. You'll do fine."

"And while I'm driving, what will you be doing?"

I gestured with the Uzi I'd taken from the guard. "I'll ride shotgun."

\* \* \*

It pained me to sabotage such fine cars . . . so I didn't. While the others pulled off distributor caps, I checked every inch of the Olds to make sure it wasn't equipped with a LoJack or some other tracking device. It had two: one very obvious on the underside of the chassis and another hidden *inside* the reservoir that held window-washing fluid. Clearly, Silver didn't want thieves making off with his automobiles. Maybe an android would regard these machines as primitive brothers and sisters. I removed both homing beacons using tools hanging above a bench on one wall of the garage. By the time I was done, my friends had also finished their missions of destruction. "Hop in," I said, opening the Oldsmobile's doors. "I've had enough of this place's hospitality."

Teresa hesitated before getting inside. "Do you think they'll just let us drive away?"

"Hard to say," I replied. "Silver is an arms dealer. He does business with crime lords and terrorists. Anyone else in that position would take stringent security precautions—nobody in or out without being checked. But Silver may not be so strict. For one thing, he's a haphazard lecher who hates paying attention to details. If he gets a whim to drive into Rio and pick up women, the guards may have orders to stay out of his way. Just let his car out, no questions asked. And for another thing . . ."

"Yes?" Lord Horatio asked.

"Silver is virtually indestructible. Why should he care about security? If someone attacks this estate—the police, a business rival, an unhappy customer—Silver can just walk away, with bullets bouncing off his back. He'll have hideouts in other countries and money stashed in Switzerland or the Caymans. Silver may let his guards slack off, because he doesn't have much to lose."

"So you're saying we could get into a colossal firefight," Teresa grumbled, "or they might let us go without blinking. Nice to have a range of possibilities."

"We'll soon narrow it down," I told her. "Let's go."

Ilya got behind the wheel and turned the ignition key.

I'd have felt foolish if the car didn't start . . . especially since we'd rendered the other cars inoperative. But the Oldsmobile's huge V8 came to life immediately. It sounded loud in the enclosed garage; I hoped it would be more subdued once we got outside.

The garage door must have had an electric eye, because it opened as soon as we approached. If that lit a warning light on some security control console, there was nothing we could do. Slowly, we started up the drive.

The driveway snaked between rows of palm trees, then along a patch of night-dark beach—likely a lagoon of the Atlantic Ocean—and finally through a thicket of profuse vegetation—rubber trees, bananas, bougainvillea—that curtained the house from prying eyes outside the property.

I told Ilya to stop the Olds just before we left the thicket. None of the guards near the house had paid us any attention; as I expected, they were used to Silver making unannounced forays into town. Before we got to the gate, however, I wanted to see what we were heading into. I left the car and quietly made my way forward, Uzi in my hand.

Rounding a final bend in the road, I grimaced as I faced a worst-case scenario: not just an iron gate that looked too sturdy for the Olds to crash through but a guardhouse with an attached garage. There could be any number of guards inside . . . and even if we got past them somehow, they'd hop into their cars and chase us. I didn't relish our prospects if it came to hot pursuit—we'd be outnumbered and outgunned, trying to escape on roads we were totally unfamiliar with. Not promising. Best to deal with the opposition before matters got out of hand.

I stole forward through the darkness.

One end of the guardhouse was a room with a plate-glass window facing the gate. Undoubtedly, the gate's open switch lay inside that room. The room also held two guards: one standing, one sitting, both visible through the lighted window. What I couldn't see, because it was below window level, was the dog—not until it started barking its fool head off.

Sometimes I like dogs. Sometimes I don't. Guess my feelings on this occasion.

The guards probably reacted as they always do, asking, "What is it, boy? What do you smell?" (Considering where we were, the guards likely spoke in Portuguese, but you get the idea.) I didn't actually hear what they said because I was too busy sprinting the remaining distance to the guardhouse and taking refuge around the corner from the big window. As I ran, I hoped the sentries' conversation would follow the usual pattern of guard-human guard-dog interactions. "Oh, he probably just smells a cat/rat/fox/opossum/fill in the name of other local wildlife. Shut up, Fido!"

But Fido didn't stop barking. Bad dog! No treats for you. And eventually, the guards did what lax security personnel always do to avoid making a decision: they let the dog out to see what would happen.

The guardhouse door was on the opposite side of the building from me. I could hear the door open. I could hear the dog raising a ruckus as he ran to where my scent was strongest. I could hear him barking in annoyance as he wondered where on earth I was.

Not on earth, Fido. My ancestors outevolved yours because we learned to climb trees.

The roof of the guardhouse had been only a few feet above my head. I'd jumped up and grabbed the edge, then pulled myself the rest of the way. My injured arm hurt like blazes. I ignored it. By the time Fido reached my previous position, I was crawling quietly over the roof's rough adobe. The dog was still yapping fiercely when I reached the other side. I peeked over the edge of the roof and looked down on the top of a guard's head as he stood in the doorway.

"Stupid dog!" the man said in Portuguese. "What are you up to?"

The dog didn't answer. It kept up its clamor. I could hear it racing around in the darkness, trying to find me.

"You'd better see," said the other guard, still out of sight inside the building. The first guard muttered a curse, then drew his Uzi and stomped off to see why the dog was raising such a fuss. A moment later, the second guard came to the doorway and looked off after his partner. The second guard also had his Uzi drawn; he was ready to offer backup in case this was more than a prowling cat or vermin.

What he wasn't ready for was someone dropping onto his head. My boots landed hard on his skull. I punched him a few times just to be thorough, but that was more a precaution than a necessity. He'd been out from the very first blow.

I ducked inside the guardroom, staying below window level in case the man outside turned back. He hadn't noticed me; the dog was still barking and the guard was yelling, "Shut up, you mangy cur!" I pulled the unconscious guard into the room where he'd be out of sight from his partner. Then I waited for the other guard to return. He did a few seconds later. "I don't know what that idiot animal is after—"

That's as far as he got before I side-armed him with my Uzi. He fell flat across his partner's unmoving body.

The dog never came back. I don't know what happened to it—off chasing shadows or looking for me in all the wrong places. I kept expecting it to appear as I sabotaged a number of Jeeps and SUVs in the guardhouse garage; but the dog's barking dwindled and the night returned to its usual ambient noise: crickets chirping, owlet moths bumping against lightbulbs, wind rustling through grass and trees.

Pushing my luck, I peeped into the rest of the guardhouse. It held a lounge kitchenette where the men obviously went for rest breaks . . . but no one was home. I couldn't resist looking inside what appeared to be a weapons locker—I had quite a collection of keys taken from various guards, and one fit the locker's lock. When I opened the door, what to my wondering eyes did appear but some dear, dear friends: Ilya's katana and AK-47; Lord Horatio's Walther PPK; Teresa's machete; and my own VADS pistols.

*Darlings!* I thought. *However did you get here?*

I should have thought about that question more seriously. But I didn't. I simply loaded my arms with weapons and flicked the gate-opening switch before going back to the car.

# 15

# RIO DE JANEIRO: INSIDE AND OUTSIDE THE CITY

It was morning by the time we reached Rio. First, we'd blundered for more than an hour on unmarked back roads trying to find a more significant thoroughfare. Then came a lengthy drive along the coast until we actually entered the city . . . and with perfect punctuality, we arrived just in time for rush hour. Or maybe it was only the usual pandemonium that fills Rio's streets twenty-four hours a day. Despite the traffic chaos, we fought our way to the Copacabana Palace hotel and settled into four suites courtesy of my own sweet smile. It's nice to be recognized by desk clerks. If anyone had asked to see a credit card, things might have gotten embarrassing.

Ilya, Teresa, and Lord Horatio immediately stumbled off to bed. They were still feeling drained from the sedative they'd been given; whatever the drug was, they'd clearly received more doses than I had. The three of them had all fallen asleep on the drive from Silver's estate and they still hadn't fully recovered. I, on the other hand, felt fine—refreshed even. So while my friends collapsed into slumberland, I dealt with other business.

First, a phone call to Poland. Father Emil sounded relieved to hear from me. We'd disappeared from Australia two days earlier, and the good father had feared we were now residing in some crocodile's stomach. When he heard we'd retrieved the leg, he whooped for joy and recited a few choice phrases of Latin—beginning with *Gloria in excelsis deo* and ending with so many *amen*s, I lost count. Next thing I knew I was talking to Bronze.

"Yes?" came the familiar grating voice.

"Mission accomplished," I said. "By the way, I met an old friend of yours."

"What old friend?"

"A chap just like you . . . except he's colored silver."

There was a pause. A long one. Then, "Where is he now?"

"A few hours ago, he was on an estate outside Rio. By now, he must have discovered I got away . . . and if he has an ounce of sense, he'll be on the run. He must realize you'll come after him."

"He has no sense," Bronze said, "but he can be sly when necessary." Bronze said something to someone . . . possibly Father Emil. Then he spoke to me again. "I will come to Brazil . . . to retrieve my leg and to begin the final hunt for Silver. Even if he's left his home base, he must have left clues where he was going."

"Do you think he's that sloppy?" I asked.

"Yes. And I excel at examining tiny shreds of evidence. Where are you now?"

"The Copacabana Palace."

"Did you check in under your own name?"

"I couldn't do anything else. They know me here."

"Then you can't keep the leg in the hotel. Silver might track you down and attempt to steal it back. He wouldn't care who got hurt in the process."

I shuddered, imagining a gang of mercenaries in Silver Shields smashing their way through the Copacabana's lobby. Bronze said, "Our Order has an agent who owns a coffee plantation outside the city. Her name is Vidonia Portinari. Phone her at this number." He recited a string of digits; I scribbled them onto the phone pad provided by the hotel. "Call her. She'll give you instructions how to reach her. Take the leg there and I'll meet you as soon as I can."

"Only if you promise to let me go after Silver with you."

"Of course."

*Of course.* His inhuman voice sounded no different saying those words . . . yet I was sure he was lying. I don't know why. Maybe he agreed too quickly. Maybe after talking to both androids, my ear was becoming attuned to the subtleties of their speech.

But I knew Bronze had no intention of letting me accompany him. He'd take the leg from me and chase after Silver, fighting me off if I tried to follow.

When Osiris fought the evil Set, he didn't let Queen Isis take part.

"See you at Vidonia Portinari's," I said.

Bronze didn't answer. He simply rang off.

I called the aforementioned Ms. Portinari—a woman with a rich voice and a soft slurring accent. Once she'd given me directions to her plantation, she said how excited she was to take part in this. The Order of Bronze had agents all around the world: seldom called into action but always keeping watch for bronze body parts in museum collections or art auctions. Vidonia told me this was the first time she'd ever contributed to the Order's work; she was looking forward to it.

Personally, I wasn't looking forward to anything. Maybe the problem was that Bronze had lied to me. Maybe it was my unresolved fear that restoring an alien hunter robot to full functionality might be a dim-witted move. I thought about it for all of five minutes—practically a record for me, considering how ill disposed I am toward introspection—and decided to take out some insurance.

I had keys to my friends' suites. I went into Teresa's room without waking her, picked up her machete, and slipped out again. Back in my own rooms I laid out the bronze leg on my dining table and watched it gleam like copper in the late morning sunlight. Pity to ruin it . . . but I raised the big knife and brought it down hard on the little toe.

Unlike in the Polynesian temple, the toe didn't break off

cleanly. I had to whack it several more times before it finally came free. I thought, *Maybe now that the whole leg's together, the parts are harder to detach.*

Sometimes I'm not very bright.

I picked up the little toe nubbin and looked at it. It looked like normal bronze—nothing special. But there was an easy way to determine what it really was. I had a friend at the Federal University of Rio de Janeiro: Professor Davida Quintero, a first-rate archaeologist with a fine little laboratory for carbon-dating organic compounds, analyzing pottery, DNA checking mummified corpses, and all the other tricks of our trade. I decided to take the toe to her on my way to the Portinari plantation . . . partly because I wanted a full scientific analysis of the thing and partly because I wanted a place to stash the toe where neither Bronze nor Silver would think to look.

Oh, what a tangled web we weave . . .

Rio de Janeiro has been many things in its history: a strategic port, a mining center, and now both an industrial city and a tourist destination. But for much of its life, Rio was most noted as a source of coffee—the second most important trade good in the world after oil. Rio de Janeiro state is still home to many coffee plantations. The one belonging to Vidonia Portinari ranked among the largest.

I reached the plantation in late afternoon . . . partly because I'd spent time in Rio getting reoutfitted: first, some money wired from home, then shopping for suitable clothes, boots, and ammunition. Ah, the relief of being properly equipped! I also ditched the Oldsmobile in a five-story car park and hired a nondescript Camry from an equally nondescript rental agency. Thus prepared, I headed into the countryside for the Portinari estate.

It took me an hour to get there. Much of that time was spent driving past field after field of coffee bushes. Years ago, the plants were only grown in shady nooks on the sides of mountains; some people claim that's still the only way to produce good quality, not to mention protecting the environment. But these days, modern farming techniques allow coffee to be cultivated like any other crop: in straight rows on flat land. I felt a twinge of regret that romantic highland farms were being supplanted by clinically efficient agribusiness . . . but if I'd ever been a coffee picker, paid by the bean and forced to slog up and down mountainsides, maybe I might have welcomed the chance to work on level ground.

Vidonia Portinari, somewhere in her fifties, greeted me with a lavender-scented kiss on both cheeks. She was large, black, and gracious, like a Brazilian Ella Fitzgerald. She was also a devotee of one of the local macumba religions . . . or so I guessed from the combination of Christian images—crucifixes, paintings of saints—and Yoruba-style fetishes—feathered medicine bags, painted chicken feet—hanging on the walls of her house. It made me wonder yet again how the Order of Bronze could unite orthodox Roman Catholics like Father Emil with anything-but-orthodox believers like a macumba spiritist; but I congratulated them for doing it. If Bronze was the one behind this peaceful cooperation of different faiths, he deserved kudos for the accomplishment.

Speaking of Bronze, Vidonia bubbled with eagerness to see his metal leg. She was too well-bred to say so—as a good hostess, she served me cakes and coffee in her elegant living room (the freshest coffee I've ever tasted), and she listened in wonder as I revealed there was a second android in the world (Bronze had never seen fit to mention Silver in all the centuries he'd worked with the Order)— but through all the conversation, I could sense Vidonia's greatest interest was seeing the leg itself. Perhaps to her it combined two types of holiness: part saint's relic, part magic fetish. She never came out and said so . . . but beneath the polite niceties, her keenness shone through. As soon as we'd finished the courtesies, I asked if she'd like to see what I'd brought.

"Oh, yes," she said. "Oh, yes."

The leg was still wrapped in the canvas from Silver's

studio . . . as if I hadn't touched it since my escape. We laid it on a worktable in Vidonia's kitchen, like a haunch of beef we intended to roast. "It's most very lovely," Vidonia said, running her hand over the smooth metal surface. "It's . . ."

Her voice broke off. "What's wrong?" I asked.

"The little toe. He isn't there!"

"What?" I said . . . with what I hoped was convincing surprise.

"The little toe is missing!" Vidonia pointed. "He is gone!"

I bent over the foot and gingerly touched the amputation site. "Silver must still have it," I said. "I don't know why he would cut it off . . ."

"Because he is evil," Vidonia answered immediately. "He wishes to use it in a dark ritual. For curses."

I shrugged noncommittally. It pricked my conscience to deceive a good woman like Vidonia. "I'm sorry I didn't notice the toe was missing," I lied. "I was just in such a hurry to escape . . ."

She waved my excuse away. "You did what you could. You seized what was there. And to miss a little toe, that is better than missing a leg."

Her words were meant to be reassuring. Her tone of voice wasn't. She seemed terribly afraid of what Bronze would do when he found out.

That made me afraid too.


Bronze was scheduled to reach Vidonia's at nine o'clock that evening. By then, I wanted to determine the location of Silver's estate . . . so Vidonia got out some maps, and I spent an hour retracing the roads I'd driven during our escape. It was hard work, made harder by maps that were thirty years old. Recently built roads weren't shown, stand-alone villages had been absorbed by Rio's ever-expanding sprawl, and a few noted landmarks— church spires, railroad tracks—had vanished since the maps were made. I felt proud for finally zeroing in on what I was sure was Silver's retreat: a "private beach re-sort" beside a tiny inlet of the Atlantic labeled Baía da Prata. My pride lasted less than five seconds. That's how long I took to realize that "Baía da Prata" is Portuguese for Silver Bay. Silver was so vain he must have pulled strings to get a chunk of geography named after him . . . like a big neon sign saying *Here I am.*

"Dear, oh dear, oh dear," I muttered. "Maybe I'm more slow-witted than I thought."

I pointed to the map. "That's Silver's estate," I told Vidonia. "And now I'm leaving."

"But why?" she asked. "Are you not supposed to wait . . . until *he* gets here?"

"Bronze won't care," I said. "All he wants are his leg and Silver's whereabouts. As far as Bronze is concerned, I'm of no further use."

Vidonia looked at me carefully. "You don't like Bronze?"

I decided to tell the truth. "He's a machine. Or a golem or a divine construct or something we don't have words for. I know he's helped the Order over the years, tracking down criminals, making the world better . . . but he's a machine. Bronze will follow his programming to the bitter end—just as Silver follows *his* programming. If Bronze hadn't been chopped into pieces, he might have caused just as much trouble as Silver. It's not hard to imagine how an implacable robot 'agent of justice' could wreak havoc."

Vidonia shook her head. "Bronze is a machine, yes, but a *good* machine. Virtuous. He has done good things . . . saved many lives . . ."

"So I've been told." I patted her hand, then turned the gesture into a parting handshake. "I hope he *is* as good as you say. But as of now, I'm an independent operator again. I don't like running errands for anyone, man or machine."

Vidonia looked me in the eye. "You'll go after Silver on your own?"

I didn't answer.

* * *

On the drive back to Rio, I debated what I *would* do. Go after Silver single-handed? That would be futile unless I had a weapon that would work against him. Most likely, I'd head for Silver's estate and lurk outside until Bronze showed up. If Silver was still there, I'd try to take part in whatever happened next; I owed that much to Reuben and all the others whose deaths led back to the amoral android. But if Silver had flown the coop . . . if, if, too many ifs. I'd go back to Baía da Prata and await further developments.

First, though, I revisited Davida at the university. If she'd learned anything in her analysis of the bronze toe—especially if she'd discovered that robot flesh had some useful vulnerability—I'd be able to play a more active role than just waiting for Bronze to handle everything. When I entered the lab, however, Davida shook her head.

"Can't tell you anything profound," she said, handing me a piece of paper summarizing her analysis. "The toe is just a common bronze alloy: 88 percent copper, 11 percent tin, 1 percent normal impurities. Probably of recent manufacture."

"Why do you say that?" I asked.

"Almost no corrosion. The only interesting thing was an odd trace chemical on the surface."

I looked at the page she'd given me. "Cyclotrimethy- lenetrinitramine? What on earth is that?"

Davida smiled. "Better known as RDX. A popular component in explosives. It's used pure in blasting caps or mixed with oils and waxes to make plastique. C-4 is about 80 percent RDX." She laughed. "Lara, you're the only archaeologist I know who excavates with bombs. The rest of us just use shovels."

"Bombs?" I whispered. "It's a bomb?" I slumped against a lab bench. "It's a bomb."

"I told you, the toe is standard bronze," Davida said. "The RDX is only on the surface. Possibly someone was working with explosives close to the toe and there was a tiny amount of transfer . . ." She stopped and looked at me. "What's wrong?"

"The leg," I said. "The leg is a fake. Booby-trapped like the statue of Osiris. Blast it!" I slammed my fist on a lab bench, making its glassware tinkle. "Silver set me up! He knew I'd escape. He put the leg in a safe that a child could open. He even left the painting ajar so I'd notice it."

"I don't know what you're talking about," Davida said. "Are you all right?"

"No. I've been used to deliver a Trojan horse. Blast!"

It'd been a charade from start to finish. No wonder we'd had such an easy time running from Silver's estate. The guards had left us alone. There were only two men on the gate, despite the large guardhouse. Our weapons had been left conveniently in that locker so we could pick them up on our way out.

And everything that happened in the dungeon . . . Urdmann coming to kill me . . . missing a point-blank shot . . . gunfire from outside the room and blood splashes on Urdmann's clothes, but his body had been dragged away before I could see whether he was actually dead . . . then the guard being foolish enough to open my cell to see if I was hurt . . .

Of course, it was possible Urdmann really was dead—Silver might have sacrificed him for the sake of realism. I could imagine Silver assuring Urdmann, "Don't worry, my friend, the guards who stop you will be shooting blanks" . . . then using real bullets after all. That might appeal to Silver's sense of humor. But whether Urdmann was dead or alive, the rest of the exercise was all a setup so I'd bring Bronze a booby-trapped leg. As soon as the RoboCop got close, the bomb would go off; and Silver would have men standing by to collect the pieces. Once again, bits of Bronze would be scattered around the globe. Silver would be safe for another few millennia. He and Urdmann—living, breathing Urdmann, wiping fake blood off his chest and laughing at how he'd duped me—would hop a private jet to who knows where and spend the entire flight drinking champagne in celebration.

I'd fallen for it, hook, line, and sinker . . . just like Reuben. But I was *especially* dim, because I'd seen Silver use the Trojan horse trick already. Stupid, stupid, stupid.

"Can I use your phone?" I asked Davida.

I couldn't get through to Vidonia. All I got was the Portuguese equivalent of *That number is not in service.* Silver must have already sabotaged the lines—he wanted the plantation isolated. I couldn't get through to St. Bernward's either; no one answered the phone. Bronze must be en route to Rio with his entire entourage: Father Emil, the two Japanese nuns, and any other attendants from the monastery. Everyone in the Order's inner circle would want to be present when Bronze finally became whole.

Wouldn't they be surprised?

"Davida," I said, "I need you to call the Copacabana Palace. Ask for Ilya Kazakov. If he doesn't answer, get the front desk to wake him. Say it's urgent. Life or death. Tell Ilya to collect the others and meet me here." I scribbled down instructions for finding Vidonia's plantation. "If the hotel staff won't help, go there yourself and bang on Ilya's door till he answers. Tell him to come armed. Can you do that? Please?"

"Of course, Lara. But what—"

"I'm going to clean up my mistakes." I paused. "Good thing I got back my pistols."

# 16

## RIO DE JANEIRO: THE PORTINARI PLANTATION

It was dark by the time I returned to Vidonia's. By daylight, the plantation had looked pleasantly spacious—all those open fields. By night, the openness grew threatening. Now it meant isolation and nobody close enough to hear you scream.

During the drive, I'd thought about calling the police. I'd decided against it. One shouldn't automatically believe the stereotypes about corrupt Latin American cops, but it *was* possible Silver had inside informants on his payroll. If not, he'd certainly have people staked out to watch for unusual police activity. The Rio authorities couldn't assemble a response team and send it an hour's drive into the countryside without attracting notice. Any such action would tell Silver I'd seen through his trick, and he'd put his men on high alert.

I didn't want that. I wanted Silver to think he'd pulled the wool over my eyes. He was the type of self-satisfied narcissist who's prone to overconfidence; he'd let down his guard if he believed he'd outmaneuvered his enemies. As Bronze had said, Silver was sly but not smart. If Silver thought he had everything under control, he'd let his underlings relax.

At least, I hoped so.

I parked my rental Camry a mile from Vidonia's property, in a small turnoff beside a stream. It was a rutted patch of bare earth, of a type that often forms beside places deemed suitable for fishing. On sunny weekends, cars would pull off the road here; and fathers, sons, maybe even the occasional daughter, would go down to the stream to catch whatever swam there: catfish, killifish, or maybe the odd eel. At night, however, the place had an air of abandonment. Unlovely bits of litter—paper cups, candy wrappers, beer bottles—lay discarded in such quantities I could see them even in the moonless dark. I watched my step as I walked back to the road; the last thing I needed was to sprain my ankle tripping over someone else's rubbish.

A short distance on, I smelled cigarette smoke. It didn't take long to spot the source: a black-clad mercenary standing under a roadside palm tree. Obviously the man was a sentry, watching for unwanted visitors. Now and then, the lit end of his cigarette glowed red as he took a puff. Nice of him to make things easy for me. In three minutes, I'd circled behind him; in five seconds more, he was unconscious.

The man hadn't been carrying a Silver Shield—drat!— but he had more conventional toys: an Uzi, a hands-free radio headset, and a pair of night-vision goggles. The fool had shoved his goggles up onto his forehead rather than leaving them in place. It was a common gaffe. IR goggles are heavy and uncomfortable; they make your eyes water and the surrounding skin sweat if you wear them for long periods of time. The gadgets are wonderful during quick night attacks, but in lengthy stints of sentry duty, people almost always take them off once in a while to let their eyes rest. As I donned the goggles myself, I vowed not to be so careless.

I was belly crawling through a coffee field when the radio headset spoke. It was Silver. "Our man at the airport says the target's plane has landed. He and his servants are transferring to a helicopter. They should get here in twenty minutes." The android didn't hide the gloating tone in his voice . . . but that wasn't what caught my attention. He'd said, "They should get *here*"—which meant Silver must be nearby.

*Not smart,* I thought. If Silver had brains, he'd be thousands of miles away—someplace Bronze couldn't find him if things went wrong. But Silver apparently couldn't resist the chance to watch his age-old nemesis blasted to pieces. Such foolhardy arrogance. Still, what did one expect from somebody like Silver?

I started forward again, crawling between the low coffee shrubs. At the edge of the field, I came to a dirt track that must have been used by the tractors, ploughs, fertilizer spreaders, etc. needed for tending the crop. I was about to cross when I spotted a car stopped fifty yards up the track: a car of such regal proportions, it had no business sitting in the farm-field dust. Unless my eyes deceived me, it was a Rolls-Royce Phantom limousine exactly like the one I'd seen in Silver's garage the previous night.

*All right,* I thought. *Now I know where the villain is.*

It was a good place to put a command post. The plantation's main buildings—Vidonia's house, barns, and equipment sheds—were clustered half a mile away from Silver's limo. Head-high weeds grew beside the track, providing enough cover that the car wouldn't be seen from the house. Silver, however, could peek through the brush and watch everything . . . including the blast of the explosion when the fake leg detonated.

I was about to start moving toward the house again when flashes of light near the car caught my attention. The blobby images in the night-vision goggles weren't easy to identify . . . but as I watched, a bright figure appeared from behind the limousine. It had to be Silver—gleaming more brightly in the infrared spectrum than ordinary humans did—and he was tossing three shiny objects in the air, juggling them.

A darker, more human, figure hurried up to the robot. I couldn't see the man's features through the goggles, but his body had the lumpish unmistakability of Lancaster Urdmann. Still very much alive. Sometime soon, I'd have to fix that.

Urdmann chased after Silver and grabbed at whatever he was juggling, catching one of the objects in the air. "What do you think you're doing?" Urdmann whispered, sharply enough that his words carried clearly. "Those things glow in the dark!"

"No one will see them," Silver answered . . . still juggling and not bothering to lower his voice. "Madame Portinari is too busy primping in front of her mirror. She wants to look good for her lord and master."

"Portinari isn't the only one down there," Urdmann said, snatching at another of the shiny objects. "She's got her farmhands on watch."

"Peasants," Silver said. "Mere peons. Do you think I fear them?"

Urdmann growled, "Didn't you learn *anything* from the French Revolution?"

"Yes. The best time to make money is when blood runs in the streets."

Silver tried to grab one of the glowing objects back from Urdmann. In the ensuing tussle, all three objects fell to the ground. When they struck the dirt, they flared up brightly . . . at least in the part of the spectrum the night goggles showed. I finally realized what the objects were: the three missing pieces of Bronze's leg—the thigh, the calf, and the foot.

Silver was playing with his enemy's severed parts. During the French Revolution, when Silver claimed he was the Marquis de Sade, I wondered if he'd juggled decapitated heads from the guillotine.

Even Urdmann was exasperated by the android's fecklessness. He picked up the hunks of bronze and quickly pressed them together before Silver could stop him. Light flared again in my goggles as the three pieces fused into a single unit. "There," Urdmann said, thrusting the reunited leg into Silver's hands, "juggle that."

The android took the leg by the ankle . . . and for a moment I thought he might use it as a metallic club to crack Urdmann's skull. Then Silver just sighed. "I wish you hadn't done that. Do you know how much energy it will take to separate the pieces again?"

"Don't know, don't care," said Urdmann. He pulled the leg from Silver's hands and strode back toward the limo. "I'm putting this away. You can monkey with it all you want once the bronze bastard is eliminated. Until then, use some sense."

Urdmann went to the rear of the Rolls. I heard the car's boot lid open and shut. Silver remained where he was, glowering into the darkness. Finally he muttered, "I'm going for a walk." He sounded like a sulky teenager who'd just been reprimanded by his parents. The android strode off across the coffee field, kicking at plants that got in his way.

When Silver was out of sight, I moved forward again: crossing the dirt track and crawling through the brush on the other side. I was tempted to head toward the limo instead. If Urdmann was there alone, I could dish out some rough justice that was well overdue. Unfortunately, I doubted that Urdmann *was* alone. The car likely had a chauffeur; Urdmann might also keep mercenaries close at hand to serve as bodyguards. One wrong move and pandemonium would break loose . . . pandemonium that could prevent me from reaching the booby-trapped leg in time. Not good. I had to delay dealing with Urdmann until I'd addressed my highest priority: getting to the bomb before it blew up Bronze, Vidonia, Father Emil, and anyone else in the vicinity.

I encountered no more mercenaries as I crept toward the Portinari house. Silver's men were keeping their distance—partly to avoid being seen, partly to stay out of the explosion's blast radius. It was only as I neared the lights of the house's windows that I realized the next few minutes could get complicated. Night-goggled eyes were surely watching on all sides. So far, I'd stayed low and out of sight, but I'd reached the end of the fields. There was no more cover between me and the house. If I went any farther, I'd be spotted . . . whereupon Silver would know his fake-leg ruse had failed.

What would he do in response? He might call for a preemptive strike, hoping to kill me, Vidonia, and all her hired hands before we could warn Bronze. Innocent blood would be shed . . . possibly including mine.

So how could I get to the house without being seen? Only one strategy sparked in my brain. I needed a diversion: something to attract attention elsewhere so no one would notice me going inside. If any of my friends were here, I could get them to raise a fuss . . . but they were still en route from Rio. Most likely, they'd only arrive after everything was over.

That left me one last option. When Bronze's helicopter arrived, it would surely draw all eyes. I'd have a chance then to race for the house and grab the leg; but I'd have to move fast and get away before Bronze got too close. Silver had bragged about creating the special detonator that could trigger the bomb by detecting distinctive emissions radiated from an android's body. I didn't want to be holding the booby-trapped leg when Bronze got close enough to set off the explosion.

*It's all in the timing,* I told myself. Get in, find the leg, get out. Nothing to it.

"I see the helicopter." It was one of the mercenaries, speaking over the radio headsets. I turned my eyes skyward and soon picked out a flying blob of light—the helicopter's engine, burning hot enough to blaze in my goggles' IR vision. Sounds came a short time later: first, just the drone of the motor, then the *thup-thup-thup* of the whirling blades.

A searchlight on the chopper's belly came to life, illuminating a circle that moved as the copter came forward. The plantation didn't have a helipad, but between the house and the barns stretched a semigraveled driveway bounded by flat green lawn. It was the obvious place for the copter to set down . . . which meant I should make my own move on the opposite side of the house. I scurried to a suitable position as the chopper flew overhead in a flurry of light and noise.

The house had no doors on this side, but there were several open windows. Screens covered the windows to keep out insects, but I had a knife that could cut through nylon or metal mesh in no time. The only challenge was efficiency: I had to get in and out while Bronze's arrival held everyone's attention. If I wasted time, either the bomb would go off or Silver would notice me and call for an all-out assault.

So where would the fake leg be? Where would Vidonia have put it? *In her best room,* I thought. As a member of the Order of Bronze, Vidonia would receive the android with every possible courtesy. She'd rush onto the lawn to welcome him personally, then she'd escort him into the finest room she had to offer: the living room where she'd served me coffee. I could imagine her creating a shrine-like setting for the leg: maybe laying it on velvet cushions atop the coffee table or building a crèche for it in front of a painting of some saint being impaled on a spiked wheel. One way or another, the leg would be lovingly displayed; too bad I had to ruin everything by stealing the center-piece.

*Feel guilty later,* I told myself. Time was of the essence.

The helicopter descended with a mechanical roar. When it was a hundred feet above the house, visible in all directions, I broke from cover and sprinted to the window I'd picked as my best way in. The living room itself was on the other side of the house, but I'd chosen what I thought was the closest entry point. Two slashes of my knife cut an *X* across the screen and I dived through the tatters of the screen as smoothly as a rabbit entering its hole.

I flattened to the floor on the other side and waited— listening for radio-set chatter indicating I'd been seen.

Nothing. No one had noticed. The copter had covered any sounds I'd made.

After a moment I moved, staying low to the ground. I'd landed in a small dining room, with a table, six chairs, and not much space for anything else. I crawled past the furniture and up to the open door, which led straight into the living room. From the doorway I could see that the leg had indeed been laid out in grandiose style: on a giant block of pine whose surface had been strewn with multicolored feathers from a dozen species of birds. A fragrance of jasmine filled the air, and Mozart's *Jupiter* Symphony played softly on a discreetly hidden stereo.

Vidonia had thought of everything to establish a sense of occasion. Unfortunately, she'd also thrown in something to ruin the mood: a man to guard the leg while everyone else greeted the helicopter.

The man was huge—probably just a farmhand, not a trained fighter or professional security guard, but a great mountain of a fellow who must have acquired his muscles carrying hundred-pound sacks of coffee beans. He wore crisp white cotton pants and shirt, obviously new, with no apparent weapons except his meaty hands. Those hands were all he needed against anything short of gunfire. True, I had my pistols and the Uzi . . . but I couldn't shoot an innocent man just because he stood between me and the leg. On the other hand, if I *didn't* shoot him, I doubted that he'd let me walk off with the leg under my arm. Vidonia had trusted him to keep the leg safe. He wouldn't let it go easily. Nor would he easily believe me if I told him what was actually happening. ("Vidonia's great treasure is a bomb. Give it to me before it goes off." Yes, that would be *so* convincing.)

So what could I do? I couldn't shoot him. I couldn't beat him in a fair fight. I couldn't tell him the truth.

Okay. New strategy.

I retreated a step into the dining room. Stood up. Set my guns on the dining room table. Walked unarmed into the living room.

"Hi, luv," I said in strong Cockney-accented Portuguese. "You all set up for the photos, yeah?"

The big man looked at me blankly.

"The photos!" I said. "You know, pictures? To commemorate the ultimate moment."

He still just looked at me.

"Oh, sorry, luv, forgot to introduce myself. I'm the bronze fella's publicist. Lara." I grabbed the big man's hand and shook it. "Vidonia didn't talk about the photo shoot? But she got you dressed up for it, yeah? I mean, those clothes you're wearing, they're new, yeah?"

"Yes . . ." he said.

"So, good, Vidonia got you dressed for the pictures." I took him by the shoulders and moved him back a step from the leg. "Now here's how it'll go. Bronze wants to document the whole thing: him coming into the house, yeah? Him walking down the hall, stepping into the room, the look on his face—got it? The whole scene. For posterity, yeah? End of a journey of ten thousand years. Not a dry eye in the house." I glanced around, then went to the nearest lamp and rearranged the angle of its shade. "We just need a few lighting adjustments. Oh, you got the camera?"

"What?"

"The camera. Vidonia promised us she'd provide the camera. You know where she keeps it, yeah?"

I gazed at him encouragingly . . . hoping like mad that a well-off woman like Vidonia Portinari had *some* kind of camera on the premises. Also hoping that this man wasn't overbright or suspicious; otherwise, I'd have to try to cold-cock him, with all the attendant risks of noise, delay, and getting walloped myself.

The man paused a painfully long heartbeat; then said, "I think the camera is in the kitchen."

"Right then, luv, you fetch it while I fix the lights. Go on, chop-chop, we need this set up before Mr. Bronze gets to the door."

I took the man by the shoulders again, aimed him

toward the kitchen, and gave him a shove. "Time's wasting, luv. Move it. You know how these high-muck-a-mucks carry on if they don't get everything their way." Without pausing, I went back to fiddling with the lampshade. I didn't turn around, but I heard footsteps heading out of the room.

As I snatched up the leg and ran, I thought, *Ten years ago, I would have tried to wrestle the big lug. Five years ago, I would have played the sex-kitten card.* I grinned. *Thank heavens, now I'm mature!*

I got away from the house without being seen . . . and without being blown up by the bomb getting too close to Bronze. Mission accomplished on priority one. Now for priorities two and three: Silver and Lancaster Urdmann.

Astute readers will have realized I was now in possession of what I needed to settle Silver's hash: a booby-trapped leg expressly designed to blast an android to pieces, triggered as soon as said android got close enough for the bomb to sense androidal "emanations." I dearly longed to lower the boom on Silver . . . but in such a way that I didn't end up dead myself. I couldn't just walk up to the metallic scoundrel with the bomb in my hands; that would kill us both. Neither could I get close to Silver and throw the leg the rest of way—I didn't know how close was too close, nor did I know the size of the bomb's blast radius.

Rather than take chances, I decided to hide the bomb under Silver's Rolls-Royce. Silver would return to the car eventually. When he did: sayonara. Furthermore, I'd seen the robot stomp off petulantly across the coffee field. I hoped that meant he was still far enough from the Rolls that the bomb wouldn't go off while I was planting it. If everything went *really* well, the bomb might take out Urdmann as well as Silver. That struck me as poetic justice—for Reuben's sake.

After all—this is important—I was *not* trying to kill either Silver or Urdmann with my bare hands. Oh, I'd wanted to do that at first . . . but I'd had long enough to cool down and reconsider.

This was not about vengeance. This was not about venting my anger or getting "closure." This was not even about making the villains pay in some suitable way for their crimes. I'd gone down the road of retribution often enough to realize it was a dead end. It eased no pain. It restored no balance. It righted no wrongs. Reuben would remain dead, whatever happened to his killers. Only fools believed in evening the score. I'd been such a fool more than once . . . but I was trying to get past it.

I was here not to pay back but to pay forward: to remove Silver and Urdmann from the world so they could never kill anyone else. I didn't want to see them bleed—that wouldn't help anybody. Forget revenge; this was simple necessity. Silver and Urdmann had to go. My role was making that happen.

At least, that's what I told myself. Another example of trying to mature.

I was halfway to the Rolls when events heated up. The helicopter had landed and turned off its engines. A mercenary had announced over the radio set: "Target is entering the house." There followed a long silence.

Ten seconds later, Silver himself came on the line saying, "What's gone wrong? Why no explosion?"

"Can't see," said the first mercenary. "They're all inside."

"Maybe the fuse was a dud." That was Urdmann, his voice sneering.

"It wasn't a dud," Silver snapped. "It was perfect."

"People are coming out of the house again," a mercenary reported. "They look upset."

"Something's gone wrong," Silver said. "Everyone move in . . . but carefully. Don't attack until the whole team's in position."

"Attack?" Urdmann said. "What's the point? If something's gone wrong—"

"We are *going* to attack," Silver answered. "This is the first time I've drawn Bronze from his safe little sanctuary, and I'm not going to waste the opportunity. Move in, everyone! That's an order."

I hurried my pace. My first priority was planting the leg at the car. As soon as that was accomplished, I could do something about the coming attack. One gunshot would warn everybody at the house to take cover. A single blank fired into the air—see how useful blanks are? Once Vidonia and the others had found refuge, I could eliminate the mercenaries one by one without risking innocent casualties.

But first, I needed to divest myself of the fake leg: put it in place, then get clear fast. Every second it was in my hands was a second it might explode.

The Rolls-Royce was in front of me now. I could see only one heat signature—a single man leaning against the side of the car. The profile was too slender to be Lancaster Urdmann. I assumed it was a driver, under orders to stay here no matter what else happened. Perhaps that's why he had none of the equipment other mercenaries carried: no gun, no radio headset, no night-vision goggles.

He never saw me coming. Oh, in the last three seconds, he probably noticed a figure approaching through the deep darkness . . . but I'd left the fake leg in the weeds by the road, so all the driver saw was a figure in black, like the real mercenaries, carrying an Uzi, like the real mercenaries, and wearing goggles that covered my face, like the real mercenaries. The man had no clue I wasn't on his side until my elbow connected with his jaw. "Quit whining," I said as I punched him to sleep, "at least you'll still be alive in the morning."

"Unlike you, Lara, dear," said a voice on the far side of the car.

Urdmann.

I hit the dirt a nanosecond before a ream of bullets ripped full auto through the Rolls. Urdmann was on the opposite side of the car. He must have been lurking there, staying low so he'd be out of sight if anyone approached from Vidonia's house. I thought, *He must have suspected I'd come.* As soon as things started to go wrong, he knew . . . and he'd gotten into position to receive me. Now, safety glass from the Rolls-Royce's windows rained down on my head in peanut-sized nuggets. The edges weren't sharp, but they hit me like a hail of pebbles.

"Hey," I shouted to Urdmann, "hasn't Silver heard of bulletproof glass?"

"The cheap bastard wouldn't pay for it," Urdmann called back. "He's bulletproof himself."

"But you aren't," I said.

I flattened myself on my belly, low enough to shoot under the car. I thought I'd see Urdmann's ankles. Instead, I saw his face and the muzzle of an Uzi pointing in my direction. We both rolled out of the way and fired at the same time, our shots going wild, slugs of lead spanging off the Rolls-Royce's chassis. *Even if the windows aren't bulletproof,* I thought, *I hope the petrol tank is.*

My roll across the ground took me to the temporary refuge of the car's front wheel. Urdmann couldn't see me with the tire in the way. I scrambled to a seated position, my back against the hubcap. Not bothering to aim, I pointed my Uzi blindly under the chassis again and fired a couple more bursts. Both tires on the far side blew out with ferocious bangs, but I heard no sound to suggest I'd hit Urdmann. I threw myself to one side just before the tire near my head blew out too. Scraps of steel-reinforced rubber slashed through the weeds along the roadside, cutting them down with the fierceness of a scythe.

"Well, that was jolly fun," Urdmann called to me. "Want to try again?"

"Can't shoot under the car anymore," I said. All four tires were gone. The Rolls was now resting on its wheel rims in the rutted dirt track, sitting too low to allow any clearance for bullets. "We'll just have to—"

I jumped in midsentence, hoping Urdmann would be slow to react. Being close to the front of the car, I threw myself straight across the bonnet lengthwise, sliding forward on the smooth metal and shooting another Uzi burst as soon as my gun cleared the far side. I hit nothing . . . because Urdmann had done exactly the same thing at the rear, leaping across the car's boot and firing at the side where I'd been.

We both realized what had happened in the same instant. Simultaneously, we turned our guns and let loose: firing at each other down the length of the car, me through the front windscreen, him through the back. Though the glass wasn't bulletproof, the two safety windows combined provided us both with sufficient protection to withstand each other's first bursts. Before he could shoot again, I rolled off the front of the car and hit the dirt in front of the Rolls-Royce's grill.

"What do you think, Lara?" Urdmann called. "Is there any other way we can shoot up this car?"

I said, "Why don't you get in the backseat, I get in the front, and we'll see if *then* we can hit each other?"

"Tempting," he said. "But first, let's try something more imaginative."

"Fine by me." I whispered to my VADS pistols, "Explosive rounds," and began backing up from the Rolls as fast as I could.

The OICWs from *Unauthorized Intervention* had computerized timers on their explosive shells, allowing for precise in-air bursts above their targets. The explosive rounds in my pistols were less sophisticated—they blew up only on impact—but my bomblet bullets had a naïve charm that might give Urdmann something to think about. As soon as I'd scrambled far enough back, I edged sideways until I had a decent shot at where the car's petrol tank would be. Thinking ahead, I took off my night-vision goggles; some things are best not seen at high amplification. Then I sighted along the gun barrel. Just as I pulled the trigger, something sailed up and over the Rolls to land where I'd been crouching a few seconds earlier: something that looked suspiciously like . . .

. . . a grenade.

It's hard to say what *really* did the trick: my exploding ammo or Urdmann's tossed incendiary. They both went off simultaneously. They both went off *with authority*. And together, they managed a feat that is actually quite difficult unless you've got a Hollywood special-effects team—they blew up the car.

It went with fiery blast, full of light and heat and thunder. I thought of the booby-trapped bronze leg, lying in the roadside weeds where I'd left it; but whatever explosive Silver had stashed inside the leg bomb, it wasn't ignited by the force of the car's detonation. That made sense—when Silver had manufactured the bomb, he would have used something that would stay safe, even if it got knocked around. The last thing Silver wanted was his booby trap exploding before Bronze arrived.

Then again, Bronze might arrive any second. Or perhaps Silver. Or anybody else attracted by light and noise. If my gunfight with Urdmann hadn't drawn everyone's attention, the Rolls going up in a fireball would.

Suddenly, the *trrrrrrr* of Uzis erupted near the house, even though no one had signaled for attack. Some overexcited mercenary must have opened fire without waiting for orders. I heard screams, windows breaking, more shots. Whatever fertilizer Vidonia used on her fields, it was all hitting the fan.

Then, beside the inferno of the burning Rolls, I saw a figure moving: a shining silvery figure on whom the surrounding fire reflected like flames in a mirror. It strode deliberately around the blaze, circling past wreckage until it stood in front, backlit by the orange conflagration. For a second I thought it was Silver . . . but then I realized the figure had Urdmann's size and shape. He was covered in a shell as glossy as mercury: yet another Silver Shield. Urdmann bowed in my direction as if to say Shall we dance?

I stood up and dusted myself off. "Okay, Lancaster. If that's how you want to play it . . . let's get this done."

I charged. Foolhardy, I know—if I'd run in the other direction, Urdmann couldn't possibly have kept up. But now was not the time to flee the scene; that would only give the enemy a chance to regroup. With a team of mercenaries to run interference, Silver and Urdmann might even manage to escape . . . unless I stopped them now.

"It's the endgame, Urdmann," I muttered. "Rule Britannia, and God save the queen."

My pistols were still set for explosive rounds. I fired six to soften him up. As far as I could see, the blasts had no effect on the Silver Shield—it held with no signs of weakness—but each detonation knocked Urdmann back a step with its force, until he teetered just outside the burn radius of the blazing Rolls. By then, I'd closed most of the gap between us. I holstered my pistols and raised the Uzi, gripping it with one hand on the muzzle, one on the butt.

" 'Some say the world will end in fire,' " I recited. " 'Some say in ice.' "

Urdmann took a swipe at me, but I dodged easily and slammed the Uzi out to catch him across the throat. The gun shattered under the force field's intense chill . . . but the blow was enough to knock Urdmann backward. He stumbled over a hunk of Rolls debris and toppled—straight into the heart of the blaze.

Hot and cold met with titanic force. The bang was even louder than the car blowing up—as loud as the sonic boom that rocked Warsaw on the night this all started. Urdmann fell sprawling amid the flames; and for an instant I hoped the clash of extreme temperatures would overwhelm the mirror shell, draining its power, rupturing its impenetrable surface.

Instead, as Urdmann struggled to stand, the fire around him died. It just winked out. Frost radiated across the car's scorched metal; ice spread from the Silver Shield, chilling the flames and choking them. Combustion is a chemical reaction that takes place only if provided with sufficient heat. Urdmann's armor squashed all heat like a smothering blanket. It leached away the thermal energy, dampening it to embers. Ice continued expanding outward, fuzzy frosty ice, until the orange firelight went completely dead.

The burned Rolls-Royce lay under its own frozen carapace, like some ancient artifact locked in a glacier.

"Okay," I said. "So much for hot versus cold. New strategy."

While the main mass of the car had frozen solid, I could still get at plenty of metal scraps strewn across the nearby field. The biggest piece was the boot door . . . or as Americans call it, the lid of the trunk. It had blown off in the initial explosion and was now several paces away from the iced-over wreck. To me, it looked like a big metal shield; and I'd need one as soon as Urdmann finished rising to his feet.

I barely got to it in time. The man in shimmering armor was faster than I expected, spurred by anger or the knowledge that his force field wouldn't last forever. No sooner had I heaved up the weighty lid than I had to swing it around to block a silvery punch aimed at my head. I blocked—just barely—and felt the jar as Urdmann's fist struck metal.

The lid cracked under the intense cold . . . but it held. The moment of impact had been brief, since Urdmann—like any good boxer—had pulled his hand back quickly after the strike. He punched again. I blocked again, shifting the lid so the blow wouldn't hit where the metal was already weakened. Once more, the lid withstood the impact . . . but Urdmann was quick to learn from his mistakes. Instead of punching a third time, he grabbed the lid by its edges and pulled hard. I might have held on if strength was the only factor; but as soon as Urdmann got a good grip, a wave of cold shot through the metal, threatening to numb my fingers. Better to let go. I did and backed away, watching the lid ice over in Urdmann's hands. The metal crackled, suddenly brittle. When Urdmann dropped it to the ground, the lid shattered as it struck the dirt.

So much for my shield. Yet it had been worthwhile com-   ·

ing here to the rear of the car . . . because from this angle, I could see into the boot's lidless interior.

Lying inside, glowing slightly in the darkness, was the intact bronze leg. The real one. Urdmann had put it in the boot after he'd taken it from Silver.

The leg was covered with the same skin of ice that coated the rest of the car. That was no problem. As I ran forward, I shouted "Incendiary!" to my VADS pistols. Two fiery rounds, one from each gun, melted the frozen layer enough for me to break the leg free from its surroundings.

Urdmann came up fast behind me. He might have believed he had me trapped against the car; he held out his arms to prevent me dodging left or right. I could even imagine a smile on his face as his silvery subzero hands closed in.

I smiled too. The last time I'd been in this position—facing Urdmann while he wore a Silver Shield and I held a piece of Bronze—I'd placed the bronze into Urdmann's hands as lightly as a feather. This time, I'd try something a little more energetic.

Holding the leg by the ankle, I swung it full strength at Urdmann's mirror-shelled head. Urdmann didn't even duck. I suppose he'd seen so many different attacks get repelled by the silvery force field, he didn't think anything could hurt him.

Surprise.

The sound of the collision rang with the perfect tone of a bell struck by a metal hammer. I could feel the vibrations tingling up my arm from where I held the leg . . . and I could *see* the vibrations in Urdmann's Silver Shield. The shiny surface quivered like aspic. The arms that had been reaching for me jerked violently as if somewhere under the glossy coating, Lancaster Urdmann had suffered a spasm of pain.

The ringing tone of bronze on silver didn't stop. The reverberations continued, both as a musical tuning-fork tone and as visible waves shivering across the Silver Shield's shell. Urdmann seemed frozen except for the vibrations trembling around him: like an immobile metal statue shaking in an earthquake.

I ducked under one outstretched arm and stepped away as the shaking increased. His body shuddered epileptically. I expected the glistening glaze surrounding him to pop like an overstressed bubble.

But it didn't. The Silver Shield didn't burst outward—it began to collapse inward. The ringing tone crescendoed, the visible tremors grew frantic . . . then the mirror shell imploded: fell in on itself like a dying star disappearing into a black hole. Urdmann shrank before my eyes, from human dimensions smaller . . . to the size of a dog . . . a mouse . . . a single drop of mercury . . . until Urdmann and his silver coating focused down to a dot. The ringing held for another heartbeat; then the silver dot vanished completely like the last vestige of a picture on an old TV screen.

Lancaster Urdmann had literally been expelled from existence; or perhaps he'd simply been removed from our universe, falling through some rip in reality into unknown realms beyond. One way or another, to one world or another, Lancaster Urdmann was gone.

Softly I murmured, " 'In the midst of the word he was trying to say, in the midst of his laughter and glee, he had softly and suddenly vanished away—' "

"But you won't do the same to me."

The voice came from behind me. I turned. Silver was standing in the darkness, holding a rapier that glinted in the starlight.

"Good evening, mademoiselle," he said, pointing the sword's lethal tip toward me. He was several yards away, but I didn't doubt he could cross the gap with inhuman speed and impale me through the heart. I lifted the bronze leg like a club and waited for him to attack.

Silver laughed. "You think my enemy's limb can damage me? Of all things in your pitiful world, I'm the one creature immune to that leg's energies. I am made of the same substance, mademoiselle: the same matter, the same harnessed forces. Bronze and I may not be the same color, but the difference is as insignificant as the distinction between blue and white diamonds." He spread his arms invitingly. "Try it, mademoiselle. Hit me and see what happens."

"Maybe later," I said. "What do you want?"

"At this moment, a glass of good Beaujolais." Silver laughed again. "But in lieu of that, I'll take the leg. Call me spiteful, but I don't wish to see Bronze made whole." He brought the rapier back to bear on me. "I have no time for complex negotiations. Give me the leg this instant, or I'll kill you."

"If I give it to you, you'll let me live?"

"Absolutely, mademoiselle. I have no need to see you dead. In fact, if I let you live, there is always a chance—a tiny, tiny chance—that at some point in future, you and I might meet again under more friendly circumstances. Who knows? Stranger things have happened. And I would not deny myself the delight of your charms, unless you make it necessary." He brandished the sword. "Now or never, mademoiselle. Make your decision. I must leave before my enemy comes."

"All right," I said, "if you want the leg, take it." I extended it toward him . . . then threw it with all my strength off into the darkness.

Silver sighed. "Women. Always the pointless gestures of defiance."

He shook his head sadly and moved away in the direction I'd thrown the leg. I moved away too—at high speed in the opposite direction . . . because I'd thrown the real leg toward the same set of bushes where I'd left the fake one.

The fake leg that was booby-trapped to explode when an android got close.

I was fifty yards away when the bomb went off. The force of the blast sent me flying into a row of coffee bushes. They scratched me like nettles. I rolled away from the rasping plants—feeling blood trickle down my skin from a dozen nicks—and I lay on my back in the dirt, staring at the stars.

*Next time I get blown up,* I thought, *I want it to be in a pillow factory.*

# EPILOGUE

The mercenaries vamoosed after I told them over the radio sets that Urdmann and Silver were dead. I don't know where the thugs went—they must have had escape vehicles standing nearby. If I'd really been a zealous crusader for justice, I might have gone after them; but I decided to let fate deal with the scoundrels. Anyone who'd work for a villain like Silver would end up in jail or worse soon enough. Some lifestyles aren't conducive to longevity.

Then again, I'm one to talk.

Ilya, Teresa, and Lord Horatio arrived in time to help gather the silver body parts strewn around the blast zone. The process reminded me of an Easter egg hunt: peeking under coffee plants, into patches of weeds, and beneath the wrecked Rolls-Royce to come up with a shiny silver hand or a hunk of torso. The helicopter hovered above, shining its spotlight to aid our search.

When I'd suggested to Bronze that picking up pieces could wait until morning, he'd just glared at me with steely eyes—all right, make that bronzey eyes. After looking forward to apprehending Silver for ten thousand years, Bronze couldn't stand any more delay.

Though Silver was in pieces, Bronze was finally whole. The blast that fragmented Silver had broken the nearby bronze leg back into separate chunks; but Vidonia and Father Emil had quickly reassembled the leg from its severed components and had presented the result to their "master." I wasn't entirely pleased at the prospect of Bronze being restored . . . but unless I wanted to shoot innocent people and run off carrying the metal leg, there was nothing I could do to prevent the reintegration.

So Humpty Dumpty was put back together again. As far as I could see, he didn't even smile as he set the leg into his empty hip socket; nor did he smile as he took his first real steps in ten millennia. Bronze did, however, venture a slight upturn of the lips as he watched us collect Silver piece by piece and lay the parts out in a row.

"No souvenir taking," he growled in his usual churlish way as I contemplated a silver finger I'd found in a muddy drainage ditch. I confess I *had* been considering tucking something small in my pocket . . . a silver pinkie to replace the bronze one that had been in my family for so many years. But even a tomb raider has to admit some antique artifacts aren't worth the trouble of collecting. If I held on to a lump of mystic metal, how long before I began to mutate and go mad like the Siberian shamans or the Carthaginian priest?

"Take it," I said, tossing the finger to Bronze. "Why should I have any keepsakes? Even though I did all the hard work. Where were you, O great avatar of justice, when I was facing off with Urdmann and Silver?"

"Facing off with their hired killers," Bronze replied. "Someone had to protect innocent bystanders like Father Emil from all those mercenaries. With only one leg, I couldn't move quickly. It took me quite some time to subdue those who were shooting at us. Besides," Bronze added, "I have a poor track record against Silver. He is . . . unpredictable. Irrational and foolish. You were far better suited for dealing with him than I might be."

"Are you saying I'm irrational and foolish?"

Bronze didn't answer. He added the finger I'd just given him to the collection of silver body parts on the ground. I felt like giving him a different finger . . . but that would be conduct unbecoming a woman of my station.

* * *

It was Ilya who discovered the main part of Silver's head. I'd found one ear and Vidonia had found the other, but the head had gone careening over the fields like a cannonball and ended up stuck in a paraná pine. I came over to watch as Ilya poked the head out of the tree with a stick.

"Ouch!" the head whimpered as it fell to the ground. Its silvery face twisted into a grimace.

"I thought you were bulletproof," Ilya said. "A drop like that shouldn't hurt you."

"It's the indignity," Silver grumbled. "I've been a king. An emperor. A god! Have some respect, you peasant."

"You're only a head and you're calling me names?" Ilya turned to me. "You're right, Larochka, this robot isn't too smart."

"I am *not* a robot," Silver snapped. "I am so far beyond your petty understanding . . ."

I didn't hear the rest of Silver's diatribe. Ilya kicked Silver's head like a soccer ball, all the way back to where Bronze was waiting.

Midnight. The moon had finally risen—only a half-moon, but enough to alleviate the pitch-blackness. At Bronze's direction, we'd reassembled most of Silver's anatomy. Now he was only in two parts: a glossy metallic body lying on the ground and a sulky whining head held firmly under Bronze's arm.

"What are you going to do with him?" I asked the bronze robot.

Bronze didn't reply at first; he stared at me as if deciding whether I was worthy enough to deserve an answer. Finally he said, "We will return to where we belong."

"Where's that?" I asked.

Bronze said nothing. Silver's head, however, moaned. "It's the worst place in the universe! It's awful! It's boring! You can't imagine—"

"Hush," Bronze said, covering Silver's mouth with one hand. "You're an embarrassment to your kind."

"So you're leaving?" Father Emil asked. "After all the good you've done, you won't stay and continue to help?"

"I must complete my mission," Bronze answered. "Farewell."

Silver screamed beneath Bronze's muffling hand, but the bronze android paid no heed. He placed his foot upon Silver's prone, headless body, then raised his empty fist to the sky. For a moment he simply stood there, like a wrestler claiming victory as he poses above his fallen opponent. Then Bronze slammed his fist to his metallic chest with the force of a hammer striking a gong.

Once more, the night air filled with reverberation—exactly the same tone and pitch as when I'd hit Urdmann with the bronze leg. Bronze and Silver vibrated in unison. Their bodies quivered with the sound, shaking harder and harder as the ringing grew louder. Then, just like Urdmann, the two metal men seemed to collapse inward, crumpling out of existence . . . or at least out of existence as I knew it.

Gone away, totally vanished. I wondered if Urdmann had ended up in the same place. If he'd been sucked into a world where creatures like Bronze tirelessly stamped out all criminal behavior . . .

"Couldn't have happened to a more deserving fellow. Bye-bye, Lancaster," I whispered.

Vidonia invited us back to the house, but I declined. I'd given the Order of Bronze enough of my time. Besides, with Bronze gone, the Order had ceased to exist. Father Emil and the others would either spend the night mourning the end of their organization or brainstorming new ideas on what to do with their money, their people, and their communication links. I wanted no part of that. If they wanted to continue, they could do so without me.

So my friends drove me back to the city. They had a rental car almost identical to the one I'd left by the fishing stream. My own rental I left with Vidonia, who promised she'd return it to the agency in the morning.

On the drive back, I let the others talk. They spent quite some time speculating where Bronze and Silver had gone. A world run by robots? A faraway planet or a magical alternate dimension? Why had Silver hated it so? If the androids had come from our own future, were we destined for a joyless tomorrow where mechanized police imposed a rigid rule of law?

I remained silent throughout the discussion. I didn't care where the metal men came from as long as they were gone. And as long as they *stayed* gone. But I worried about that. Silver had found a way to Earth once; he might do so again. As for Bronze, I still didn't trust him. Who was to say that after he'd taken Silver home, Bronze wouldn't return to our world? He saw Earth as a cesspool of crime. Now that he was whole, maybe Bronze would come back to "clean up" human civilization . . . to regulate us into orderly citizens. Isn't that what his programming dictated?

The thought made me shiver.

But I couldn't hold on to that sense of foreboding. After twenty-four hours of being awake, fatigue was catching up with me. I was floating in a sleepy haze when someone asked what I was going to do next. Go home to Surrey? Or off on another adventure?

"Let's go back to Silver's hideout," I mumbled. "It had a nice beach. We'll kick out the mercenaries and spend a year or two lying in the sun."

"A year or two?" Ilya said. "Larochka, you'll be bored within a week."

"Will not," I said. "I'll look around Silver's house for something to read while lying out on the sand. He told me he knew where to find plenty of wonderful loot. Excalibur. The ring of the Nibelung. Incan gold. If he kept maps somewhere . . ."

I fell asleep, dreaming of tombs and treasure.

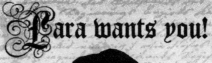